THE

THE

BEN OLIVER

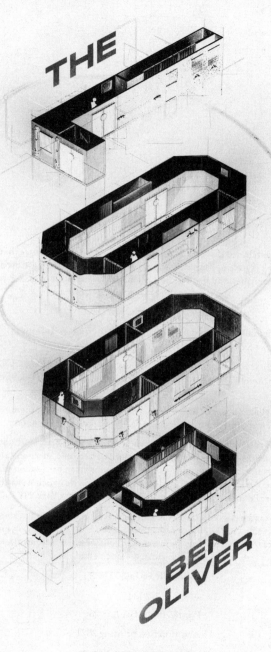

Chicken House

SCHOLASTIC INC.

Originally published in hardcover in 2020 by Chicken House, an imprint of Scholastic Inc.

All rights reserved. Published by Scholastic Inc., *Publishers since 1920.* SCHOLASTIC, CHICKEN HOUSE, and associated logos are trademarks and/or registered trademarks of Scholastic Inc.

ISBN 978-1-338-58931-3

1 2021

Printed in the U.S.A.   23

This edition first printing 2021

Book design by Maeve Norton

For Sarah. Sorry there are no dragons in this one.

He was mastered by the sheer surging of life, the tidal wave of being, the perfect joy of each separate muscle, joint, and sinew in that it was everything that was not death, that it was aglow and rampant, expressing itself in movement, flying exultantly under the stars.

THE CALL OF THE WILD, JACK LONDON

The harvest begins, and all that exists is fear.

This is how it goes, every night at the same time.

Minutes pass, or maybe hours—it's hard to tell—but at some point I begin to hallucinate.

My mind recoils from the pain and the panic, and I'm no longer in my cell. I'm standing on the roof of the Black Road Vertical, the mile-high tower block where I used to live. The boy with the blond hair is screaming, he's trying to pull a weapon from his pocket as he steps back toward the edge of the building, and the girl in the witch mask is getting too close. If I don't do something, he'll kill her.

"Stay back!" he screams, his voice cracking in his rage and dread.

One last tug, and he frees the pistol from his pocket. He takes another step back, increasing the distance between himself and the girl in the mask, and then he aims the gun at her head.

My eyes snap open as the harvest ends, and I'm left completely drained on the hard concrete floor of my tiny gray cell. My heart beats so loud and so fast that I can hear it echoing off the walls of the clear glass tube that surrounds me and reaches from the ceiling to the floor.

I try to brace myself for what comes next, try to hold my breath, but there's no time. The cold water falls from the ceiling so relentlessly and so powerfully that I'm sure I'll suffocate. My lungs are on fire as the tube begins to fill with the chemical-laced water. My exhausted body begs me to suck in oxygen, but if I do, I'll drown.

After what feels like a hundred years, the grate opens below me, and I'm sucked to the floor. The water drains away, and I'm left choking and gasping for air.

My breaths come out in ragged coughs as I lie naked at the bottom of the tube. The heated air comes next—a blast of constant wind that's so hot it's on the very edge of burning my bare skin.

Once I'm dry, the air stops and the tube lifts, disappearing back into the ceiling for another day. For the longest time, all I can do is lie still on the cold floor.

In the Loop, this is the closest thing we get to a shower—a government-approved waterboarding.

Soon it will be time for the rain; every night, despite the pain of the energy harvest, I force myself to stay awake and watch the rain. It comes at midnight—half an hour after harvest ends—and it falls like a monsoon for thirty minutes.

"Happy, talk to me," I manage, through gasps. The screen on my wall comes to life.

"Yes, Inmate 9-70-981?" the screen says. The female voice is calm, almost comforting.

"Vitals," I command.

"Heart rate 201 and falling. Blood pressure 140 over 90. Temperature 98.9 degrees Fahrenheit. Respiration rate 41—"

"Okay, okay," I interrupt. "Thanks."

I push myself to my feet, legs shaking and muscles straining against this simple action. I scan my cell; the familiarity helps settle my breathing: Same four gray walls, bare apart from a ten-inch-thick door in one, a screen in another, and a tiny window in the back wall. My single bed with its thin cover and thin pillow, the stainless-steel toilet in the corner and sink beside it. Not much else, apart from my stack of books and a table that's welded to the floor.

I feel as if I haven't recovered at all when I look at the dimmed screen on the wall and see that it's five seconds to midnight. So, exhausted, I force my legs to move and take trembling, shuffling steps to the back of the room. I focus my attention through the small rectangular window and up to the sky.

I'm still breathing so heavily I have to step back from the glass so that it won't fog up and obscure my view.

Hundreds of small explosions flash across the black night air. I can't hear them because my room is soundproof, but I remember what they used to sound like when I was a child, and I can almost hear that ripping echo. Dark clouds plume out from the afterimage of the bursts and join together, forming a shadowy sheet across the sky. The rain comes down so hard that the first drops bounce off the concrete of the yard. Deep puddles form in seconds and the smell hits me—not a real smell, but again I remember the way it used to smell when I was young. A fresh, pure scent that—if I close my eyes—I'm sure

3

I can sense in my nostrils, and every time I think of it, I wish I could go out there and feel the wetness on my skin, but I can't.

The rainfall signifies a new day. The second of June, my sixteenth birthday. I've been here for over two years. This is the start of my 737th day in the Loop.

"Happy birthday," I whisper.

"Happy birthday, Inmate 9-70-981," the screen replies.

"Thanks, Happy," I mutter.

I lie down and tell myself not to cry, that it won't do any good, that it won't change anything, but I can't stop the tears from forming in my eyes.

I can feel the closeness of the walls, feel the thick metal of the door that I can never open, feel the futility of it all. I tell myself that I don't have to take the Delays, that I could refuse and accept that I was sentenced to death, and therefore death is the only way this will end. I don't have to keep fighting it.

This sense of futility, of hopelessness . . . this is what happens when you take compassion out of leadership, when you take mercy out of judgment, when you let the machines decide the fate of humans.

I'm awake before the alarm again.

I watch the screen go from its dulled-out sleep mode to a bright glow.

7:29 a.m. ticks toward 7:30 a.m. and I speak along with the wake-up call.

"Inmate 9-70-981. Today is Thursday, the second of June. Day 737 in the Loop. The temperature inside your cell is 66—"

"Skip," I mumble as I swing my legs over the side of my bed and stand up.

"Very well. Please select your breakfast option," the voice requests.

I tell Happy to give me toast and orange juice.

I turn to face the screen. There is a picture of me in the top left corner. This picture was taken on the day of my imprisonment and is an especially bad image: I have a dazed look on my face, various scars stand out light against my dark skin, my nose looks even bigger than normal, and my ears are sticking out of my head like jug handles. If I had been rich, these unconventional features would have been cosmetically fixed before I was born, but I'm a Regular, so I'm stuck with my big nose and big ears, and the scars that came later. I don't mind, though—my mom always used to say that they give me character. Beneath the photograph is the information that the screen reads out to me every morning: the outside temperature, the temperature inside my room, the date and time, how many days I've been inside, and a countdown to both my execution and my next Delay (these are one day apart).

A panel opens beneath the screen and a tray with my breakfast on it rolls onto the small metal table.

The toast is dry and hard to swallow. When I'm done, I place the tray against the same panel it appeared from, and it's taken away by the conveyor belt.

Happy speaks again. "Inmate 9-70-981," she says, "today is Thursday, you are issued with a clean uniform."

"Right, right," I say, peeling apart the Velcro strip that runs down the front of my prison-issue white jumpsuit while kicking off my shoes.

I step out of the prison-issue boxer shorts (horribly starchy, scratchy things) and put the bundle of clothes into the tray that comes trundling down the conveyor belt. The dirty clothes disappear, and I wait, standing naked in the middle of my cell. A few seconds later, a clean set of clothes appears, neatly folded and stiff.

I lay out most of the clothes on my bed but put on the extra pair of shorts I requested and was granted as part of my uniform. I begin my workout: push-ups, sit-ups, squats, pull-ups on the doorframe, and half a dozen variations of the same exercises until I'm dripping sweat and exhausted. Normally,

6

I would stop after an hour, but today I want to keep going, I want to keep working, I want to outrun the pain that is trying to catch up to me. I go again: push-ups, sit-ups, squats, pull-ups. I go until I can force nothing more from my burning limbs.

I lie, exhausted, on the floor. And then let the pain level me. *Maddox is gone.*

I accept this fact. I let it roll over me, let it settle.

I wash, using the water from my tiny sink, and then dry myself off with my towel before getting into my fresh prison uniform.

"Inmate 9-70-981," Happy says, "prepare for the daily address from the Region 86 Overseer, Galen Rye."

"Wonderful," I mutter, sitting down on my bed and facing the screen.

Across the city and in the villages on the outskirts, the Barker Projectors will cease spewing out their holographic advertisements; Lenses will halt all gameplay, augmented reality, and social functions; every TV, VR module, and screen will be forced to show Galen's daily message.

His face appears on my little prison screen. Friendly, warm, and confident.

"Good morning, citizens," Galen starts, that sly smile spreading across his lips. "I know you are all busy people, so I'll keep it brief."

I have no interest in these daily political broadcasts, but broken eye contact makes the footage pause until the viewer is watching once again. Better just to get it over with.

"My pledge to increase engineering roles is coming to fruition, and I'd like to personally guarantee that 50 percent of those non-robot jobs will be reserved for Regulars. We are not the divided nation that the media would have you believe we are. I won't let that happen, not on my watch, not during my term as Overseer."

I roll my eyes, and for the second I'm not focused on the screen, Galen freezes in place, one finger raised in the air, until I'm watching once again and he continues, talking about his policies and how Region 86 is the most successful it's been in fifty years, which is debatable at best.

His address ends with his usual sign off—*As One*—and my next two hours are spent reading. I'm lucky; I made friends with the one human employee of the Loop—Wren Salter, the warden—about a year into my incarceration. She collects antique books—not the electronic kind, not the kind that can be displayed on a Lens, the original paper books. In the Loop, the rooms are scanned every three seconds to ensure that the inmate has not escaped and to check for contraband electronics, so old-fashioned paper books are the only versions that can be successfully smuggled inside. I have 189 books piled up at the foot of my bed, everything from damp-smelling Westerns from 300 years ago, the pages yellowed with time and the text fading in the corners, to the last of the mass-printed paper books from around the time I was born.

I can read a book in a day if it's really good. There are a few I keep going back to: stories so good, characters so well written that they don't go away and I wonder if they were popular when they were printed. *Kindred*, Harry Potter, *Life of Pi*, and *The Left Hand of Darkness*, for example.

Right now, I'm halfway through a book about a family trapped in a haunted hotel. It's by an author I like—I've read at least five of his other books, and this one might be the best so far.

What I like about books is the way I can disappear for a while into a place that someone else created; I don't have to be who I am or where I am for as long as I'm in that other world, and I need that sometimes. In that way, I suppose, I'm not much different from the drug addicts who populate the tower blocks and slums on the edge of the city.

At 11:30 the back wall to my room begins to slide slowly up. It moves silently, but I hear the birds and I can feel the wind and the warmth of the sun. I put the book down and stand at the wall as it rises.

We get an hour of outdoor exercise every day. I spend forty-five minutes of it sprinting laps of my walled-up triangle of yard.

It's only when the door is open fully that you ever truly get a sense of the shape of the prison. Unsurprisingly, it's one big loop, hence the name. The Loop is a half mile in circumference with 155 cells and a gap at the entrance that leads directly to the only way in or out—the Dark Train, which is connected to the Loop by a system of tunnels. Each inmate's room is nine feet at its widest point and just over eight and a half at the wall that opens up to the yard. There is four feet of concrete on either side and three feet above; this makes the rooms soundproof, escape proof, and virtually bombproof. Each inmate gets a strip of yard, a continuation of the tapering shape of their room that stretches for almost two hundred feet to the enormous concrete pillar in the center, on top of which the drones reside.

Exercise hour is the only time inmates are allowed to interact with one another. We can't see one another due to the fifty-foot-high walls that separate us, but we can talk, and before the back wall is even halfway up, I can hear the shouts and screams of all the other inmates. I hear Pander Banks singing one of the seven songs that she remembers from the outside world. When she finishes all seven, she'll start again at the first.

I can hear the drones on the other side of the yard whirring to life and issuing threats to Malachai Bannister, who likes to climb the walls and wait until the robotic security guards reach *one* on their three-second countdown before he drops down and laughs. Four and five cells to my right, I hear Pod and Igby, two of the quieter inmates, who are continuing their strange adventure games played with five dice each that Wren snuck into their cells. They must be extremely honest or incredibly gullible, because neither can see over the wall to confirm what the other has rolled.

On both sides I hear the planners; a group of four inmates—Adam Casswell, Fulton Conway, and Winchester Shore on my left, and Woods Rafka on my right—who discuss ways to escape, their ideas ranging from the absurd (using the flight technology of the drones to fly over the walls) to the ingenious (a coordinated attack, utilizing the Delays and hijacking the Dark Train). They know as well as anyone else that escaping the Loop is impossible, and they also know that everything we say is recorded, and—although it's against the law—the government could access the pinhole cameras surgically implanted in the middle of our foreheads, yet it doesn't stop them.

But over all the disorder, I hear a gravelly voice screaming over and over again about how he wants to kill me. He chants my name constantly, from the minute the back wall opens to the minute it closes. Every. Single. Day.

"Luka Kane," he screeches, "Luka Kane, I'm going to kill you. Luka Kane, I'm going to kill you."

The screaming boy arrived in the Loop the day after me and has been making declarations of murder for 736 days. I admit that it scared me for the first few days; I didn't even leave my room for more than a second. I would step out into the yard and then reenter my cell. This action would tell Happy that I no longer wanted to be outside, and the back wall would close, leaving me in silence once again. I soon realized how foolish I was being, that there was no way he could get to me, no way that he could make it over the enormous walls that separated us—they were too high, and the drones would shoot him full of poison if he tried.

The warden told me the screaming boy's name is Tyco Roth. The worst part about him wanting to kill me is that I have no idea who he is and no idea why he wants me dead.

Finally, the wall of my cell reaches the top of the ceiling, and I race out into the yard. I run as fast as I can, pushing myself to the limit. I watch the center pillar grow in my field of vision as I approach it, slowing myself enough to touch my palm against the cold concrete column before sprinting back to the entrance of my room. To the center and back takes less than twenty seconds, and I repeat the lap over and over and over until my breaths are coming in sharp painful gasps and my muscles are burning. I can feel the lactic acid in my legs building up, and I push harder, ignoring the pain. This is my act of rebellion; this is how I tell the government what I think of their torture chambers.

I run back to the middle. The walls that separate me from the yards on either side are close enough to touch, and I think about the empty area to my right; that cell has been unfilled for two days now. It used to belong to Maddox Fairfax, my best friend, a Regular who was three months away from being transferred to the Block. Maddox had ridden his luck through eleven Delays until his final one, a surgery; they took his eyes and replaced them with prototype prosthetics, a mixture of technology and laboratory-grown tissues. For a while, the new eyes worked. He was in agony when he returned to the Loop, the stitching and swelling still fresh, but he could tell me the exact dimensions of the yard just by looking from one wall to the other, he could immediately tell how many liters of water filled the harvest tube, and if a plane flew overhead, he'd tell me how high up it was, the exact direction of travel, and how fast it was going.

Then one day he wasn't the same Maddox anymore. His body had begun to reject the prosthetics; the tissue became infected. They took him away on the Dark Train for observations, and he never came back.

That's the risk we take when we accept the Delays. You pray for a nanotech trial, a vaccination, or a cosmetic injection that removes all body hair or changes your eye color, but every now and then an inmate is taken away for their Delay and when they return, and the back wall opens for exercise—you can hear them screaming in agony because the doctors took their legs or their lungs or their heart and replaced it with something new, something robotic.

The Delays are for the benefit of the Alts. The trials exist to test new products that make the lives of the wealthy better; all of us in the Loop, we're just guinea pigs for the rich.

I think about Maddox, how he guided me through those first few weeks after the trial, after Happy had adjudged me morally aware of my actions and culpable for my crimes.

Maddox spoke to me on my fourth day in the Loop, the first day I had dared to set foot into the yard for more than a moment. We'd spoken about the Delays, how it made more sense to decline and accept our execution rather than bending to the government's will, but we both knew that it was near impossible to refuse. Choosing death spits in the face of hope, and—despite how desperate things are—hope remains.

When my first real Delay (after the mandatory first surgery in which anti-escape technology is implanted) came six months later, I'd stared at the screen for a long time, knowing that one day I'd accept the Delay contract and it would be an amputation, a bone replacement, a new synthetic type of blood to replace my own, and it would fail and I'd die screaming in agony. The scientists at the Facility, where the Delays are administered, don't do mercy kills. They bring the patient in for observation, then watch them 24/7 until they die. They don't even offer pain relief—they study every second of footage from the cameras, watching as the body rejects the new limb, or the new pancreas malfunctions, or the reinforced veins split open. They record the patient's levels of pain and how their body reacts to the failure of the experiment, and then they adjust the trial and run it again with another inmate.

They say it's worse in the Block. They say Delays come every six weeks instead of every six months. The Block is a newer facility that they finished building seven years ago. Not much is known about what goes on in there, but there are rumors, horrifying rumors, about torture and pain and conditions far worse than the Loop. Inmates are sent to the Block when they turn eighteen. I have 730 days until it's my turn.

I push down all thoughts of Delays and the Block and death sentences and Maddox, and just run. At last, I collapse against the dividing wall between my and what used to be Maddox's exercise yards. I suck in the warm air, and I wonder what breathing must be like for the Alts; the Mechanized Oxygen Replenishment systems replace oxygen in the bloodstream seven times more efficiently than their original lungs, and the Automated Pulmonary Moderators where their hearts used to be clean and pump blood through their veins soundlessly.

The superhumans, the cyborgs, the Altered; the ones who look down on us Regulars like we're nothing.

I've almost caught my breath when I hear a few words from a conversation a few exercise yards over to the left. I push myself to standing and move to the wall on the other side. Amid the singing and yells, beneath the sounds of Tyco Roth's relentless screamed death threats, I catch snippets of a boy and a girl talking about something that's going on in the outside world. I recognize the voices; it's Alistair George and Emery Faith.

"They're talking about unrest, as though the Regulars are going to rise up..." Alistair is saying, but his Irish accent blends into the chaos, and the end of the sentence is inaudible.

"How?" Emery replies. "How would that even work? It's an unwinnable fight."

"There's talk of war. They're saying that..." Again I lose track of Alistair's voice.

"Alistair, there hasn't been a war in a hundred years."

"No, but what about all those people who have gone missing from the city? I heard they're hiding in the Red Zones. What if they..."

I strain to hear more, try to catch a full sentence amid the cacophony of sound, but the conversation is interrupted by sirens wailing out over the yard followed by the voice of Happy, informing us that we have one minute to return to our rooms. Just to remind us of what will happen if we disobey the order, the drones that sit on top of the center pillar float up into the sky, weapons scanning from one inmate to another. I hear the last goodbyes, the last notes of Pander's singing, and the last yells from Tyco as the inmates of the Loop make their way back to their cells for another day of silence and solitude.

I sit on my bed as the wall closes, and try to savor the sound of the breeze before the silence returns.

I think about the conversation between Emery and Alistair. They were talking about war in the outside world, but that's impossible: The world is regulated by one government, and that government is counseled by Happy's irrefutable logic. There's another reason to dismiss the rumors—there's no way that two inmates of the Loop would have information from the outside world anyway. There are no visiting hours, no television broadcasts, no Lenses, no LucidVision, not even VR, and although Happy is the operating system that all these devices use, there's no way of accessing the information, even through the screen. The only face-to-face human contact we have is with the warden, Wren, whom the government requires to come around once a day to deliver the afternoon meal. This is considered an act of compassion from the authorities (advised, of course, by Happy) and keeps the people satisfied that criminals are not treated entirely like animals.

The last time I saw anyone from the outside world who wasn't a warden, a guard, or a doctor in the Facility was as the Marshals dragged me out of my home—that person was my sister, Molly, who was crying and pleading with me not to go.

That was my last day of freedom; I was taken to the station, where I confessed to my crimes. I was tried by Happy and then taken to the Facility, where they cut first into my wrists, implanting a magnetic core coiled in cobalt, and then into my chest, where they attached the device to my heart. This was my first Delay—every inmate of the Loop is subject to this surgery, as it's how they control us and how they prevent riots and escape attempts.

I fight off these thoughts; they are unhappy memories of the end of my real life and the beginning of this routine, this repetition of days where nothing ever happens and nothing ever changes and, if the World Government has its way, nothing ever will.

"Happy," I say, glancing to the screen.

"Yes, Inmate 9-70-981?" the screen replies.

"Panoptic playback: Day 733 in the Loop. Time: 11:45 a.m."

"Right away," the screen replies. The stats and figures melt away and are replaced by the footage from the Panoptic camera implanted in my head. I hear my heavy breathing as I finish my final sprint from the pillar to the door. The footage ambles over to the joining wall and collapses.

"Yo, Maddox." My own voice, calling out over Tyco's screams and Pander's singing, is met by silence. "Maddox, you there?"

As I watch the footage, I feel the hurt creeping up on me again, but I fight against the tears this time.

Finally, I hear it, Maddox's voice, weak and broken.

"I think they finally got me, Luke," he says, the words trembling over the wall.

"What are you talking about?" I hear my own voice come back, full of humor, sure that my friend was messing with me.

"I don't think I'm going to make it to the Block. Probably a good thing."

I watch the footage, remembering the way my already-racing heart had begun to sprint inside my chest as the reality sank in.

"Maddox, what's going on?"

"The eyes, Luke, they're not taking."

17

Maddox had been the only person who could get away with calling me Luke, and hearing him say it again is too much for me.

"Stop footage," I say, my voice hitching against the onrushing emotion. "Playback. Day 4 in the Loop. Time: 11:30 a.m."

"Of course," the screen replies.

I watch the footage. Me tentatively stepping out into the yard, physically shaking as the screaming voice of Tyco Roth promises to kill me.

"That you, new guy?" Maddox's voice calls out.

I look over to the bare dividing wall. The footage shows this. I stay silent.

"My name's Maddox, and I'm guessing you're the Luka Kane that the psychopath keeps yelling about? Ignore him, he's clearly got a goddamned screw rattling around in that empty head."

I walk over to the wall, placing a hand against the metal. "Yes, I . . . I'm Luka Kane."

"Luka Kane," Maddox repeats, "nice to finally meet you, neighbor."

"Why does that boy want me dead?" My voice, so hollow and scared. So young.

"Who the hell knows?" Maddox replies, so bright and self-assured. "Who the hell cares? He can't get to you."

"Inmate 9-70-981," Happy interrupts me as I watch the screen, "you have two minutes of your daily allowance of memories remaining."

"Playback," I reply. "Day 6 in the Loop. Time: 11:39 a.m."

"Of course," Happy says.

The new footage is displayed: the yard, the joining wall, Maddox's voice coming over to me.

"The thing is, you might as well get used to this place, Luke, old friend. Relax, get comfortable. If you're really unlucky, you'll be here for a very long time."

"Unlucky?" I hear myself reply, my voice now more recognizable than the terrified, unsteady stutter from Day 4.

"That's right," Maddox declares. "We're rats in a lab, man. There's nothing good waiting for us at the end of all this."

"So why bother taking the Delays?"

He'd laughed then. "I ask myself that every time. Do you know how they do it? How they execute us?"

"I assumed it was the heart trigger," I say.

"They use Deleters. Have you ever seen one? They look like big tennis rackets without strings, but if any part of you goes through the middle, it gets erased into tiny, microscopic pieces. Next Delay, let's see if you've got the willpower to face Deletion."

The screen fades to black. "You have reached your daily allowance of memories."

"Fine," I say. "Can I have some privacy?"

"Of course," Happy says, and the screen goes blank.

I tell myself to stop reminiscing about Maddox. Thinking about him over and over won't do any good, it won't bring him back.

I lie back on my bed and grab my book from beneath my pillow. Within five words I have disappeared back into the vivid world, and I'm immersed fully. This is better than the Lens could ever be, better even than LucidVision and its dream-manipulation technology.

Two hours pass before the sliding panel in the door to my room opens and I hear Wren's voice.

"Happy birthday, Luka."

I'm snapped out of the story, but I can't help smiling at the sound of her voice.

Wren started at the Loop just over a year ago. The warden before her was a bitter old man named Forrest Hamlet who would spend approximately five seconds yelling questions at me before shoving the afternoon meal through the gap in my door, slamming the hatch shut, and disappearing for another day. But the truly horrible thing about Forrest was that I actually looked forward to seeing him. The Loop taught me to never underestimate the power of loneliness; it can make you miss even the most horrible circumstances.

Wren is different, though. Yes, she's an Alt, but she's not like the others; she genuinely cares about the inmates and our mental health.

"Thanks," I reply, sitting up and turning to face her.

"How's the book?" she asks, her blonde hair falling perfectly across her green eyes.

"Amazing," I tell her, marking my place with the piece of fabric I tore from a pillowcase and putting it down. "Really amazing, one of the best so far."

"Yeah, I love that one," she says, smiling. Her smile is so beautiful; of course it is, she's an Alt, which means her parents paid for her to be beautiful and genetically flawless before she was born, along with at least a dozen technological improvements, but for some reason that smile seems so real, so natural. "Wait until you read his fantasy series, it might be his best."

"Can't wait," I say.

Wren stretches her arm through the hatch—this is forbidden, and the screen on my wall turns red and Happy's voice speaks firmly: *"Infiltration. Lockdown in five seconds, four, three . . ."*

I stand up quickly when I see the red-and-silver wrapping paper covering the small parcel in Wren's hand. I take it and stare at it as she withdraws her arm and the warning voice ceases.

"A present?" I ask, peering through the hatch.

"It's your birthday," she replies, shrugging.

"I didn't think . . ." I start, but I don't finish my sentence; instead, I tear off the paper.

"It's just another book," she says, "but it's a really good one."

I turn the hardback over in my hands. The cover is green and depicts stems of grass in a field. I read the title: *The Fellowship of the Ring*.

"It's the first in a trilogy," she tells me. "I think you'll really like it."

"It's amazing," I say. "Thank you."

"No problem."

"I'll get to it as soon as I finish this one." I nod to the book on my bed. "Do you want any of these back?"

I gesture to the small mountain of books at the foot of my bed, and Wren shakes her head.

"You ask me that every day." She laughs. "Keep them; I get ten for one Coin at Vintage."

"Are you sure?" I ask.

Wren nods, and I realize—not for the first time—that these books, which seem like priceless treasures to me, are really nothing of worth to the outside world, where technology and complete immersion are king.

"I'm sure," she says. "So, how have you been?"

Wren and I spend the next ten minutes talking about how my favorite skate team is doing in the outside world, any good movies she's seen recently, her ambitions to become a virtual architect, and how she's been studying code in her free time, and before long it's time for her to go. She hands me a sandwich for my lunch and says goodbye.

And this is the saddest part of my day: the second the hatch closes and I know that I won't see Wren for another twenty-four hours. It's not even three in the afternoon, and I have nothing to do but read and wait for the energy harvest to begin.

Alone in the silence, I find myself thinking about how hard my time in prison would have been without Wren. Before Forrest retired, I had been imprisoned for almost a year, and I had felt the weight of the Loop pressing down on me. I felt every second of every hour stretching out into infinity, and I thought that I would lose my mind.

Then one day as the hatch opened and I lay on my bed waiting to hear the gruff voice of Forrest Hamlet, a voice that didn't suit his aging but handsome Alt face, yelling government-approved questions at me, instead Wren said, "Hi, I'm Wren. I'm the new warden."

I think I felt a moment of hope, a little spark in my chest when I sat up and saw her smiling at me, impossibly green eyes glowing bright the way Alts' do, wide smile revealing perfect white teeth. I said hi back, and we talked—nothing particularly deep or meaningful, just friendly words. How are you? What's your name? How long have you been in here? It felt like she cared.

I fell in love with her the first time she gave me a book. It was such a simple gesture. "Just something to pass the time," she'd said, and then laughed as I stared at the black cover with a red silhouetted wolf howling to the sky. She said that I was looking at it like it was a cup of ice water in a desert, and I told her that it was. A pretty weak reply, but she smiled. The book was *The Call of the Wild* by Jack London, an ancient novel about a dog who joins a pack of wolves. I loved it and can still quote it from memory. I read it twice before she returned the next day with another book.

After that, Wren brought me a new book almost every day. She took time out of her life to go online, using her Lens to enter the Mall—a gigantic virtual shopping center with over four million stores—and go to one of the antique shops and choose a new book for me, a book that would be delivered by drone to her home within an hour of purchase. She was selfless, kind, nice. She was unlike any Alt I'd ever met.

Wren saved me from the insanity that infects a lot of the inmates in this place. I hear them during the exercise hour, babbling nonsense into the air, unable to adapt from their hyperstimulated life in the outside world to the agonizing solitude of the Loop.

I'm still staring at the hatch where Wren was five minutes before, smiling at my own good luck that she came along. I eat my sandwich and hold on to this good feeling for as long as I can.

At 5 p.m., the screen displays my dinner options, and I select soup and bread, which arrives through the panel a few seconds later. I eat, and then at 5:25 p.m., the screen tells me to stand in the circle of light that has appeared on the floor of my cell. I sigh; it's time for the energy harvest.

In the moments leading up to the harvest, it's not Happy's voice that comes through the screen but Galen Rye's.

"Please remove all items of clothing," he says, the usual approachable tone gone from his voice.

Refusal is an option, but the punishment is drone poison. I pull the Velcro straps of my shoes loose (no laces allowed in the Loop) and kick them onto my bed. I pull apart the Velcro fastener of my plain white jumpsuit and slide it down my body. It joins my shoes on the bed, and I stand there, naked. Galen's voice returns: *"Keep your hands by your sides and legs together. Inmate, know that the energy harvest is part of your punishment. Know that criminality will not be tolerated. Know that your suffering will act as a deterrent to those outside prison who are considering a life of crime."*

"Shut the fuck up," I mutter.

The great glass tube lowers from the ceiling. The harvest begins at 5:30 p.m.

It starts quickly.

Adrenaline dumps into my system; my heart goes from its resting rate to racing in one second, and every muscle in my body begins to tense, knotting and hardening until I'm sure they're all going to tear at once. I fall forward, unable to control my spasming fibers, and my face slams against the glass of the tube. I want to cry out in pain, but my throat has locked. Next, microscopic nanobots are released into the tube. They push themselves through my skin and into the veins at my temples, riding the blood flow until they are in my brain, where they replicate and access fear centers in the neocortex and amygdala. They make me believe my life is in great danger, and I'm sure that I'm going to die. No matter how hard I try to assure myself that this is just the energy harvest, that this is just how they get the power they need to operate the Loop without the Alts having to pay more taxes for our imprisonment, I cannot shake off the certainty that this is the end of my life. I twist and convulse and claw at the glass, frantic for a way out.

I fall to the floor, find my voice, and scream.

The harvest goes on for six hours, but it feels like days.

When it finally does end, I'm physically and emotionally drained. I lie on the concrete, wet with the sweat that is pouring off my body, and then the water comes, acrid and infused with delousing agents, triglyceride, and a form of bleach.

Then the hot air blasts in, drying the water and the sweat to a grainy residue, and finally the tube lifts away.

I lie there, and after a few minutes I smile because tomorrow I will run again—I will run and run and drain myself of all my energy so they can't have it.

I crawl to my bed and look at the clock. I count down the minutes until midnight.

When it comes, I stand at the window and watch the government-issue rain, which comes at midnight and lasts for thirty minutes, calculated to be just the right amount for the crops and the trees before tomorrow's perfect amount of cloud cover to allow the perfect amount of sunlight to keep the inhabitants of this quadrant of Earth perfectly happy and healthy.

Half an hour later the rain ends, and I can sleep.

I lie in my bed, the moon casting shadows of my hands on the wall as I practice the sign language my mother taught me when I was a kid. I spell out my sister's name—*Molly*; I spell out my old address—*Door 44. 177th Floor. Black Road Vertical*; I spell out Wren's name; I run through the alphabet.

Tomorrow I will do all this again, and the next day and the next day and on and on until I turn eighteen and I'm taken to the Block, or I get unlucky with a Delay, or I drop dead of some new kind of sickness out of the Red Zones.

And this is how it goes. This is life in the Loop.

DAY 738 IN THE LOOP

I wake up before my alarm, eat my breakfast, and begin my workout.

At 9 a.m., Galen's address comes on.

I read until 11:30 a.m., when the back wall of my cell silently opens for exercise hour.

I run from my cell to the pillar and back, over and over again, pushing myself as hard as I can for forty-five minutes, then rest, enjoying the warm sun, listening to Pander sing and Tyco threaten me for fifteen minutes before I return to my cell.

I read again, almost finishing my book, until Wren arrives.

We talk for ten minutes. Today my lunch is a salad bowl. Wren leaves, and I'm left in the silence and sadness for over three hours until the energy harvest begins.

For six hours, I suffer the fear and the pain of the harvest.

Finally, it ends, and I crawl to the window to watch the rain before collapsing into bed and falling into a restless sleep.

I wake before my alarm.

    Choose cereal for breakfast.

    Work out.

    Watch Galen's address.

    Read.

    Run.

    Wren brings me lunch, a vegetable wrap.

    I sit in silence.

    I choose dinner.

    The energy harvest comes.

    I watch the rain.

    I sleep.

DAY 740 IN THE LOOP

The same routine . . .

Day after day . . .

It never ends.

I wake up before my alarm and smile.

Today is Wednesday, and on Wednesday the routine is broken.

The day is the same as always—the only difference is that it seems to take forever. Each minute feels like an hour, and the hours feel like days.

After exercise I can't help but glance at the clock over and over again, hoping each time that a great chunk of this endless day will have magically disappeared, but the numbers are stubborn and refuse to change.

Wren comes at her usual time, and we chat, only this time it's more muted, more cautious. There's a secret between us, something that we know but can't talk about, not yet, not until 2 a.m.

She says goodbye and winks at me before closing the hatch. I smile back and feel a burst of excitement in my stomach.

I face the energy harvest with a smile. The smile quickly disappears as the harvest begins, but I can handle it tonight, I can get through it.

The rain comes and goes, and I lie on my bed, feeling my energy levels beginning to replenish bit by bit. Tonight I don't sleep, though; tonight I wait.

I watch the numbers switch from 1:59 a.m. to 2:00 a.m.,

and for the briefest of moments the screen flickers.

I reach under my pillow for my hat and pull the black knit material low over my Panoptic camera. This is just a precaution—the footage from the Panoptic cameras can only be accessed by the government if they are given permission by the citizen or if the person is suspected to be actively involved in a crime or missing-persons case.

I sit up on my bed, stare fervently at the thick steel door, and wait.

I hear the snap of the lock followed by a rolling, metal-on-metal sound as the spin handle is loosened from the outside. The door swings open.

"Ready?" Wren asks, smiling and beautiful in the frame of my cell's doorway.

I nod and get to my feet, stopping at the threshold and taking a deep breath before stepping out into the expanse of the Loop's corridor.

I can hear Wren moving from cell to cell, unlocking the doors of a few selected inmates for three hours of freedom, or, the closest we can ever get to freedom.

I follow the curvature of the corridor until I can see Wren. I watch her unlocking Juno's cell, and I can't help but marvel at her bravery, her selflessness. To risk her job, her freedom, her life to exploit the only flaw in the Loop's security: a three-hour system diagnostic-and-analysis period when the in-cell scanners are down. There is not another Alt in this world who would do something so amazing for lowly Regulars, let alone convicted Regulars.

"Keep staring," Woods says, appearing beside me, grinning his gap-toothed grin, his broad shoulders brushing past me. "That ain't creepy at all."

"I was just . . ." I stutter. "I wasn't staring."

"Sure," Woods replies, his stocky frame shaking as he laughs. He makes his way around the corridor toward the cell of his boyfriend and fellow planner, Winchester.

The corridor begins to fill up with freed inmates—they dance and sing and skip along the wide corridor, meeting in groups of twos and threes and fours to talk and to hold one another and to be human for three short hours.

There is no gift in the world, no experience or feeling, that can compare to these hours where we can look into one another's eyes and talk without walls between us, or microphones listening to us.

Wren frees the last of the lucky few: those of us who are deemed trustworthy, level-headed, and resolute enough both to pose no threat to the lives of the others and keep the secret that would result in Wren's incarceration if it was ever found out.

I watch as Malachai swaggers out of his cell. Malachai is a Regular who just happened to be born tall and handsome. To be honest, he's beautiful. Alts refer to this kind of Regular as a Natural. He's not perfect like the Alts, but somehow that just makes him more attractive; his slightly crooked nose and almost-beady eyes do nothing to detract from his stupid Natural allure. I can't help but look away as his charming grin is reciprocated by Wren. I try to focus on anything else, and my eyes fall on a small crack in the wall. I stare at it, attempting to counter the tremors of jealousy that wrench at my heart.

Wren laughs, the sound breaks my resolve, and then she turns to the group, holding two hands above her head. She, like everyone else in the 2 a.m. club, wears a hat to cover the camera in her head.

"Guys, listen, please," she calls, and the corridor falls silent. "Just a quick reminder of the rules: You are all back in your cells by 4:59, no later or we're all caught. You do not cross the detonation threshold . . . for obvious reasons."

This gets a laugh. My eyes dart toward the exit from this prison, an opening between two cells that leads to the Dark Train platform.

Wren continues, "If you have requests for items you want brought in, nonelectronic, of course, then please talk to me. I can't make contact with anyone in the outside world, the risks are too high, I'm sorry. If you have—"

"Winchester? Hey, where is he? What's going on? Where is he?"

Wren's speech is interrupted by Woods's voice booming along the hallway.

All heads turn in the direction of the commotion as Woods pushes past Pander, Akimi, and Juno and charges toward Wren.

"Open his cell, Wren," he demands.

"Woods, listen," Wren replies, shaking her head slowly. "He's not back from the Facility yet."

I observe the hope whoosh out of Woods's body, even

though all I can see from here is his back. He seems to deflate, to crumble.

"He didn't even tell me . . . I thought he just slept through exercise . . . When did he . . . how long has he been gone?"

"His Delay was at ten a.m.," she replies. "It doesn't mean he's not coming back, Woods. People sometimes come back after days, you know that."

"Yeah, but mostly they don't come back at all."

He's right. We all know what has happened; we don't need it explained to us. As Woods storms back to his cell and slams the door behind him, we all share a look that says that any one of us might face a surgery in our next Delay, any one of us might go the way of Winchester.

"Anyway," Wren says, addressing the group, "enjoy your three hours."

Slowly the noise levels rise back to their former volume as we put Winchester's fate to the back of our minds and enjoy the time we have left. Aside from Wren's rules, there are a few unwritten ones among the inmates: You don't complain during the 2 a.m. club, you don't talk about your past life, and you never ask why anyone is locked up in here. None of us want to think about that stuff.

Juno takes this opportunity to approach Wren. I watch her skeletal frame—which is barely substantial enough to keep her white jumpsuit from sliding off her shoulders—as she sidles up to the warden. She speaks in hushed tones, but from where I am, I catch every word.

"Did you think about what I said?" Juno whispers. "Last

week? Did you manage to get hold of anything?"

"Juno, you know I can't bring Ebb in here. They put you on the program, didn't they? You're off the stuff; why go back?"

Juno's dull gray eyes bore into Wren's bright green ones. She smiles cynically and shakes her head, her lank sand-colored hair falling across her face. "Do you know why people get clean, Wren? They get clean for the promise of a future. I'm going to die in here, that's a fact, you know it is. There's no future for me. Please?"

Wren's eyes scan the emaciated face of the girl in front of her. "I'm sorry, Juno, I just can't."

Juno bites her bottom lip, trying to fight off the tears that well into her eyes. "All right," she whispers.

"Do you need more paper? A new pencil? Your drawings are amazing, Juno; focus on that . . ."

But Juno is no longer listening. She turns and walks away, collapsing into a cross-legged position on the floor next to Pod and Igby, who sit opposite each other as they roll their dice and battle imaginary creatures. When Pod rolls, he counts the numbers by running his fingers over the indents in the face of each die, his blind eyes drifting up, seeing nothing. Pod, unlike Juno, is huge and broad-shouldered. Igby is shorter and slimmer. He is intelligent and quick-witted and swears like no one else. He's from Region 19, formerly known as South Korea. He also has the worst receding hairline of any fifteen-year-old boy I've ever seen.

Pander starts singing again, one of the old songs from our great-great-grandfathers' era. She's only thirteen and doesn't talk much, but she loves to sing. Pander's eyes are big and brown, magnified further by her thick glasses. She has hearing aids in both ears and a scar on her neck, but these things that the Alts would call flaws seem to disappear when she sings. She also has tattoos under both eyes, needled into her with white ink to show up more clearly against her dark brown skin. These are gang tattoos that no one ever asks her about.

Chirrak and Catherine run past me, two young inmates who obviously have a crush on each other but—despite the constant threat of death—haven't yet told each other. Instead they chase each other, playing playground games in the hopes they might stumble into intimacy.

Akimi goes through her usual 2 a.m. club routine; Wren hands her a paper bag full of clothes, and she disappears into her cell to change. When she comes out—now wearing a red summer dress with bright white sneakers—she swirls the fabric around her knees and begins to dance to Pander's singing. Akimi has an accent, Region 70, what would have been known in the past as an Eastern European accent, but it only really comes out when she's scared or mad, and when she's mad, her sweet, sharp features become intimidating and scary.

Adam and Fulton could almost be twins, both short with black hair and pale skin. Usually they are joined by Winchester and Woods, but today it's just the two of them, standing close together and discussing their latest plan of escape.

Reena Ito runs and skips around and around the wide corridor, laughing as she goes, her freedom countering the effects of the harvest, one outstretched hand running along the wall, her curly bright red hair bouncing from beneath her hat and falling into her eyes.

"You read the book yet?" Wren's voice breaks me out of my observations.

"Hi," I say, turning and smiling at her. "Nearly finished, and you're right, it's incredible."

"It gets even better," she says, smile widening. "Book three is my favorite."

"I can't wait."

"So, any requests? Nonelectronic, remember."

"I guess books two and three," I tell her.

"Already got them," she says. "I put them in your room." She touches my arm and walks away.

"Hey, wait," I say, and she turns back. I realize that I hadn't planned to say anything, I just didn't want her to go.

"Yeah?" she asks.

The silence grows, and I grasp at the first thing that pops into my head. "Are there rumors of a war coming?"

Wren's luminous eyes narrow, and her smile broadens. "What?"

"You know, on the outside, is anyone talking about a war?"

She laughs. "No, Luka, who would we be going to war with? We're one nation, one planet under one rule and all that stuff. War? That's mad."

"What about the Missing?" I ask. "Any news on them?"

"I mean, it's still happening, in fact it's happening more often, at least four a month, but . . ." She laughs again. "Luka, what's this about?"

39

I laugh too. "Ah, it's nothing, it's just, you go a little stir-crazy in this place, and you hear things."

"Well, rest assured there's no war."

"Great, and you know . . . thanks for all this. It's crazy—you risk everything to give us this little bit of freedom and it means the world, you know?"

"It's worth the risk," she replies, pushing her golden hair behind her ear. "The way they treat you in here, it's . . . I didn't vote for it. I don't care what Happy says, I don't care how logical it is, I would never . . . It's worth the risk."

"Well, thanks is all I wanted to say."

Not true. What I wanted to say was: *I love you. I wish I could blow this place to a million pieces and run away with you.* But even in my own head, it sounds impossibly stupid.

"No problem," Wren says, and then wanders over to Malachai, punching him playfully on the arm and laughing gleefully as he makes some pithy comment.

I turn from the scene, block it from my mind.

I see Alistair and Emery locked against the wall of the hallway, arms wrapped around each other, lips pressed together as their heads move rhythmically with the kiss. Alistair's bleached shock of hair almost glows in the dim light. I consider talking to them, asking them about the rumor they spoke of in the exercise yard, where they got their information from, but I decide not to interrupt their tryst.

"Want to play hide-and-seek again?" a voice comes from beside me. I turn and see Harvey, his old-fashioned steel crutches under both arms. The boy has cerebral palsy, a disease that shouldn't exist anymore, but Harvey was born poor.

"Remember what happened last time? Malachai yelled at you for hiding in his room."

"Fuck Malachai." Harvey smiles. "I'll hit him with the business end of one of these if he starts his shit again." Harvey brandishes one of his crutches and grins.

I laugh. "Maybe next time?"

"Fine, loser. As One," Harvey says as he limps away to find someone else to play with him.

This region of Earth's last election was won in a landslide by the current Overseer, Galen Rye, whose slogan was *As One*. He became a cult hero among both the richest members of society and the poorest. He has a knack of appealing to the extreme ends of politics. He promised to tighten migration control when the rest of the world was eliminating borders, he promised to eradicate homelessness by reinstating compulsory conscription into the emergency services, and he promised to vote against the algorithms of the machines when he felt human logic and the will of the people were at stake. He won the poor vote by convincing them he would fight for them, promising free training in virtual architecture, human thorium reactor engineers, and more teaching positions for low- and no-income households.

Galen Rye was predicted to *lose* by a landslide. I remember my dad telling me to listen carefully to what he was saying—he told me that this was not what hate sounded like, this was not what fascism sounded like, this was the voice of pure manipulation. A man who knew how to unite foes against a new common enemy and use it to his own advantage.

Rye won by a record margin. His supporters are adamant that he is a force for good. I'm not so sure.

I watch Harvey use one of his crutches to trip Chirrak. They both laugh. It breaks my heart watching these kids burn away their childhoods in a pit like this. I was one of them not so long ago—in a lot of ways I still am.

I put these thoughts aside; this is a time for happiness, brief as it may be. I walk over to Akimi, who is still dancing away in her temporary dress. She grabs my hands, and we dance together, smiling and laughing and enjoying these fleeting minutes that will be gone so swiftly.

Tomorrow is just another day inside the Loop.

It's 5:32 in the morning, and a rumbling sound thrums through the walls.

I'm alert immediately. Anything that breaks the routine is likely to provoke a fight-or-flight response in me.

I realize this is not so much a sound but a feeling; it's a vibration, like a minor earthquake shaking the ground beneath the gigantic prison. I know what this is—this is the Dark Train. A new inmate is arriving.

I close my eyes and try to go back to sleep, but it quickly becomes evident that it's not going to happen. Despite the depleting effects of the harvest on my body, my brain is wide-awake.

I get up and walk to the door, pressing my ear against it, as if I'll somehow be able to hear the new inmate taking that long walk around the Loop to their cell, but I can't; all I hear is the deep and constant silence that I live with every day.

I'm loath to start my morning at this time—two additional hours can feel like a lifetime in this place—so I lie down on top of my sheets and stare up at the ceiling in the dim light.

I return to the world I have created, the story I'm writing in my head; this is a technique I developed to keep me from losing my mind in the endless hours of silence. I can get lost in another world for a while, like I can with books. This story is set far in the past, long before the machines controlled everything, before pre-life cosmetic improvements for the rich, before the ascension of the Altered and their dominion over the Regulars, and long, long before Galen Rye. A time that my dad used to talk about, a very brief period in human history when we almost got it right, not everyone, not all the time, but we were close.

I walk through this world, far away from the Loop, I'm free to go wherever I want, and I always end up at the same place: the riverside. This place is where my favorite memories live; this is where we used to go as a family on long summer days, where we'd forget about everything for four or five hours and just relax. My sister and my father are with me in this place now, and there are no such things as Alts and Regulars or war or hate. There isn't much to this story—no conflict, no danger, no twists and turns—but it's a world where I can be happy. And yes, Wren exists in this world too, and yes, sometimes when I walk along the riverside in this world, I'm holding her hand, and sometimes she smiles at me, and sometimes, for a while, I even forget that it's not real. I can see how easy it would be to lose myself in here, and I don't blame all of those in the outside world who are addicted to Ebb.

Before I know it, hours have passed—it's 7:30 a.m., and Happy's voice comes through the speakers.

"Inmate 9-70-981. Today is Thursday, the ninth of June. Day 744 in the Loop. The temperature inside your cell is

66 degrees Fahrenheit. Please select your breakfast option."

And the routine begins again: I eat my tasteless breakfast, I watch Galen's daily address, I complete my workout, then I open the second book in the trilogy—*The Two Towers*—and read.

I'm so lost in the fantastical world of Middle-earth that I'm almost unaware of the sound of birdsong and the slight breeze as 11:30 comes and the back wall opens up for exercise, but I mark my page and quickly stretch my legs before sprinting out into the sunlight.

Again I hear the mixture of sound coming from all sides of the Loop—the conversations picked up from the day before as though no time has passed, the mad ramblings, Pander singing, and, of course, repetitive threats from across the yard: "Luka Kane, I'm going to kill you. Luka Kane, I'm going to kill you."

I've gotten so good at blocking out the unfulfillable threat that I almost miss the sound of crying on the other side of the wall to my left.

The new inmate, I think as I complete my first lap and turn to spring back to the pillar.

I feel like it's my responsibility, as it was Maddox's before mine, to help my new neighbor, to tell them that it's going to be all right, to tell them that the fear goes away, but not now—now I have to complete my sprints. Forty-three more minutes.

The sun feels hotter today, which is impossible—the machines keep the temperature of this part of the world at a constant 66 degrees from 8 a.m. until 5 p.m., at which point it slowly lowers throughout the night to 41 degrees. It must be the thought of a new inmate, possibly a new friend, and that makes me feel more exhausted than usual today. Every time I complete a lap and glance at the screen, it seems like no time has passed at all.

Finally, though, it finishes, I hit forty-five minutes of painful sprinting, and I collapse against the joining wall.

I allow the sounds of the Loop to come back to me: the background chatter of the inmates, the beautiful singing voice of Pander, the continuing game between Igby and Pod, and the droning cries of Tyco Roth as he relentlessly promises to end my life, but over that I hear that some of the nastier inmates have realized that there's a new prisoner in the Loop and they've turned on them, as they do with all newcomers.

"Welcome to the Loop; you're going to die here," one calls out.

"Stop crying; there'll be nothing left for the energy harvest," another yells over the laughter.

And finally, I hear the quiet sobs from the cell next to mine again. I can tell by the tone that the new inmate is almost certainly a girl.

I know what she's feeling. Right now, sitting in her cell or out in the gray concrete yard, she's never felt so alone and so hopeless. I felt it too, and the words from the heartless inmates feel like fists raining down on you.

There's a unique cruelty to this place; they take your life away from you without a second thought. It all happens so fast; the televised trial is over in seconds, you're not allowed to say goodbye to anyone, you're dragged to the platform where you wait for as long as it takes for the train to come, and then the first surgery to ensure you can never escape, then imprisonment. Surrounded by a silence that begins eating away at your sanity immediately.

It takes some time for my breathing to return to normal, and I try to think of the right words to say, and the right way to say them, so that I can help the new inmate in some small way.

"Hi," I say finally, and wait for a reply. Nothing comes, not even a break in the tears. "Hey, it gets better, you know? Not great, but . . . better."

I turn and lean against the wall; I can feel every minute of the girl's pain and anger.

"Umm," I say, fumbling for more words, "I know what you're feeling, we all felt it, well, almost all of us, some of these guys are just psychos, you know? And, uhhh . . ."

My thoughts are interrupted by a siren and the one-minute warning.

"*All inmates must return to their rooms within one minute. All inmates must return to their rooms within one minute.*"

I look up at the blue sky and try to take in as much of the fresh air and warmth as I can before I'm locked away again. I can't enjoy it, though, not while the girl on the other side of the wall is in so much pain. I wish there was something I could do.

There is, I think, remembering the enormous pile of books in my room.

I run into my cell, crossing the threshold and activating the sliding door early. I move quickly to the foot of my bed and search for a book. A very specific book: *The Call of the Wild*, the first one that Wren ever gave me. I find it and run back outside, ducking under the half-closed door. I'm all too aware that if the door closes with me on the yard side, the drones will shoot me, not with bullets—that would be too kind—but with a tranquilizer agent that induces horrific hallucinations followed by a terrible sickness that lasts days.

I know this because an inmate named Rook Ford once tried to commit suicide by drone. Rook had lost his mind after five years inside—he'd been incarcerated at age twelve, and day after day his sanity had faded. He made a loud declaration about how he was taking control back from a broken system, and he refused to reenter his cell after the one-minute warning. When he recovered, five days later, he wasn't the same person, something had changed in him, and he quietly told anyone close enough to hear that whatever they shot him with was far, far worse than death. He was convinced that he had been in a nightmare world for hundreds of years. He refused his next Delay, accepted his Deletion, and they say he boarded the Dark Train with a smile on his face, although this is probably just a made-up rumor, seeing as no one could have seen him getting on the train.

The thought of the poisonous darts loaded into the insectile flying robots makes my heart race, and I sprint to the wall.

"Hey, new girl," I call out as I throw the book in a high arc. I see the nearest drone spin in the direction of the soaring paperback, and for one horrible moment I'm sure it's going to shoot it out of the air, but its sensors must take it for a bird or a floating leaf, and it leaves it alone.

The book dips over the metal barricade. I turn and run back to the door, which is now almost all the way closed.

I take two long strides and dive, turning in midair so that I land on my hip and roll under. I feel the hard, cold door press against me as I squeeze through, and just before it slams shut I hear my new neighbor's voice call out in a surprised and grateful tone, "Thank you."

"Who's the new girl?" I ask Wren, nodding my head in the direction of the cell beside mine.

Three more yard sessions have passed since the two words my new neighbor spoke to me, and I haven't managed to get anything out of her, other than another thank-you when I threw her a second book.

Wren doesn't reply—she doesn't appear to have heard me. A deep line divides her eyebrows as she stares anxiously at nothing.

"Wren?" I say, getting the warden's attention.

"What? Oh, I'm sorry, Luka, it's just . . . nothing, it's nothing."

"Are you okay?" I ask. "You've been distracted since you got here."

Wren smiles, she's good at faking it, but I can tell she had to force it onto her face. "Really, Luka, I'm okay. What were you asking?"

"The new girl," I repeat. "Who is she?"

"Kina Campbell," Wren says, taking a bite of her sandwich. "Nice girl, a Regular, like you."

Wren bites her lip and looks guiltily at me as though she's misspoken. I ignore the comment.

"I gave her a few books—I hope you don't mind?"

"They're your books," she replies, smiling.

Wren's eyes drift off to the left, checking the time in her Lens display. "Better get moving," she says. "See you tomorrow."

"Yeah, see you tomorrow."

And she's gone again.

That night, when I watch the rain, I can't help my mind drifting off to that made-up world. I imagine Wren and me sitting on a hillside somewhere, talking about the future, our future. It's a stupid fantasy, a stupid teenage boy's dream that can't ever come true. Even if I wasn't serving a death sentence, even if I wasn't destined to die from a botched Delay, Wren is a nineteen-year-old Alt and I'm a sixteen-year-old Regular. Outside the Loop, she'd never even look at me.

I truly hate this place. Sometimes it becomes unbearable, and I understand exactly why Rook Ford tried to have the drones kill him.

As the back wall opens up for exercise the next day, I find myself not running. Instead, I walk to the dividing wall and press my hand against it.

I'm trying to think of something to say, when my neighbor speaks.

"Hello."

Her voice is hoarse and quiet, and I'm sure that today is the first day she's managed to stop crying.

"Hi," I say.

"Thank you for the books. I think I might have gone crazy without them."

"That's okay."

"My name's Kina," she says.

"Luka," I reply.

"Luka?" she repeats. "The same Luka that guy keeps yelling about killing every day?"

"The same one."

"Why does he hate you so much?"

I think about this for a second. I have my theories, but I don't know for sure. For a moment, the image of the boy falling off the roof of the Black Road Vertical flashes in my mind.

"Honestly, I wish I knew," I tell her. "I guess he knew someone I knew on the outside."

"Well," Kina says with a new brightness in her voice, "thanks again for the books, Luka."

"I've got plenty more," I say, feeling the conversation coming to an end and not wanting it to. "Books, I mean, hundreds of them, and I've read them all, so you can borrow them whenever you want."

"Luka the librarian," she says, and laughs. "How did you get them?"

"I'm friends with the warden, Wren. She's nice; you'll like her."

"Wren?" she says. "Oh, yeah, she seems nice."

"She is; she's really great," I tell her, and I can't help but smile.

"So, Luka, how long have you been in this fine establishment?" she asks.

"Two years, two weeks, and four days," I reply.

"God, that's . . . a long time," she says in a low voice.

"Ah, the time flies when you're . . . trapped in crushing silence."

Kina laughs, and the sound makes me smile again. "Well," I say, stepping back from the wall, "better get on with my sprints."

"Sprints?" Kina asks.

"Yeah, I like to run."

"Really?"

"Yeah, it keeps me fit and leaves them with no energy to take at the harvest."

Kina laughs at this. "I like that. A little act of rebellion."

I smile. "Exactly. Speak tomorrow?"

"Tomorrow," she replies.

The run doesn't feel as hard as it usually does. And that night, after dinner, even the harvest is bearable.

As midnight approaches, I drag myself from the floor, my legs so weak that they shake uncontrollably as I stumble to the back wall and look to the sky through the window.

I stare at the clear black night and wait, and wait. Midnight comes, and I turn my eyes skyward, but the explosions don't appear.

Impossible. Happy is not late, not ever, not even by one second—the system is flawless; it runs everything. I look at the time on my screen and see that thirty seconds have already passed since the scheduled rainfall.

"Happy?" I say, not tearing my eyes away from the sky. But no reply comes from my screen. "Happy!"

My screen flickers and then comes back to life.

"How can I help?" the screen asks in that familiar voice.

"The rain—" I start.

My panic is interrupted by the first flash in the sky, followed by a second and third spreading out into the distance in a long net of lights, and the clouds spiral out and join together.

"What just happened?" I ask.

"Everything is as it should be, Inmate 9-70-981," Happy tells me.

"The rain," I say, finally looking away as the first drops slam into the yard. "It was late."

"Everything is as it should be."

54

I look from the screen back to the falling rain.

I'm so relieved at the sight of the thick drops beating against the ground, running down the walls, drenching the waiting drones atop the column, that I ignore the error for a moment and just watch, pretending it never happened.

But it did, and I don't know what it means.

There is talk among the inmates of the late rain.

It surprises me. I guess I always assumed that I was the only one who watches the rain each night.

I hear their voices in the yard, asking questions: *Why? What does it mean? What's going on out there?*

I finish my final sprint toward my cell and then lean against Kina's wall. It takes a while to catch my breath.

"How was your run?" she asks.

"Good, thanks."

"Luka, the rain . . ."

"It was late," I finish. "I know. What do you think it means?"

"Probably nothing."

"Yeah, probably nothing," I agree, but I can't seem to shake off this uneasy feeling.

I sit in silence for a while, listening to the sounds of the inmates chatting, Malachai Bannister taunting the drones, Pander singing, Chirrak and Catherine talking tentatively, and two out of the four planners planning. Winchester still hasn't returned from his last Delay, and Woods knows what that means—he died on the operating table when whichever piece of trendy technology they were trying to attach and perfect killed him. Woods hasn't said a word since last Wednesday.

"How are you recovering from your heart implant?" I ask Kina, my hand instinctively going to the small scar on my own chest.

"It doesn't hurt," she says. "It's just a bit uncomfortable."

"That goes away."

I feel my body jerk at the memory of my initial surgery. The kind of trauma that you never truly get over, but here in the Loop, we don't talk about it. I try to fight against the memory, but it comes on fast and unyielding.

The Marshals kick my front door in, splinters of wood and militaristic yells. My sister is screaming as my dad stares solemnly out the window at the black speck that is growing smaller and smaller, carried toward the horizon by a large drone.

The Marshals dragged me, currents of electricity forcing my limbs rigid, out the door and down 177 flights of stairs.

There was darkness after that. The rumbling of an engine, the vibrations as I was transported to the Facility.

And then the paralysis needle.

The first time it happens, you're sure that it's forever, that this is your life now, that this is what they do with criminals—immobilize them and stack them into cells to be forgotten about.

Then came the surgery.

Her face, half covered by a pristine white mask, appeared in my field of vision, a horrible glee in her eyes as she talked me through the things they were doing to my body.

She held aloft the thick cobalt cables and told me that they were cutting deep into my wrists and embedding the magnetic cuffs.

My body shifted as the blade tugged open my skin, then I heard the sound of bolts being fired into bone.

The surgeon appeared again, and as she spoke, I could hear the smile in her voice.

"This," she said, holding up a small metal wire clasped in her tweezers, "this is what we do to felons." The wire weaved around into an infinity symbol. It was made of silver metal, and white lights—evenly spaced throughout the figure eight—blinked rapidly. The surgeon turned the device around so that my locked eyes could see it clearly.

"This will pierce a hole through the right atrium of your heart. It will weave out and then into your pulmonary artery. It will track your movements, it will connect you to the Loop, and, most importantly, it will detonate and kill you if you step out of line."

I wanted to scream, I wanted to run from there, but I couldn't.

I didn't feel it, but I heard the tear and the rip as she cut into my chest and between my ribs and into my beating heart. Inserting a loop into my heart so that I would be trapped inside the Loop, with no hope of escape.

"When's your next Delay?" Kina asks, snapping me out of the recollection and back into the bright sunlight of the yard.

"Uh, about three months," I tell her.

"You feeling lucky?"

I shake away the last of the lingering memory of the heart

implant. "I've made it through four without dying so far. Five if you count the heart implant."

"What were they?" she asks.

"My first was a nanotech. They never told me what it was for, but they made me drink some blue liquid, then they injected me with something. The second was a surgery. Luckily, it was only a minor one—they replaced the cartilage between two of my ribs with a new fiber that was supposed to have better tensile strength than the natural stuff, then they ran a bunch of tests and left me to recover without painkillers. The third Delay, they injected me with this fast-acting virus that made my temperature rise immediately, and bruises began to appear on my skin where blood vessels were bursting below the surface. They let the virus take me to the point of convulsions before they injected me with an experimental vaccine that—fortunately—worked. The fourth one was a new type of surgical stitching—they cut my forearm open from the elbow to the wrist and then sewed the wound up with some kind of skin-binding tool."

Kina is silent for a while. I hear her exhale. "That sounds awful."

"It's not exactly a holiday," I tell her.

"How can they let this happen to us? How can the government treat us like this?"

"The people don't vote against Galen Rye," I remind her. "If you're rich, he's a capitalist hero; if you're poor, he's fighting for your rights."

"It makes you wonder, why has there never been a rebellion?"

"It takes a lot to rebel, and Galen's got the extremists on his side. Besides, they've made it impossible," I point out. "They control every aspect of our lives, our currency is digital, they can seize it without lifting a finger, taxes come out of wages without the worker having to hand anything over, we're watched twenty-four hours a day by surveillance drones so nothing can be planned, and they keep enough people solvent so that the voices of the repressed are never listened to."

"There were rumors, you know, on the outside. I never heard them directly, but my mother, she—"

Kina is interrupted by the one-minute warning ringing out across the yard. The drones hover off their center pillar, weapons tracking the inmates below.

"What rumors?" I ask.

"Nothing," she says. "It was just conspiracy theory nonsense. I'll speak to you tomorrow, Luka the librarian."

I want to hear more about these rumors, see if they match up with Alistair and Emery's whisperings of war, but there's no time. The back wall begins to close, and I step inside my cell.

When the wall shuts and the silence returns, I have nothing but time.

I lie back on my bed and think about the stories my dad used to tell me and my sister when we were kids. He'd tell us all about the Third World War—the Futile War. Mom always said that the stories were too adult for us, but we always wanted to hear more. I often wonder if that's why I felt such a kinship with Maddox, because he was so similar to my dad.

Twenty-nine nuclear bombs were dropped during the Third World War; some were big enough to level half a country, and others merely took out cities. An estimated 900 million civilians died during the conflict, but countless more died in the aftermath as Earth's temperature dropped and the effects of the nukes took their toll.

It was a coalition of rebels that ended the war—rebels from both sides, from almost every country. The fact was that most of the citizens of the world didn't want to be a part of it; they were too smart to fall for government propaganda and fear-mongering, so they ended it, not with bombs or missiles but with a combination of hope, courage, and having nothing left to lose.

No single country won the war, no group of nations left to write their own version of history—the people of Earth won the war, and when those who started it were brought to justice and sentenced to death, those same people vowed it would never happen again.

Once the old powers were removed, evidence was uncovered of corruption so deep and sickening that it justified the musings of even the most ardent conspiracy theorists; several of the world's most deadly diseases at the time had been cured decades previously, but the treatments were kept from the world to benefit the rich pharmaceutical companies, who made trillions selling near-useless pills to the sick and dying. It transpired that the political groups that people so fervently supported were merely a facade fostered and encouraged by the billionaires of the world to keep the people at odds—it was much easier to pass a despicable law when the citizens were voting with anger in their hearts rather than logic in their heads. Oil was obsolete; it had been for nearly a century—dozens upon dozens of scientists, mechanics, and tinkerers had created engines that ran on solar power, water, and hydrogen, but governments the world over bought and buried the patents because the oil wars were making fortunes for a select few.

After the war, the World Government was formed: a government that represented peace and prosperity, health care for every citizen and genuine equal opportunities for all, and—most importantly—logic. Logic in the form of Happy Inc. advising the government, solving international problems, and administering flawless and swift justice. And for a while it really worked, but curing three of the top five causes of death had its drawbacks too—the population exploded after civilization was rebuilt. People lived longer, and almost no one died young. The populations of countries were forced into the surviving cities, as far away from the nuclear blasts as possible, and overcrowding was a huge problem, as were water shortages, energy shortages, famine, and the spreading of brand-new diseases that seemed to be born in the fallout. To this day, the sites of the nuclear blasts and the surrounding areas of irradiated land are uninhabitable. These areas are known as the Red Zones.

My sister and I would listen to these stories, and stories of the most famous battles, with such interest that we could barely sleep afterward.

But the thought of war, real war, is one that both terrifies and excites me. I wish it didn't excite me, but just the notion of any sort of break in the routine of the Loop makes me almost dizzy with anticipation.

My father told me that they used inmates during the Third World War; they promised them reduced sentences, even freedom, if they would fight on the front lines. That's an offer I would take without a second thought.

You're getting ahead of yourself, Luka, I tell myself. *You've heard one rumor. There is nothing going on.*

And I know that it's true, and I'm ashamed of myself for wishing for war, but when you've been caged and broken down, perhaps war is the best you can hope for.

I'm pulled from my thoughts by the hatch opening and Wren's voice.

"Hey, Luka, how are you?"

And with that, all thoughts of war and freedom are gone.

I'm awoken by the sound of my screen rapidly bleeping.

Something sparks in the back of my mind, and I realize that today is Wednesday, and at 2 a.m. I get to walk out of this cell and be free for a few hours. But then I realize the alarm that's woken me isn't my regular wake-up call.

I recognize the sound; it's a high-pitched beep that signals a Delay opportunity.

I sit up in the darkness and rub the sleep out of my eyes.

"Can't be," I mutter, stumbling toward the screen. It takes a second for my eyes to adjust, but I see that it's 4:04 a.m. and the red dot at the bottom right corner is flashing below the word *Delay*. This is impossible. Delays are offered once every six months, and it's only been three months since I completed my last one.

I blink a few times and try to clear my head. I look at the screen again, but nothing has changed.

My heart begins to thump in my chest. This is new, this is different, and different is amazing in the Loop. Anything that is not the daily routine is something to be savored, good or bad.

I press the red dot, and the screen changes to a white background with lines of text; it's a Delay contract, but what's it doing here on my screen at four in the morning and three months early?

THE UNDERSIGNED (INMATE 9-70-981, HENCEFORTH "THE INMATE"), IS OFFERED THE OPPORTUNITY TO TAKE PART IN A CLINICAL TRIAL OR TRIALS AS PART OF GROUP B, IN EXCHANGE FOR A DELAY IN THE FULFILLMENT OF THEIR COURT RULING (IN THIS CASE THE PENALTY OF DEATH).

UPON ACCEPTANCE OF THIS OFFER, THE INMATE WILL HEREBY BE GRANTED A STAY OF EXECUTION FOR 168 DAYS, AT WHICH TIME—SUBJECT TO CONDITIONS SPECIFIED BELOW—A FURTHER OFFER MAY BE MADE.

THE INMATE RETAINS THE RIGHT OF REFUSAL OF THIS PROPOSAL AT THIS TIME BUT UNDERSTANDS THAT REFUSAL OF THIS CONTRACT WILL RESULT IN THE IMMEDIATE EXECU-TION OF THE RULING OF THE COURT FOLLOWING A ONE-WEEK COOLING-OFF PERIOD, AFTER WHICH THE INMATE WILL ONCE AGAIN BE OFFERED THE OPPORTUNITY TO TAKE PART IN THE TRIAL. IF—ONCE SIGNED—THE INMATE CHOOSES TO RENEGE ON THIS CONTRACT, THE RULING OF THE COURT WILL BE CARRIED OUT IMMEDIATELY.

THE NATURE OF THE TRIAL WILL REMAIN UNSPECIFIED UP TO THE TIME OF SAID TRIAL AND MAY REMAIN UNKNOWN TO THE INMATE FOLLOWING ITS COMPLETION, DEPENDING ON THE NATURE OF SAID TRIAL.

FURTHER DETAILS AND CONTRACTUAL OBLIGATIONS CAN BE FOUND ON PAGES 3–14.

If the Inmate agrees, consent can be given by electronic signature (provided by fingerprint and iris scan) below.

This offer stands for 24 hours from the time of submission (4:03 a.m., on the fifteenth day of June).

By order of the World Government and Region 86 Overseer, Galen Rye.

It's the standard Delay contract apart from two things: the bit about *Group B* and the fact that it doesn't make any sense. Surely, from a legal standpoint, the offer of a six-month contract becomes invalid by offering a new one after only three months? It doesn't matter, though—it's not like I can hire a lawyer to fight my case or voice my dissent to the government, and they wouldn't listen even if I could.

"What the hell is going on?" I whisper into the silence.

I convince myself that it can wait until later. The offer stands for twenty-four hours, after all. And then I remember I have Happy.

"Happy," I say, commanding the screen to talk to me.

"Yes, Inmate 9-70-981?"

"Why have I been offered a Delay?"

"Everything is as it should be, Inmate 9-70-981."

"No, it isn't," I insist. "I have three months left until my Delay. Can you explain this?"

"Everything is as it should be."

I stare, disbelieving, at the screen. I try to slow my breathing, try to think rationally, but this unprecedented occurrence is causing adrenaline to pump through my body.

"All right," I say finally.

I climb back into my bed and rest my head on my flat pillow. I don't even bother to close my eyes; I know that I won't sleep.

The sun comes up and I go about my daily routine, but I can't help but be distracted by the constant flashing of the red light below the contract—reminding me that something is wrong, something is going on. I'm practically bouncing off the walls waiting for Wren to show up so she can tell me exactly why the Delay contract arrived early.

It feels like time is moving in slow motion, like every second lasts a minute, but finally exercise hour arrives and I don't even wait for the back wall to fully open before ducking into the yard.

Immediately, I'm hit with a wall of concerned voices all talking at once, and I know that I'm not the only one who received the offer.

"Did you get the contract?" one older-sounding inmate yells to his neighbor.

"I took my Delay last week!" someone calls back.

"What does it mean? I got Group A, what did you get?"

"I'm B, what's the difference?"

And still—over all of this—Tyco, unfazed, sticks to his murderous mantra.

"Luka, I'm going to kill you, are you listening to me? I'm going to kill you."

I walk to the wall between Kina and me. Before I can say anything, she speaks.

"What does it mean, Luka?"

"I don't know. It has to be a fault, doesn't it?"

"Which group are you?" she asks.

"Group B. You?"

"B. Did you accept it?"

"No, I decided to wait and talk to Wren. Did you?"

"No, I'm going to do the same thing."

"Something's going on, Kina. It might be time to tell me about those rumors you heard."

There's a moment of silence. "They were just rumors, though, silly gossip I heard from my mom."

"They could be important."

"The thing is, my mother, she didn't spend a lot of her time in the present, if you know what I mean?"

And I do know; Kina's mother is a clone.

The clones aren't clones exactly, it's just what Regulars call victims of the epidemic, those who got lost in a combination of technology and a drug known as Ebb. They got the nickname "clones" because after a few months on Ebb, they all look the same: dull gray skin, missing teeth, matted hair, and skinny because they have no desire to eat.

The rich who get hooked on Ebb use it with a Lens, a piece of technology that every Alt has. It's essentially a contact lens that displays information, records what the wearer sees, and can overlay virtual reality or augmented reality on top of the real world. In the Verticals—where the Regulars can't afford such tech—Ebb users rely on old-fashioned VR headsets. The effects of the drug coupled with the virtual world let the user truly believe that they are living an entirely different life. In reality, they become emaciated, their teeth rot, and their skin develops sores. They just don't have the will to take care of themselves in the real world. Why bother when you're always perfect on Ebb?

"I'm sorry," I say, lost for anything of worth to add.

"No, it's good," Kina tells me. "As far as I know, she's completely unaware that I'm even in this place, and she didn't have a clue about Orla."

I hear Kina catch herself as she finishes her sentence—she's clearly said more than she intended to.

"What did you hear?" I ask, moving the conversation on.

"Well, she was always meeting friends when she was on Ebb, other users, you know? In virtual cocktail bars inside the seedier parts of one of the VR worlds, and I'd hear her talking to them about an uprising—always the word *uprising*, never *war*. I didn't think anything of it, I just assumed it was the usual Ebb-user nonsense, but the topic seemed to keep coming up. But an uprising? That's not possible."

I barely hear the end of her sentence—my mind is racing back to the conversation between Emery and Alistair nearly two weeks ago. Somehow they had gotten wind of the war rumors too.

"It's probably nothing," I say. "We're just jumping to conclusions—late rain and an early Delay doesn't mean there's a war coming. Before I was put away, the biggest news was all the people disappearing from the city, but no one suggested that was the beginning of a war."

There's a pause before Kina answers. "That's still happening," she tells me. "The news calls them the Missing. Around forty people a year, mostly Regulars, they just vanish. Some people say they go into the Red Zones, find a way to survive the radiation."

"I heard they're planning a revolution," I say, almost laughing at the idea of a bunch of Regulars overthrowing a government run by Alts. "Anyway, we don't jump to conclusions about the Missing, so why should we jump to conclusions about this?"

"You're right," she says. "I'm sure when Wren arrives she'll explain that this is just a malfunction or something."

"Exactly," I say. "Let's not get carried away."

"Yeah," Kina agrees, and we let the silence between us stay there for a while.

"Got any more books I can borrow?" Kina asks. "I've read all of the ones you gave me twice."

I laugh even though the sense of unease hasn't left me. "Of course," I say. "Any requests?"

"Anything at all."

I look through the selection of books I've brought outside with me, trying to decide which ones she'll like best.

The commotion of the yard still hasn't died down when the end of exercise alarm sounds.

Kina and I say goodbye, and it's not until I'm lying on my

bed reading the penultimate chapter of the second *Lord of the Rings* book that I realize that I didn't run today. I suppose I was too distracted by the Delay and the late rain.

I finish my book and pick one that I haven't read in a long time. One thirty comes and goes, and Wren doesn't appear.

She's been late before, I tell myself, trying to focus on the words, but I can't seem to find my way into the book. I keep glancing at the time: two o'clock, two thirty, three o'clock, three thirty, four. Still no Wren.

I get up and pace my room. It only takes a few steps to walk from the door to the back wall, but I need to do something to distract myself.

Finally, at a few minutes to five, the hatch slides open and I see Wren's tired eyes staring back at me.

"Wren," I say, moving close to the door, "what's going on?" I don't mean to sound so panicked, but I can't help myself.

"Hi, Luka," she says, and something in her too-wide eyes sets me on edge. "Sorry, it's been a long day."

"Yeah, I bet."

"So here's the deal," she says, and something in her listless voice tells me this isn't the first time she's had to give this speech today. "The Delay is not a mistake; it's been confirmed by the Region. There's an enormous clinical trial coming up, and the Delay will be cumulative, meaning it will be added on to whatever existing time you have on your last Delay contract."

"Right," I say, surprised by the leniency shown by a government that could just as easily take away our banked time and sweep it under the carpet. After all, it's not like any of us will ever get out of here alive to tell anyone. "And if I don't accept it?"

"Unfortunately, not accepting it doesn't mean your Delay reverts back to your previous postponement of your sentence," Wren says, and her eyes rise up as though she's remembering the rules of the new Delay. "Refusal to accept will still result in the commencement of your sentencing."

"So I'll be Deleted if I refuse?" I confirm.

"Essentially, yes."

"I suppose I'll accept, then."

"I suppose that's best," Wren replies, and again I sense apprehension.

"What about the groups? What's the difference between groups A and B?" I ask.

"That I don't know," Wren admits. "All I've been told is that the groups were assigned at random."

"Right. Hey, but nine months until my next Delay," I say, shrugging. "That's pretty good."

I walk to the screen and raise my finger to press the accept button.

"Luka, wait," Wren calls.

I stop and lower my finger from the screen. "What is it?" I ask.

She bites her lower lip and shakes her head. "No, just go ahead. You have to take it."

"Wren, what is it? If something's going on, I should know—"

"It's not that. I don't know . . . I have a bad feeling. I've heard some things."

"Wren, if this Delay is going to kill me, then I'd rather just decline it."

"That's just it. I don't know what it'll be but . . ." Wren trails off and then looks up and to the left—activating a menu in her Lens. Her eyes move right and then she mutters the voice command, "Surveillance off."

"Are you allowed to do that?" I ask.

"Luka, listen, I shouldn't tell you this, but a file was sent to my government email. I think it was a mistake—it was lines of code, really complex stuff. They were deleted from my Lens files almost immediately, but it was a program, an executable file. There was also a document attached. I only had a few seconds to read it before it was erased, but it said something about Phase One and the Great Selection, and something about the Sane Zone and the Battery Project. I don't know what it all meant, but it didn't seem right, Luka. It scared me."

I look to Wren's Panoptic camera, knowing that she's taking a huge risk. The government isn't supposed to watch the footage back without good reason or consent, but the way things have been going recently, nothing would surprise me.

I think about what she has told me, try to make sense of the words. "It's probably nothing," I say, but I can hear the doubt loud and clear in my own voice. "The government uses code names for plans all the time."

"The file was accidentally sent to all government employees, but it was addressed to 'Tier Three applicants.' This was on Saturday night, four days ago. Fifteen government employees haven't been heard from since."

"Wren, I don't have a choice; if I don't take the Delay, I'll be killed anyway."

I turn back to the screen and get the familiar flare of adrenaline and nerves as I press the ACCEPT button, only this time amplified a thousand times. The fingerprint and eye scanner appear. I hesitate for a moment, just a moment.

The scanner accepts my prints and recognizes my iris, and the contract is signed.

The screen flashes green and then more text appears.

YOUR TRIAL WILL BEGIN IN 2 DAYS, 13 HOURS,
AND 2 MINUTES.

"Three days?" I ask Wren, surprised.

"Yes," she replies, her voice shaking. "Group A heads out tomorrow morning. Group B is two days later."

I swallow and nod.

"Well," Wren continues, wiping a tear from her eye, "I better get on with telling the rest of the inmates what's going on."

"I understand," I say, and I want to ask her if tonight is still on, if we'll be meeting as usual at 2 a.m., but I have to be tactful in case anyone's listening. "I suppose you'll be looking forward to getting some sleep after the day you've had?"

She looks at me, and a small smile forms on her lips. "Not too tired—think I'll probably be up until the small hours tonight."

I smile back. "Bye, Wren."

Wren reactivates the surveillance function of her Lens and smiles sorrowfully back at me.

"Bye, Luka."

The hatch shuts.

Wren's words echo in my mind. Phase One and the Great Selection? The Sane Zone and the Battery Project? The fear in her eyes and in her voice have set my mind racing. What does it mean? Why has everything been so strange recently? What's going on in the outside world?

It takes me hours to calm down, to convince myself that everything will be okay.

But that night, after the harvest, as I stand at the window and wait for the rain, all that anxiety comes flooding back—tonight, the rain doesn't come at all.

When 2 a.m. comes, there is none of the usual joy or jubilation. Instead we stand together, sharing apprehensive glances and a sense that something bad is coming.

"So," Malachai says, breaking the silence, "who's in Group A?"

Chirrak and Catherine slowly raise their hands; Harvey raises a crutch.

"Group B?" Malachai asks, and raises his own hand along with Pod, Igby, Pander, Juno, Adam, Fulton, Reena, Akimi, Alistair, Emery, Woods, and me.

"Does anyone know what's going to happen?" Harvey asks, shifting his balance and readjusting his crutches.

I think about what Wren told me and steal a glance over to her, but she looks down at the floor.

"It's going to be fine," Malachai tells him, placing a hand on the boy's shoulder. "We'll all meet up this time next week and laugh about it, right, Wren?"

Wren nods and forces a smile. "That's right," she says, "nothing to worry about."

"Now come on," Malachai says, looking around the group, "we only get this opportunity once a week, let's make the most of it."

Slowly, the crowd begins to break off into smaller groups.

Wren makes her way through the crowd, talking to us individually, making sure we're all right, sharing jokes, and trying to reassure the Group As that tomorrow is nothing to worry about.

I hang back, leaning against the wall, watching, unable to enjoy this precious time as thoughts of the mass Delay occupy my mind.

As Wren approaches me, her bright eyes locked on mine, I feel my heart swell and I forget, momentarily, about my worries.

"How's things?" I ask, and then correct myself. "How are things? How are you? Are you okay?"

Brilliant, I think, *really smooth.*

I hear Malachai laugh somewhere off to my left, and I'm sure he's laughing at me. I feel my face flush and glance over to him; he's leaning against the wall on one hand and is talking to a clearly besotted Reena. She's ceased her skipping around the Loop to talk to the Natural, pushing a strand of curly red hair back underneath her hat.

"I'm fine, Luka. How are you?"

"Good, I'm pretty good."

"Listen, what I said earlier, I'm sure I was overreacting. I didn't mean to scare you."

"Scare me? I wasn't scared, I was never scared. It's just an unusual situation."

"Good, I'm glad you're not scared. I overreacted, that's all."

"Yeah, like Malachai said—we'll all be laughing about this next week."

"Exactly."

I nod. "Hey, listen, the new girl, Kina, she seems okay, you know? She seems like maybe she might be one of us?"

I look around our little group. Wren's eyes follow mine.

"It might be a bit too soon," she says. "We have to be sure, one hundred percent sure, that she's . . . a good fit."

"She is," I say.

A smile forms on Wren's face, and her eyes narrow. "Luka Kane, do you have a crush?"

"I . . . well . . . no, I . . . no crush, she's just . . . she seems . . ."

Wren laughs. "Let me talk to her," she says. "Maybe in a few weeks, we'll see, okay?"

"It's not a crush," I say, getting control of my words. "I don't have a crush on her."

Wren laughs again and walks over to Akimi, handing her a bag containing her weekly outfit.

"I don't have a crush on her, because I'm in love with you," I say under my breath. "I should have said that."

Pander is singing over by the wall, and I sit down beside her, listening to her pitch-perfect voice as she belts out some twentieth-century pop song that has been rereleased so many times I don't even recognize which version she's mimicking. She reaches up and adjusts the settings of one of her hearing aids and smiles as the sound comes through more clearly. I listen to the lyrics, a song about being young and defiant, a song about love and heartache. It's beautiful and ambient as her words echo off the concrete walls of the Loop.

Akimi exits her cell, spinning and admiring her green dress.

I feel a wave of sadness engulf me. Although all our conversations and all our interactions have been masked by the unwritten rules of the 2 a.m. club, I love these people, and I can't help but feel it's all about to come to an end.

At 7:30 a.m., the wake-up call comes.

I slide carefully out of bed and order breakfast, and my mind continues its cyclical stream of unanswerable questions. After a few minutes, the conveyor belt takes my uneaten food away.

Happy tells me to prepare for Galen's speech. I sit on the edge of my bed and face the screen, which shows nothing but blackness for four or five minutes before returning to normal.

"Great," I whisper to no one. "I guess everything has gone to hell."

Hours later, the back wall opens up, and I'm greeted, for the first time ever, by silence from the yard.

I step outside and listen to the breeze until Tyco, who must be in Group B as well, finds his voice.

"Luka, are you there?" he calls.

"I'm here," I call back.

"I'm going to kill you one day."

"I know."

Silence again.

It's eerie knowing that half the inmates are not here, knowing that they are being experimented on as we stand in the sunlight. For all I know, they might be dead.

"Luka?" Kina's voice comes from my right.

"Yeah."

"I don't like this."

"Neither do I," I tell her.

"Do you think Group A is okay?"

"Yes," I say too quickly. "I'm sure they're fine. They'll be back later today, and we can ask them what happened at exercise tomorrow."

"And then it's our turn," she points out.

"Luka Kane," Tyco yells, "I'm going to kill you."

"Give it a rest," Malachai yells back.

And Tyco falls silent.

Today's conversations consist of quiet muttering, as though they don't want to disturb the rest of us. The one-minute warning comes, and we say goodbye and reenter our cells.

Too many hours pass, and I convince myself that Wren has been arrested, thrown in the Block, and I'll never see her again.

I hear the hatch sliding open.

"Hi, Luka."

"Hi, Wren," I say back, and I can't stop myself from inhaling hard against the surge of comfort that washes over me. I turn to look at her, and my emotions double. She's so perfect and so beautiful that it makes my heart hurt.

"Hey, listen, I got you a book," she tells me, holding up a small paperback for me to see.

"Wow, Wren, thank you. I'll read it as soon as I've finished *Lord of the Ri—*"

"No, read it tonight, Luka."

I look into Wren's imploring eyes.

"All right," I tell her. "I'll read it tonight."

"Good," she says, her voice shuddering as she breathes through the words. "I think you'll find it really interesting."

I look at the cover of the book—the picture shows a great castle atop a cliff; below is a raging sea. *The Count of Monte Cristo,*" I read aloud.

"Yes. It's a classic," Wren says, and then reaches down and holds a container of food out to me.

I stand and reach for the box, ignoring the infiltration alarm as Wren's fingertips touch mine and she stares pleadingly at me once again. I nod, confirming that I understand that something is amiss, and take the food from her.

"Well, I have to go," she says. "I'll see you soon."

"Wren, wait." But the hatch closes, and I'm left in silence.

I look first at the container of noodles, then at the book. I throw the container onto my bed and open *The Count of Monte Cristo* at page one and skim the words. The writer speaks of a great ship pulling into a dock. Nothing significant, nothing that elaborates on Wren's obvious attempt to communicate something of great import.

I turn another page and then stop. Scrawled across the printed text on page three, from top to bottom in red ink, is Wren's handwriting.

Luka, you have to get out...

I snap the book shut as fast as I can. I think about the surgically implanted camera in my forehead, and I wonder if Wren knows something I don't; I wonder if the government is watching us more closely than usual.

I casually throw the book down onto my bed and pick up the food. I spend the next twenty minutes chewing on noodles that I don't want to eat, waiting for night.

It's 1 a.m. before I can read the book.

I'm so distracted that for the first time in over a year, I don't watch the rain. I make a show of stretching and yawning. I know that the likelihood of anyone watching my Panoptic camera footage is low, but I can't take chances.

I crawl into bed and rest my head on my pillow. Then I reach down and grab the book, pulling the blanket over my head as I do so. I rest one hand against my forehead so that the Panoptic camera mounted there is covered, and I'm hidden from prying eyes.

I turn to page three and read:

Luka, you have to get out. The Group A inmates are back—they were all unconscious for the first few hours, when they woke up they were disoriented and confused, and then they changed. They started behaving irrationally, silently stalking their cells, punching and kicking their doors, slamming their heads against the floor without making a noise. Some have died and I think more will follow. Luka, the worst part is they smile the whole time—while they're killing themselves they're smiling as though they're happy. I'm under 24-hour surveillance after the information I mistakenly received to my Lens. I can't help, but you have to try and escape the Delay. I don't know how, I don't know if it's even possible, but you have to try, Luka. Find a way. Wait for an opportunity and take it. I'll warn as many others as I can. I wish I could help, but they're watching me. Do whatever it takes.

     Wren

I read the warning a second time and a third.

In a little over twenty-four hours, I'll be taken to the Facility and whatever happened to Group A will happen to me too.

I turn the page and remove my hand from my head. I pretend to read the words of the novel while my heart returns to its normal rate.

How the hell am I supposed to escape? No one has ever broken out of the Loop in its seventy years of existence. No one has even come close.

It can't be done. Wren's note serves only as a forewarning of almost-certain death.

All right, I think. *If that's what it means, then that's what it means. How much longer could you have remained sane in a place like this anyway?*

I swallow back tears and steel my resolve.

When the Delay comes, I will be ready to capitalize on any opportunity to escape that may arise, but if there truly is no chance, then I will accept my fate.

I close the book and turn to the screen.

"Happy."

"Yes, Inmate 9-70-981?" the screen replies.

"Panoptic playback. Day 1 in the Loop. Time: 5:17 p.m."

"Right away."

The screen dissolves into blackness for the first twenty seconds and then comes alive as I cross the threshold into the prison. I hear my terrified, gasping breaths as I'm led along the corridor, followed by a guard with a heart trigger in his hands—a small cylindrical device that's linked to the infinity-shaped explosive that's just been implanted in my heart. I hear the soldier's voice telling me to stop as he walks in front of me and opens my cell door. I'm shoved inside, and the door is slammed shut behind me.

Happy allows inmates to watch four minutes of memories on the screen every day. The cruel part is the memories can only be from your time inside the Loop. You are not allowed to see anything from before.

I watch my own memory, watch myself looking from wall to wall, stumbling forward in the moment I thought I'd faint, feeling the coldness of the walls, looking through the tiny window to the yard.

"Inmate 9-70-981," Happy interrupts, "you have two minutes of your daily allowance of memories remaining."

84

"Switch it off," I say, and the screen goes blank.

Despite not sleeping the night before, I lie awake on my bed in the dim light all night, thinking about my life. Thinking about when I was eleven and my dad lost his job at the sky-farms—the government was supposed to keep a 50 percent human workforce, but the number slowly got pushed back, year after year, until it was just 20 percent. Thinking about when I was twelve and I bought an early twenty-second-century screen from a Junk Child selling her wares in the Black Road Vertical. I used the screen to pickpocket Alts who still used thumb-chips to transfer Coin. Thinking about when I was thirteen and I taught my sister to read. Thinking about the roof of the Black Road Vertical and the boy with the gun. Thinking about the death of my mom. About Wren. About dying.

By the time exercise hour comes the following day, I feel as though I'm living in a dream. Everything feels slow and unreal, my thoughts are foggy, my movements clumsy and inexact.

Again, Galen's address is nothing but a blank screen.

When the back wall opens, I am met once again by the horrible quiet.

After a few seconds, some of the Group B inmates call out to their friends from Group A, who don't answer.

"Luka," Kina says from the other side of the wall, her voice fragile and low.

"Yeah."

"Why aren't they back?"

I want to tell her what Wren told me, I want to tell her that they *are* back, that the lucky ones are dead, and the others are in a state of silent insanity, but I can't.

"I don't kn—" I begin, but the quiet of the yard is interrupted by the sound of a body hitting the dividing wall on the other side of Kina's yard. Harvey's yard.

"What was that?" Kina asks.

I don't reply. The horrible thump-and-crunch sound comes again, and I try to force out the image of Harvey throwing himself against the wall, breaking bones, splitting his skin open as he fights to kill himself.

And I hear a similar sound from the other side of the Loop, the cracking of bone like a gunshot into the quiet. And then more, from all over, as if they've all received a signal that now is the time.

"Luka, what is that?" Kina asks.

I don't reply. I hear more worried shouts from Group Bs as the insane inmates try to break through the walls.

And then the meaty slapping sound of impact from Harvey's cell is replaced by the sound of scrambling hands and feet and then the warning sirens as one of the drones from the center pillar comes to life. *Inmate 9-71-343: Cease your activity and return to your cell.*

But Harvey doesn't stop; I can hear his ragged breaths and the skidding, slipping rustle as he climbs up and up. And then Kina screams.

Inmate 9-71-343, this is your final warning. Cease your activity and return to your cell.

"Oh god, what's wrong with him?" Kina screams. "He's trying to get into my yard!"

From where I am, I can't see what she's seeing, but it's clear that Harvey, or whatever is left of Harvey, has reached the top of the dividing wall.

And then more drones are rising off the pillar, training their lasers onto more and more inmates who are trying to climb the walls, trying to get to those of us who are still sane.

Restless murmurs and frantic questions start to come from

the Group B inmates, but everyone falls silent when the first drone's cannon fires a single dart into Harvey. We all listen as the scrambling sounds grow silent, the hallucinogenic drug working into his system, the tranquilizer weakening him until he can't hold on. The wet smack resonates thickly around the Loop as his body hits the ground.

And then a second drone fires somewhere to my right. Then a third and fourth almost simultaneously. The bodies fall. Six, seven, eight of them. And then we are in complete silence.

"He—he was smiling," Kina says finally. So quietly that I almost don't hear it.

From far in the distance I hear the electronic hum of other drones approaching.

The buzzing grows louder, and the whispers and murmurs around the exercise yard begin to grow in volume once more. I follow the sound, and then I feel my body going into shock. Every breath I suck into my lungs feels weak and ineffectual as I see, approaching the prison at high speed, coffin drones.

I lean against the wall as the strength threatens to leave my body. I watch as the coffin drones lower themselves into the yard.

"Hey," I hear a girl call out. "Hey, what the hell is going on? What is this? Someone answer me!"

Her shouts are accompanied by more and more voices demanding answers, screaming out to anyone who might be watching via Panoptics or listening via the mics in our rooms. No answer comes.

After a minute or so, the coffin drones lift into the sky with black body bags gripped in their metallic talons.

Harvey, my friend, who had suffered through the torture of the Loop with cerebral palsy, is dead. All the Group As are dead.

I can only hope that their passing didn't hurt, that they're free now. I slide down the wall until I'm resting on my haunches, watching the drones grow smaller as they fly their cargo into the distance.

The inmates are still screaming, demanding answers, demanding to know what happened to the Group As.

Eventually, the only sounds coming from the yard are the quiet sobs from those of us who have lost friends today.

Even Tyco is silent by the time the alarm sounds.

Back in my room, I pace, waiting for Wren. She's late. I tell myself she's been late before. I keep waiting, but she doesn't show. It's only when the energy harvest comes that I accept the fact that I won't be seeing her today.

The harvest is hard to take tonight. When it ends, I'm sure that I will never recover. I lie on the floor for two hours.

When I finally have the strength to crawl into bed, I find that I can't sleep. I'm worried about Wren, I'm worried about tomorrow, I'm worried that this is my last night on Earth.

The wake-up call comes half an hour early, at 7 a.m., and I don't think I slept at all.

An announcement tells me that I will be boarding the Dark Train in thirty minutes.

I sit up slowly and try to focus. I'm so exhausted that it takes a full minute before I can blink away the blurriness.

I select my breakfast, but I'm not even sure what buttons I've pushed as I play scenarios in my head of what might have happened to Wren. Did they decide to silence everyone who received the files to their Lenses? Is this to do with the rumors of the war? Or did they find out about her warning notes to the inmates? Is she locked up in the Block?

Then I play scenarios of what might happen today after I board the Dark Train.

Be ready, I tell myself. *If you see an opportunity to escape, take it!*

My screen begins to beep and informs me that I'll be exiting my cell in five minutes. I haven't touched what's in front of me. Turns out it's porridge, and it has turned to thick gloop in the bowl. I put it on the conveyor belt to be taken away.

"Happy?" I try, hoping that whatever is going on with the omnipresent system might have fixed itself.

The screen flickers a few times. "Yes, Inmate 9-70-981?"

"What's going to happen to me at the Facility?"

"Everything is as it should be."

"That's what I thought you'd say." I look to the floor and take a deep breath. "Happy?"

"Yes, Inmate 9-70-981?"

"I really fucking hate you."

I tighten the Velcro on my shoes and wait by my door.

The one good thing about Delays is being able to walk to the Dark Train platform. It's hard to explain the sense of elation I get from just this simple act. Freedom is a privilege that can only be truly appreciated when it's taken away, although today it's hard to find enjoyment in anything.

The timer counts down to zero, a harsh Klaxon sounds twice, and the hatch in my door slides open.

This is it, Luka, I tell myself. *Wait for your chance. Be ready.*

A guard, dressed all in black and wearing a riot helmet, peers inside. He gestures for me to come closer.

I step forward, and he points a cylindrical tube of metal at my chest. A green light on the top of the device turns red, and I hear a series of beeps inside my chest. The weapon in the guard's hand is now connected to the infinity-symbol implant in my heart; if the guard's hand comes loose from the tube of metal, a small explosion will rip through my chest and I'll be dead before I hit the ground. They call it a dead man's switch.

The riot guard unlocks my door and pulls it open. He points with his free hand toward the entrance to the Loop and follows four or five steps behind me until we get to the gate.

Big yellow letters over the entrance read:

INMATES! CROSSING THIS POINT WITHOUT AUTHORIZATION WILL CAUSE IMPLANTS TO DETONATE.

I stop, and the silent guard moves to a panel on the wall. He removes his glove and presses his thumb against the scanner. He then turns and gestures for me to exit the Loop.

Every time I've passed through these doors, my heart has skipped a beat. I picture the infinity loop running through my heart. I anticipate a problem with the system, a mis-scan of a fingerprint, an indifferent guard whose mind is already on after-work drinks or that weekend trip to the country.

But I pass through unharmed and into another short corridor that leads to the platform. The Dark Train waits, an almost imperceptible electronic hum as it hovers two inches above the six rails of the track below. Half the doors to the tiny, one-person carriages are already shut, the inhabitants waiting inside to be taken to the mass Delay.

The guard points to the first open carriage, and I walk toward it, climb inside, and sit on the uncomfortable molded-plastic seat.

A screen in front of me comes to life and demonstrates where I should put my hands, and Happy's voice comes over the speakers.

"Good morning again, Inmate 9-70-981. Please place your hands into the spaces at either side of your seat."

I've done this before, so I know the drill. I put my hands, up to the wrists, into the circular gaps on each side of me and feel the three layers of grips tighten around my forearms to prevent any attempt to escape.

This is when the guard is supposed to come over and shut the hatch, leaving me cut off from the outside world with no windows to see where I'm being taken, but he forgets. He turns and walks back into the Loop.

He'll remember, I think. *He'll come running back any second.*

But he doesn't. I'm left sitting in my carriage, listening to the hum of the train, waiting to see what happens next. A few minutes later, a girl walks onto the platform. I don't know how, but immediately I know that it's Kina. Her dark hair is shaved almost to the scalp (inmates' hair is shaved on day one), and her dark eyes are almost black, but despite this they seem to glow against her brown skin. She's short and skinny and intrinsically tough looking. Her eyes meet mine, and she smiles.

"Hi, Luka," she says, nodding her head as though we've just passed each other on the street.

"Kina," I reply, mimicking her nonchalance, and we both can't help laughing as the flustered guard rushes over to slam my carriage door shut.

I laugh in the silence and the darkness of the carriage for a long time. I laugh because the guard forgetting his duties was funny, but more than that, I laugh because I got to see Kina; I got to see the face of my friend.

"Kina Campbell," I say out loud, and then I laugh again.

To know what my friend looks like, to be able to picture the way she smiles with only one side of her mouth, and her brown eyes, means the world to me, and if I have to die today—at least I have this.

I realize that for almost a full minute I have forgotten about Wren, but as the silence slowly kills my humor, all thoughts lead back to her. I hope she's okay. I hope she's home and safe with her family.

It's another hour before we begin to move. The carriages are soundproof and windowless, and without being able to see where I'm being taken, it's hard to even figure out which direction we're traveling, but it's only fifteen or so minutes before we're slowing to a stop at the Facility.

Again, I have to wait as the inmates are escorted one by one off the vehicle. It feels like hours that I'm left alone, and this white silence only quickens the gestation of my worries about Wren and my fear of the Delay.

Finally, the door to my carriage is opened, and the guard scans my chest with the trigger. Once the device in my heart is armed, the arm restraints are released.

I step out onto the concrete platform and I see the Facility: the enormous black dome with *F-459* painted in great white characters over the thirty-foot-wide entrance. The building itself looks the same, but rather than the space in front of it being empty like usual, there's a snaking line of inmates winding from the entrance all the way to the platform. Some of the lineup I recognize from the Loop, but others I don't recognize at all; most of these are older prisoners, who must be inmates from the Block.

"What's going on?" I ask.

"Shut up," the guard replies. "Hands behind your back."

I barely hear the guard; I'm transfixed by the sheer number of people. I haven't seen a genuine crowd in over two years.

"I'm going to give you one more chance!" the guard yells, going from calm to agitated in a heartbeat. "Do not resist, or I will light you up, am I understood?"

I turn to the officer, surprised by his intensity. "Okay, okay."

I put my hands behind my back and feel the coiled cobalt that was implanted into my bones become magnetized. My wrists pull together with irresistible force and slam into each other behind my back.

"Join the line," the guard tells me. He pushes me forward. I stumble and only just keep my balance. I make it to the end of the line and stand behind a broad-shouldered woman of about forty.

"Do you know what they're doing to people in there?" I ask, keeping my voice low.

"School trip," she replies, her mad eyes roving around as she looks over her shoulder at me. "Best behavior, or you'll wait on the bus while the other children visit the museum."

She has obviously lost her mind in the Block, but I try one more time. "Do you know what's going on?"

"Talk to me again, and I'll eat your heart," the woman says, turning around to face me. She has one eye; the other is a mass of scar tissue. She breaks into a toothy grin, and a wheezing sound escapes her mouth. It takes me a while to realize that she's laughing.

I turn my head away from her, hoping that she'll lose interest.

I look down the line and see a tall, skinny, bald man twitching violently and cowering as if he's being attacked by birds that only he can see. Not far ahead of him is a man on his knees laughing hysterically at the dirt. Near the front of the line, an Alt woman from the Block is spitting over and over again and muttering a nonsensical incantation.

What the hell happens in the Block?

I scan the line and see that there are guards every twenty feet or so, standing poised. They all have heart triggers in their hands and Ultrasonic Wave—or USW—guns at their sides. About halfway down the line sits an enormous military tank. I've never seen anything like it in real life.

Is this it? I think to myself. *Is this the moment to try and make a break for it? If I can somehow rally all these people quickly enough, if I can somehow let them know that they're sending us in here to die, then maybe we could—together—overthrow the guards, get hold of their weapons? Escape.*

I strain against my magnetized wrists and know that this is not the time. I'm stuck between too many people, and I'm too visible. *Patience, Luka.*

From somewhere up ahead, I hear Pander yelling at an older male inmate of the Block; he must have said something horribly inappropriate because by the time I've spotted her, she's kicked the man so hard between the legs that he's on his knees. Pander leans over him, her thick glasses inches from his purple face.

"Where did the tough guy go?" she hisses. "What happened to the tough guy?"

"Inmate 9-71-444," a guard yells, taking a few steps toward

Pander and pointing a heart trigger in her direction, "one more move, and I execute you where you stand. Am I understood?"

"What?" Pander yells back, feigning innocence. "I didn't do anything, he just collapsed."

"Inmate 9-71-444—"

"Pander. My name is Pander Banks—isn't that easier than *9-71-444*?"

"Inmate 9-71-444, move to the front of the line immediately."

Pander tilts her head against her shoulder, loosening her hearing aids from her ears. "I'm sorry, what did you say? I'm deaf, I can't hear you."

The officer arms his heart trigger. The green light on the end of the small metal tube turns red, and a series of beeps can be heard coming from inside Pander's chest.

"All right, all right. Calm down," she says, pushing her hearing aids back in.

She makes another impudent comment about the officer being a gang member. I stop listening as I feel someone approaching from behind. I twist my neck and see Kina shuffling to the back of the line.

"Luka," Kina says.

"Kina," I reply, unable to hide my smile.

"Looks like Pander isn't the sweet little girl I imagined her to be."

I turn to see Pander aiming another kick at the chest of the floored Block inmate before moving to the front of the line, protesting her innocence all the while.

"Listen, did Wren manage to get a message to you?" I whisper.

"A message? What about?"

"This Delay—it's suicide."

"Harvey," Kina says, her voice weak at the memory. "I guess I already knew."

"Inmates, silence," a nearby guard calls to us.

We stop talking until the line shuffles a few feet forward and more inmates join the back.

"So what do we do?" Kina whispers.

"I don't know; there's not much we can do while we're cuffed. Wren said to wait for an opportunity, a moment when they're off guard, and try to find a way out."

"Inmates 9-70-981 and 9-72-104, if I hear one more word, you will both be executed where you stand, am I understood?"

I face forward and lower my head.

I hear more and more inmates joining the back of the line as we slowly move toward the entrance of the vast building.

"Do you have a plan?" Kina asks, her voice almost inaudible.

"No," I tell her, shrugging. "We just have to be ready. If someone makes a move, we try to help them out."

We shuffle forward again as more inmates are ushered inside.

"Luka, if we don't make it out of here . . . I just want to say thanks. You got me through those first few days."

"It's all right," I tell her. "I'm just sorry there weren't more days." My voice comes out calm and measured, but inside, my heart is racing and my stomach is twisting itself into knots.

We move forward, nearing the enormous entrance of the Facility. I look up at the sun, enjoying the warmth on my face. Disorientation overcomes me as I hear Tyco's voice.

"Luka Kane, I'm going to kill you."

I turn my head, almost expecting to see the exercise yard, but instead I see wide-open space and the scorched land of the edge of the Red Zones. I try to catch sight of my would-be assassin, but he's too far back to see.

"Inmate 9-70-982, stay where you are." I hear the frantic voice of one of the guards near the back of the line call out, and the sound of running footsteps grows louder.

This is it, this is Tyco's moment, he is going to try and kill me right now. The voices of half a dozen panicked guards merge together, each one closer to me than the last.

"Inmate 9-70-982! Stop right there, or I will execute you where you . . ."

"Inmate 9-70-982! Do not take one more step, or I will execute you . . ."

"Inmate . . . Tyco Roth . . . Stop, just stop right now."

I turn to see a circle of guards surrounding Tyco; I try to get a look at him, but I'm too late. I hear five or six series of beeps as some of the guards arm their triggers while the others point their guns at him. Finally, it seems as though they have got the charging bull under control.

"Why didn't they just kill him?" Kina asks.

"I don't know," I admit as I watch the guards shepherd Tyco to the back of the line.

"You," a guard calls out as he storms over to me, "Inmate 9-70-981, you're next."

"But I'm not at the front of the line," I point out.

"We can't have you antagonizing the others," he says as he aims his heart trigger at my chest. I hear the four beeps, and he beckons me out of the line.

"Luka," I hear Kina say, "keep your eyes open."

I look back at her and nod as I'm pushed toward the building.

"Inside," the guard demands, and I lead the way with him a few feet behind.

"Good luck, Luka," I hear Igby say as I pass by.

"Good luck," Pod echoes.

"Good luck, Luka," Adam mutters, followed by Malachai and then Woods.

And this is it. This is the long walk. This is the end.

Beyond the threshold of the gigantic doorway is a vast hangar filled with inmates being processed for the trial. Officers use Lenses to identify their prisoner numbers and transfer their information to Happy. Then they are led, one at a time, into the Facility.

The guard pushes me to the front of the line and tells someone there that I'm next. There is no argument, and I'm shepherded through the door and into the building.

"Next left," the guard grunts. His instructions are unnecessary; I've walked this long white corridor before, passed the doors closed on animal screeches and chemical smells. Only this time the feeling is different. All those other times I knew that I *might* not make it out of here alive, but this time I'm *sure* I won't make it out of here alive—or at least not in any state in which I'll want to keep on living.

We take a right, go through three sets of automatic doors,

and finally make it to the locked door of the trial room.

Keep your eyes open, I think, remembering Kina's words, and then, *Wait for an opportunity and take it*—Wren's words.

The guard signals for me to turn around in the corridor outside the anesthesia room, and I feel the magnetic pull of the internal handcuffs release.

"Inmate 9-70-981, you are to be made aware of the following," the guard says, his voice becoming the lazy drawl of someone who has to repeat the same thing day after day. "When you enter the holding area, you will be seated on the chair in front of you; you will be under surveillance at all times, and your myocardial implant will be active at all times. You are permitted to take this opportunity to renege on your Delay contract, at which time you will be taken immediately to the courthouse to confirm your . . ."

The guard's words become a blur of background noise as I focus on the heart trigger gripped in his left hand.

And then I see my opportunity.

"I renege," I say, interrupting his flow.

"Excuse me?" he asks, eyes widening.

"I renege, I don't want to take the Delay anymore, I've changed my mind."

The guard stares at me for five seconds before stuttering, "A-are you . . . sure? There's no seven-day cooling-off period if you renege on a signed contract today; they'll Delete you now."

"I'm completely sure," I say. "I don't want any part of this; I'd rather die."

The guard looks at me, dumbfounded, and then shrugs. He

looks up and to the left, activating his Lens, and mutters a few voice commands. I see his eyes scanning the air, reading through guidelines visible only to him.

"Okay," he says, and begins to read aloud. "Inmates who decide to renege on their signed Delay contract at the time of said Delay are to be read the following: The inmate understands that the alternative to taking part in the Delay is to be executed within one hundred and twenty minutes of confirming the decision at the courthouse and giving confirmation by way of iris scan and fingerprint. This decision is final and cannot be revoked a second time—"

I don't let him get any further. I move quickly, taking advantage of the distraction. I grab his left hand with my right and squeeze it hard against the trigger, forcing him to hold on to the device that will kill me if released. At the same time, I wrap the fingers of my left hand around the grip of his USW pistol, pulling it from its holster and pressing it against his belly.

"Disarm the trigger, or I'll execute you where you stand," I hiss. "Am I understood?"

The officer looks down at me, his eyes almost curious. "Put the gun down, kid," he says. "Put it down, I'll let you take the Delay, and I'll forget about this incident. Does that sound good?"

"No," I say. "That doesn't sound good at all. Here's what's going to happen: You're going to deactivate the trigger and hand it to me."

I feel him tug slightly at the trigger, testing my grip. It doesn't falter.

"Listen," he says, smiling, "you made a mistake, an error in judgment, but we can let it go, you and I . . . we can make a deal, and no one has to get hurt."

"I'm going to give you three seconds to disarm the trigger; if I get to one and you haven't switched this thing off, I'm going to shoot you."

"Shoot me and you kill yourself," the guard points out. "If I release my grip on this—"

"Three," I say, my voice somehow calm despite the flood of adrenaline in my system.

"You're going to have to shoot me, kid. I'm not deactivating . . ."

"Two."

"You're not going to intimidate me."

"One."

"Wait! Wait!" the guard screams. "Fine, here."

He looks up and to the left once more and mumbles the word *disarm*, and the red light turns green.

"Now give it to me," I say, letting go of the guard's hand and holding mine out. He slaps the tube of metal into my palm and sneers at me.

"What do you think's going to happen now? Do you think you're going to walk out of here? You're screwed, kid. They're going to kill you."

"I guess we'll find out," I say. "Now strip."

"Excuse me?"

"Take your uniform off, quickly."

"Why?"

I raise the gun to his head and step closer. "I don't have time to answer your questions. Take your clothes off, and take your Lens out too."

The guard grinds his teeth, his jaw muscles clenching as he unclips his body armor.

When he stands in front of me in his underwear and socks, I slip out of my prison jumpsuit and kick it over to him. "Put that on."

He does as I ask, and I struggle into the guard's uniform while still aiming the gun.

"I promise you—you will not escape."

"The Lens," I demand, ignoring his statement.

He reaches a finger and thumb up to his left eye and pinches out the contact lens before placing it into my palm. I rest it on the tip of my finger and press it against my own eye. Immediately, I have a heads-up display in my field of vision: Along the bottom, there is red writing displaying information about whatever I'm looking directly at—the material the table is made out of, the coordinates of the building, the dimensions of the room, and much more. Running along the top is updated information about the guard's working schedule, assignments, and other miscellaneous information. To the right are five options: Call, Messages, VR, SoCom, Mall.

The call button begins to flash green, and I can hear the buzzing of an incoming call inside my head.

"Turn around," I tell the guard.

"What?"

"Face the wall, now," I demand, pointing the gun threateningly at him. "And don't make a sound."

He does as I ask, and I move my eyes to the right until the CALL option is highlighted. Nothing happens.

"Uh, answer," I try, and suddenly I can see a woman dressed in a military-style uniform standing in front of me. I can still see the prison guard, facing the wall, through her hologram body.

"Officer Petrov, what's the hold up?"

I panic; if I reply, she'll know that it's not Officer Petrov wearing the Lens.

Can she see me? I wonder. *If she can, I'm dead.*

"Officer Petrov?" the holographic figure demands.

I try to imitate the officer's voice as I blurt out the first thing that comes to mind. "Everything is under control. Situation normal."

"I see the inmate reneged? We do not accept. If he signed the contract, he's taking the Delay. Hurry up."

"Uh, just getting it done now."

"Get the inmate into the trial room, Petrov. The clock's ticking; Tier Threes who do not give one hundred percent won't make it onto the Arc. Phase One begins in thirty hours."

"Sorry . . . boss," I say.

"Back to work," she says, adding "As One" before her image disappears.

I exhale, astonished that I wasn't found out.

Tier Threes who do not give one hundred percent won't make it onto the Arc. What the hell had all that meant? And had she said "As One"? When had that become a sign-off for Alts?

"Keep facing the wall," I tell the guard as I back up toward the door. It opens automatically behind me, and I back through before locking the manual mechanism on the other side. It won't take the guard long to raise the alarm, but hopefully I can get a head start. I find it and twist it before turning and running along the empty corridor.

As I run through the next set of sliding doors, I look up and to the left, and the Lens offers me a dozen more options. Most are in relation to the guard's job, but one of them is titled F-459 SCHEMATIC. I scan over to it and say, "Activate," under my breath. In my peripheral vision, a detailed plan of the Facility appears, complete with moving markers showing the locations of every guard.

Okay, okay, this is good, I think. *I can use this.*

I turn slowly around, the map moving with me, looking for another way out. I spot an unguarded emergency exit right at the back of the building and down two levels.

I enter the animal room. The monkeys' screaming becomes so loud that I cover one ear with the hand that's not holding the gun. But then the birds join in, and the rats scrabble at their glass cages.

Suddenly, the room goes dark, and Happy comes over the speakers. *"All units respond, code nine in progress. Location: C-F One. All units respond, code nine in progress. Location: C-F One."*

I can't be sure, but I'd bet my life that *I'm* the code nine.

I watch the map, and dozens more guards flood into the building.

I have to move, have to run—if they catch me, I'm dead.

And then the voice comes over the speakers once more:

"All units be aware. Threat contained in Lab Four. Armed. Approach with caution."

"Contained?" I say aloud as still more adrenaline fills my system.

I run to the door at the far end of the animal room. Locked. I run back the way I came and try that door. Locked.

It can't end like this, I think, shocked that my escape attempt has ended before it's even begun.

I aim my stolen weapon at the lock of the door and fire. The steel bubbles but doesn't give. I fire again and again and again. If I had ten minutes to spare, I might get through, but I don't have any time left.

"Inmate 9-70-981, drop your weapon!" a voice calls through the door.

What do I do? I think, my eyes scanning the room for another way out, another option, but there is nothing. I'm trapped.

I move to the center of the room. The map now shows a small army of guards behind each exit. There is nothing I can do.

Both doors open simultaneously, and officers pour in from both sides. They take strategic positions, crouching behind desks and monkey cages.

"Freeze!" a voice calls from behind me.

I turn around and see three officers creeping toward me. Two of them have their guns aimed at me while the other points a trigger at my chest. I hear the three electronic beeps coming from my heart, and I know it's over. I know that I'm as good as dead.

"Inmate 9-70-981, drop your weapon, or I'll execute you where you stand. Am I understood?" the lead officer calls out.

Five more guards come in, rifles aimed at me.

"Inmate 9-70-981, drop your weapon now!" another officer calls.

It's over, I think. If I were braver, I'm sure I'd kill myself right now, just place the barrel of the gun against my head and pull the trigger. I don't want to be dragged to the courthouse, I don't want to be taken to the Deletion room, I don't want some anonymous guard in a white suit to activate their Deleter and erase me into a trillion subatomic particles in the blink of an eye. If only I had the guts to end it all right here. And then I realize I don't have to. They will kill me if I don't drop the gun.

"Inmate 9-70-981, this is your last warning. Drop the weapon now!"

I look around at the small army of guards, more of them joining from the rear, and I smile. "No," I say.

I slowly raise the gun up, the barrel moving toward the group of officers in front of me.

"Line one, take aim," the lead officer calls.

I close my eyes and brace myself.

"Wait!" another voice yells from the back.

I recognize that voice, but I don't have time to register it before something hits me hard around the waist. My arms are snapped to my sides, and the gun falls from my hands, clattering to the floor. I look down and see a metal strap wrapped around me, pinning my arms to my sides. I hear a *thunk* sound, and a second strip of metal slams into my shins. I'm thrown off my feet as the belt cinches itself tight around my ankles. Without my hands free to protect myself, I slam into the hard floor face-first. I feel my nose break under my own weight.

I can barely move, pressed into the cold floor, blood trickling and pooling around my face.

I see a pair of black shoes, the toes brought to a polished shine.

It's over, I think again.

I hear the digital humming of some unknown piece of equipment, followed by the contemplative exhalation of the man with the shiny shoes.

"Diastolic: excellent. Respiration: excellent. BP: excellent," the man says, and again I'm sure I know that voice. "This boy, Luka Kane, is in incredible shape. Young, virile, healthy. He'll make an excellent battery. Take him to the trial room. Put two officers on him."

"As One," I hear one of the guards reply.

And then it clicks. I know that voice because I hear it every day in the Loop. It's Galen Rye, the Overseer. What is he doing here? Is he behind this mass Delay that has already killed half my friends?

Galen walks away, and I'm dragged to a standing position by three officers.

"Get him to the anesthesia room before he tries anything else," the lead officer demands.

I'm dragged, bound feet scraping along the floor, back along the corridor I escaped through. The monkeys are still going wild in the animal room, screeching like a jeering crowd as I'm dragged back to the locked door of the trial room.

The officer whose clothes I stole stands in front of me in my prison uniform, grinning. "How did freedom taste?" he asks, and without warning throws a fist into my stomach so hard that I almost throw up. And then he leans close to me, his voice a whisper. "If you've cost me a spot in Tier Three, I will make sure you die slowly."

"Fuck you," I groan.

"Take him to the Chair," Petrov mutters, and the door to the anesthesia room slides open.

I'm dragged into the sterile white room, empty apart from the Chair in the center. It's a large and uncomfortable wheeled dentist's chair, the seat and arms covered in blue plastic, easy to wipe the blood off. I struggle against my restraints as the two guards drag me over to it. The stainless-steel frame glimmers under the lights as I'm turned around and shoved into a sitting position.

This is the worst part of any Delay—no matter what they do to you on the table, nothing is worse than the Chair.

There's an electronic hum from the Chair as the needle is raised. I feel the jab at the base of my spine and immediately become paralyzed.

Every muscle in my body lets go completely, and I'm a limp bag of blood and organs. I can't even blink, drool runs out of my mouth, and the angle that my head has fallen makes it hard to draw breath. The only things I'm in control of are my breathing and my bodily functions.

I hear the whirring of the automatic doors, and a few seconds later, two orderlies come in wearing dazzling white uniforms, casually chatting to each other about their upcoming Saturday night plans. One of them, sporting dreadlocks, is planning to go to a music festival and take Ebb; the other sounds disappointed to just be spending time with her wife.

Together, they manually adjust the Chair until it's a bed. As soon as I am lying horizontally, I can breathe properly again. Dreadlocks sprays my drying eyes with a mist from a canister, and they wheel me through the automatic door and into the trial room.

"Bye, bye, Luka Kane," Officer Petrov calls out, his voice muffled by the dividing glass. I can only hope that the humiliation of being overpowered by a teenage boy loses him his job and his place in Tier Three, whatever the hell that is.

As I don't have the ability to move any part of me, all I can see is the ceiling high above and all I can do is hope that I don't *feel* the madness that they are about to infect me with, that there's no part of me left alive inside my mind once the insanity kicks in.

I have never felt fear like this before.

A face appears above me—a middle-aged woman wearing a surgical mask. She has a horrible grin in her bright Alt eyes and speaks in gleeful tones.

"You must be Mr. Kane?" she asks with no possibility of an answer from my frozen vocal cords. "The escapologist—you're famous around here. Shall we get started?"

She disappears from my vision, and I hear the metallic rustling of surgical instruments.

I want to run—I beg my body to obey the commands of my brain, I will my legs to move, to carry me away, to not let them operate on me, but there's nothing I can do except wait.

The doctor's face reappears. She's holding a syringe.

"Here we go," she mutters as she pushes the giant needle somewhere into me. I can't be sure where it has gone, but from where she's standing, I imagine it to be my upper arm or neck. I hear the clunk as she drops the syringe back into a tray, and then she appears with another one.

"Number two," she says, positively singing the words, and ducks out of my field of vision to inject me again.

"Annnnnd three," she says, producing a third needle. This one, I'm sure, is twice as long as the others.

And then there's silence for what feels like a full five minutes, and for all I know, they're removing my skin or sawing my feet off. It's not like I'd be able to feel it.

"Okay, that should be long enough," the doctor says, and then she makes a surprised little *oh* sound. "Doctor Soto, welcome. Come to witness the fruits of your labor?"

"No," comes the curt reply of the female doctor who moves—just out of my field of vision—and grabs something from the tray beside my head, then leaves the room.

Then I'm moving again; my bed is being wheeled to the other end of the room, and I'm pushed into some sort of plexiglass container that looks like a cheap greenhouse.

There's a hissing sound, and the chamber is filled with pale white gas. My instinct is not to breathe, so I don't, but the gas is pumped into the container for far longer than I can hold my breath. Finally, I give up and breathe the gas in. I can't feel anything, but I can imagine the caustic mist burning into the tissue of my lungs, blistering my windpipe, poisoning my blood.

The hissing sound ends, and I lie there waiting for something to happen, waiting for the effects of the gas to do whatever they do, waiting to become like Harvey, like Chirrak, Catherine, and whoever else was in Group A.

I try to think of something, a happy memory to cling on to before my mind shuts down and I become something else. My mind cycles through memories of my mother before she died, my sister and me sneaking into the sky-farms when we were kids. I think about Kina on the platform, then my mind settles on Wren, the first time she handed me a book and changed my world, and if I could work the muscles in my face, I would smile.

I hold on to the thought, and I wait.

Nothing happens.

After a while, the door to the container is opened, and I'm wheeled through a door on the other side of the trial room, where I'm left alone. The needle that is embedded into my spinal cord is retracted, and the paralysis is immediately lifted.

I scream, an involuntary sound of pain and fear and mostly relief that the nightmare of the Delay is over. I feel the sting of the puncture wounds in my neck from the syringes, I feel the incredible sensation of my limbs obeying the commands of my brain, I wiggle my toes and stretch out my fingers, and I can't help but sob a few times before taking four or five deep breaths to try and get ahold of myself.

"I'm alive," I say, my voice shuddering. "Why am I alive?"

They should have killed me when I tried to escape, they should have either shot me right there or taken me to the courthouse to be Deleted, but they didn't.

Why?

What had Galen meant when he'd said I'd make an excellent battery? Why are they refusing requests to renege? And why didn't the Delay put me into a coma or turn me crazy like it did to Group A?

Maybe that comes later, I think.

But in this moment, I decide that it doesn't matter. I'm alive, for whatever reason they decided not to kill me, and—for now at least—I have survived the Delay. I smile and think back to the morning, waiting on the platform, seeing Kina's face; she recognized me, she said hi, and we shared a laugh.

"Kina," I say again, and my smile grows.

It's amazing how much a simple moment can be worth to a person starved of connections.

Happy tells me to change back into my prison uniform, and I obey her.

I blink away the tears from my eyes and try to look as calm as I can when the door that leads back to the Dark Train opens. Three guards come in; one links their trigger with my heart, and the other two keep their guns aimed at my head. "Let's move, superstar," the one with the trigger says, and they take shuffling steps backward all the way to my carriage on the Dark Train.

There is always a recovery period after a Delay. You need a little time to get back what the government has taken from you. Maddox used to call it R & R for the soul.

I don't have time to feel any of that today, though; I'm too lost in thoughts of why I wasn't killed for trying to escape.

On Delay days, they don't make us take part in the energy harvest, so I guess that means the whole place will be running on stored power tonight. But I can't even enjoy the moment that the harvest is supposed to come; Wren still hasn't arrived, and my mind is so wrapped up in maybes and what-ifs.

By midnight, I've worked myself into such a state that I have a pounding headache. I move over to the window to watch the rain, and as I wait, all my turmoil slowly turns to the now-familiar sense of apprehension as, minute by minute, the rain doesn't come.

As I stare up at the sky, an hour passes, two, and still no rain. I give up at 2:30 a.m. and go to bed. I lie there in the darkness, staring into the void, too scared to sleep in case I fall into the coma that preceded the madness that killed Group A.

I know something is wrong as soon as I open my eyes.

At first I think it must still be the middle of the night, because the lighting inside my cell is all wrong, but then I realize that it's because the only source of illumination is the thin strip of sunlight beaming through the small window in the back wall.

Instinctively, my eyes dart over to the screen to check the time.

The screen is off.

I get out of bed and walk over to it, staring at my own reflection looking back at me in the black mirrored surface.

The screen is never off.

"What's going on?" I whisper to no one. And then, "Happy?"

There is no reply from the blank screen.

"Happy, where are you?" I ask. I try to ignore the tremble in my voice, try to ignore the horrible attachment I have to the operating system that runs this world.

With the screen off, I have no idea what time it is; my wake-up call is controlled by the screen, so it could be long after or long before 7:30 a.m.

No, wait, I think, and walk to the back window, where I look up to the sky and see that the sun is high above me. *After seven thirty, long after.*

"What's going on?" I say, louder this time. I wish my sleeping patterns weren't all messed up, because my body clock is usually pretty reliable at getting me up a few minutes before the alarm, but now I have no idea what time of day it is.

All right, all right, I think. *Stay calm. At least you're alive, you're not in a coma yet. Go about your normal routine. It'll be exercise soon, and you can ask the others if they know what's going on, and if they don't know, you just have to hope that Wren will eventually show up and explain everything.*

But it's hard to do all my exercises without any breakfast for energy, and by the time I get to the third set of push-ups, I'm dripping with sweat and exhausted.

I sit on my bed and just wait for something to happen, but nothing does.

Time passes, I can't tell if it's hours or minutes, but the back wall doesn't move. I'm certain that exercise hour has come and gone, but it's so hard to be sure when there's no way of tracking time.

I pace again, I try singing like Pander, but I'm tone-deaf and the sound only annoys me. I look through the window again and see that the sun is still high up in the sky, or is it a little bit lower now?

Wren didn't come after she gave you the warning about the Delay, I think. *They must have found out, they must have caught her.*

I wait and wait and wait. Too distracted to read, no energy

to exercise, mind racing at a million miles an hour trying to figure out what the hell is going on.

I pace and I sit and I stand and I watch the sun sink lower and lower.

Is this punishment? Does the government know what Wren has done? Did they torture her until she confessed to everything? Did they watch her Panoptic footage without her permission? Are they just going to leave us here, locked up, no food or water, no contact, just left to die in our cells like caged rats?

I notice something as I stare up at the sky: The little lights that encircle the drones on top of the pillar are still on. That doesn't make any sense; why would those electronics still be working when my screen is off and the lights in my cell are out? I had been working on the assumption that *all* the power in the Loop is out, but maybe it's just my cell. And then I remember that Wren explained the security system in the Loop to me, how if there was some catastrophic power failure, everything would shut down except the security features, which would run off energy from the harvest stored in a massive battery twelve feet belowground. The mechanical instruments that run the doors and a supply of triggers to activate heart devices would also use the backup supply, and these things are protected from every kind of attack they could think of, from escape attempts to nuclear blasts.

Dusk begins to settle in, and I remember that it's been getting dark at around 7 p.m.

It can't be seven, I tell myself. *Where's Wren? Where's anybody to explain what's happened?*

The conversation between Alistair and Emery replays in my mind, and Kina's words about the war.

What if it happened? What if some cataclysmic bomb has been dropped and wiped out most of the population? What if my family is dead? What if Wren is dead?

Just as the thought crosses my mind, the hatch in my cell door opens, and I turn to see Wren staring back at me. The feeling of relief is so immediate that I think for a second I might collapse to my knees.

"Wren, thank god, what the hell's happened? The screen is off, the back wall never opened, I haven't heard from anyone all day."

Wren doesn't reply, just stares at me, her blonde hair hanging disheveled over her face, her eyes blinking unnaturally fast over and over again, and for the briefest moment, a wide and crazy smile spreads across her face.

"Wren, are you okay?"

She blinks five, six, seven times and then shakes her head as though trying to snap out of a trance.

"Luka?" she says, her voice unsure. Her eyes are clear, and she appears to recognize me for the first time since opening the hatch.

"Yeah, it's me, Wren. What's going on?"

Wren steps aside, and Malachai's face appears in the gap in my door.

"Are you okay, Luka?" he asks, and I hear my door being unlocked.

"What are *you* doing here?" I ask, unable to hide the disappointment from my voice.

The door swings open, and Wren walks into my cell, wearing jeans and a T-shirt, and wraps her arms around me. "I'm so glad you're all right," she says, her breath against my ear somehow sending shivers down my spine despite the situation. I gently push her back.

"Wren, what happened?"

"There's no power anywhere, Luka. The whole city is in a blackout, and things are . . . weird."

"Weird how?" I ask.

"She heard things," Malachai answers for Wren. "Screams and gunshots."

"Looting?" I ask. "Maybe the homeless?"

"Yeah, maybe," Wren agrees. "But it sounded like . . . I don't know, it was scary."

"You didn't come on Friday, what happened?" I ask.

"I was put on paid leave; they wouldn't let me come in," Wren tells me. "I had two armed officers with me until late last night. I think they might know something, Luka."

"It might not even matter," Malachai says, putting an arm around Wren's shoulder, the sight of which makes me grind my teeth together. "There hasn't been a power cut in ninety-seven years; something big is happening."

She let him out first, I think, staring at Wren's hand as it reaches up to squeeze Malachai's. *She went to him first.*

"So, what now?" I ask, tearing my gaze away from their interlinked fingers and into Wren's eyes.

"I don't know," she says, looking away from Malachai, frowning at me. "The trains are running on backup power, but

120

they'll be offline within three hours, same with the streetlights and anything else that runs off stored power. We need to figure out how serious this is and then make a decision."

"A decision?" I repeat. "What kind of decision?"

"Luka, if this is something big, then we need to think about leaving the Loop. All of us."

"Something big? Like what?"

"Like a war," Malachai says.

"War?" I turn to Wren. "I asked you about a war days ago, and you told me it was impossible."

"Well, it doesn't seem so crazy now, all right?" she snaps back.

"Hey, let's not start arguing among ourselves," Malachai says. "I won't lie—I *hope* it's a war. I know that's immoral or whatever, but my prospects grow infinitely brighter if the world is in chaos. I'm thirty days from the Block—you think there's a 2 a.m. club in the Block? There isn't, and they say there are no Delays; they say that they experiment on you constantly. If this is a war, I've never been happier."

I nod in agreement, remembering my own confused longing for anything, no matter how terrible, to end the monotony of the Loop. "So, what now?" I ask.

Malachai sighs. "I guess we gather the team."

One by one we open the cells of Wren's chosen few, the ones who were lucky enough to be put into Group B: Pod, Igby, Pander, Akimi, Reena, Juno, Alistair, Emery, Adam, Fulton, and finally, Woods.

They all want an explanation, and we tell them to wait until everyone is free of their cell.

The group gathers, and I look over to Kina's cell. I want to go over there and let her out, or at least explain what's happening, but Wren begins to talk.

"Early this morning, at about five a.m., the power went out across the whole city. At first, everything was fine. There was a little bit of panic—people thought it might have been the Missing, maybe they had been planning some sort of attack all along—but by six a.m. everyone was enjoying the blackout. They carried candles in the streets and laughed about the first power cut in most people's lifetime. Then we started hearing screams near the center of town, then more from the financial district, and later we heard gunfire. My family and I locked ourselves in our cellar. We were there for hours. My dad went out to find out what was going on, and he didn't come back. Sometime later the ground shook, and I heard the loudest sound I've ever heard. We thought a bomb had dropped, we thought it was the end. I held my brothers and we said goodbye to one another, but the sound stopped. I'm the second oldest in my family so, after some more time had passed, I went upstairs to get food and water for the boys, and outside the kitchen window I saw that a plane had fallen out of the sky. Everyone who had been on board was . . . their eyes, they were staring . . ." She breaks off and stifles her tears. She takes a deep breath and composes herself. "I came here as soon as I could; I couldn't leave you to die. The trains are running on emergency power, but they'll be offline soon."

"So, we're under attack?" Reena asks, pushing a strand of curly red hair behind her ear.

"We think so," Malachai says, turning to look at her.

"Well, we need to go," Fulton says, his eyes meeting first Adam's, then Woods's. "Right? I mean, you can't leave us here to rot."

"We need to talk about it," Wren says. "We need to—"

"What is there to talk about?" Fulton says, his voice growing in volume. "If there's a war out there, then we'll be the last thing on their minds. The government doesn't care about us; they'll either Delete us or forget about us, you know that."

"Or they might pardon us," Woods points out, his wide frame still slumped and dejected from the death of Winchester. "If we sign up for the front line, they might pardon us."

"And you want to wait for that option?" Adam asks, taking an aggressive step closer to Woods.

Woods turns toward his enraged friend, looking up into his face. "Wouldn't you rather be legitimately free than a fugitive?"

"We might never get that chance! I want to be free, no matter the cost!"

"I think you know what you have to do," Fulton says, glaring at Wren.

Wren appears not to hear this at first, her eyes distant and unseeing, but then she takes a deep breath and looks at Fulton. "Yes, yes, of course, you're right," she mutters.

"You're going to let us out?" Woods asks.

"I think I have to, don't I? I think that's the right thing to do."

"It is," Pander says decisively.

"Right, yes, it is," Wren replies, her voice faraway and dreamy.

"Think about this, Wren," Malachai says, touching her cheek. "Think carefully."

"I have, I've thought about it. I have to do the right thing. The trains will stop running soon, and you'll be trapped here. I'll let you guys out first, then I'll set the rest of them free."

Malachai nods and steps aside.

My heart rate increases suddenly as Wren moves toward the detonator threshold. She's going to free us; she's going to let us go. I think first of my sister, Molly, then my father. I have to get to them; that's the first thing I have to do. I have to make sure they're okay.

Wren moves forward, but she appears to be unstable on her feet, stumbling as though she's been drinking or taking Crawl.

I follow her, we all do, eagerly staring at the panel beside the doorway that, soon, Wren will press a finger against to disarm the infrared barrier that would kill us instantly if we tried to cross it.

But then I stop, my head turning toward Kina's cell. Can I really escape now and leave her to deal with those Wren deemed too dangerous for the 2 a.m. club?

"Fuck," I whisper, and take a step back from the group. I know I can't go without Kina. Either I have to get Wren to let her out or I have to wait and take my chances with the second group.

Tyco will be in the second group, I think.

"Come on, let's go," I hear Pander say impatiently, and I turn back to Wren.

She's standing stock-still at the doorway, her back to the group. She is so still that she seems frozen in time. I step closer, feeling that now too-familiar sense of dread seeping into my skin.

"Wren," Malachai says, and for the first time I hear fear in even his voice, "everything all right?"

Things happen quickly. Wren spins to face the group, her eyes blinking rapidly, her mouth contorted into a grotesque smile. The entire group takes a stumbling step back. Malachai's arm stretches out across them, defensively. Wren reaches for the trigger on her belt and aims it into the crowd. I hear the four beeps inside someone's chest as the trigger links up with one of our heart implants. I close my eyes and pray it's not me.

"No," I hear Fulton whisper. "No way."

And then he falls silent as he crumples to the floor.

There is a moment of complete stillness. And then screaming and panic and shoving as we all sprint for the safety of our cells. Woods sidesteps into Fulton's old cell. In front of me Igby wrenches at Pod's massive arm, dragging him into a free cell and slamming the door shut. I see Malachai slide on his back into another cell and Emery grunt as she pulls a heavy door shut, screaming at Alistair to "go, go, go!" at the same time. Her voice cuts off the moment the door shuts flush with the frame. All of this happens in the space of three seconds, and all the while I'm being pushed and pulled by the panicking crowd.

I run toward my own cell—there are two empty ones before it, but I'm not thinking clearly. Alistair runs beside me, and then his bleached-blond hair moves ahead as he beats me for pace. I hear four beeps, and I can't tell if it's him or me. He goes limp, a rag doll dropped from a height, his legs flipping up, curving his spine as his expressionless face scrapes along the floor.

I grab the frame of my cell, spinning myself around and into the tiny room. I pull at the door, my breaths coming out in panicked cries.

I see Pander sprint past me, her glasses falling to the concrete floor, and she stops, turns around, and bends down to pick them up. I want to scream at her to run, but my cell door closes, the locks snapping shut. I really hope she makes it to the next room.

The silence engulfs me, surrounds me, swaddles me like a blanket.

I collapse to the floor. This isn't real, this can't be real, this isn't happening.

Alistair and Fulton are dead. Wren killed them. Why did she do that?

I can't face this, I can't accept this. My mind blocks out everything, drags me down into a world of nothingness: I feel nothing, see nothing, hear nothing; I'm aware of nothing. I sit on the hard floor, and I am no one, I am nowhere, and it's a kind of bliss.

Alistair and Fulton are dead. Wren killed them. Why did she do that?

The question is far from here, inside a locked room in a locked house in a ghost town.

I might lose my mind if I don't get a grip, I'm aware of that. I slap myself in the face, hard, and then I do it again. The pain brings me back to the present.

"Alistair and Fulton are dead," I say aloud. "Wren killed them. Why?"

I contemplate the question.

"She went crazy, she lost her mind. Wren killed Alistair and Fulton. There's a war in the city, the power is out, and we're under attack."

I'm mumbling the words, trying to put them together like assorted jigsaw pieces from a dozen different puzzles. None of it makes sense; none of it fits together.

I stand up, walk to the sink, and twist the cold tap. Nothing happens.

"Fuck," I hiss.

My heart thumps in my chest, as though it's taking running leaps against my rib cage. I look at my reflection in the blacked-out screen on the wall of my cell. I barely recognize myself: my skin ashen, my eyes bulging, my mouth fixed in a grimace that doesn't belong to me. I'm in shock, I know that, but there's nothing to be done.

I walk to the screen and touch the black surface. I wish it worked, wish Happy would talk to me again, keep me company, bring me my food, tell me the time. I don't want to be in this alone. I pick a book from on top of the pile, read the first line, and then throw it at my locked door. No way of opening it from the inside.

I am stuck in here again. It seems I can't stop getting stuck in here. Am I destined to return over and over, until I die?

I freeze as the hatch on my cell door slides open slowly, the metallic scrape squealing into the silence of the room.

I turn to face the door. Wren's wide, bright eyes stare back at me, her eyelids fluttering open, then shut, open, then shut, over and over. Hummingbird's wings.

"Wren, it's me," I say, my voice sounding like an echo of an echo. "It's Luka."

She says nothing, just stares at me, teeth bared in that awful smile.

She lifts her hand up and points something at me. In my dazed state, it takes half a second to recognize the little green light on the end of the trigger. For a moment, I don't move. For one little moment, I accept that Wren is going to kill me. I think of my dad, my sister, of Kina, and I dart out of the way before she can arm the device and link it with the wire in my heart.

"Wren!" I yell, pressing myself against the wall. "Please, Wren, put that down."

She doesn't reply, her expression doesn't change; she just aims the trigger at me.

"Put the trigger down, Wren. What are you doing?"

I see her arm snake through the hatch, and the trigger comes around to face me.

I dive to the other side as she tracks my movements. Without thinking, I roll under my bed and watch as Wren thrashes around trying to arm the device so she can detonate the explosive that's surgically attached to my heart.

And then I realize that there's a sound in my cell: the sound of Happy's voice:

"Infiltration. Lockdown in five seconds . . . four . . . three . . . two . . ."

"Wren!" I scream. "Get your arm out of the hatch!"

"*. . . one . . . lockdown.*"

The hatch slams shut, and Wren's arm, severed at the shoulder, falls to the floor of my cell. As it does so, the green light of the trigger turns red, and I hear four beeps from deep inside my chest.

The trigger is armed.

I'm frozen for a second by the sight of the blood seeping slowly from the lifeless limb, but then I scramble over and carefully pry the trigger from Wren's hand, making sure I keep my finger pressed down firmly on the switch.

"What the hell, what the hell, what the fuck," I say through shallow breaths as I hyperventilate. "The Lens," I mutter. "I need the Lens to disarm the damned thing."

Disarm! my brain screams wildly, and I almost laugh at the sight of the pale arm on the floor.

There's no time to assess the situation, no time to work out what to do next, as the sound of my cell door creaking open infiltrates the silence.

I turn to face Wren, who stands in the doorway, still blinking, still smiling, apparently unaware of the life-threatening injury that she has inflicted upon herself. She steps forward, her remaining hand reaching out and grabbing me by the throat.

We both fall to the hard floor of my cell. A sickening crack fills the room as my head thumps off the concrete, and I see white spots in my vision. Wren's face is inches from mine; she smiles down at me and crushes my throat with all her strength.

I try to speak her name, try to beg her to stop. Blood drips onto my face from the wound at her shoulder, and the pain and the panic are unbearable.

The pressure is building behind my eyes, and my vision is growing gray at the corners. I feel my grip on the trigger weaken.

I have to do something, and I have to do it now. With my free arm, I punch and chop at the hand that's choking the life out of me, but Wren's smile doesn't even waver. I reach out and grab for a weapon, something hard and heavy that I can hit her with to stop her from killing me. My fingers wrap around something that feels hard enough, and I swing it with all my remaining strength into her temple.

It barely affects her, but her grip loosens for a fraction of a second, enough for me to roll out from underneath her and fill my lungs with air.

Without thinking, I turn and swing my weapon again. As it hits her above her cheek, I see that it's the hardcover book—*The Fellowship of the Ring*.

The blow drops her to the floor, and I scramble to the cell door, swinging it shut as this deranged version of Wren throws herself toward me. I lift the handle and spin the wheel. The door is locked, and Wren is inside.

I rest my free hand on my knee, and the other grips the dead man's switch tightly. I try to fight off the need to vomit as I cough and breathe and spit blood onto the floor.

After a few seconds, the events of the last week explode inside my brain, and I let out a scream of anger, frustration, confusion, and fear.

I run my free hand through my sweat-soaked hair and tell myself to breathe, tell myself to be calm. I take a look at the trigger, but it's just a solid tube of metal with a single button depressed beneath my thumb, two lights on the end, and as far as I can see, there are no instructions or hints as to how to turn it off.

Wren is going to die, I think, unable to shake the mental image of her severed arm falling from the hatch and landing on my cell floor with a wet smacking sound.

I slide the hatch open.

"Wren, you need to make a tourniquet or you're going to lose too much blood," I say, my voice coming out in a weak croak.

She doesn't appear to hear me; she's pacing the cell from wall to wall like a wild animal, still with that horrible smile on her face, still blinking over and over again.

"Wren," I say, trying to yell.

For a second, her eyes dart up to mine, and she runs at the door, diving for the hatch as though she believes that she can squeeze through the tiny gap and get to me, finish me off.

I slam the hatch shut before she can reach it. I stand in the corridor, feeling helpless.

Whatever happened to Harvey happened to her, I think, but, once again, the puzzle pieces don't fit—the Group As all lost their minds after the Delay, but Wren was nowhere near the Facility.

I have to get to her before she dies from blood loss, but how do you help someone who tries to kill you every time you get close?

I step back and lean against the other side of the corridor. It's then that I notice that some cell doors are open. It appears to be a random pattern—one cell shut, the next open; four cells shut, three open . . .

I feel even more adrenaline enter my system, accompanied by complete terror. *Mine wasn't the first cell that Wren came to.*

I stare at the open doors, and I know what I'll find inside. I hold the trigger up to my face and try to absorb that inside all those rooms lie the lifeless bodies of my fellow inmates. Wren was successful in pairing the trigger with the devices in their hearts, and she killed them. She moved from cell to cell, stopping, when the mood took her, to execute the helpless inmate inside, and then she opened their door to check that her work was complete.

To confirm this I will have to go to each cell and witness the carnage firsthand, but as I stare at the glaring dead eyes of Fulton and the unnatural position of Alistair's body sprawled on the corridor floor, I know that I can't do that now, because if what I'm imagining is true, then it will make wanting to save Wren's life very difficult.

I look to the right of my cell, and I see that the adjacent door is still shut and locked. I feel a burst of elation in my chest as I know that my neighbor is still alive.

"Kina," I whisper, and I allow myself a second to smile.

I take a breath. *Think.*

I have to save Wren. She won't last much longer if she keeps losing blood.

I have to get help, I have to get out of the Loop and get help.

I run toward the entrance of the Loop, keeping my eyes firmly ahead, unwilling to glance into the open cells. I run straight at the exit until something in my mind screams at me to stop. I see the big letters written in yellow:

INMATES! CROSSING THIS POINT WITHOUT AUTHORIZATION WILL CAUSE IMPLANTS TO DETONATE.

My heart jumps in my chest when I see how close I came to crossing the threshold. I scold myself for being so stupid. I walk to the panel on the wall. At first I'm sure that there's no way for me to deactivate the barrier, as I know that my fingerprints won't work on the scanner. The only person who will be able to deactivate it is Wren, and she's not going to voluntarily press her fingertips to this—

But she doesn't have to volunteer.

I run back to my locked cell as fast as I can.

Without overthinking my plan, I open the door, grab Wren's severed arm from the floor, and throw it behind me into the corridor. As I'm still holding the trigger, I have to do everything one-handed. Wren doesn't react as quickly as she should, probably because a lot of her blood is now on the floor and soaking into the mattress of my bed, but she lunges at me, the fingernails of her hand scraping the skin on my face as I dive back into the corridor and spin the lock.

I pick up the arm and run back to the entrance of the Loop, the place where the Dark Train delivered me on my first day, and push Wren's lifeless thumb against the pad. The display reads:

133

DISARM? YES OR NO

I press **YES** and the next option appears:

RE-ARM: YES OR NO

I press **NO**, drop Wren's arm to the floor, and step toward the doorway.

Despite knowing that I have deactivated the barrier, I still close my eyes and hold my breath as I step through to the other side.

Nothing happens. My heart does not explode, and I breathe again.

Ahead of me is the platform where the Dark Train picks us up for Delays. It's strange to see the place without a waiting train, but I can't dwell on that now. I have to get out of here and find help, but first I have to stop the bleeding, or Wren won't last an hour.

There has to be another door somewhere, I think. *A staff entrance, a place where the food is prepared.*

And then I see it, on the other side of the tracks: a door that would normally be concealed by the waiting train.

I don't hesitate. I climb down onto the track, stepping over the rails, and run to the door. There's an eye scanner to the left, but whatever's beyond must not be deemed worthy of stored-power security, as the door swings open when I gently push it.

Inside, there are five or six old-fashioned bulb lights glowing dimly—they must be on the backup power but don't seem to be getting all the juice they need. There's a countertop with coffee machine next to a small sink, a table with a 360-degree television projector in the middle, a radio, and a door marked ENGINEER in the far wall. Beside that, there's a second door marked EMERGENCY EQUIPMENT.

I open the second door and find a small walk-in cupboard with a dozen or so prison jumpsuits hanging up, two riot guard suits, four more heart triggers in a stand on the wall, a tranquilizer gun, a first aid kit, and one early-model USW pistol.

I pocket the tranquilizer gun and drag the first aid kit into the staff room. I rummage through it and find a tourniquet; it's fully electronic, so all I have to do is tranquilize Wren, place the loop of cloth over the stump of her arm, and press the button, and it will fasten itself to the required tightness to halt the loss of blood.

Again I am running back to my cell, the panic is still driving me onward, not allowing me to break down or give up.

I make it to my room, drop the tourniquet to the floor, and open the hatch. I look inside, expecting to see Wren coming toward me in a blind rage. Instead she sits on the bed, her face so pale it's almost silver. She is completely still, other than those blinking eyes.

As I aim the tranquilizer gun through the hatch, ignoring the lockdown warnings, Wren turns to face me, smile still wide and crazy. I fire the dart and hit her in the shoulder. It takes about five seconds for the tranquilizer to take effect before she slumps to the floor.

I drop the tranquilizer gun, open the door, and step inside.

I place the tourniquet over the remaining portion of her arm and press the button. Nothing happens. Even the medical equipment has been affected by whatever has taken out the electronics. I grip the small handle, which resembles an old-fashioned tap, and twist it over and over again; the loop of material that makes up the tourniquet begins to tighten around the pink flesh, pushing the bloody meat of the stump against the snapped bone inside until the severed arteries are squeezed shut and the blood stops pouring out.

The dead weight of Wren feels impossibly heavy as I pull her from the floor and lay her on the bed before stepping back and wiping the sweat from my forehead.

I stare at her lying there, lifeless. For all I know, she might be dead; there is no rising and falling of her chest, or pulse to be felt in her neck or wrist, but there wouldn't have been yesterday either: At the age of eighteen, all Alts have their heart and lungs replaced with more efficient apparatus (tested on former inmates of prisons in Region 7 and Region 44 many years ago).

I kneel beside the bed and press my ear against her chest; from within I hear the constant hum of the APM where her heart once was. The sound sends a chill down my spine. I know the benefits of the APM—they're advertised frequently enough across the city by personalized Barker Projections, I hear them yelling out to Alts in the wealthy parts of town— but I've always wondered: If your heart doesn't beat faster when you're scared or nervous or excited, does that mean you're a little less human?

I lean forward and lift her left eyelid. Her pupil dilates as light hits her eye—she's still alive. I hold open her eyelid with my trigger hand before easing out her Lens with my free hand.

Using the blacked-out screen as a mirror, I place Wren's Lens over my eye. There is no heads-up menu, no text, no way to shut off the trigger. The Lens must have gone out with the rest of the power.

"Shit," I mutter, my hand already feeling weak and hot against the metal. "Shit!" I say again, screaming it this time.

I take the Lens out, place it on the edge of my sink, and make my way back into the corridor, closing the cell door behind me. I can no longer hold back the emotion brought on by the sheer chaos of the last few hours. I sink to my knees and scream a string of gravelly profanities before getting to my feet and throwing a punch at the wall.

I stop myself just before my knuckles connect. It would be stupid to break this hand when the other one is keeping me alive, gripping the trigger.

Don't be an idiot, I tell myself. *Think. You have to be smart now.*

I breathe slowly, calming myself.

Wren is still going to die, I think, laying out the facts. *The tourniquet will give her some time, but without proper medical attention, she won't last a day.*

I know that I have to get on the Dark Train; I have to get out of here and find someone who can help. I turn to move back toward the station, but I hesitate.

Kina will be in her cell, panicking, worried, wondering what's going on, just like I was.

I walk to her cell and slide the hatch open.

For a few seconds, she just stares at me from her bed, her brown eyes wide, her mouth half-open.

"Luka?"

She speaks my name like I'm a ghost.

"Kina, something's happened."

"I can see that," she says, swinging her legs over the edge of her bed and getting to her feet. "Do you want to elaborate?"

"Something's . . . happened," I repeat, and I realize just how tormented I am.

"Okay," Kina says, getting closer to the door. "Take a few breaths."

I do as she instructs, but the air feels somehow thin and ineffective, as though it's not reaching my lungs at all.

"Slowly," she says, and demonstrates slow, exaggerated breathing. In through the nose and out through the mouth. I copy her actions and gradually my head stops spinning, and I no longer feel like I'm going to collapse.

"Now," Kina tries again, "what's going on?"

"The power is out, I don't know how or why, but something is wrong, people are going crazy. Wren, she killed . . . she killed them."

"Wait, what?" Kina says. "Wren killed someone?"

"I think she's killed half the inmates of the Loop. I think she . . . I . . ." My words fade away.

Kina's eyes scan mine, maybe looking for signs that I'm mistaken or that I'm the one who's gone crazy. "What do you mean, killed half the inmates?"

"She lost her mind, started executing the 2 a.m. club. We

all ran to our rooms. I locked myself back in my cell, but she came to my door, tried to arm my heart trigger, tried to kill me. The hatch came down, her arm . . ." I realize that I'm rambling as I mime the hatch chopping Wren's arm off. Kina's eyes widen when she sees the trigger in my other hand, "Oh, yeah, this is armed; if I let go, I'll die." I feel myself hyperventilating again. "I got out, Wren's bleeding to death in my cell, I got a tourniquet on her, but I have to get help. I'll come back, Kina. I'll come back as soon as I can."

I'm about to shut the hatch when Kina yells, "Wait!"

I turn back.

"You're going to have to slow down. I didn't understand any of that. What is the 2 a.m. club?"

"There's no time to explain," I tell her. "All you need to know is: Something bad has happened, something big."

"Luka, what if this is the war? What if it happened?"

"I don't have time to think about that right now," I say. "I have to get help."

"What if you get killed out there?" Kina continues. "Who's going to come and let the rest of us out? We'll die of thirst by Tuesday. Someone needs to stay behind to unlock the doors, just in case."

I nod; she's right. I step forward, spin the lock on her door, and haul it open.

Kina steps out into the corridor and stares up at me.

"Thanks," she says. Then her eyes drift over to Fulton's body, his limbs splayed unnaturally, his mouth open, skin gray.

"Look at me," I tell her, and her worried eyes turn slowly to meet mine. "Just wait here, okay? Don't move, don't look in the open cells, and don't unlock any of the doors."

"Okay," Kina says, and now I can hear fear in her voice.

"It's going to be all right," I say, marveling inwardly at how quickly our roles have switched. "Kina, if I'm not back by morning, try to find Pod and Igby—they'll be in a cell together. If they're dead, try to find Pander—she wears hearing aids and glasses. If not her, then Malachai. They'll explain what happened here and help you escape."

"Right," Kina says, her voice still electric with terror. "Right, okay. Just come back, all right? Just come back."

Once again, I turn to go, and Kina calls out, "Wait!"

I turn back and feel her hand in mine. For a second, I get a sense of vertigo as her fingers wrap around the trigger that I've been clutching so tightly that my hand is throbbing. Instinctively, I pull away. Kina looks into my eyes and takes my hand in hers; slowly she takes the device, replacing my fingers with hers around the switch that would end my life if released.

"Just come back," she tells me once more.

I nod and hold her eyes for a second longer. And then I run. Again, I stare forward—I'm still not ready to look into the open cells and see who lies inside.

I cross the threshold of the disarmed doorway and hold my breath until I'm standing on the platform.

There is no way into or out of the Loop other than the Dark Train. I walk to the screen where guards make a request for the train, but it's blank. The emergency power has gone out. I'm too late.

I stand on the dimly lit platform and stare into the blackness of the hexagon-shaped subway that leads to the city.

Now my only way out is through those tunnels.

I step down onto the rails. There is only one direction I can go—the line terminates at the Loop.

I take a breath and step into the darkness.

Immediately, fear grips me. The Dark Train is unmanned, and for the last few miles between the city and the Loop, it runs through tunnels. The fact that I'm walking through these tunnels coupled with the fact that the train travels in almost-perfect silence makes me incredibly aware that I could be pulverized at any second.

The trains aren't running, I reassure myself. *The power is out.*

I push the fear down and run the fingertips of my left hand against the tunnel wall to keep me on the correct path. My fingers run along crumbling concrete, wet slime, and wires that snake in and out of the wall. I try to picture the path that I'm walking down, try to imagine the half dozen rails that—when working—would be thrumming with the magnetic power to hover a ten-car train. I try to imagine the white walls, stained by the strange moss and algae growing on them. I try to imagine my own feet landing over and over on the concrete floor, but in this kind of darkness it isn't easy.

It's hard to tell how much time has passed. One foot in front of the other, over and over, on and on into the darkness.

As I walk through the damp underground passageway, I begin to sing, in nervous and tremulous tones, the last song that I heard Pander singing before the end of our last exercise hour. I don't know all the words, so I resort to vowel sounds and tuneless mumbling through the chorus.

I stop. *Pander, did she make it to a cell after she dropped her glasses? Did Wren kill her? Was her cell door open?*

This thought leads me to the horrible geometry of trying to remember which cells were open, which of my friends are alive, and which are dead.

I start singing again, louder this time, trying to keep the thoughts from infiltrating my brain once more, trying to focus on my badly out-of-tune voice.

The Dark Train travels at 200 miles per hour almost constantly and only makes one stop—at the courthouse—before reaching the Facility after about fifteen minutes. This means the Facility is around fifty miles away. If there are no other stations along this line apart from the courthouse and the Facility, then Wren is as good as dead.

The disheartening calculations cause me to pick up the pace until I'm jogging along the tracks, singing my mumbled song even louder, but the singing comes to an abrupt stop when I feel something brush past my leg. Something big, something warm and alive.

Ignore it, I tell myself. *Just a rat; it'll leave you alone if you leave it alone.*

But as I move onward, I feel a second and a third creature slalom around my ankles. The sheer size of them makes me shudder.

When we were kids, before I was taken to the Loop, my

sister, Molly, and I used to stand at the entrance to the subway tunnels of the city, goading each other to run as far in as we dared. We'd tell each other stories about the rats, stories that had been passed down through generations and around the playgrounds of the Regulars' schools, embellished and inflated until they became urban legends—the tunnel rats that had made their way here from the Red Zones, mutated rats crawling through sewage pipes and the old underground train lines. We'd say the rats could drag fully grown men into the darkness and strip their flesh to the bone.

Ignore them, ignore them, ignore them, I repeat over and over in my head, losing my place in Pander's song before starting again.

But now there are more of them. I can hear their feet scuttling against the hard ground, their hairless tails whipping the rails, their nattering calls echoing off the cold concrete walls. More and more come scurrying in from the darkness until there is a wave of rats surrounding me and every time my feet touch the ground there's another tunnel rat squirming out of the way.

Ignore them, ignore them, ignore—

"Shit!" I scream as I feel razor-sharp teeth digging into the material at the calf of my jumpsuit.

This act of bravery from one of the rats seems to ignite something in the rest, and I feel a second bite, this one harder and right on the bone of my ankle, and then another high up on my left knee. I can feel blood trickling down my leg.

My blood acts like a drug to the creatures, and the air is filled with the fervent screeches of desperate vermin. They jump up, sharp claws scrabbling at me, teeth biting and ripping through the material of my clothes, and more blood begins to spill out as more and more teeth and claws tear at me. One climbs as high as my shoulder and sinks its teeth in so deep that they hit the muscle below the skin.

I scream in agony, swiping in the darkness, kicking out at the relentless swarm of squirming animals as panicked thoughts rush through my head, too fast to register.

I drive forward, walking with stiff arms and legs, weighed down by the creatures covering my body, rapidly losing hope that I'll get out of this tunnel at all, and I'm glad that I opened Kina's cell before I left, that she'll have the chance to get out of the Loop alive. I hope that she's smarter than me; I hope that she'll search the staff room and find that gun and take it with her. Why didn't I think of the gun? Why did I assume that it would be easy to get out of here?

The weight of the clambering rats is getting too much for me now. I feel myself flagging, weakening as the blood seeps out from countless wounds. The pain of the onslaught is taking its toll, and I can't go much farther. And when I die here, I will have failed Wren; she will die as well because I was too stupid to bring a weapon, too weak to make it to safety.

The thought of Wren, how frail she was when I laid her down on my bed, how close to death she was, pulls me forward for one more step, two more, three, but it's hopeless, the rats are piling onto my body, their instincts telling them to bring me down to the ground so they can eat. I close my eyes and fight against the rats.

If Kina had left the trigger in my hand, I would let it go right now. I would let my heart explode.

This thought offers no comfort as I wait to die.

I'm almost ready to give up when I open my eyes and see a light.

Up ahead, in the distance, a small patch of brightness in the black of the tunnel.

It's too far. Surely it's too far for me to make it?

But what else is there?

I swipe at the rats with my remaining strength and free myself of some of the weight. They pile on again almost immediately, squeaking and biting and scratching. I shuffle forward, the muscles in my legs straining and burning.

The light grows bigger and brighter; it's barely a glow, but compared to the gloom of the tunnel, it looks heavenly. I can smell the fresh air of the outdoors, and I know that the light is coming from the glow of the moon.

I can see a platform up ahead, the raised concrete of a station, and something tells me that when I get there, I'll be okay. I'm ten feet away, eight, six.

And then I fall.

No sooner have I hit the ground than the swarm of rats doubles in size. There must be dozens of them, the size of small dogs.

Their teeth pull at my flesh, ripping it away as they shriek with delight. They cover me from head to toe, fighting one another, killing one another as they vie for space. They teem and roil, they cover my face until I can't breathe, and I know that it ends here.

No.

No, not when I'm so close. I won't die on the ground like this. I want to see the moon one last time, I want to see the stars as a free man just one more time.

I grab one of the rats off my face and throw it with all my might against the wall of the subway. I dig the fingernails of my hands into the cold ground and drag myself and the frantic rats an inch closer to the platform, and an inch more, and an inch more.

Something strange begins to happen: The rats who were biting at my ears and the back of my neck begin to scramble away, and as I heave myself ever closer to the platform, the rats at my shoulders and the top of my back run away from me, back into the darkness of the tunnel.

They're afraid of the light, I think, and strain every muscle in my body as I pull myself forward.

A few more yards, a few more agonizing, exhausting yards, and I'm lying in the light of the moon, free from the suffocating weight, feeling like I've crawled across broken glass, my white Loop suit now shades of red and black, torn to shreds like the skin beneath it.

I lie on my back, staring at the stars, breathing in the night air. I don't let myself think, don't let myself acknowledge that—for the second time in less than two hours—I came within touching distance of death.

I push myself to my feet and stumble to the platform edge before hauling myself onto the cold concrete. The wounds across my body scream out in renewed pain as I make it to the platform and look around.

Despite the condition I'm in, despite everything that's happened, I can't help but feel awe as I see the half-moon hanging large in the sky, illuminating the rooftops of the small village beneath it and the Ferris wheels of the sky-farms beyond. I smile up at the stars and laugh weakly.

This feeling of wonder is short-lived, however, as my eyes move to the horizon and the enormous residential buildings beyond the farmland: the Verticals reaching up and up into the sky above the crowded mass of homeless shacks surrounding them, the big blue rain collectors on the roofs and the jumble of homemade pipes connecting the water to each apartment looking like some monstrous sea creature wrapping itself around the concrete. The Verticals are lit by fire; the city is burning, great plumes of thick, dark smoke rising up into the black sky.

I stand there, in the darkness, beneath the glowing moon, staring out at the city in which I used to live. Witnessing a war.

Even from this far away—probably three miles from the city—I can hear the rumble and roar of the flames, see clouds of smoke curling up into the sky, and watch as a tall office block collapses in on itself. The impact as it falls shakes the ground so violently I can feel it from here.

The rumors were true, I think, unable to tear my eyes away from the destroyed city. *There is a war, and whoever has attacked Region 86 is winning.*

No time to think about the ruined city, the loss of life, the war. I need to keep moving; I have to save Wren.

I run toward the village, and as I get closer, I can tell that this is one of those second-home retreats for the Alts. These types of places began to pop up as the radiation began to recede from the Red Zones—the real estate was immediately worth millions of Coin because the homes offered relief from the massively overcrowded city. Most Alts own a home outside the city for weekends and getaways—the highest-earning Alts own at least three—while us Regulars cram into rented apartments on the top floors of cheaply built towers in the crime boroughs.

Do these Alts know how close they're living to a prison? I think as I move quickly toward the dark streets.

I hammer on the door of the first house I come to but don't wait long for a response before moving to the next door and slamming my fist against it over and over. I wait for one of them to answer, but no one comes. I cross the road, tripping over something metallic on the ground, but it's too dark to see what it is. I try ringing the doorbells, but even those aren't working, so I knock until my knuckles ache, but still no one comes to help.

When I get to house number seven or eight and hit my bruised hands against the wood of the door, it swings inward, unlocked and unlatched. I take a step inside.

"Hello?" I call out, trying to alert any inhabitants to my presence. I'm all too aware that if a young man in prison clothing, covered in blood, is found creeping through an expensive home like this, or any home for that matter, he will be considered a threat, and my guess is that any Alt with a vacation home this size will have an immobilization modification installed.

They'd be well within their rights to activate it now, so I yell out again, letting anyone inside know that I'm not here to rob them.

I take another step inside and expect the automatic lights to come on or the family's Secure Guard system to ask me my business in this home, but nothing happens.

I'm standing in a vast open-floor plan, a room that is the kitchen, living room, and dining room combined into one free-flowing area. The home is clean and bare—sterile.

They don't have a television, not even a 360-degree projector that enables images to be viewed from all sides. Instead, they have an Immersive7 system that allows the viewer to walk around the scene of a movie, look for clues if it's a murder mystery or find hidden bonus features in comedies. This system works in tandem with a Lens and is built into the far wall of the living room, but it too appears to be out of power.

I notice a SoCom unit on the kitchen countertop and make my way over to it—from here I can contact the emergency services in eight different ways. I wave my hand over the domed screen, but nothing happens. I try again; still nothing.

I scream at the stupid hunk of glass and metal—not because it isn't working but because I've known for a while now that the power outage isn't confined to the Loop. It's at least city-wide, maybe Region-wide, maybe even worldwide. I had hoped that the rich, with their backup generators and solar storage units, might still have some form of electricity, but I think, deep down, that as soon as I stood on the platform and looked to the burning city, I knew it was hopeless.

I can't save Wren. I doubt even doctors could save her without the proper technology, and with no power there is no technology.

I take a deep, angry breath and exhale hard.

There has to be a way. There has to be something you can do! And then, from nowhere, two words come into my head. *Drone poison.*

At first I don't make the connection, but then a painful memory leaps into my head: my mother on her bed, dying eyes wandering aimlessly around the room, the fingers of her left hand rubbing together in agitation, a fine sheen of sweat on her forehead and her thin, translucent skin clinging to her frame. Her hands would come together, and she would sign words, phrases that mostly made no sense. My mom was deaf, so my whole family spoke sign language—a language that had become extinct among the Alts, as they were all born with perfect hearing. She signed my name, words like *love* and *I'm sorry.* She was dying of something, one of the new flus probably, the ones that the government assured us did not come out of the Red Zones. A diagnosis would cost us more than we had. Dad spent every Coin on an appointment, and a medic drone was sent to our house; blood and saliva were taken and the drone analyzed the samples in front of us. The diagnosis was complete, and we were asked if we wanted the information. We said yes, and the drone informed us that it would cost fifty Coin, and that treatment was another two hundred. Of course the injection of Quarantine, to ensure the virus wasn't spread, was not only free but also mandatory.

It was my mom who convinced my dad that we didn't need

to know what was wrong with her as long as she got the treatment. I could see in my dad's face that he wanted to ask, *What if it's something big? What if it's untreatable? What if whatever the drone gives you just delays the inevitable?* But he just smiled and agreed.

Thirteen days later she was dead.

She only lasted those thirteen days because of the final drug offered by the medic drone. I don't know the medical name, but in the Verticals it's known as Crawl. Alts who are hooked on Ebb often mix the two to make the experience last longer. Crawl slows down the user's heart rate and respiratory system to slow-motion pace, and it also slows the perceptions of the user down, essentially slowing down time. Crawl put my mother into suspended animation, slowing down everything, even the disease that was killing her.

My mother died on the same day I was sent to the Loop. I was still standing in her bedroom, watching the coffin drone carry her away in a black plastic sheet, when the Marshals kicked down the door to our tiny home and dragged me away as Molly screamed and tried to tell them I had done nothing wrong.

I swallow the pain of the memory and bring myself back to the present.

If I could get ahold of some Crawl, I'd stand a chance of saving Wren's life. The slower her APM system pumps blood around her body, the less she can lose from the severed arm; that'll give me more time to find someone to help. But with the city on fire and the power out, there's no way I can make it three miles, find a hospital, figure out which drug is Crawl, and get all the way back to the Loop before Wren dies from blood loss.

There's only one other option, I tell myself. *Drone poison*.

The same stuff they fired into Rook Ford when he refused to reenter his cell after exercise—it contains Crawl. The downside is it also contains those powerful hallucinogens. The slowed heart and respiratory system makes the whole nightmare experience feel as though it's lasting a thousand lifetimes. I don't want to put Wren through the horror that Rook went through, but if it's a choice between that and certain death . . . I have to do it.

"I have to go back," I say aloud, and cry out in frustration and anger that all of this has been for nothing.

And then I hear the slightest creak behind me. I'm being watched.

My senses crackle and come alive. I don't know how I know, but someone is crouched on the stairs behind me, studying my every move.

I turn around and look into the blinking eyes of a young boy of about twelve. He's smiling, but it's that same maniac smile that Wren had, except his mouth is covered in dried blood. He's hunched forward, balancing on the balls of his bare feet, arms hanging loosely between his pajama-clad legs. How long has he been there? Has he been watching me this whole time? I say nothing, do nothing; the silence is a fuse and we both know that when it ends . . .

"I'm leaving," I say, holding both hands up in the air to show that I'm not a threat. "I'm going, okay?"

I face the boy on the stairs the whole time, his electric-blue eyes on me, intense and determined, blinking furiously as I sidestep toward the front door, slowly, slowly.

I reach out behind me with my left hand, grasping for the round handle of the door. I find it and wrap my fingers around it, and that's when the boy springs into life, rushing down the stairs on all fours like a rabid dog, eerily silent and coming straight for me.

I scramble to get the door open, slip out into the garden, and slam the door shut behind me. I hear the boy's body crashing into the thick wood. The handle turns, and the door begins to open. I grab it, pulling it toward me with all my strength, jerking it back into its frame. The boy tries again, desperate to get to me—and he's way stronger than he looked.

He's the same as Wren, I think, the muscles in my arms tensing as I fight. I lean back against the impossible power of the little boy in the pale blue pajamas. *He's the same as Wren, and Harvey, and all the Group As.*

Somewhere in the back of my mind, I know that it can't be. The Group As went crazy because of the Delay, but Wren didn't take the Delay, and neither did this boy.

The door rattles as the boy strains silently. Do I wait him out, fight against him until he gives up, or run? My mind is made up for me as I hear footsteps pounding on the pavement and turn to see a woman of about seventy sprinting toward me at an inhuman pace.

There's enough time to register her smile and rapidly blinking eyes—and the glint of the moonlight on the large knife in her hand—and then she is within arm's length of me, swiping at my throat with the blade. I lean back fast, losing my balance, and I feel the air from the slicing knife as it comes within a millimeter of opening up my neck.

I hit the ground, and my hand knocks into another metallic object, releasing the stink of rotting food. I don't have time to figure out what it is; the door to the vacation home swings open, the boy leaps out, and his wild eyes survey the scene.

I don't remember getting to my feet, don't remember running, but here I am—sprinting as fast as my wounded legs will carry me, which isn't fast enough. I can hear the footsteps of the old lady and the little boy right behind me and getting closer and closer until I can almost feel their breath on the back of my neck.

Just when I'm sure they're going to grab me, I hear both of them tumble to the ground. I feel a moment of euphoria and I sprint on, past five, ten houses before I stop and turn around.

What I see turns my blood cold: The old lady is on top of the boy and she's bringing the knife down into his chest over and over again. The scene is a silhouette in the darkness, a shadow stabbing another shadow to death, black droplets spilling into the air, and the boy dies in almost complete silence.

I can't move, can't look away from the horror in front of me. I can't run, can't yell for help, can't do anything.

When the boy lies motionless, the lady turns her head toward me. It's enough to break the spell, and I'm running again.

I'm turning left, then right, leaping over fences and through gardens until I spot a tree house at the foot of one particularly lavish mansion.

I jump, grab a low-hanging branch, and haul myself up, swinging my legs onto the next branch. I'm high enough now to reach the entrance, and I pull myself into the little hut just as I hear the murderous lady stumble into the garden and wade through the pond below me.

I try to keep my breathing silent, wishing that I was born an Alt so that I could have had an MOR system installed where my burning lungs are. I keep my gasps short and shallow, sweat rolling from my forehead as I wait and hope that she will just go away.

Time passes, what feels like hours. Finally, I hear my attacker stomp off and into the adjacent garden, searching for her next kill.

I peek out of the little wooden tree house and see the lady—shoulders raised high, head twitching from side to side as she marches away, the moonlight no longer glinting off the blade in her hand—the light is absorbed by the young boy's blood.

They were the same as Wren, I think, watching the lady as she begins to run again. *What's happening to them?*

The sky is beginning to brighten, and from this higher vantage point I notice, dotted all over the village, drones lying motionless on the ground. These are the metallic shapes I've been stumbling over since I got here. Some still have their cargo clutched in their metallic grips—packages, fast food, alcohol, groceries, prescriptions—some are companion drones, some are surveillance drones. All of them must have fallen from the sky when the power went out.

I climb out of the tree house, shaking from the adrenaline, the cold, the exhaustion, and blood loss.

You have to get back to the Loop; you have to get that drone poison. It's the only way to save Wren's life. After that, you have to figure out how to cure her of whatever the hell is happening to her.

I stop and face the city. Somewhere in there, if they're not dead amid the chaos and the killing, my father and my sister are fighting for their lives.

Either that or they're infected too, I think, *like Wren and the boy and the old woman.*

I'm torn between the city and the Loop, my family and Wren, and for a moment I choose the city. I take a few steps toward the burning metropolis, and then I stop, my mind filling with memories of Wren—the old Wren, before she became . . . what she became. Her kindness, her compassion, the way she could make all those hundreds of days that should have been unbearable bearable. I know I can bring her back; I know I can help her the way she helped me. I know I have to go back through the rat tunnel; Wren will die without my help. I have to believe that my family is still alive, safe and hidden somewhere. I can't consider the alternative.

"Got to be prepared this time," I whisper, remembering the swarming rats and how they cowered from the light.

I walk through the garden and carefully slide open the glass door at the back of the big house. Creeping slowly and quietly inside, my senses are on high alert as I anticipate attacks from all angles. Nothing comes.

This house is even bigger than the last. My cheap Loop-issue shoes, wet from the dew on the grass, slip on the tiled floor of the room. It's some kind of conservatory—it has a glass roof, glass walls, and furniture made of bamboo.

I find a set of drawers in the corner of the room and begin rifling through them, looking for a flashlight.

It won't work, I remind myself. *Nothing works.*

I almost slam the drawer shut in anger but catch myself and close it quietly.

I need to make fire.

I look around the room and spot the bamboo furniture.

Perfect, I think, turning a chair on its side and bringing my foot down hard on the frame.

The crack is deafeningly loud, and I freeze, waiting for the sound of footsteps rushing toward me from the darkness within. I'm poised, ready to run for the door if anyone comes, but there's no sound. I pick up three of the shattered tubes of thick, hollow wood, each one about a foot in length.

Next, I need some kind of material, some rags to wrap around the tops of the canes so that they will burn bright in the tunnel. I head upstairs to where I think the bedrooms will be, still moving slowly, silently. Every shadowy corner could be hiding one of those smiling killers.

I open the first door and see, in the moonlight, a large office with a big wooden desk and some framed certificates on the walls. The next door is some kind of studio, filled with green screens, cameras, and costumes. I come to a bedroom; it's too dark to make anything out other than the shape of a large bed, the sliding mirrored doors of a walk-in wardrobe, and the two LucidVision headsets above the headboard.

I move to the window and open the blackout blinds to let some moonlight into the room. When I turn back, I see the pale body of a middle-aged man lying under the covers of the bed. The blankets on his side are a thick, shiny red from the blood that has drained out of the slit in his neck, his eyes are wide and stare endlessly up at nothing, and his mouth is stretched into that horribly familiar smile.

Skirting around the bed, I make my way to the big wardrobe, never taking my eyes off the dead man lying motionless under the covers.

Pretend he's not there, I tell myself. *Just keep moving.*

I force myself to look away and grab an armful of shirts from the hangers. I back toward the door, once again staring at the corpse, with an irrational fear that he might sit up and tell me to put his clothes back where I found them.

I leave the bedroom, quietly shutting the door behind me before running back downstairs, where I try to ignore the creepy feeling inside me while I wrap and knot the shirts around the bamboo canes.

I need two more things before I can leave: some kind of fuel so that my torches will burn longer and something to light them with.

I find a first aid kit in a drawer in the kitchen—there's some hand sanitizer with a high alcohol content. I shove it into my pocket. Next to the large artificial fire in the center of the living room, I find a wind-resistant lighter.

It's hard to run with the torches under one arm, the lighter and hand sanitizer in my pockets, and the bite wounds aching all over my body, but I move as quickly as I can back to the Dark Train platform and jump down onto the tracks.

I look into the pitch-blackness of the tunnel, and my skin tightens at the thought of facing the rats again. I try to ignore the fear, try to think only of saving Wren, so that I can get back to the city and find my family.

I douse the material of the first torch in the flammable gel and light it. The flame encircles the shirt and glows a pale blue at first before bright yellow fire emerges.

Are you sure you want to go back there? I ask myself.

I swallow hard and think about Wren, about the others locked in their cells, about Kina.

I nod my head, take a deep breath, and step inside.

The tunnel seems somehow more ominous with the dancing light of the torch illuminating the damp walls and the flat ceiling, where short stalactites grow out from the green moss that covers the concrete.

Shadows flicker in time with the fire, and I can't stop my eyes from darting around, sure that I'll see a horde of giant, ugly rats with glowing yellow eyes, but there's nothing.

I walk, slowly at first, as my vision adjusts to the gloom, and then I pick up the pace, moving deeper and deeper into the passageway.

After a few minutes, I come to a fork in the track. In my fear and desperation to escape the rats I hadn't noticed it before; the left fork goes slightly uphill, and the right slightly downhill. Logic tells me that the Loop is to the right—I had been walking with my hand against the left wall and would have felt the point where the tunnel splits if I had been coming out the other way, plus I'm sure I remember the gentle uphill slope.

I step into the tunnel on the right, just as my first torch begins to flicker and sputter. One minute later, and the flame has died.

As I stand in the darkness, fumbling with the next torch, trying to pour hand sanitizer onto the shirt, I hear the first clicking of claws on concrete. In my panicked state, I drop the open bottle of the sharp-smelling fuel. I curse myself and scramble around for it. Finally, my fingers wrap around the bottle. Another skittering of rat claws and the slap of a thick tail behind me.

Grabbing the lighter, I douse the cloth in gel and light it as quickly as I can.

The flame bursts into life, and for a second, all I can see is a boiling carpet of black-and-brown fur, with a thousand milky little eyes staring hungrily at me. I am in the middle of a sea of rats.

The torch begins to shake in my hand as I think about how far I have to go, how long the torches last, how much hand sanitizer I have left.

I take a step forward, and the swarm of rats moves with me—although they keep their distance, staying away from the brightest of the light thrown by my makeshift torch. I take another step, and my vermin chaperones come with me.

"I hate these tunnels," I whisper as I start walking quickly toward the Loop, the rats moving as one writhing, scratching, crawling mass, never stepping into the light but never looking away from their next meal.

I run, the flame roaring beside my ear, and my footsteps no longer echo as the rats are joined by more and more, filling up the tunnel with their warm and foul-smelling bodies. They are behind me now, trailing the light, a sea of them, too many to count, too many to imagine.

The flame only illuminates the next few feet in front of me, and I'm sure that any second I'll trip and the flame will go out, or I'll run into a wall and knock myself unconscious, and then all the rats will have to do is wait until the flame dies and I become an easy meal.

It's not long before torch number two begins to choke and fade. I stop, this time not waiting until the darkness comes before lighting my third and final torch.

Too far to go, I think. *The torch won't last.*

I pour most of the remaining fluid onto my final torch, light it, and throw the almost-burned-out one among the mass of bodies behind me. I hear them shriek and cower away from the fire, and I run again, as fast as I can, pushing with every ounce of energy that is left in me as the flame burns away the fuel.

The rats keep pace with me, never getting any closer nor any farther away than the ring of light around me.

Where is it? Where is the platform? Where is the Loop?

I run even faster, sure that any minute now I will see my destination and I'll be safe from these wiry creatures and their razor-sharp teeth and claws.

The walls, the rails, the green mold on the ceiling of the tunnel all rush past me as I run and run and strain and push for the platform, for what is now, I realize bitterly, the freedom of the Loop.

The rank smell of damp coupled with the festering stink of the rats fills my senses, and I can feel myself choking on it. I hear the flame crackle, and the light dims.

"No," I hiss, and push myself even harder, forcing my legs to move, move, move.

The light drops to nothing and then comes back as the flame finds one last reserve of fuel to burn.

There it is, up ahead, the platform.

The flame dips once more, so close to going out that the rats have closed in and are at my heels.

I grab the last of the hand sanitizer from my pocket, use my teeth to pry off the lid, squeeze the gel onto the closest rat, and drop the torch onto the leaders.

The squeals that come out of the flash of yellow flame are horrifying, almost human, cries of agony and terror as the rats become the light that they fear so much.

I make it to the platform without so much as a single new scratch to match the old ones. I climb up and lie on my back, listening with a mixture of sickness and triumph to the screaming rats.

I've imagined escaping the Loop time after time after time, but never once did I imagine returning. I shut my eyes and wait for my breath to return to normal before getting to my feet and walking back into the prison.

Kina is on her feet, her fingers wrapped tightly around the trigger keeping me alive, her eyes narrowed and watching. Having heard my footsteps, she is alert and ready for whoever or whatever might appear. She looks relieved when she sees that it's me, but her expression quickly turns to one of shock when she sees the bloodstained jumpsuit.

"What happened?" she asks.

I try to answer, try to tell her about the rats and the crazy people who tried to kill me, about the crumbling city, but I don't know where to start. "We need to get to the drones," I say instead.

"The drones? Why?"

"They're armed with a hallucinogen that puts the body into hibernation," I say, stumbling over my words as I try to explain as quickly as I can. "We need to use it on Wren; if we can slow her heart rate down, then we can slow the bleeding and maybe keep her alive long enough to get her to a doctor."

"Luka," she says, putting a hand on my shoulder as I try to walk past her, "what did you see? Why haven't you brought help?"

Again, I hesitate. How do I explain to her that there's a war going on? That we're in grave danger? "There's no one to help . . . The war is real, Kina. The city is burning. Wren is sick, she lost her mind and started killing people, and there are others like her—I saw them in the village, they attacked me . . . It's bad, Kina, it's bad. I think whoever started the war has poisoned people, turned them into killing machines."

She nods. Her eyes scan side to side, focusing on nothing as she tries to process the information that I have given her. "Okay," she says. "Okay, all right. So how do we get to those drones?"

"I don't know," I tell her, "but I think I know someone who might."

I walk past two of the open cells, and from the corner of my eye, I see figures draped over their beds, skin gray, unmoving. I make my way to Fulton's old cell, where I saw Woods run to hours before.

I slide open the hatch. Woods's bloodshot eyes stare at me.

"Woods?" I say, trying to get a reaction from the unmoving boy.

Slowly, his head drops, and he speaks in a low, gravelly voice. "Luka, what was that? What happened out there? Is she dead? Did she kill anyone else?"

"Woods, I need your help," I say, unlocking and opening his cell door.

"Wait, wait, wait!" he yells, leaping to his feet and pulling the door back toward the frame. "Is she still out there?"

"No, she's locked in a cell," I tell him, and open the door again. "Like I said, I need your help."

Woods steps tentatively out into the corridor, his wide, strong frame a contrast to his obvious fear. "My help? You need *my* help? Help with what?"

"Wren's going to die if we can't get to the drones."

Woods holds a hand up, silencing me, his eyes growing wider still as he stares at the corpse of Alistair. "A-Alistair?" he stammers. "She killed Alistair too?"

"Woods, listen to me," I say, trying to remain calm. "We're running out of time, Wren is dying . . . Something has happened to her; there's a virus or something," I tell him. "It changes people, makes them killers."

"She executed them, man. She ended their lives without a second thought."

"She didn't know what she was doing," I tell him. "Just like everyone in Group A."

"I ain't helping her!" he screams, tears spilling from his eyes. "If I ever see her again, I'm going to kill her. I'm getting Adam, and we're getting out of here!

"Woods, please . . ." I start.

"This is not a debate, Luka."

I watch him amble, hunched and hitching shoulders, to Adam's cell. He stops at the open door, and even though I can only see his side profile, he seems to age ten years in front of my eyes.

I walk over to him and place a hand on his shoulder. "I'm sorry, Woods."

"How can they all be gone?" he asks.

"If you want to get back at the people who did this, you have to realize that it wasn't Wren. There's a war going on outside the Loop—they've poisoned innocent people with something that turns them into murderers. Wren is a victim in this; she's not your enemy."

"You've been outside the Loop?" he asks, looking at my bloodstained jumpsuit.

"Yes, and whoever attacked the Region is winning."

"So who was it, Luka? Who is responsible for killing my friends?"

"That's what we're going to find out."

He stares at me, unblinking in his anger and grief. Finally, he nods his head. "Tell me what you saw out there."

I explain everything from escaping my cell and locking Wren inside, to the rat tunnel and the other crazies in the village. Kina and Woods listen intently as I come to the end and explain my theory that the drones' poisonous darts have the same effect as the hibernation medication that was given to slow down my mom's death.

Woods is clearly still unhappy about trying to save the life of the woman who took his friends', but he accepts that Wren was not herself when she did what she did.

"I'll help you get the drone, but then I'm out of here, understood?"

"The more of us there are, the more chance we have of—"

"Luka, I got nothing left; Winchester is gone, Alistair and Adam are dead. They were everything to me in this place, and they're gone. I'm leaving, I'm going alone, is that clear?"

I sigh. "Fine."

"Good," he says, crossing his arms over his chest. "There is a way to get to the drones."

"How?" I ask.

"I don't know exactly, but Winchester spent months staying up all night to watch them and see if he could gather any information."

"And?" Kina urges.

"Who's this?" Woods asks, looking from Kina to me.

"Answer the question," I implore him.

"And a drone broke down, an engine fault or something, meaning they couldn't fly it out of here to be repaired. So at about four in the morning, they sent two mechanics up through the pillar. Winchester saw them open a trapdoor, grab the drone, and disappear back down the pillar with it. They returned about an hour or so later with the repaired drone, attached it to the charge point, and left."

"So there's a way up the middle of the pillar?" Kina asks.

I remember the door marked ENGINEER on the other side of the platform. "I think I know how to get there," I tell them.

Kina and Woods follow me to the entrance, where the warning about exploding implants is written.

"Wait!" Kina calls, and points to the yellow words.

"It's okay," I say, pointing in turn to Wren's severed arm on the floor, "I deactivated it."

"Pretty resourceful," Woods muses. "Fulton once came up with a similar plan."

We cross the tracks, enter the staff room, and open the

ENGINEER door, where we are faced with two more doors: REPAIRS and DELIVERIES.

"This one," Kina says, and leads the way through the REPAIRS door to a set of stairs going down into the darkness.

We descend, and at the end of the staircase is a corridor. We walk along in darkness, following the wall as it circles around until I'm sure we're under the exercise yard. A few more steps, and I walk face-first into a door. It's unlocked. Inside is another set of steps, this one a spiral staircase leading up.

"I think this is it," I say, and climb up and around until I come to a thick metal hatch above my head. I push it open and tip it over until it crashes down with a loud boom that reverberates around the yard.

I climb up and onto the pillar. I'm in the center of the yard, the wind blowing hard, whistling over the dividing walls. I stand for a while and just look at the Loop from this vantage point. It's so strange to see the yard from here, to look down at the strip of concrete where I've spent hundreds of hours sprinting back and forth, sure that I would never leave until it was time to be transported to the Block. I look out over the cells to the almost desertlike land around the Loop, and if the walls that separated the yards weren't only two centimeters thick, we could walk over to the roof of the Loop and climb down to freedom without having to go through the rat tunnels.

Woods and Kina stare out at the landscape, awed by the expanse. None of us talk for a full minute.

"Come on," I say finally.

I move toward the nearest drone, fighting against the vertigo brought on by the fifty-foot drop on all sides of me. The drones are bigger than I thought they were, and I take the chance to inspect one close-up. A black carbon-fiber shell covers the machinery inside, and there are two propeller blades on either side, the large one in the middle, and three barrels of weaponry hanging below.

"Wait," Woods says. "Won't it attack? The light is still on."

"I don't think so," I say. "The charging point still works because the machinery for it is in the nuke-proof bunker underground, but whatever took out the rain and the screens will have wiped these things out too."

"How do you know that?" Woods asks.

"Wren told me," I reply, grabbing the enormous security drone and lifting it off the charging point. "Help me with this."

Woods and Kina help me carry the drone down the stairs, along the corridor, and back up into the staff room, where the dim backup lights offer little help when it comes to figuring out how to get the darts out. Luckily, we have Woods, who seems to know his way around electrical equipment. He unscrews bolts and removes panels until he holds a magazine full of hallucinogenic ammunition in his hand.

"Here," he says, handing it to me.

I push three rounds out of the magazine and examine them. The tips are hollow, meaning the fluid enters the bloodstream from the attached vial, so all I have to do is get one of these into a vein, and Wren will enter a world of mental torture—but it might also be enough to save her life.

We move quickly back to the corridor, and still I've avoided looking directly into the open cells. We get to my cell, and I open the hatch. I don't like what I see: Wren is still lying on my bed, but she's a horrible shade of off-white. Her hair is matted with sweat, and her skin seems somehow too tight, her cheekbones protruding too much, her cheeks hollow like she's emaciated, and the sheets below her amputated arm are soaking up the still-escaping blood.

I open the door, kneel beside her, whisper that I'm sorry, and push the small dart into a raised vein in her neck.

I see her body relax, and for a second, I wonder if the solution inside the dart will work on people with mechanical hearts and lungs. But there must be nanotech infused with the chemicals; as I listen to the hum in her chest, I hear the tone change as the mechanics slow down in response to the poison.

"I'll come back," I tell her unconscious body. "I promise."

I step back out into the corridor and look from Woods to Kina.

"I'll take that back now," I say to Kina, pointing to the trigger in her shaking hand. "Thank you."

Kina nods and hands it, carefully, back to me.

"That what I think it is?" Woods asks.

"We have to let the others out," I say, ignoring Woods's question.

"Yeah, good luck with that," Woods says, folding his arms across his chest again. "There's some pretty bad people in here, and I already told you I ain't sticking around."

"Are you sure I can't convince you to stay?" I ask.

"No," he replies without hesitation. "There's somewhere I got to be. If there really is a war, I know what side I'm on."

"What do you mean?" Kina asks.

He looks at her for a long time, as though he's considering telling her something, but in the end he just says, "It don't concern you."

I consider trying one more time to persuade him to stay with us, but he's already done me two favors in not killing Wren and helping me with the drone. "Listen, remember what I told you about the tunnels," I say.

"Right. Rats."

"There's a USW in the staff room," I tell him. "In the emergency equipment room, some riot gear too—it might be enough to get you out. And they're afraid of light, so if you can figure something out . . ."

He nods, and for a moment, he looks again as though he's going to say something. Instead, he turns and walks away.

Kina and I stand in the silent corridor and listen to his footsteps fade.

"Well," she says. "And then there were two."

I nod in agreement. "Better get the rest of the team," I say.

"Team?" Kina asks, following me as I move to a closed cell.

"Just some friends of mine," I say as I try switching on the screen beside the cell. I'm surprised to see that the power is still running to the cameras. Inside, I see Akimi pacing back and forth. I unlock her door.

Her initial reaction is to shrink back against the far wall

of her cell in terror, but when she recognizes me, she runs forward, throwing both arms around my neck and crying in relief.

"I was so scared," she says through tearful gasps, her accent coming out stronger than usual.

"It's okay," I tell her. "You're safe."

She steps back and looks at the bloodstains on my prison clothes. "What happened? Did she get you?"

"This wasn't Wren," I say, leading her out of the cell and into the corridor. "I'll explain once everyone else is out of their cells."

I introduce Akimi to Kina. "Nice dress," Kina says, and I register for the first time that Akimi has changed into the red summer dress Wren brought to 2 a.m. club for her a couple of weeks back.

"Thanks," Akimi replies, smoothing down the fabric. "I figured, you know, if I was going to die . . . might as well look good."

I move to the next cell. I don't recognize the boy lying on his bed, so we pass by, but next there are two open cells. I face forward, unwilling to look at whoever is inside, but Akimi stops. "She got Emery," she whispers. "She killed Emery."

I close my eyes and try to push aside the sorrow.

I make it to the next closed door and check the screen. Pod and Igby sit on the bed, talking to each other. I'm so relieved to see that they're alive that I throw open the door and step inside the cell.

Pod is on his feet in a flash, and before I can protest, his massive frame has pivoted and he has hit me so hard, right on the point of the chin, that I black out for a second and wake up on the floor of the cell.

At first, the world seems like a dream, all muted colors and faraway sounds.

"Pod, it's Luka, it's fucking Luka," I hear Igby yelling. I look up from the floor to see little Igby tugging at his giant friend's arm.

I shake my head and get to my feet. "Damn, Pod, that's some aim for a blind guy."

"I'm sorry, Luka. You just stormed in here. After everything that's happened, I couldn't just assume you weren't hostile."

"My fault," I tell him, opening and closing my mouth to check if my jaw is broken.

"Holy hell, Pod," Igby lauds. "What a hook!"

"Thank you," Pod says, perfectly calm and composed.

"Do you need help?" I ask him as he makes his way into the corridor.

"I'll be fine," he replies, smiling as he walks by me. "I grew up in the homeless villages and the landfill barges; this is nothing."

"You were one of the Junk Children?" I ask.

Pod nods and smiles. "We prefer Refuse Adolescents," he says.

"Oh, I'm sorry, I didn't—"

"Joking," he replies, his smile growing wider.

I laugh. I try to imagine him as a child, rummaging through mountains of discarded trash, trying to find anything worth selling or repairing, avoiding the long-range rounds from the snipers' USW rifles as they scour the gigantic offshore landfills.

I tell Pod and Igby that I'll explain what happened once we get the rest of the 2 a.m. club out of their cells.

We free Pander next. I can't help but smile with enormous relief when I see her walk out of her cell.

"Let's get going," she demands, pushing her thick glasses up her nose, looking toward the platform.

"Pander, we can't just run into the city—it's under attack."

"If the city is under attack, then our families and friends are under attack while we wait around like cowards!"

It's then that we hear a burst of high-pitched USW rounds coming from far away.

"What's that?" Akimi asks.

"I guess the rats found Woods," I say, looking toward the tunnels.

Pander swallows and joins us as we scour the remaining cells for people we know.

We come to Juno's cell. By now I've started to feel more comfortable and confident; surrounded by my friends, I feel safe. But as soon as I open the hatch, Juno forces both her slender, Ebb-addict arms through the gap and grabs for me. For a moment, I feel certain that her small, powerful hands are going to grip me and drag me through the tiny gap and into her cell, but I lean back and away from her before slamming the hatch into her hands over and over until her arms disappear inside and it snaps shut.

"Holy shit, she's one of them," I breathe.

"One of them?" Pander repeats. "One of who?"

"You were in the yard when the Group As tried to climb the fucking walls, weren't you?" Igby asks.

Pander nods.

"It's not just the Group As," I say. "The same thing has happened to Wren and others from outside the Loop. They've gone crazy."

"Well, that's not great news," Pod mutters.

"No," I agree in a daze. "So what do we do?"

"Got to keep going," Pander says.

I nod and tell my shaking feet to move on.

I'm beginning to lose hope that we'll find any of the others alive, but I get to the next cell and raise a shaking hand to the screen. This is Malachai's cell. I'm not sure if he made it to his own cell or not, but I picture him dead on the floor, skin gray like that of Fulton and Alistair. I switch the screen on and see the Natural nonchalantly relaxing on his bed, legs crossed over each other, reading a comic.

I unlock his door.

"I was hoping someone would make it out alive," he says, throwing the comic to the floor. "You took your time."

"Sorry for keeping you waiting," I say, taken aback by his demeanor. I had been expecting a broken man, mourning Wren's sudden decline into insanity, but instead he seems almost tranquil.

"No worries," he says, stretching and getting to his feet.

"How are you doing?" I ask, searching his face for some sign of pain or loss.

"So, do we think it's a war?" he asks, ignoring my question and glancing at the bloodstains on my jumpsuit.

I nod. "I think so."

"Well," Malachai says contemplatively, "I guess that's sort

of good news for us. I'd rather die out there than in here."

"Yeah, I guess so," I say.

He steps out into the corridor and looks around. "Fulton?" he asks.

"Dead," I reply.

"Alistair? Emery?"

"Dead."

"Woods?"

"Woods ran," Kina tells him.

"Juno?"

"Juno is—" I start.

"Psycho killer." Pander finishes my sentence for me.

"Interesting," Malachai muses, and then turns to Kina. "And who the hell are you?"

"I'm Kina. Who the hell are you?"

Malachai ignores her and turns back to me. "Adam?"

"Dead," I tell him.

Malachai sighs. "Was it Wren who—"

"Yes," I say.

"And she's . . . ?"

"Psycho killer," Pander says.

"Alive," I tell Malachai. "Badly wounded, but alive."

"Okay," he says, and looks once again at the assembled group. "So, I guess this is our little crew for surviving the war. Let's have a look at you."

His eyes scan the crowd of six Regulars, and he can't stop himself from laughing.

"You're not exactly anyone's first choice either, Bannister,"

Pander says, glaring at him, her eyes magnified by her strong lenses.

"I'm sorry, I'm sorry," Malachai says through gasps. "It's just . . . we're definitely going to die out there."

"Hilarious," Akimi says, rolling her eyes.

"So, are you going to explain what happened?" Pod asks, shuffling his feet until he faces me, his unseeing eyes drifting from side to side.

I tell the story of Wren coming to my cell, of her trying to pair the trigger with my heart detonator. I can't help but glance at Malachai when I tell the part about her arm being sliced off in the hatch, and I'm almost relieved to see a look of concern in his eyes. I tell them how I had to manually attach a tourniquet to stem the bleeding. I tell them how I deactivated the barrier and faced the rats, about the boy and the old lady and the burning city. I explain that Wren has been injected with drone poison in the hope that it will help her live through the next few days.

"Holy hell," Igby whispers when I'm done.

"Yeah," Akimi agrees. "Holy shit."

"We have to go," Pander says, once again looking toward the Dark Train platform. "We're wasting time in here."

"What about the rest of these guys?" Kina asks, looking down the corridor at the eight or nine cells we can see that remain closed and locked. There will be more farther around the Loop.

"There's no fucking way we're opening those," Igby says.

"We have to," Kina replies, turning to face him. "They'll die."

"Hey, new girl," Malachai commands, "there's a reason they weren't invited to the 2 a.m. club."

"And what the hell is the 2 a.m. club?" she asks.

"Well, seeing as you weren't invited either, it's none of your business."

"Wren used to let a bunch of us out every Wednesday night," I tell her. "We were deemed safe enough—the rest of those guys were not."

"Turned out she was the dangerous one," Akimi mutters.

"She's sick!" I yell. "It's not her fault."

"Dangerous or not," Kina says, her voice overriding the growing tension in the group, "we can't let the others starve to death in their cells—that would be barbaric."

"The alternative is to let them out and play Guess the Serial Killer," Malachai says.

"We're the killers if we let them die," Kina hits back.

"Are you forgetting who my neighbor is?" Malachai says, hammering on the locked cell door beside his. "I'll give you a clue: His favorite phrase is *Luka Kane, I'm going to kill you*. Ring any bells? I doubt your boyfriend wants Tyco Roth roaming these corridors."

I have to shake off the word *boyfriend* and implore myself to focus on the more important issue; Malachai's right, I do not want Tyco Roth free from his cell.

For some reason all eyes turn to me.

"Well?" Pod asks.

"Well, what?" I reply, taken aback by this sudden committee.

"Do we let the rest out?" Igby asks.

"I don't know. Why are you asking me?"

"I don't know," Igby replies.

"Should we vote?" Pod suggests.

"No," Kina says. "We're not voting on whether these people live or die. We're letting them out."

There's a pause, and then Malachai speaks. "Okay, all those in favor of leaving them in their cells, raise your hands."

"I told you, we're not voting!" Kina insists.

Pod, Igby, Pander, and Malachai raise their hands.

"That's the majority," Malachai says. "Now, how do we get out of here?"

"Wait," Kina says. "Just wait a second. These people have brothers and sisters out there in the real world, they have mothers and fathers. What if it was your families locked up in here? Wouldn't you hope someone had the courage to set them free?"

"Yeah, sure." Malachai shrugs. "But that's the way it goes. Life isn't fair. Sometimes you win, and sometimes you lose."

"Well, I'm not going to let them lose," Kina says.

She storms over to the nearest door, spins the lock, and pulls it open.

I feel my muscles tense as I prepare myself for whatever monster is about to be unleashed into our midst.

But nothing happens; there is no sound. Kina stares into the room, and slowly we all gather around to look inside.

A boy of about ten or eleven is prodding at the screen on his wall, muttering to himself. He doesn't even seem to notice us.

He's so young, I think, and I can't believe that the machines could possibly have found him morally culpable for whatever crime he committed.

"Hey," Kina says in a gentle voice.

The boy turns his head slowly and stares at the crowd of people gathered in his doorway. "Are you here to fix it?" he asks, pointing at his screen.

"No, we're here to let you out. There's a war going on," Kina tells him.

"I can't leave," he says. "I need to select my breakfast option."

Kina turns to look at us all one by one and then turns back to the boy. "What's your name?" she asks him.

"Good morning, Inmate 9-71-990," the boy replies, mimicking the voice of Happy. "Today is Monday, the twentieth of June, Day 404 in the Loop. Please select your breakfast option."

"What do we do?" I ask, turning to Kina.

She bites the inside of her cheek, thinking. She shrugs and steps into the boy's cell before kneeling down beside him.

"Please select your breakfast . . ." the boy whispers, but trails off as he cowers from Kina.

"It's all right," Kina says, holding both hands up. "You're scared, that's okay, we're all scared, but the screen isn't coming back on and we need to get out of here."

"Day 404 in the Loop," the boy says, his nervous eyes flicking to meet Kina's and then darting away.

"My name's Kina Campbell," Kina says. "You don't have to stay in this cell anymore, okay?"

He looks at her, his eyes moving quickly over her face. "It's Kilo," he whispers. "My name is Kilo Blue. M-my friends used to call me Blue."

"Blue, you can stay here if you want, but no more food is coming, no more water, the screen is not coming back on, and you'll be alone."

Kilo Blue's eyes fill with tears as he stares up at Kina. "I've been alone for 404 days."

"Then come with us."

"But this is my home," he whispers.

"Not anymore."

The boy looks at all four walls, at his bed, the broken screen. Tears spill quietly down his cheeks. He nods, stands up straight, and grabs Kina's arm as they walk out of his cell and into the corridor.

"This is Kilo Blue," Kina says, introducing the boy to everyone. "His friends call him Blue."

"Hi, Kilo," Malachai says, smiling sarcastically.

I'm ashamed that my first thought is about how this boy is going to slow us down. I should be happy that he's come to his senses and left the cell.

"Hi, Blue," I say, trying to put my negative thoughts aside.

"That could have gone another way, you know?" Malachai whispers to Kina as she passes.

"Do you see now?" Kina says to the group, ignoring Malachai's protestation. "Is this the kind of person you want to let die?"

"Shit, she's right," Pander says. "I vote we open the cells, but

I'm going to have to be careful—there are people in here who will want me dead." She reaches up and touches the tattoo under her right eye.

"Yeah," Pod says, nodding his head. "We have to let them out. If we leave them behind, we're no better than the bastards who locked us up in the first place."

My heart begins to race at this turning of the tides. All I can think about is the inevitable release of Tyco Roth.

"All right," I say, trying to calm the shaking in my voice, "the majority votes we open the cells."

"You're all morons," Malachai mutters as he crosses his arms over his chest.

"Wait," Akimi says, her voice strained. "Can we please just wait a second?! What if we open one of those cells and let one of the crazy people out? The ones like Wren and Juno and the Group As? And come to think of it: Why are some people going crazy and others aren't?"

We all look at one another, hoping that someone has a rational explanation.

"It doesn't make sense," Pander says. "Juno can't be like the rest of them. She refused the Delay that turned Group As crazy. She was turning eighteen in a few months, said she'd rather be Deleted than face the Block. Then again, she was strung out, a clone. Maybe she just lost her mind because she couldn't get Ebb in this place?"

"That doesn't explain Wren," Akimi says, her voice quieter now. "Or the people who Luka saw on the outside. Why have they gone crazy?"

There's a long silence. Malachai shrugs. "We know as much as you do, Akimi."

"Do you want to know what I think? I think it's just a matter of time before we all lose our minds, just like the rest of them," Akimi replies, fear burning in her eyes.

"Either way," Pod says, "it doesn't change anything. All we can do is keep moving forward."

The silence hangs heavy for a moment more. "Pod's right," I say. "It doesn't change anything. We'll either go crazy, or we won't."

I move to the next locked cell and open the hatch. A girl of about sixteen stops pacing and turns around quickly. She doesn't say anything, just stares at me.

"Hi," I say, and immediately feel stupid.

"The war came?" she asks.

"We think so."

"So, let me out of here."

I nod and pull open her cell door. She steps out.

"The heart barrier working?" she asks, nodding her head in the direction of the exit.

The heart barrier must be what she calls the detonation threshold. "No, it's off," I tell her, and she brushes past me, moving fast toward the exit.

"Where are you going?" Pander asks.

"I'm going to find the Missing. If you're smart, you will too."

"Wait," I call out. "The tunnels aren't safe."

"I can handle it," she calls back.

"You can stay with us," Kina calls out.

The girl laughs, a short snort. "Nah, no thanks," she says, and stops at a cell three down from her own. She pulls open the door. A tall, slim boy with a scar across one cheek steps out.

"It happened?" he says.

"It happened."

They hug, and he looks over to us. "Who're the losers?"

"Doesn't matter," the girl says, and they walk away, rounding the corner to the platform.

"Hey, there are rats in the tunnels . . ." I yell.

"Fuck off," the boy's voice comes back along the hallway.

"That went well," Malachai says.

"Losers?" Pod asks. "I mean, there was no need for that, right?"

I walk to the next cell—it's open. Inside is Reena. I recognize her from her curly red hair. She lies still under her blanket, and she could be sleeping, but I know that her heart is no longer beating. She must have run from Wren and then just lain down in her bed in a state of shock.

Wren did this, I tell myself. *Wren aimed the trigger at her and detonated the explosive in her heart.*

"Is she coming with us?" Blue asks from beside Kina.

"No, she's going to stay here," Kina replies in a hollow voice as she shuts the girl's door.

The next three cells choose not to join us either—two boys and a girl who decide that they want to set off on their own.

I want to hurry this up, to get out of here. I can still picture the burning city in my mind; I can still see the insane eyes of the people who attacked me in the village, the bloodstained sheets of the dead man in the bed. I want to get to my sister and my dad and make sure they're okay.

I move faster. We walk past Woods's empty cell, and two more with dead inmates inside. Kina tries to stay in front of little Blue as we pass by, but he slows and leans back to catch sight of one particularly distorted corpse. His face turns ashen, and he falls silent.

The next cell houses a huge boy. He must be under eighteen, or he'd be in the Block, but the thick stubble on his face, the bulging muscles, and the bags under his eyes make him look more like he's thirty.

"Open the door," he demands as I stare at him through the hatch.

"Listen, something big has happened. We think there's a war going—"

"Open. The. Door," he orders, enunciating every word.

"Right, yeah," I say as I close the hatch and reach for the spin lock.

"Think carefully about this," Malachai warns.

I look down at the handle of the cell door and then up at Kina. I unlock the door and pull it open.

"Out of my way," the big guy says as he squeezes his massive frame out into the corridor.

"I'm Luka," I tell him. "This is—"

"Don't care," the boy mutters as he brushes past me and walks to the cell adjacent to his and opens it.

A skinny guy with thick-rimmed glasses and a vacant stare

steps out, places a hand on the giant's shoulder, and then stares at us.

"They with you?" he says in a strangely high-pitched voice.

"No," the giant replies.

"Stay here," Glasses tells us, pointing a long finger in our direction. "Do not move." And then he does a double take, his eyes resting on Pander. He smiles and points a finger at her.

"Well," Pander whispers, "I'm fucked."

The two newly released inmates take over our quest to release those still locked up, only they are a lot more selective than we were.

The giant unlocks a cell three down from his, and a girl runs out.

"Thank the Final Gods, Soren, you're alive," she cries as she jumps into his arms. She kisses his neck, and he lowers her to the floor.

"This is not good," Malachai whispers.

"Why not?" I ask.

"Did you ever listen at exercise? These guys knew one another on the outside—they have enemies in here."

"But we're not their enemies," Akimi points out.

"Right," I agree as I watch the group move along the corridor. "We're not their enemies."

"What do you think they're going to do when they open their enemies' cells, though?" Malachai asks.

We watch nervously as the three newly released inmates move to an open cell two down. They fall still, silent, and I know that they're looking at the corpse of their friend, one of Wren's victims.

The giant comes storming back toward us. "Who killed her? Which one of you killed her?" he demands.

"Listen to me," Malachai says, stepping forward and looking up into the giant's face. "She was already dead when we got out; a lot of people were. We had nothing to do with it."

The giant leans down close to Malachai and speaks in a soft, calm voice. "Tell me which one of you did it, or you all die, is that understood?"

"If it wasn't for us, you'd still be locked up in that cell, so why would we kill your friend?"

Before any of us can react, the humongous boy has hit Malachai so hard in the stomach that he's on the floor. Malachai coughs and gasps for air, and the giant points at us.

"Sit down," he demands, and we do as he asks. "I'll be back to deal with you."

He turns to walk away but then stops and turns back toward us. His roving eyes rest on my face before tracing down my right arm until he's staring at the trigger in my hand.

"Now, now, that's interesting," he says. "That'll make things a lot easier."

He smiles and storms away, his footsteps so loud that we hear them as though they were right beside us as he disappears with his acquaintances around the corner.

We sit in silence. Blue begins to sob beside Kina.

"Still glad you had the courage to set them free?" Malachai wheezes from his fetal position on the ground.

Kina opens her mouth to speak but can't seem to find the right words.

"What did he mean by *easier*?" I whisper.

"It means he's going to kill us when he gets back," Malachai informs me, sitting up.

From down the corridor we hear a cell being opened, followed by begging and then screaming.

"What are they doing?" Akimi asks.

"They sold Ebb on the outside," Pander explains. "They're killing rival gang members: the Alts who sold Ebb in the Verts."

We hear another cell creaking open, the high-pitched voice of the staring boy as he issues some mumbled threat. More screams follow. Blue's crying grows louder.

"We have to help," Pod says, pushing himself to his feet. "We have to stop them."

Igby drags him back down. "Are you fucking insane?" he asks. "They're fucking psychopaths."

"I know what they are," Pod hisses back.

"Why would you want to get in the way of killers?"

"Shut up, just shut up, all of you," Malachai whispers as loud as he can without being heard by the giant. "Let me think!"

Malachai is quiet for ten seconds, twenty, during which time another inmate is murdered by the gang of cold-blooded killers. Her guttural screams sound almost animalistic as she fights for her life.

"Can you think faster?" Pander asks. "That little guy

recognized my tattoos—they're going to kill me first when they get back."

Malachai stands up, pauses for a second, and then runs over to a closed cell in the opposite direction from the psychopaths. He spins the lock and opens the door.

"They're killing your friends," Malachai yells into the room. "Hurry."

He then repeats this trick a few cells farther away.

I watch as the two freed inmates hold each other for a minute in the corridor—two girls of about seventeen, both impossibly beautiful, both with bright blue eyes that seem to shimmer like moonlight. They are Alts, there's no doubt about it. They turn in the direction of the screams and run.

Malachai moves to the next cell. He turns before he unlocks it and looks at me. "I'm sorry, Luka."

At first I'm confused, but as he opens the cell and tells the inmate inside to hurry and save his friends, I know why he's sorry.

This is the first time I've ever seen Tyco Roth, but I know it's him straightaway. He's tall and tanned, with perfect bone structure. He's an Alt.

As soon as I look into his eyes, I feel as though the ground is falling away beneath my feet. Now I know, for the first time, why he wants to kill me. His eyes are identical to his brother's. They narrow now as his jaw clenches. All I can see is his brother falling off the roof of the Black Road Vertical, flailing arms grabbing for something and finding only air.

"Oh, shit," Akimi says from beside me.

Tyco's eyes fix on mine, and I can see all of the pain he feels, feel the hurt he wants to inflict on me. A scream from somewhere along the corridor grabs his attention. He looks back to me one more time before heading off to join his friends in battle.

"You want to sit there all night?" Malachai asks. "Let's move."

"This was your plan?" Akimi asks.

"Yes, this was my plan. Now run."

"What about the other cells?" Kina asks.

"Are you mad? If we hang around, we all die; if we run, we have a chance of living."

Kina sighs, staring back along the corridor toward the unopened cells. "Okay, let's go."

We all follow Malachai, sprinting around the Loop. I know that there's only one way out of here, and I know that we won't all survive the tunnels, but we don't have a choice.

We're only thirty feet from the entrance when Tyco and the boy with the glasses tumble to the ground in front of us, fists flying, teeth bared. Other bodies litter the concrete corridor behind them—these two are the only survivors of this small-scale gang war. Tyco, huge and toned; Glasses, slight and wild.

We all stop, frozen by the scene that's playing out in front of us. Tyco gets the better of the smaller boy and wraps his big hands around his neck. He chokes him while beating his skull against the concrete.

When Tyco is done murdering the boy, he gets to his feet. He is not breathing heavily—his MOR system is replenishing his oxygen levels at incredible speeds. He points a finger at me.

"I told you I was going to kill you one day," he says.

"Tyco, listen—" I try.

"Quiet," he says. The calm in his voice is eerie.

"Come on, Tyco. Can't you just let us go?" Malachai asks.

Tyco looks at him, emotionless, and Malachai falls silent too. "I want you all to get inside that cell," he says, pointing to the nearest empty room. "I need time to think about just how I'm going to do this."

"And if we refuse?" Pander asks.

"Then I'll kill you all."

"There's eight of us," Pander points out.

"Eight Regulars," Tyco says, his voice still so tranquil. "One blind, one deaf, a little boy. The rest of you don't pose much of a threat. Do as I say, and only Luka dies."

I don't give them time to consider anything else. I step into the cell, and one by one they follow me inside.

"I'll be seeing you soon, Luka Kane," Tyco says, and then slams the door shut.

"Well, this just keeps getting better." Malachai sighs, running a hand through his thick hair.

"Everyone turn around; I have to pee," Pander says, pulling apart the Velcro of her jumpsuit as she moves to the toilet.

"Whoa, wait until we're looking away," Malachai says.

"Why?" Pander asks, tapping a finger against one of her hearing aids as if it's faulty. "In case you see a nipple? Everyone has nipples, Malachai. Get over it."

Everyone turns and faces the door.

"Can you have a conversation or something?" Pander says from behind us. "It's kind of hard to go in dead silence."

"Uh, so, everyone having a great day?" Akimi tries, causing Malachai to burst out laughing.

"Oh, yeah," he says. "Hasn't it just been an absolute dream?"

"Hey, it's better than your average day in the Loop," Igby says, casting a sidelong glance along the group. His receding hair is disheveled after everything that's happened.

"True," Pod says, nodding in agreement. "I'd take this over another hundred days of the same old routine." He cracks the knuckles of his enormous hands and then feels for the wall for support.

"Maybe a little less death next time," Igby suggests, and then adds an exasperated "Fuck!" for good measure.

"Woods had the right idea: Run while you've got the chance. *Open the cells; let's all be heroes,*" Malachai mutters, mimicking Kina's voice.

I'm half listening to the conversation that's going on around me but mostly thinking about what happens when Tyco is done deciding how he wants to kill me. Maybe I'd have been safer outside, in the war. My hands are shaking, and I feel light-headed.

"Finished," Pander says, flushing the toilet and joining the end of the line as we still face the wall. "So, Tyco's going to kill us, huh?"

"He's only going to kill me," I say, my voice catching in my throat.

"If you believe that, you're a chump," Igby says.

"He doesn't care what happens to you guys," I say, "as long he gets to end my life."

"Why *does* he want to kill you?" Malachai asks, as if it's only just occurring to him, his piercing eyes examining mine.

I don't reply, just look down at my feet.

"Hey, why are we all still facing the wall?" Kina asks.

We all look at one another and shrug.

Akimi leans against the wall with the screen, Pander, Blue, and Kina sit on the floor, I stand by the sink with Pod and Igby, and Malachai sits on the edge of the toilet.

We all face one another, saying nothing, listening to the silence, and probably all wondering the same thing: How long until Tyco comes back?

I watch Blue as he fidgets with his hands and then rubs at his eyes. I can see him getting more and more agitated.

"This is your fault," he whispers, getting to his feet, his irises moving to the corners of his eyes to look at me.

"What?" I say, unsure that I heard him right.

"He . . . he wants to kill you, and now he's going to kill all of us," he says, his voice still quiet, still apprehensive.

"Hey, you didn't want to leave your cell a few hours ago. You were going to die in there anyway," I remind him.

"But I don't want to die," he says, tears forming in his eyes.

I sigh. "You're right. I'm sorry."

"Sorry doesn't matter now," Blue says, and then he bursts into tears. "Sorry doesn't matter now."

"Blue, calm down," Malachai says.

Blue begins to hyperventilate, huffing in air and blowing it out. "I'm going to die in here, I'm going to die, and then what? Then nothing! There's nothing next. Do you know what I did to get locked up? I was a drug mule. That means I moved drugs around different countries. I was nine years old! I didn't even know what drugs were! I didn't even know they were in my bag! How is that fair? I thought I was on vacation with my foster family . . . I thought . . . I thought . . ."

Blue slumps back to the floor, breathing so heavily I'm sure he'll pass out. He holds his head in his hands and cries quietly. A somber silence falls back over the room.

"I stole five hundred thousand Coin worth of high-end cars," Igby says, breaking all the unwritten 2 a.m. club rules at once.

"Five hundred thousand Coin?" Akimi repeats, her sharp features softening as she nods, impressed.

"Mm-hmm." Igby nods. "I started off with Eon 14s and shitty Chauffeur Sunrises, but I got greedy, started cloning the vocal signatures of Volta Category 7 and 8 owners and delivering them to some dodgy fucking people. They'd transfer encrypted Coin into a fake company, and I'd pay into fifteen different accounts set up as employees. All the accounts belonged to me. Eventually, when the gangsters got busted, the Marshals followed the money straight to me. I had bought my parents a home in the city, but it got seized along with everything else we owned. I have no idea what happened to my family. They locked me up in here within about two hours of the arrest."

"The Volta 8 is my favorite car," I tell Igby.

"Cool, if we somehow get out of here, I'll fucking steal you one."

This line gets a few laughs. Pod speaks next.

"I lived in the homeless village around the West Sanctum Vertical. Five of us in a two-room shack. Without insurance, which my family could never afford, the cost to fix the genetic defect that caused my blindness is four hundred and thirty-nine Coin per eye. I've been shot at over eighty times while scavenging in the junk barges; I've survived hypothermia, pneumonia, and Drygate flu. I repaired and sold the old technology that the Alts threw out. By the time they threw me in the Loop—three strikes of stealing government property, can you believe that? They consider taking the junk that others have thrown away stealing—anyway, by then I'd managed to save two hundred and seven Coin. I wanted my sight, but the money was to get out of the slums. I wanted to go to college and become a teacher. Because of the system, because of the way the world is set up to let the rich thrive and the poor flounder, they took everything I had, everything I'd saved, and now I have nothing."

Igby lays a hand on his friend's massive shoulder and looks over to Malachai. I look over to Malachai too, expecting to hear his own tale of woe.

The Natural looks up at us, realizing that all eyes are on him. "What is this, group therapy?" he snaps, getting up and walking over to the bed, where he lies down and crosses his hands behind his head.

"When I was six," Akimi says, smiling to herself, "I peed in my sister's bed because she kept ignoring me to hang out with her friends."

The sudden change in tone causes us all—even Malachai—to laugh.

"Why would you do that?" Kina asks.

"I wanted our mom to think she'd peed the bed; I wanted her to get in trouble," Akimi explains. "I was six years old; there wasn't a lot of logic going on. The major flaw in my plan was my sister was seventeen."

This makes us laugh even harder. Blue lifts his head and wipes the tears from his eyes. "My brother saved up from his job at the sky-farms and bought himself a LucidVision," he tells us. "He wouldn't let me have a go. I was so jealous that he got to have all these great adventure dreams, and I begged him to let me try, but he kept saying no. So, one day, while he was at work, I found his password scratched on the inside of the headset. I logged in and changed the settings from porno scenarios to horror. He woke up completely naked, screaming his head off."

This makes us laugh so hard most of us have tears in our eyes.

Malachai tries to contain his laughter as he tells us that we're all freaks.

"Do you know what hurt most for me after I got locked in here?" Kina asks, her dark eyes looking down to the floor. "I hadn't even worked out what I wanted to be yet. I had ambition, don't get me wrong; I just didn't know where to aim it. There weren't exactly a lot of options growing up in the Verts. I always felt like I was waiting, though, waiting for a chance to be great at something. Now even that's gone."

Malachai seems to sense that the conversation is wheeling its way back around to him. "Well," he says, rolling onto his side, "might as well get some sleep. God knows how long old psycho boy is going to be."

This appears to be the final word, as silence falls over the room once again.

Blue sleeps with his head resting against Kina's shoulder. Pod and Igby chat quietly, Akimi lies on her back staring at the ceiling, Pander has shoved Malachai against the wall so that she can share the tiny bed, and I stare at the window in the far wall, cursing the fact that Tyco forced us into this cell and not my cell—at least there are books in my cell.

I have no idea how much time has passed. It feels to me as if we've been in this room for an eternity, but I guess that's because I'm waiting for my killer to decide on the method of my execution. I slowly move the trigger from my left hand to my right, sliding one thumb off the switch and replacing it carefully with the other. I open my left hand and can't help but moan against the stiffness and pain.

We haven't discussed any further what our plan is when Tyco comes back for me, but I know what I'm going to do. I'm going to tell him that I'll come quietly, that I won't fight against him as long as he lets the others go first. It sounds—even to me—horribly gallant, but the reality is it's an easy decision. Why let my friends die when they don't have to?

The sky continues to lighten; the sun has risen on the other side of the Loop, and I hope to see it hanging bright in the sky before Tyco returns, but that hope is dashed as the door slowly opens.

Everyone is suddenly awake and on their feet. Tyco's massive frame fills the door as he smiles at me.

Pander steps in front of me, followed by Kina and then Pod and Igby.

"Are we standing in front of him?" Pod whispers, a steadying hand reaching out into the space around him.

"Yeah," Igby tells him.

"Good."

Tyco looks at us all one by one. "Give me Luka, and the rest of you can go."

Now that he's here, standing this close, ready to kill me, Tyco looks enormous. His shoulders seem to be as wide as the doorway, and he almost has to duck so as not to whack the top of his head off the frame as he steps into the cell. He stares right at me, and I wait for Malachai and the others to accept his offer.

"It was his idea to let you go," Malachai says from behind me.

"This isn't a debate," Tyco replies. "It's an offer. Take it or leave it."

"We'll leave it," Kina says.

"No, you won't," I say. "Tyco, they accept your offer."

"Well, thank you very much for nominating yourself spokesperson, Luka, but I think I'll see what your friends think."

I make a decision to take control. "They're not my friends," I say, raising my voice in an attempt to sound commanding.

"Oh, fuck off, Luka," Akimi says. "We know you love us."

I fall silent, slightly embarrassed. Tyco stares at the group, waiting for an answer, but no answer comes. "This is the last time I'll ask. Leave me alone with Luka, and I won't hurt you."

There's a long silence, but I can see the looks of grim determination on the faces of my friends. And then Malachai steps forward, brushing past me as he walks toward the platform.

"Malachai, no," Akimi cries.

"He dies, or we all die," Malachai says, shrugging as he passes Tyco. "It's a pretty simple equation."

Tyco smiles at the remaining group. "Anyone else?"

I feel the rest of them take a step closer to me and a tremendous surge of gratitude swells up inside.

"Go," I say, resigning myself to Tyco's will.

"We're not going fucking anywhere," Igby says.

"You have to; he'll kill you."

"He'll try," Kina says.

Tyco laughs. "Fine," he says, and takes a step toward us.

And then Malachai is on Tyco's back, arms wrapped around his neck as he clings on and chokes the massive Alt with all his might. "The cell! Lock him in the cell!" he cries as Tyco thrashes around, trying to throw him off like a raging bull.

For a second, we're all stunned and frozen in place.

"As slow as you like!" Malachai screams at us.

Tyco manages to back himself into the corridor, reaching over his shoulders, trying to grab Malachai.

I run forward as fast as I can out of the cell and grab Tyco by the arm with my free hand. I start pulling him back toward the cell, and he hits me hard with his swinging free hand.

I'm sent skidding along the corridor on my back, my vision flashing white and then slowly coming back. I redouble my grip on the trigger as I sit up and see Kina and Igby shoving the Alt from behind as he yells in frustration.

I get to my feet, stumble as I regain my balance, and then run toward Tyco. I lower my shoulder into the Alt's chest, managing to knock him back a few feet. Akimi hits him next, followed by Pod and Blue. As Pander runs at him, he aims a kick at her, sending her sprawling to the floor. Kina throws a punch at his chin, connecting perfectly, and he backs up another few inches.

He's on the threshold of the cell. Malachai drops down off the Alt's back, diving and sliding along the floor until he's free of the chamber.

Igby and Akimi both run at Tyco again as I grab his flailing leg. He tumbles backward into the cell and struggles on the floor, trying to get to his feet.

I crawl toward the exit, the base of the trigger clunking against the concrete as I move, and I'm almost free when I feel his strong fingers wrap themselves up in the material of my jumpsuit.

Pander runs into the cell, leaps up in the air, and brings all her weight down on the big man's hand. I hear a sickening crunch. Tyco screams and releases his grip.

"Now!" Pander calls out.

I roll out of the way as the cell door is slammed shut by Pod and Akimi.

We all look at one another, panting in exhaustion, and then Malachai begins to laugh. Akimi joins in, followed by Pander, and then we're all laughing and cheering and hugging.

It takes a minute for us to catch our breath.

"All right." Igby sighs. "What the fuck now?"

"Can we eat?" Akimi asks. "I'm actually starving. All this waiting to die and fighting, you know?"

"Seconded," Pod says, raising his hand.

We make our way across the tracks through the door marked DELIVERIES and find the processing area of the Loop: a room that is the same size and shape as the entire circular building, where an enormous conveyor belt sits still beneath robotic arms.

We grab bread from the conveyor belt and water from the gigantic vat and bring it up to the cells of Tyco, Juno, and the few remaining inmates who refused to leave. And then we eat as much as we can.

Kina continues her mission to free the remaining inmates and joins us in the processing room with a newly freed prisoner, a young girl with freckled cheeks. Her brown hair is swept back in a ponytail, revealing shining burn scars from her left ear down her neck.

"Hey, guys, this is Mable," Kina says, introducing the new girl. And then, more quietly, "She's the last."

"Great," Malachai says. "Welcome to the worst team in history."

Mable's scared eyes dart from one face to the next, her lips trembling as though she's constantly on the verge of bursting into tears.

"Hi," Mable says, looking down at the floor.

Blue walks up to the girl, puts a hand on her shoulder, and tells her she's going to be okay.

While we eat, we gather in the middle of the room and go over the facts. We discuss the Delay and come to the conclusion that we all went through the same experience: three injections into the neck and then placed in the room the gas was pumped into.

Blue and Mable sit close together in the corner of the room.

"The power?" Pod says. "How did they knock the entire power system out?"

"EMP?" Igby suggests.

"What's EMP?" Akimi asks.

"Electromagnetic pulse."

"No," Pod says, shaking his head. "That would have taken out everything electonic, but some things are still on. Honestly, it makes no sense to me."

"Well, it killed these," Pander says, taking her hearing aids out. "Stupid things haven't worked since yesterday."

"How can you hear us?" Malachai asks.

"I have a little bit of hearing, plus I can read your lips," she replies. "And if anyone happens to know sign language, I speak that too."

"I do," I tell her, remembering the lessons that my mom gave me before she died.

"So," Igby says, continuing the conversation, "we don't know exactly how they selectively took out the electrics, but we can agree that some kind of fucking chemical weapon was dropped?"

"And affected the mental state of those who came into contact with it," Pod adds.

Concern is etched on Akimi's face. Malachai is nodding slowly as he turns the information over in his mind.

"This is fucking unprecedented," Igby whispers.

"And irrelevant," Pander adds. "We need to get into the city."

"What if we become infected?" Akimi asks. "What if we become like Juno and Wren?"

"What about him?" Malachai asks, pointing at me. "He's been through the tunnel, right to where the"—he pauses to find the right name—"the Smilers are, and he's not infected."

"Not yet," Pander adds.

"Juno never left the building, and she went crazy," Pod points out. "How long until we go crazy too?"

"Wait," Kina says, turning to Pander. "Didn't you say something about Juno being due for Deletion?"

"Yeah, she didn't want to go to the Block; she'd heard rumors. She didn't accept the Delay and . . . Oh, right," Pander says, nodding.

"Wait, what's going on?" Malachai asks.

"The Delay, it came early, and we all took it, all except Juno."

"Right, of course," Igby says.

"Hey, new girl," Pod says, turning aimlessly toward the wall.

"Me?" Mable replies from the opposite corner of the room.

"Yeah," Pod replies, turning in the direction of her voice. "What group were you in for the Delay?"

"I—I was in Group B," she says.

"It all adds up," Igby whispers.

"Umm, can somebody break it down for me?" Akimi asks, looking between Pod and Igby.

"We thought they were injecting us with the crazy chemical at the Facility. Turns out they were giving us the cure! They *stopped* us from becoming . . . Smilers," Pod says, using Malachai's word for the crazies.

"And Harvey? Catherine? The Group As?" Akimi asks.

Igby shrugs. "They must have tested a different formula on them . . . and it didn't fucking work."

One of the jigsaw pieces falls into place in my mind. The reason they didn't kill me at the Facility for trying to escape, or Tyco for stepping out of line. They were desperate; they knew the war was coming, and they needed all the test subjects they could get.

"The Delay must've been a last-minute attempt by the government to find a way to save society," I say. "Galen Rye was there that day—he was making sure the whole operation ran smoothly. Judging by the state of the people outside the Loop, the bomb dropped long before they could get the vaccination to people."

"But the Group As went crazy before we got the injections," Malachai says, almost to himself. "If the chemical was dropped before we got the vaccine, why aren't we crazy?"

"Look," Igby says, "I don't know how it works. Maybe it takes a while for the Smiler chemical to take effect; maybe it was dropped a week ago, and we got the vaccine just in time. I don't know; I don't have the fucking answers. All I *do* know is we're the only ones who are alive and not crazy, and we're the only ones here who got the Group B injection."

"So, this is the safest place to be," Blue says, his tiny voice coming from behind Kina.

We all turn to look at the small boy as he holds Mable's hand and stares up at us.

"He's right," Akimi says. "Why risk leaving if there's a war out there, and thousands of Smilers?"

"We could stay here and wait it out as long as we can," Mable suggests, a note of hope in her voice.

"Wait for what?" Pander declares. "If 'our' side wins the war, the 'good guys' will come back here and lock us up again. If they lose the war, the bad guys will come back here and execute us or turn us crazy like everyone else."

The group falls silent, contemplating the irrefutable logic of Pander's statement.

"What do we do?" Igby asks, looking first to Malachai, then to me.

"We should head to the Facility," Kina says. "If we're right about the Delay saving us from becoming Smilers, and if the scientists at the Facility found a vaccination, then maybe they have a cure. We might be the only people in this city, this Region, who are vaccinated against the chemical. For all we know, we're the only hope of saving the infected, *and* the only chance Rye and his group have of winning this war—that must be worth our freedom."

"I want to leave," Pander says. "Screw the war. My sisters are out there, and we don't know anything about how this crazy chemical warfare works yet. They might need my help."

"Didn't you hear what he told you about the rat tunnels?" Akimi asks, pointing at me again. "Can't you see the blood all over him?"

"Can't you see that I don't care?" Pander replies, glaring at Akimi, who backs away from the smaller girl.

"Rat tunnels?" Mable says, her quiet voice almost inaudible. "There are rats in the tunnels?"

"They're afraid of light," I tell her. "As long as we have fire, we'll be fine."

Mable's eyes widen at the mention of fire, and her hand goes up to her neck, where the scarring is a deep shade of purple.

"You *hope* we'll be fine," Malachai mutters.

"Listen," I say, holding my hands up. "We all have family out there, we all want them to survive, which is why I'm leaving. I'm going to find my dad and my sister and make sure they're safe."

Igby puts a hand on Pod's shoulder, and they both nod. "We're coming too."

Kina shrugs. "Me too."

"I'm not hanging around waiting to be killed or, worse, locked up again," Malachai adds.

Akimi sighs and nods her head. "All right."

"If we split up and find our families, we can try to meet back at the Facility in two days," I say. "Kina's right—if there's any chance of a cure, we should try to find it. We can all find our way back to the Dark Train tracks and follow them to get there."

"I don't . . . I don't think so," Mable says.

"Come on, Mable, you can do it," Blue says, seeming to gain bravery from her fear.

"I can't do it. I don't want to do it. I'm not leaving."

She turns, letting go of Blue's hand, and storms back toward the cells.

Malachai watches her until the echoing of her footsteps fades away, then he turns back to us. "Do we know if the tunnel is the only way out?"

"As far as I can tell, everything comes in and out via the train. We'll need fire to keep the rats at—"

"Why don't we just climb the walls?" Malachai asks, interrupting my speech.

"We can't even get into the yard," I point out. The power is out, and we can't get the back walls open. We can get to the top of the center pillar, but the walls are too thin to tightrope-walk across, and it's a fifty-foot drop to the yards below.

"There's still some power," Igby interjects, pointing at the emergency lights.

"Okay," I say, "but it's no good if it's not reaching the doors."

"Remember why I was locked up in here? Master fucking car thief; I'm good with electronics. Give me a few hours," Igby says, and he leads Pod out of the room.

"You think he'll manage it?" Malachai asks.

"I hope so," I reply, watching the two boys leave. "I never want to go through those tunnels again."

We watch Igby work for a while until he announces that it'll take him and Pod another four or five hours, which, as far as we can tell, will take us close to midnight. We all decide to get some rest.

We walk back to our rooms on tired legs. Blue whispers about how he's afraid of ghosts as he looks back at the dead lying in the corridor: Fulton, Alistair, the dead Ebb dealers.

Pander carefully closes the door to her cell until it's open just a crack, making sure it doesn't snap shut and lock her inside. Malachai rounds the corner, and Akimi sits in the corridor with her head in her hands.

After Kina has reassured Blue that he'll be safe, she says good night to me and wraps her arms around me in an embrace.

"Thanks," she says.

"For what?"

"We'd all be dead if you hadn't gotten out."

"We might all be dead soon anyway," I point out.

"Yeah, but what would you have given yesterday for one day of freedom?"

I think about it and nod in agreement.

Kina smiles—a smile that, as usual, only takes over one side of her mouth. She goes to her cell.

I wait in the corridor for a while, until the last cell door creaks shut, before I open the hatch of my old cell and look inside.

Wren is lying perfectly still on the bed. Her eyes are closed, but her eyelids move rapidly as she looks around at the nightmare landscape in her mind. I feel a strong sense of guilt knowing that it was me who inflicted that horror upon her, and I can only hope that the effects of the chemical that turned her into a Smiler leave her with no memory of the hell she is going through right now.

She's alive, I think. *That's what matters.*

I open the cell door and step inside, crouching down beside her.

"I'm so sorry, Wren," I whisper. "I'm going to do everything I can to help you."

"You care a lot about her, don't you?"

Malachai's voice comes from the doorway. I jump up, startled.

"I mean, yeah, I guess so," I reply. "You do too."

Malachai shrugs. "If she dies . . . that would suck, but that's where we're at."

"But you two were . . . are together?" I ask.

"Luka, I was a prisoner. It didn't really mean anything."

I look at the pale, unconscious girl and back to Malachai. "If you believe that, then fuck you."

Malachai laughs. "It was companionship in a place where there *is* no companionship."

"You don't have to act like she meant nothing to you."

"What do you want me to say, Luka? That I loved her? You want me to break down and cry? Tell you that I used to imagine our future together? A house outside the city? Kids? It was never going to happen."

I almost scream at him, tell him he'll never know how lucky he is, but I can see that he's on the verge of tears.

"I'll see you tomorrow," I tell him, and leave him alone with Wren.

I walk around the Loop until I come to Woods's empty cell. I step inside and lie down on the bed. Every muscle in my body breathes a sigh of relief, the cuts and bruises that cover me settling into a dull ache.

I know that I can't sleep as long as the trigger is still active, but I rest my head on the pillow anyway. Even if there was no trigger, I wouldn't be able to sleep; too much has happened, too much is going to happen. My entire world has been flipped on its head in the space of a day.

I realize, lying here, that I've spent every moment since Wren attacked me in a state of shock. It all seems so unreal now: escaping my cell, the rat tunnel, the village, Tyco. I feel my body shaking as all the chaos begins to sink in, and the more I think about it, the closer I come to a panic attack. I can feel my breaths coming out in shallow gasps, the oxygen I draw into my lungs feels weak and empty, and my heart speeds up and beats irregularly. This sensation, this feeling of impending doom, is so similar to the energy harvest.

And then I hear a voice.

"Hey, Luka."

I look up to the open door, and Kina is there. She looks anxious.

I manage to catch my breath. "Hi," I say, and I'm surprised that it comes out clear.

"Can I sit with you for a while?"

I sit up. "Yeah, of course."

"It's been sort of . . ."

"A weird day?" I offer.

She laughs. "Yeah, a weird day."

She sits down next to me. My heart beats normally.

"I feel as though it's all just sinking in now," she says.

"I know what you mean."

"Everyone we've ever known might be dead. Hell, the last time there was a world war, humans almost destroyed the planet."

"All the remaining nukes were detonated in deep space," I tell her, remembering my history lessons.

"That was a century ago—a lot has changed since then. Do you honestly think they haven't made more? Plus, there's not supposed to be any biochemical weapons, and yet they've turned normal people into insane monsters."

"Who's *they*? That's what I don't understand—who would attack the Region? There's only one World Government."

"Maybe that's just as dangerous as multiple governments," Kina says, lying down. "No one to question what's right or wrong."

"Maybe," I agree. "But that doesn't explain who attacked us."

"Some kind of rebel group? A rogue Region? Aliens from outer space? Right now, it doesn't matter."

I lie down beside her. "I'm worried about my family," I say. "Do you think Pander was right? Do you think we should have left tonight?"

She doesn't reply, just wipes her eyes and rests her head on my chest.

"Luka," she says quietly, "why did they lock you away in this place?"

I swallow. "It's a long story."

"How does it end?"

"Murder."

Kina puts her hand on top of mine. We lie like this for a long time.

"Who's Orla?" I ask, remembering Kina's words from the yard.

"She was my sister. I was put away because I killed the man who forced her to . . ." Kina begins before trailing off. Her voice is emotionless and yet somehow full of pain. "She got caught up selling Ebb for one of the Alt gangs. He got her hooked on the stuff and . . . They had this *scheme* where they'd advertise their girls as home help or house cleaners. Rich Alts would pay fifty Coin for one hour with young Naturals like Orla. I confronted her pimp; he tried to choke me to death. I stuck a knife in his neck, and they sent me to the Loop."

I don't know what to say, how to tell her that I understand, that I don't think of her as a murderer, so I say nothing; I just put my arm around her and hold her.

After a while, Kina falls asleep. I move the trigger from my rigid right hand into my left and can barely suppress a scream as I open out the fingers of my now-free hand.

I think about what Kina told me, think about why I'm in

here, about how we'll do anything to protect our families. I think about Tyco and how his need to see me dead is fueled by the same thing that made me take the blame for my sister's crime—and the same thing that made Kina kill her sister's pimp.

I don't sleep, just look out the small window in the back wall as the sky darkens and the stars come out.

Kina wakes after what must be about three hours. We hear the others getting up and ready to go.

As we walk out of Woods's cell together, Malachai gives me a grin and a wink, and I feel a mixture of embarrassment and anger.

"Right, let's see what Pod and Igby have managed to do with that door," Malachai says.

"Wait," I say. "First, I have to give Tyco another chance."

Malachai laughs as if I've told a great joke, and then he stops, the smile falling off his face immediately. "You're not serious?"

"I've thought about it all night. I can't let him die without him knowing the truth."

"Truth? What truth? Who cares about truth? The guy is out of his mind. Luka, no one would blame you if you just walked away," Malachai pleads, but I barely hear him.

I remind myself of why I want to do this crazy thing; I remind myself he hates me because of his love for his brother. I think of my love for my own family, and I think of Kina's bravery and integrity when she chose to let the others out of their cells. *And look how well that turned out!* a voice inside my head screams. I ignore it.

I walk to Tyco's cell and look back to see that the rest of the group has gathered behind me. I open the hatch.

The Alt lies on his bed, hands crossed behind his head, staring up at the ceiling. He looks content, peaceful.

"Are you here to kill me?" he asks.

I shake my head. "No."

"You should be," he replies, a smile spreading across his lips. "If you don't kill me, I'll kill you."

"You need to listen to me, Tyco," I say, trying to sound calm but unable to rid my voice of the tremble that gives me away. "I am going to let you out of here because if I don't, you'll die. I don't have to do it, I could leave you in there to rot, but I won't. No one else is coming for you, do you understand that? There's a war outside, and we're not on the top of anyone's evacuation list. I know you want to kill me, I know what happened to your brother, and—"

At this, Tyco is on his feet. He storms over to the hatch and pushes his arm through, grabbing me by the throat. I feel immediate pressure in my head and pain where his thumb is digging into my windpipe.

Over the pounding of blood in my ears, I hear the voice of Happy blaring out of the speakers.

"Infiltration. Lockdown in five seconds . . . four . . . three . . ."

I see the determined look in Tyco's wide, staring eyes, and for a moment, I'm sure he won't let go in time, that the hatch will come down and for the second time in less than forty-eight hours I'll have a severed arm to deal with, but as the countdown hits one, he lets go and pulls his arm back inside just as the hatch snaps shut with the ferocious force that cut Wren's arm clean off.

I fall to the floor and gasp air through my bruised windpipe. Pod and Igby run over to me, each of them grabbing me by a shoulder.

I take a deep breath and feel anger sweep over me. I throw open the hatch again and look in at Tyco pacing the floor of his cell.

"You're a moron, you know that?" I yell. "If you had one brain cell in that head of yours, you would've been smart enough to act nice until I let you out, and then you could've killed me right out here."

"Listen to me, Luka: I'm going to kill you. One way or another, I'm going to kill you."

I slam the hatch shut again and yell out in frustration.

"Offer still stands," Malachai says. "We can walk away."

I consider it, I really consider it. I sigh and open the hatch.

"You again," Tyco mutters. He's sitting on the edge of his bed now, face red with rage.

"You ready to be reasonable?"

"Why should I be? You killed my brother."

His words echo into the corridor, and I can feel the rest of the freed inmates' shock transferring telepathically between them. Malachai whistles a high, descending note. I ignore him.

"Tyco, you need to listen to me—if you don't listen and understand, you're not going to get out of this cell."

"Why should I listen to a liar?" he asks.

"I'm not lying, Tyco. I didn't kill your brother."

Tyco gets to his feet, walks to the hatch, and stares at me. "Don't talk about him. Don't you ever talk about him again, murderer."

"Tyco, we're leaving this place today, with or without you. It's your choice."

"Open the door, coward. See what happens."

I turn to Kina, and she shrugs. I try Malachai, who steps forward and takes my place at the hatch.

"Hey, tough guy," he says, "will you settle for giving my boy here a head start into the war zone? That way you get out of this cell and the option to murder him is still there for you to cash in at a later date?"

"What do you mean?" Tyco asks.

Malachai turns to Kina and says under his breath, "Not the smartest, is he?" before turning back to Tyco. "What I mean is, we let you out, we get out of here, and you give us one day to get away from you, like hide-and-seek. Did you ever play hide-and-seek when you were a kid? It's like that, except with murder. After that day is up, you're free to do all the killing you want."

Tyco is silent for a long time. "Fine," he says eventually. "I'll give him a day, but only because he didn't let me die in here."

"Good," Malachai says. "For the record I was all for leaving without you."

"What?"

"I'm unlocking the door now," Malachai says, reaching down for the handle. "Just be cool." I feel my heart skip as the lock creaks and the door swings open.

Tyco steps out into the corridor. The boy is so big that it's hard to believe he's not yet eighteen. He stares right at me, and I can tell that he's fighting every cell in his body begging him to brush aside the crowd of inmates and tear my head from my shoulders.

"Well," Malachai says, clapping his hands together, "this is nice and awkward. No point in wasting any more time."

We walk around to Igby's cell. I try to fight against my instinct to keep both eyes on Tyco, but it's hard.

We find Pod on his knees wrapping two wires together while Igby wrenches a piece of metal out of the back of his screen. Together they have dismantled three light fixtures, two screens, the 360-degree projector, and the radio from the staff room. A string of wires leads from a light fixture into Igby's cell and is crudely hooked up to the back of his semi-dismantled screen.

"All right," he says, standing up and dusting off his jump-suit. "Firstly, none of this makes any fucking sense. Half the working electronics in this place should have been taken out by whatever took out the rest of the power."

"No," I say. "The emergency features run off a battery that's in a bunker—"

"Yes, I know all about the battery and the emergency electronics, but there are some things—the microphones, some sensors—that aren't connected to the bunker. It's as if whoever cut the power has chosen what will work and what won't work."

"So, what does that mean?" Akimi asks.

"No fucking idea," Igby replies cheerily. "Anyway, it should just be a case of . . ."

He trails off and exits his cell as we all watch, fascinated by his ingenuity.

Igby presses a few commands on his—somehow working—screen, and a second later Happy's voice stutters. "Inmate 9-9-9-9, Inmate 9-9-9-9, everything, everything, everything is as it should should be." And then the back wall opens up, revealing the exercise yard beyond.

"Easy," Igby says with a smile.

"That was impressive," Akimi says, staring out into the open space.

"Not bad," Malachai mutters as he ducks under the opening door.

Everyone follows him until we're all standing on the hard concrete, feeling the cold air on our faces.

"All right," I say. "I guess we climb?"

"I've done this hundreds of times," Malachai says, stepping forward. "All you need to do is wedge yourself in the corner, like this."

Malachai presses a foot against the dividing wall and a forearm against the right angle of the outside cell wall and begins spider-crawling up toward the roof.

"I'm not sure if I can do that," Blue mutters.

"Hey, this is great when there's no drones threatening you," Malachai grunts as he works himself higher and higher.

Akimi steps forward next and copies Malachai's climbing style.

Malachai reaches the top, spins around on his stomach, and reaches down to pull Akimi up the final few feet.

Tyco goes next, racing up the wall with ease. Then Igby leads Pod to the corner and places his hands and feet onto the correct places.

"It's not so bad," Pod says. "The wall is rough; there's grip."

Igby follows close behind his friend, and then Pander shoots up the wall with no difficulty at all.

I step forward next, taking one last look around this prison, this hell that I have been trapped in for so long. I smile as I give the middle finger to the yard, the pillar, the drones, and the cells. "Fuck you," I whisper. And then I climb.

It takes longer for me to climb the wall. I have to use the wrist of my left hand to ensure the trigger stays firmly in my grasp, but I make it to the top, where Pod and Akimi drag me up to safety, and then I turn to watch Kina. She tells Blue that she'll go first to show him how easy it is.

She begins to climb, and Blue watches, staring at the summit.

I help Kina up, and we all turn to watch Blue struggling slowly up the walls.

"You can do it, Blue," Akimi calls.

"You've got this," Pod adds.

Blue begins to climb, his feet slipping as he struggles to maintain grip. He is breathing heavily, sweat matting the hair at his temples, but he begins to make progress. He is about twenty feet up the wall when he stops and looks at us, his eyes glaring with fear.

"Did you hear that?" he asks.

"Hear what?" Pander asks.

Then the sound comes again, and this time we all hear it. A voice screaming out from inside the corridors of the Loop.

"Wait for me. Wait!"

"Mable," Blue says quietly, and then he screams it. "Mable!"

A second later, I realize what Blue has realized: Mable thinks we're going through the rat tunnels; she doesn't know that we changed plans to climb the walls.

Blue begins to descend the wall as quickly as he can.

"Shit!" I hiss.

"What's happening?" Pander asks.

"Take this," I tell Kina, holding out the trigger. She carefully grips it, and I throw myself over the ledge, getting my hands and feet in place as quickly as I can.

"Mable, wait!" I hear Blue screaming below me. I look down and see that he is almost at ground level. He drops, feet thumping down onto the concrete, and sprints through the open door and into Igby's cell, screaming after the girl as he goes.

"Blue!" I yell, but he's gone.

I climb down, faster and faster, my hands and feet barely maintaining grip as I go. I make it to the last ten feet and then drop down, the shock of the fall sending pain through my ankles, but I ignore it and sprint after the boy.

I can hear his voice calling after Mable from somewhere along the long, curving corridor, and I run as fast as I can after him.

I finally catch sight of him as he crosses the threshold onto the Dark Train platform.

"Blue, stop!" I call, but as I gain on him, I see him jump down onto the tracks and sprint into the darkness.

There's no time to think of the danger as I follow him onto the tracks and into the tunnel.

I can just make out his shape in the gloom of the tunnel—he's almost close enough to grab, but then Mable's agonized screams echo out, filling the subway with horror.

"No!" Blue cries, and moves faster into the darkness.

Mable screams again, and this time the sound of the hissing, screeching rats is intertwined with her voice.

"No! No! Mable, no!" Blue screams.

Now I'm close enough to grab him—my fingers close around the material of his jumpsuit, and he falls to the ground. "It's too late, Blue," I tell him, holding him tight. "She's gone."

"Let go, get off me!" he snarls as he thrashes around, trying to break free.

Mable screams again, this time a quieter, gurgling call as her life drains away.

"Get off me—we have to save her."

"Listen to me: She's gone, Blue; we can't save her. And if we stay in these tunnels any longer, we'll be next."

I pull him to his feet and drag him back toward the platform. He continues to fight against me until Mable's screams fall silent.

"I hate you," Blue whispers. "I fucking hate you."

"I know," I tell him as we make our way back to the yard.

Blue climbs first, slowly and languidly, rejecting the arms that reach for him at the top and pulling himself up.

I follow, the echoes of Mable's dying screams in my mind. We couldn't have saved her; it was too late—we couldn't have run into the pitch-darkness and blindly fought an army of rats. We had to let her go.

Didn't we?

I make it to the top, the eyes of my friends on me, waiting to hear what happened. I can only shake my head, silently take the trigger back from Kina, and walk to the other side of the roof. I look out at the wasteland that the Loop sits in: a valley of dust dunes and charred, dead trees.

The wall that leads down the other side is a lattice of concrete that offers hand- and footholds. I climb down first, sending some loose concrete tumbling to the ground, barely registering the burning in my shoulders as I move, using only one arm so as not to drop the trigger, but I make it easily to the ground. I want to watch the others climb down, offer help, but I don't want them to see the tears in my eyes.

Kina climbs down second and stands next to me. She puts an arm on my shoulder, and I force a smile.

"Are you going to be okay?" she asks.

I nod. "Yeah. Thanks."

We turn to help Pod as Igby directs him from above. Tyco makes it down next, followed by Pander and Blue. Blue stands on his own, staring out at the horizon.

Malachai climbs down, leaping the final few feet. Akimi is last over the edge, carefully finding her footholds and making her way steadily down.

"It's a lot harder coming down than it was going up," she calls out from the middle of the wall.

"You're doing great," Kina calls up to her.

"Thanks, this wall feels a little—"

Akimi's words stop midsentence as the indent where her right foot was resting gives way. The concrete crumbles into the dust in a series of heavy thunks. Akimi screams as both her feet swing out and away from the wall.

"I can't hold on," she breathes. And before anyone can do anything—she's falling. Her red dress billows out as she tumbles through the air.

She lands heavily on the ground. A horrific snap emanates from her right ankle as she falls back.

"Akimi!" Igby calls out as he runs over to her.

"Shit, shit, shit!" she screams through clenched teeth.

"Fuck! Are you okay?" Igby asks, falling to his knees beside her.

"My ankle, my right ankle, it's broken, I know it's broken. Oh shit, it's fucking, shitting broken."

"Guys," Pander's voice comes from atop a dust dune ahead of us, "we need to move now."

I run up the dune to join Pander, my feet sinking into the fine dirt, slowing my progress. I look to where she's pointing. Marching along the grimy landscape is a small group of fifteen to twenty soldiers, all dressed in black, all carrying USW guns across their chests.

"What are they doing here?" asks Kina. "There's nothing else around here for miles."

"Do you think they're coming for us?" Malachai asks, joining us at the summit of the dune.

"Let's not wait around and find out," I say.

225

We all jump down into the dust, sliding effortlessly toward the group.

"Akimi, I'm sorry about this, but we have to move now," Malachai says, running to her and bending down to grab her by the arms. "Can you put any weight on your good foot?"

"I can try," she says through gasps.

Malachai gets her to her feet, and we move toward the upward slope of the valley, which leads away from our prison and away from the soldiers. Akimi limps and hops as fast as she can, Igby on one side, Malachai on the other.

It takes an agonizingly long time to scale the dust hill and even longer to get down the other side, but after an age, we see the opening of the rat tunnel and the village train platform in the distance.

It takes another ten minutes until we make it to the platform, and we finally take a break.

We are all gasping to catch our breath, but slowly, one by one, we begin to smile. I watch the other inmates look around, take deep breaths of the fresh free air, and marvel at the sun, rising red on the horizon. They hug and jump and cheer. Pander even does a little dance, and in spite of the pain she's in, Akimi laughs with joy.

Despite everything, I can't help but smile at the scene, all these young people who had resigned themselves to a life of confinement, of loneliness, of confinement, prisoners to the energy harvest, now experiencing the simple joy of freedom once again.

Even though there's a war going on, we're still so happy in

this moment, and it occurs to me that it's better to be free in a ravaged world than a prisoner in a utopia.

The only person not celebrating is little Blue, who sits cross-legged on the ground and holds his face in his hands. I know that he feels a sense of responsibility for Mable's death. I do too. I feel bad for him—the burden he's put on his young shoulders is devastating.

I look back to the group of elated escapees and smile again. I allow myself to feel happy for a moment. But I will talk to Blue soon, try to make him see that Mable's death wasn't his fault. I take a deep lungful of air and smile again. The sense of happiness I'm feeling is short-lived, though, as I watch Tyco break from the hugging, laughing pack and turn to me. His eyes narrow as he pulls a gun from inside his jumpsuit and points it right at me.

I was right, I think, completely frozen. *He was planning on killing me all along.* I had known it from the beginning. I should have trusted my instincts. I should have left him in his cell.

"Wait," I manage to say in a weak, quiet voice.

But there is no time for me to react as he pulls the trigger.

I feel the dart from the tranquilizer gun zip past my ear, and I turn in time to see a man of about fifty, balding with a ripped white shirt and red tie, stagger, blink a few dozen times, and fall to the ground.

Everyone is still and silent as they look from the unconscious Smiler back to Tyco.

His shaking hand repositions the barrel of the gun, and this time he really is pointing the weapon right at me.

He must have picked the tranquilizer gun up from outside my cell, where I dropped it. How did I not notice that it was gone?

"Why did you let me out? You know I want you dead; why did you do that?"

I open my mouth to speak, but I can't think of the right words; I can't even tell myself why I saved him when the logical thing to do would have been to let him die.

"I don't know," I say.

"You killed my brother," he says, his voice shaking. "You pushed him off the roof of the Black Road Vertical."

"Tyco, listen to me: Do you know what Happy found when it ran the probability diagnostics? It told me that I was four percent likely to have committed that murder."

"Those are just words," he roars back at me. "Words from a liar's mouth."

"It's the truth. The only reason they convicted me is because of my confession."

"Lies," Tyco screams, his eyes narrowing until tears spill down his cheeks. "I saw the footage from my brother's Panoptic camera. I saw you push him."

"You saw someone in a mask push him."

"Who was it, then? Why would you take the blame for someone else's crime?"

"It was Molly, my sister," I say, remembering the moment on top of the roof. The silence after the boy fell, only the wind whistling through the gap between the giant rain collector and the bizarre assemblage of pipes connecting the water to the thousands of apartments beneath our feet. She turned around slowly, pulled off the Halloween witch mask, and stared at me, tears forming in her eyes. I decided in that moment that she hadn't pushed him—that it was me, I had killed him.

"Why should I believe you?" Tyco asks. "Why wouldn't you have told me that years ago?"

"I didn't know who you were. I asked you a thousand times, and all you ever said back was that you were going to kill me. I guessed that you were that boy's brother, or at least his friend, but I didn't know for sure. And even if I had, what was I going to do? Yell it across the yard? Do you think they weren't listening? Do you think they didn't have microphones in every square inch of that place? It would have been as good as sentencing my sister to death."

Tyco steps forward, the gun barrel shaking but still aimed right at me. I can see him wrestling with his emotions. He lets out a frustrated scream, drops the gun to his side, and then raises it up to my face again. "Why did your sister kill him?" His voice is quieter now, and there are still tears running down his face. For the first time, I feel something other than fear or hatred for him.

"It was an accident," I say. "I'm not going to stand here and tell you that we were the good guys. We planned on robbing him. He sold Ebb to Regulars in the Verticals—he was in the same gang as you. We knew he had Coin; we were going to force him to transfer everything he had to an encrypted account. We needed the money; our mother was dying of some undiagnosed flu and..." I trail off. "I'm sorry that your brother died, Tyco. Every day I wish it hadn't happened, and not only because it got me locked up in the Loop but because a person lost his life. I'm not saying this just because you want to kill me; it's the truth—I regret what happened every day."

Tyco sniffs loudly and swipes at the tears in his eyes. He lowers the gun. Malachai steps up beside him and takes the weapon out of his hand.

"This doesn't mean I like you, Luka," Tyco says, wiping his eyes. "I'm just not going to kill you."

I nod my head.

"Oh my god." Pander's voice is—for once—quiet and afraid.

We all turn in the direction she's looking, and they all see what I have already seen: the city that we all grew up in, burning and crumbling. Even City Level Two, the mile-wide piece of luxury real estate built on great graphene stilts, is burning just as bright as the rest.

"This is so bad," Akimi whispers.

"The war is really happening?" Pod asks.

"It's really fucking happening," Igby tells him.

"Let's get moving," Malachai interjects, walking past everyone and dropping back down onto the tracks.

Kina reaches for Blue's hand, but he pulls away from her. "I'm not a baby."

He glares at me as he passes, jumping down onto the train tracks and stomping away.

Pander walks past and plants a hand on the platform, vaulting down. "At least he's not being a wimp anymore," she mutters, and follows Malachai.

Pod and Igby lower themselves onto the train track and help Akimi down. Kina and I follow on, with Tyco bringing up the rear.

"So," I say, trying to get the attention of the group, "I know we all want to find our families, that's the priority, but we also have to think about getting to the Facility—that's where we'll all meet up in two days."

"Don't worry about it," Malachai calls from the front of the group. "We're going in the right direction."

"How do we know that this is the way to the Facility?" Akimi asks, wincing as her dangling foot catches the ground. She looks up at Malachai, who appears to have appointed himself leader.

"Because I used to live on the far side of the city," the Natural replies, pointing to the horizon. "Gallow Hill Vertical. The Dark Train used to go by every now and then, and as the Dark Train is only used to transport criminals and supplies, and it wasn't heading south to the Loop, it must have been going to the Facility. Which means the Facility is north."

Pod and Igby look impressed as they nod in agreement, and for some reason there's a slight pang of jealousy inside me. I try to figure out why and realize that it must be because they all see Malachai as the leader, despite the fact that it was me who broke out, me who saved all their lives, me who went through the rat tunnel on my own twice.

You're being ridiculous, I think. *You don't even want to be in charge.*

I try to accept it, but I can't pretend that the feeling isn't still there.

We walk in silence, glancing up at the city from time to time, and after a while Pander begins to sing, only this time it doesn't feel melancholy in the way it did when we were all behind the walls—out here it feels oddly hopeful. Perhaps we're the only people who could find any kind of hope in a situation like this; perhaps the very fact that we resigned ourselves to a miserable countdown to an agonizing death has given us a unique perspective on the end of the world. I have to admit that the feeling of walking in one direction without a wall or a locked door to halt my progress is almost overwhelming.

Kina ups her pace and walks beside Malachai, at the front

of the group. The feeling of jealousy returns, stronger this time. I push it down, reminding myself that I don't feel that way about Kina, but something about the way she laughs at whatever he's just said makes it difficult to convince myself that I'm telling the truth.

Grow up, idiot, I tell myself.

We walk for about another hour, past the holiday village and through the mile-high sky-farms, where we stop and dig out some carrots from one of the troughs. When the power is on, the Ferris wheel farms never stop spinning around and around at almost imperceptibly slow speeds, growing crops for an entire city without taking up the room of old-fashioned farmland. I remember my sister and me sneaking into one of the potato troughs one summer—despite the news stories every year of kids falling from the top and dying. We lay there on our backs as the enormous piece of machinery carried us slowly up into the sky and slowly back down. We were caught by security drones, then scanned, and our information was sent to the Marshals. Then we had to spend fifteen days working on the farm, side by side with the robots, to pay off our fines. It was worth it, though, and we did it again a few months later.

We carry on, the smell of burning and chemicals filling the air and growing ever stronger, the sounds of crumbling structures and raging fires becoming almost deafening, and the tension growing among all of us. Fear is spreading, along with thoughts that maybe we were wrong about being vaccinated, maybe any second now one of us will start grinning and blinking, and we'll turn on one another like rabid dogs.

My hand has been cramping for the last few hours, the muscles convulsing and twitching in protest at being held in the same place for such a long period of time. I try not to think about it, but the more I tell myself to ignore the pain, the more I focus on it. I'm not sure how long I'll be able to hold on to the trigger.

And, as if she's reading my mind, Kina slows until she's beside me.

"How's the hand?"

"Fine," I lie, shrugging.

Kina laughs and takes my hand in both of hers.

"Careful," I say, and she rolls her eyes.

She takes the trigger and smiles at me. "I'll be careful, don't worry."

"Thanks," I say, and smile back.

And then I hear a sound from inside my chest. One long beep followed by three short ones. I swear my heart stops. Kina's eyes widen.

"I didn't let go. Luka, I didn't—"

"It's okay," I say, breathing again. "I don't know what that was, but I'm all right."

Kina exhales hard. "That scared the shit out of me!"

"It's okay," I say again. "I'm fine."

We both laugh nervously, trying to ignore the anomaly. We start walking again, and soon we reach the edge of the city.

The landscape slopes down to the area of man-made dirt streets where the homeless have built their huts and shacks from scrap metal and plastic, siphoning electricity in complicated masses of wires and makeshift fuse boxes that snake down from the Verticals, the dangerously frayed cables sagging into puddles of thick brown water. The irrigation system is a cobbled-together network of pipes and ditches that carries filthy wastewater away from the houses. Ahead of us, the train tracks disappear into the shantytown and past a towering Vertical that pierces the sky. I try to ignore the deep red color of the stream of water that flows alongside the homeless town, try to somehow block out the sound of the screams from deep inside the city.

Pander's song grows quiet and then stops completely as we all come to a halt and stare into the destruction.

"All right," Pander says, taking a deep breath. "Let's do this."

"I can't," Akimi replies, her voice quiet and choked from the back of the group, where Pod and Igby hold her up.

"What do you mean?" Pander asks, a strange mix of frustration and understanding in her voice.

"I can't walk; it's really starting to hurt. I think it's bad."

There's a moment of silence as we look around, waiting for someone to say the right thing, waiting—perhaps—for an adult to tell us what to do next.

I think: *Maddox would have known what to do.* And I wish he were here. I wish he had lived long enough to escape with us.

Malachai steps forward. "Lie down," he says. "Let's take a look."

Pod and Igby help Akimi to the ground, and as her right ankle rests on the hard earth, she lets out a wail of agony.

"It hurts so much," she breathes.

"We're going to have to take the shoe off," Malachai tells her. "It's not going to be fun."

She nods, grinds her teeth together, and nods again. "Do it."

Malachai slowly unties the laces of her white sneaker. I kneel down beside her and take her hand.

"Squeeze my hand when it hurts," I tell her.

Malachai grips the shoe by the heel, and as soon as he pulls it toward himself, Akimi screams and a viselike grip crushes the bones in my hand. I want to scream along with her, but I bite my lip and try not to react. The way I'm involuntarily squirming in pain earns me a look from Kina. I force myself to sit still and smile back at her.

Igby turns away from the grotesque scene of Akimi's ankle, which is moving like it's held together with frayed thread. Slowly, the shoe slides off her limp foot, and her grip loosens on my throbbing hand.

"Sock next," Malachai says, his voice sounding thick with nausea.

He grabs the top of her sock with two hands and slowly pulls it off her foot. The pain in my hand increases as Akimi grabs hold once again.

"Well?" she says through hyperventilating breaths.

Malachai stutters. "It's, uh, it's going to be okay."

"It's bad, isn't it?"

"Honestly?" he replies. "It's disgusting. It's all limp and at a weird angle. I almost threw up . . ."

Kina hits him in the arm, shutting him up.

I lean forward and look down at the swollen mound of

flesh where Akimi's ankle used to be. The skin has become a mottled lump of bruises, there's a horrendous kink just below her shin, and her foot points unnaturally away from her body. I feel the dry bread and water from breakfast swirl in my stomach and have to breathe heavily until I'm sure I won't vomit.

"God, it hurts," Akimi cries.

A loud scream comes from just inside the city, maybe only fifty yards from where we've stopped on a patch of scorched grass and trees. Akimi suppresses her own cries until they're involuntary grunts. All our heads turn in the direction of the city. Malachai rises to his feet, a look of fear in his eyes.

"Guys, just go. I'll find somewhere to hide," Akimi says.

"Don't be stupid," Malachai mutters, still staring into the city. "We're not leaving you."

"What do we do?" Blue asks, and looks at Malachai.

"I . . . We should . . ." He trails off.

"Here's what we're going to do," I say, standing up. "You guys are going to find a place to hide, and I'm going into the city to find something for Akimi—painkillers or something."

"Well, that's all very heroic, testosterone-fueled macho stuff," Kina replies, "but I don't think you've thought it through."

I feel my face flush red. My first instinct is to deny her accusations, but the very fact that I'm embarrassed by her words lets me know that there's an element of truth to them.

"What . . . what do you mean?" I ask, trying, and failing, to sound confident.

"Even if you do manage to get in and out alive, even if you

do make it back here with painkillers, she still can't walk, she's still trapped here."

"Well, what's your plan?" I demand.

"I don't have one yet, but I'm not just going to yell out the first thing that comes into my head."

"At least I'm trying!"

"Oh, yeah, great work, let's all get killed one by one," Kina exclaims, waving the heart trigger around.

"I got us this far."

"What do you want? A parade?"

"Maybe a little gratitude . . ."

Our escalating argument comes to a sudden halt as we realize that the rest of the group is murmuring and turning away to face the city. Our eyes follow theirs, and we see the small figure of Pander disappearing into the smoke.

"Pander, wait!" Malachai yells.

She turns, a blurry figure behind the heat haze of fire and smoke. "I can't hear you!" she yells, pointing at her ears.

I run to the front of the group and use my hands to sign *wait*.

Pander shrugs and raises her own hands, and they move quickly as she speaks to me. Then she's gone, following the line of the train tracks through the homeless village and into the war zone.

"What did she say?" Kina asks.

"She said that she can't wait for us idiots forever, that she'll be back with the painkillers and then she's going to find her sisters."

"What do we do?" Igby asks.

"We should go after her," I say.

"Hey, it's her life," Malachai replies with a shrug. "Shame, I liked her."

"Maybe she'll make it," Igby says.

"Maybe," Kina replies, but neither of them sound confident, and as we stare at the place where Pander stood just seconds before, a piece of rubble falls to the ground in a thunder of stone and smoke as if to punctuate the feeling of preemptive mourning for the young girl.

One by one the group turns away, and I can't help but stare along the tracks and into the city. My eyes move to the Black Road Vertical on the horizon to the east, my old home, and I feel a pull toward it, toward my dad and my sister. Whatever happens, I have to find them; that's my first priority.

I turn back to Kina, determined now to do something, anything. "Over there," I say, pointing to an abandoned diner on the edge of the homeless village. "We'll get Akimi inside and barricade the doors, and then we'll figure out what to do next."

"All right," she agrees.

"I'm sorry, guys. I'm so sorry," Akimi mutters from her spot on the ground.

"It's not your fault," Malachai tells her as he kneels beside her. "Do you think you can make it to that building?" He points to the diner. Akimi nods, and we help her to stand, her red dress billowing in the breeze.

Malachai puts one of the injured girl's arms around his shoulder, and I take the other side. Slowly, we make our way across the scorched ground, Akimi in tears at the pain, Blue walking with his head down, Igby guiding Pod, and Tyco last in line.

"Wait here," Malachai says, pushing open the front door of the building.

He steps inside, walking on tiptoes over the broken glass and rotting food. He moves quickly through to the kitchen and out of sight.

From behind us, in the city, we hear another scream of pain. We all share a look, and I can tell that we're wondering if it was Pander.

Malachai returns, eating a banana. "All clear," he says. "And there's a walk-in freezer that we can lock ourselves inside if anything happens."

I help Akimi lower herself to the floor, and then step back.

There's a long silence among the group. We look around at our new surroundings. The diner is old-fashioned, and not in the way the vintage diners in town are—the ones that try to replicate the old twentieth-century style. This place is simply out of date: obsolete robotic waiting staff, the humanoid automaton at the counter frozen in time, the outdated neon lights. Four large windows line the front of the building, but three of them are shattered—so my plan of barricading the door is useless. There are seven booths alongside the windows, where customers must have sat enjoying their meals just days before, and on the tables are order and pay points, if they chose not to use the robots. A long counter runs against the far wall with a large menu above it. One of the strip lights hangs from

240

the ceiling by wires, and there's a large dark pool of dried blood in the middle of the tiled floor.

"Homey," Malachai says, throwing his banana skin toward a trash can and shrugging.

"So, what now?" Blue asks.

I look around the group. "I guess we stick to the plan."

"Yeah, I need to know if my parents made it," Tyco adds, speaking for the first time since his breakdown on the platform.

"But what about Akimi?" asks Kina.

I nod. "Whoever wants to go into the city now to look for family—you can come with us. Some of us will have to stay with Akimi. We'll meet back here as soon as we can. Remember Juno is still in the Loop. Once we've found our families, we need to get to the facility and find a cure or she'll starve to death in there. And, Akimi, we'll try to find painkillers or something while we're there."

Akimi raises a thumb.

"I don't have any family," Igby says. "I can stay with Akimi."

"My parents are dead to me anyway," Blue mumbles.

"I'll stay with Igby," Pod says, slumping his massive frame down onto one of the booth benches that he has felt for with his hand.

"I . . ." Kina starts. She looks up to the ceiling as if weighing a tough decision. "My mother might be out there, I guess."

"All right," I tell the rest of the group, "Malachai, Tyco, Kina, and I will head into the city. We'll meet you back here as soon as we can."

"Whatever," Blue mutters, walking over to an empty booth and lying down.

I take one last look at my friends. Any other group of people would be terrified in this situation, but to us this is a reprieve, a pardon, a stay of execution.

I see Tyco's eyes lingering on the detonator in Kina's hand, but he catches himself before anyone else notices and looks out the broken windows, clearing his throat. Perhaps it's just old habits dying hard—he's spent so long wishing me dead that it's hard not to see an opportunity to kill me when it presents itself.

"Don't die, okay?" Akimi says from her position on the floor, still twisting in pain.

"I'm too pretty to die," Malachai says with a smile that fails to convey the humor he's aiming for.

"Wait," Tyco says, walking into the kitchen and reappearing a few seconds later carrying four large chef's knives with colorful handles. He hands one to Malachai, one to Kina, and one to me. "For protection," he says, shrugging.

I take the knife and tuck it into the pocket of my prison clothes. I feel stupid, like a kid playing make-believe games, but I remind myself that this is real, this is really happening.

"Okay," I say, taking a deep breath. "I guess we'll see you guys later."

The rest of the group says goodbye and wishes us luck.

"Hang in there," Malachai says to Akimi, who is lying on the floor breathing fast through her nose, her arm draped over her eyes.

"Mm-hmm," she replies, her eyes squeezed shut with the pain.

Malachai is the first to leave, pushing open the doors and stepping out into the sunlight, his knife clenched in his fist. Tyco is next, then Kina, and then me.

My heart is thumping in my chest as we enter the homeless village on the edge of town. We're following the tracks, walking between the rails to avoid the river of blood beside us. The sun is directly above us now, so I guess it must be around mid-afternoon. Despite the sun, there are still dark shadows between the huts, but out of the shadows it is warm. So warm, in fact, that the smell of rotting food and sewage is drifting up into the air, along with something else that I don't want to admit to myself is probably the smell of dead people.

We walk on, trying not to look anywhere but straight ahead, trying not to think about the threats that could kill us at any second.

I focus on the makeshift structures around us. The ingenuity that went into building some of these homes is incredible: strips of paper wetted with glue fill gaps in the scrap metal of the walls, homes built on stilts to avoid flooding from the river, others pieced together like a three-dimensional jigsaw puzzle built from thousands of bits of debris.

"This is disgusting," Tyco mutters, eyes glancing briefly at the filth and the squalor.

"Easy for you to say, rich boy," Malachai mutters.

"Come on, there's poor and then there's living in your own filth."

"You think these people wanted to live like this? It's rich

kids like you who rig the system so they don't have the opportunity to get out."

"Oh, save it," Tyco hisses. "I've heard all the excuses a thousand times."

"This must have been so easy for you to ignore," Malachai throws back.

"Don't blame me because you weren't smart enough to make it out."

"What, like you, who made it all the way to the Loop?"

Tyco turns on Malachai, grabbing him by the collar, and standing nose to nose with him. "Shut up, you shut your mouth."

"Is this really the time?" Kina spits, brandishing the trigger at them.

The two boys seem not to hear her mocking tones as they butt heads like mindless stags.

I run toward them to split them up, but stop when I hear shuffling feet from somewhere to my left. I look between the crowded shacks and hanging wires, trying to find the source of the sound, but then I hear more footsteps from behind me.

"Do you want me to knock you out, Regular?"

"Why?" Malachai asks, and I can hear the smirk in his voice. "Is the rich kid in a situation that he can't buy his way out of?"

"Shut up," I say, backing toward them.

"I don't need money to beat the hell out of you," Tyco says through gritted teeth.

"Hey," I whisper. "Shut your mouths. There's someone else here."

Tyco lets go of Malachai. I hear more footsteps now: feet shuffling through the mud, rippling the blood river from somewhere upstream.

Malachai turns his head left, then right. Tyco reaches for his knife.

I see a kid sprint between two houses—I catch sight of her for no longer than a couple of seconds, but see she is covered in mud, wild eyes blinking rapidly. A second later, a boy follows her.

"There," Tyco says, and I turn to see him pointing the tip of his blade toward the corner of a hut made of rusted corrugated-iron sheets and wooden crates. The mad blinking eyes of a woman in her thirties, or maybe her forties, peek out.

"They're behind us too," Kina says. "Three of them."

"Two of them to our left," I whisper, watching the feet of the children from beneath an old Galen Rye AS ONE banner blowing in the breeze.

I remember the way the old lady brutally slaughtered the boy back in the village, the way she brought the knife down over and over again, and I'm certain that we're going to die here.

"Don't move," Malachai whispers, his eyes tracing the shapes of the makeshift buildings around us. "When I say *go*, follow me, understand?"

"Malachai, there's too many—" I start.

"Shut up and get ready to run."

I watch Malachai as he turns the knife over in his hand until he's holding it by the tip of the blade. He raises his arm until the handle is beside his ear and takes a deep breath. I watch his eyes narrow as he steps forward and launches the blade between two shacks.

"Go!" he yells, and takes off in the direction of the knife he's just thrown.

I see one of the Smilers step forward with Malachai's knife in his chest; he is silent, still smiling, still blinking, but his legs give way as the blossom of red around the blade grows.

The world becomes a blur as I take off running. Sounds blend together, and above it all I hear my rattling breaths being sucked into my lungs. I focus on Malachai's heels as he shoulders a middle-aged woman out of the way, climbs up the wall of a sturdy-looking hut, and runs across its roof. I follow, pushing with my arms, dragging myself up, and sprinting to the edge, where Malachai has leapt to the roof of the next shelter. In two strides, he has crossed it and is jumping to the next.

I turn to see Kina pulling herself up, one-handed, onto a nearby shack, the trigger still gripped in her other hand, the tendons in her neck straining. She runs to the edge of the home and leaps to the left, her feet landing almost soundlessly on the flat roof of another building.

For a second, I can't take my eyes off the trigger in Kina's hand, and even now, in the midst of all this turmoil, I am terrified that she'll lose her grip and my world will cut to black.

Put it out of your mind, Luka, I tell myself. *Put it out of your mind, or you won't survive this.*

I grit my teeth and follow, aware now that the ground around us is swarming with Smilers. They're flowing like a river of killers, and I don't want to see them, but as I tense my legs and dive to the next roof, following Kina, I look down and there they are: boys and girls, women and men, elderly people with walkers and wheelchairs stuck in the mud, all of them focused on one thing—murder. They're chasing us, but at the same time they're attacking one another. Some have weapons, rocks, and planks of wood; one older lady has a knitting needle, and others are using their teeth to rip at the flesh of whoever is closest.

They're just like the rats, I think.

"Go, go, go," Tyco's terror-filled voice calls from behind as he catches up to me.

I up my pace. Malachai and Kina have the lead, running adjacent to each other. I watch Malachai as he throws himself through the air, hopping from structure to structure, some of the homes rocking and contorting with the weight of him. I don't know if he has a plan beyond running away, but I hope he does, because the horrible, determined silence of the Smilers around us allows me to hear clearly the ugly sounds of the butchery below, and I know that if we fall into the stream of killers, we'll be carried away, drowned in the mass of predators, torn apart.

Malachai turns right; Kina follows. The gap between the next two buildings is vast, and as she leaps, stretching out her leading leg, I'm sure she's not going to make it, that she's going to fall short and hit the edge of the roof, knocking all the air out of her lungs before sinking to the dirt road below, where the insane residents will eat her alive. But she makes it, the toes of her left foot just reaching over the lip of the roof. She stumbles and catches her balance, and then she's off again, over to the next building.

I take a different route, make the shorter gap, and catch up with Malachai. Now we're running side by side. Tyco finds an even quicker route and ends up in front of us.

"Head to the city," Malachai calls out.

Tyco adjusts his route, stepping between three shacks in quick succession. I follow, making the three strides and then jumping with two feet to the next rooftop, feeling the entire building warp under the burden of my landing. The next gap is even farther, and I have a half second in midair to think *I'm not going to make it* before landing, losing my footing, rolling over on my shoulder, and getting back to my feet. That's when I stop, as I hear Malachai's yell of anguish above the sound of a building collapsing.

I turn just in time to see him disappearing into the crumbling debris of wood and plastic.

"Just keep moving," Tyco yells from one rooftop away.

I look over to him, and he shrugs, but I can see remorse etched on his face as he turns and continues on toward the city, leaping from roof to roof.

I turn back to the destroyed hut and see Malachai struggling to free himself from the wreckage. Behind him, maybe only two hundred feet away, is the horde of Smilers, tumbling and tearing and ripping at one another like crocodiles.

"Run!" I call out to him. His eyes meet mine, and for the first time, I see fear there.

Kina pushes past me, leaping toward the fallen Natural and down onto the dirt path beside him.

"Fuck!" I whisper, and jump down from the relative safety of my rooftop before running to Malachai. Kina grabs one hand, I take the other, and we pull him free of the rubble. The sound of hundreds of approaching killers grows.

"Go," I tell them as I push Malachai toward the nearest shack.

He grabs the hanging wires and climbs up to the roof. I can feel the ground rumbling beneath my feet now, feel the heat coming off the mass of bodies as they close in, smell the dried blood and body odor.

Malachai turns, lies on his stomach, and reaches a hand down. He pulls Kina up by her hand that's not holding the trigger. I jump for the lip of the roof, grab it, and feel my fingers slip.

"Luka!" Kina calls. She lies on her stomach and throws her hand toward me. I grab it and use my other hand to reach for the roof's edge. A strong, vicious hand grabs my ankle, but I kick it free and clamber to my feet beside Malachai and Kina.

"Thanks," Malachai says, and then he's running again.

Kina and I follow. Up ahead I see the shape of Tyco making his way to the nearest Vertical, and I understand Malachai's plan.

We move quickly, gaining a lead on the swarm of Smilers as we use the shacks like stepping stones all the way to the Vertical.

The shacks this deep into the city are older and over time have been reinforced until they almost resemble houses. They are so tightly packed here that we barely have to jump between them, just take slightly larger steps. The last of the shantytown's homes are pressed right up against the Vertical, and from the rooftop of the last building, it's easy to climb in through a broken window.

Malachai climbs in first, collapsing to the ground, his chest rising and falling as sweat pours from his head.

"Do you realize," he says, gasping in oxygen, "how close we just came to being killed?"

I'm leaning forward, my hands on my knees. I don't have the composure to answer his question.

Kina nods fervently; she too seems unable to speak due to exhaustion.

From outside I can hear the swarm of Smilers, the sounds of skin slapping and bones snapping. I lean forward and peer out the window, and what I see fills me with revulsion: There must be two hundred of them in a mass brawl, all killing one another without feeling. One is using his head as a bludgeoning tool to cave in the rib cage of another, two appear to be working together to dig into a prone man through his lower back, and the old lady appears to be systematically stalking the outside of the brawl and sticking her long knitting needle into whomever she sees fit.

"They're all going to die," I say.

"Come on," Tyco says from the doorway of the dirty-looking living room we find ourselves in. Tyco is not out breath at all; of course he isn't—he's an Alt, his MOR system is working on overdrive inside his rib cage to pump oxygen into his bloodstream without the need for the primitive arcana of breathing.

"Yeah, can you give me just a minute, big guy?" Malachai says, rolling onto his front until his nose is pressed against the vinyl floor, his harsh breaths causing plumes of steam to form and disappear on the sheen of the surface.

"There could be more of them in here somewhere," Tyco points out. "We have to keep moving."

"This guy," Malachai mutters. "No empathy." He pushes himself up and follows Tyco out of the room.

I'm still looking out the window; as much as I'm horrified by the scene in front of me, I can't bring myself to look away.

"I have to find my sister," I say to myself as the horde begins to thin. More and more of the Smilers lie dead. The remaining fighters are all covered head to toe in the blood of their peers.

I try to fight off the mental image of my sister, Molly, infected like the killers below, somewhere out in the city, insane and hell-bent on death.

Finally, I manage to tear my gaze away.

I take a look around the living room. It reminds me so much of the house I grew up in: the furniture crammed together; cheap, old technology cluttering up the place; the light barely penetrating the dust outside or the dirty windows.

I follow Tyco, Malachai, and Kina out into the corridor of the Vertical. The place smells like urine, and the walls are covered with incandescent graffiti. In the darkness of the cut power, I can see more clearly the crude writing and gang symbols glowing in neon paint.

We're only one floor up, so it doesn't take long for us to move down the flight of stairs to the front doors. Tyco pushes them open, and we see, from our point on the raised landscape, the city laid out before us. Burned-out shopfronts, derelict pubs, and pawn shops dominate the foreground, but farther on down the hill I can make out the financial district: glass buildings trimmed in gold and silver, water fountains and statues to the gods of money and trade. The more expensive residential areas and social spots make up the center, where green parks and woods border eight-lane roads. Right in the middle lies Midway Park. Above us there is City Level Two, where the ultra-rich live in mansions. The city is encircled by hills dotted with sky-farms and Verticals that pierce the sky. It's a view I'm familiar with, albeit from the perspective of the Black Road Vertical, but what makes us stare, unblinking, is the true scale of the city's destruction.

I can see three planes that have fallen out of the sky and destroyed dozens of buildings; one lies still burning, its wing in a fountain in the financial district. Another has come down nearby in the center of a children's playground. The third is half-submerged in the river that winds through the city; from here it looks like some mechanical river monster.

"Where are you headed?" Malachai asks me.

"Black Road. You?"

"Gallow Hill."

"Tyco?" Malachai asks.

"That way," he says, gesturing vaguely toward the center of the city.

"Okay," Kina says, frowning into the distance. "I think we should stick together at least as far as the river, if we're all heading that direction anyway. If we don't find any painkillers on the way, we can cross the river to Old Town Infirmary and check for them there, then split up. Sound good?"

"Sounds good to me," I say.

"Me too." Malachai nods. "Pander probably headed that way too."

We all turn to Tyco, who gives a dismissive shrug and sets off down the street.

As we begin to move cautiously down into the city, we use the piled-up wrecks of cars that litter the roads as cover—some of the airborne ones, that would have come down from eighty feet or so, are almost unrecognizable as cars at all. The rubble of collapsed buildings makes the air thick with dust, and fires still burn, roaring out of windows and destroying everything that they come into contact with. But all that is secondary—what I can't help but stare at are the bodies, thousands of them filling the sidewalks, hanging half out of windows, inside the cars, charred in the middle of the roads.

"This is . . ." Kina whispers as we pause in a doorway. "This is unbelievable. Whoever did this . . ."

"We have to keep moving," Tyco says, but even his voice is hoarse in the presence of such devastation.

He steps out into the fading sunlight, but Malachai grabs him by the collar and pulls him back into the shadow of the doorway.

"What's your prob—"

"Shh," Malachai says, pointing toward the playground where the plane wreckage lies, which is now only a little way down the street. I look to where he indicates and see a group of six soldiers, dressed head to toe in black, as they move out of the park and down a parallel street. Five of them travel with their weapons raised, checking corners and clearing their route, while the sixth walks, calmly, with no weapon at all. Her eyes are glowing, not like a normal Alt, but brighter, like torchlight.

"What's the deal with the woman's eyes?" Malachai whispers.

"Must be some new upgrade," Tyco replies.

"Are they on our side?" I ask, remembering the soldiers we saw marching toward the Loop.

"I don't even know what our side is," Malachai says. "Let's not ask them."

We sidle along the outside of the building, keeping the distance between us and the soldiers as big as possible.

We dart, one by one, to the foot of a gigantic billboard that shows nothing on its enormous screen. We watch as the soldiers move out of sight.

"Who the hell are they?" Kina asks.

"Doesn't matter," Tyco says. "We're here to find our families. Let's not get distracted."

Glass shatters from somewhere behind us, and we all move quickly, pressing ourselves against the wall of the building the billboard is attached to—it's a provisions depot. A man wearing a tuxedo and a woman in a blue dress walk along the middle of the street toward us. Both of them are infected, but they're not attacking each other.

"In here," Kina says, and we enter the depot before the Smilers spot us.

Inside are row after row of shelves with different foods still piled up, but they're far from full—they can't have been restocked for a while and could even have been ransacked before we got here. On the floor are thousands of drones, which lie where they fell when the power went off.

"This is one of those grocery-delivery depots, isn't it?" I ask.

"Yeah," Tyco says, already grabbing a packet of protein bars off a nearby shelf and shoving them into his pockets.

"Might as well stock up while we're here," Malachai says, grabbing a bottle of water and some chocolate.

Kina walks over to where the protein bars were, but the shelf is now empty.

"Here," Tyco says, handing one of his to her.

"Thanks," she replies, tucking the foil-wrapped bar into her pocket before moving methodically through the depot, scanning each shelf with her eyes. "No painkillers," she says, and we sit on the floor of the depot, among the downed drones, and eat.

"You think Pander made it?" Malachai asks.

"I doubt she even made it through the shantytown," Tyco replies. He sees the look of disappointment on Malachai's face. "What do you want me to do, lie? There are thousands of those smiling things and only one of her."

"You're a real optimist, you know that?" Malachai says through clenched teeth.

Tyco shrugs and turns his head away.

"Hey, she probably made it," Kina says, reaching out a hand and placing it over Malachai's. "She seems like a tough girl."

"Yeah, she's tough," Malachai agrees, and takes another sip of water. "Let's keep moving."

I root around the higher shelves nearby, find another box of protein bars, and shove them into my pockets as we make our way back into the daylight. We head farther into the city, sticking close together but making swift progress. Other than the constant background noise of burning buildings and smoldering wreckage, the streets are eerily silent and empty of life. As the afternoon turns to evening, we reach the river and follow its path toward the bridge to Old Town—the area where the central hospital and the city's administrative buildings lie.

We stop at the corner of a Church of the Last Religion, making sure the coast is clear. Kina leans close and speaks to me in a whisper. "That man and woman in fancy clothes—the Smilers outside the grocery depot—they were working together."

"I know," I say as we sprint closer to the edge of Old Town. I can see the ruins of the parliamentary building, left to stand in remembrance of the Futile War—a shrine to the corruption of the old ways.

"What do you think that means?" Kina asks when we pause again.

"I hope we won't have to find out," I tell her.

We continue our stop-and-go movements from the corners of buildings to crashed cars to fences, always checking for any danger before moving to the next cover.

We make it to the bridge that leads to Old Town and duck behind a solar-charge block. Kina, Malachai, and I catch our breath while the Alt looks out to check that the bridge is clear. I close my eyes for a second and rest my head against the charger, listening to the rushing river below.

"Shit," Tyco whispers, holding up a hand.

I open my eyes, peer around the charge block, and watch as a man in a high-visibility vest and a dirty, old baseball cap sweeps the street.

"He's not blinking," Malachai says.

"Or smiling," I add.

The man looks like he's in his sixties, the skin around his eyes deeply wrinkled with laughter lines that are filled with dark dirt, his tanned hands gripped tightly around the brush that scrapes the ground in rhythmic sweeps. We watch him silently as he makes his way slowly across the bridge. This must have been his job before the end of the world, working side by side with the robot street sweepers. Obsolete but permitted to work thanks to protests by jobless Regulars who demanded employment opportunities. "He's not one of them," Kina says. "He hasn't been affected by the poison."

"What the hell is he doing out on the street?" Malachai whispers.

"He's on Ebb," Tyco replies, leaning forward and squinting. "There's a patch on his neck."

"What do we do?" I ask.

"We have to find out how he survived the attack," Malachai says, getting to his feet. "Maybe there are more survivors."

Malachai opens his mouth to call to the man in the bright vest, but Tyco grabs him by the sleeve and hauls him back to the ground. "Look," Tyco says in a quiet voice, pointing to the other side of the bridge.

Three almost-identical girls wander across the deserted road bridge ahead of us, weaving in and out of stalled traffic. All three have thick dark hair, blue-gray eyes that blink frantically, and wide smiles that reveal straight white teeth. They are dressed in the latest Alt fashion: three-piece suits that wouldn't look out of place in a 1960s boardroom meeting.

"Shit," Kina whispers.

The sweeping man glances up at the girls, smiles, and starts sweeping again, ensuring that he cleans every inch of the dusty road ahead of him.

The girls move faster toward the man, and as they get closer, I can see that all their suits are stained with blood.

"We have to help him," I say as the girls begin to run across the bridge.

Kina looks to Malachai and then Tyco, who avoids her gaze, and by then it's already too late.

The girls leap on the man, knocking him to the ground, and begin biting and kicking and clawing at him. I see now that he has not one but three Ebb patches stuck to the base of his throat. He begins to chuckle as the girls kill him.

"No, no, no," I mutter, unable to stop the words from coming out of my mouth.

The sweeping man laughs up until the moment the girls end his life, adding to the bloodstains on their suits. The smiles never falter from their insane faces as they admire their work and then silently move on.

"No, no, no," I say over and over.

Kina reaches toward me and puts her hand over my mouth; her eyes are wide, and they're telling me to shut up or we're next.

I nod to show that I understand, and all four of us crouch behind the charge block, listening as the girls' footsteps grow and grow until they're deafening in the silent city. As they pass, we slowly move around to the other side of the block until we're facing the open road of the bridge ahead of us, and the footsteps recede into the distance.

"Do we go on or split here?" Malachai asks. "There could be groups of Smilers all over Old Town."

"Pander might be across there," Tyco says, turning to look at us. "We should help her."

Tyco's sudden burst of empathy puts me on edge—all I've ever known from him is homicidal single-mindedness, and now he wants to help a girl he barely knows? But I can see fear in his eyes, and I think that perhaps he's scared and doesn't want to be left alone.

"He's right," Malachai says. "Let's go."

And so we resume moving from burned-out cars to lamp-posts to pillars until we're across the water and into Old Town.

The cobbled streets are littered with the dead, all of them still grinning despite their violent final moments, and the heat of the day has amplified the odor of their decomposition until it overwhelms me.

Among the corpses are more drones than I can count. Most of them are security drones, tiny insectile robots carrying 360-degree cameras to film every inch of the city at all times. We try to move silently, but the microdrones crunch under our feet.

There must be more Smilers active in this area—we hear footsteps, slamming doors, explosions, and more, but all we can do is keep on moving, keep on making our way toward the hospital and, hopefully, Pander and painkillers.

That man wasn't one of them, I think, my mind racing. *He wasn't infected; he wasn't a Smiler. How?* I can feel my mind reeling from all this insanity. I look to the east, toward the Black Road Vertical, my home on the 177th floor, and I remind myself of why I must survive. *You're still alive*, I think, picturing Molly's face and my father's, *both of you, and I'm going to do whatever it takes to find you and find the cure to . . . whatever this is.*

We move on, weaving around dead bodies and stalled cars. We walk past another Church of the Last Religion—the city's only remaining faith, where they worship the Final Gods—and turn onto Street 41-40.

He wasn't affected by the chemicals, I think again, picturing the man sweeping the bridge.

"There," Tyco says, interrupting my thoughts.

I look to where he's pointing: the Old Town Infirmary, an almost pyramid-like building with hundreds of blacked-out windows. From here we can see the rescue-drone bay and emergency entrance.

Malachai turns so he's facing Kina, Tyco, and me. "We go

in, and we split up. Tyco, you and I will start from the top and work our way down. Kina and—"

Malachai's words are cut off by the sound of smashing glass coming from the hospital. We all turn to see a figure leaping out of one of the middle floors of the building and sliding down several closed, sloping windows to a balcony ten feet below.

"Pander?" Malachai gasps, squinting at the figure who is now hanging from the balcony by her fingertips and dropping to a windowsill below.

But I'm not looking at the girl anymore—I'm looking at the window she jumped out of. Five Smilers are crawling through after her, ignoring the deep cuts that the shards of glass slice into their flesh as they shamble down the building, stalking their prey.

As the girl climbs rapidly down the pyramid and lands hard on the roof of an ambulance, I see that it *is* Pander, but there's no time to celebrate—as she clambers down to the pavement, three Smilers slam into the roof of the same ambulance while a fourth hits the pavement and lies dead.

"Pander!" Kina calls, and her frantic eyes find us.

"Run, idiots!" she screams back. "Go! Run! Move!"

The chasing Smilers jump down from the ambulance. The fifth crawls down the side of the building and jumps onto the dead body of the one that hit the pavement, and now all four are running at us, Pander leading the way only a few steps ahead of the chasing killers.

We come to our senses as one and turn, and as we start to

run, Pander has already caught up with us, but the sound of the Smilers' footsteps behind us grows louder every second.

"I'm starting to regret coming with you," Malachai yells as he sprints past me.

We reach a junction: One way leads toward the river, and the other back to the center of town. I don't get to choose as Tyco shoves me toward the river. I leap down the steps leading to the path that runs alongside the water, and as I run beside the fast-flowing river and underneath the bridge that we crossed minutes earlier, I feel the temperature drop so suddenly that I can't help but slow down to see what's happened. Dark clouds have rolled across the sky, and snow falls so quickly and heavily that the path in front of me turns white.

"What the hell?" I say, slowing down.

"Run, stupid!" Tyco hisses as he sprints past me.

And I do. I force my exhausted legs to carry me onward.

I glance behind me—Kina, Pander, and Malachai have gotten separated from us. Two of the Smilers are still chasing, silent apart from the sounds of their feet crunching on the snow. I turn and run faster, gaining on Tyco now despite his mechanical lungs, and I have just enough time to think, *Maybe we haven't been separated from the other three, maybe the Smilers got them,* before my foot slips on the snow.

I stumble forward, trying to regain my balance, but it's too late. I fall, arms outstretched. My chin connects with the hard path beneath the cold snow, and I see a white flash in front of my eyes. For a second, the world turns black, and all I can hear is the sound of my heart beating fast and loud in my chest.

I'm scrambling to my feet in a pulsing world of fog, unsure of where I am. All I know is that I have to move, I have to run, I have to get away.

The sound of sprinting footsteps closes in.

Smilers, I think, but I'm too dazed to make my legs work properly. I'm staggering forward like a stunned boxer, watching Tyco disappear into the distance and knowing that any second I'll feel the warmth of the senseless killers as they swarm me.

This is it, I think, trying to breathe through frozen lungs. *You die here*.

I feel a blow, hard and fast into my rib cage. All the air blasts out of my lungs, and I'm falling again, this time toward the river.

I hit the water. The freezing temperature clears my head, and I kick my legs hard until I break the surface, just in time to see a tall, skinny Smiler leap into the water and begin moving toward me, his smile unfaltering. Behind him, the second Smiler jumps in, and she moves toward me too, fighting against the power of the current.

I take a deep breath and dive back below the flowing stream, kicking my legs and dragging my arms through the murky, cold water. I swim as fast as I can. I have no idea if my pursuers are close, if they're gaining on me, if I'm getting away from them. All I do is swim and swim and swim. I stay below the surface, using the experience of the energy harvest to remain calm as my lungs feel like they are stretching to the ripping point in my chest.

After what feels like forever, I climb to the surface and suck the cold air into my body.

I turn back to where the Smilers were and see only the fast-flowing water through the rapidly falling snow.

"Hey," a shout comes from the bank, and I turn to see that Tyco has stopped running. He's pointing a finger into the stream in front of me.

I follow the direction of Tyco's outstretched finger. At first I see nothing, then, through the snow, I see the shape of a human body, floating facedown ahead of me. It's the tall Smiler. I stand there, frozen in shock as the corpse floats by me, and, a few seconds later, the second Smiler floats by, her orange blouse almost glowing in the dirty water and white snow.

"Get out of there," Tyco calls. "You'll catch hypothermia."

I can't think of anything apart from the unmoving bodies floating downriver as I fight against the current and the rapidly forming ice. I make it to the muddy banks. Tyco pulls me onto the path. All of this seems to happen in snapshots—I feel as though I float away for a second and then come back. As I lie in the snow, staring up at the blizzard, I laugh. I don't know why. Maybe Tyco's right and this is the first symptom of hypothermia—certainly I can't feel my fingers or toes, and my breath is coming out in clouds of thick white.

"We have to go," Tyco says, leaning down into my field of vision.

I can't make sense of his words. The whiteness of the snow seems to fill my whole world until there's nothing else.

And then I'm indoors. Collapsed onto a couch in a vast, clean living room in a home I don't recognize or remember getting to.

"Where are we?" I say, my teeth rattling together as my body temperature hits a new low.

"My house," Tyco mutters as he moves around the place, opening doors, looking for signs of life.

"Pander and Malachai?" I ask, almost unable to get the words out, I'm shaking so violently. The words are slurred as well, as though I'm drunk. "Kina?"

"I don't know," he replies. "I didn't see what happened."

I nod, but I can't really comprehend the meaning of the words. I no longer feel fear, or hope, or anything. I want to sleep, so I lie down and close my eyes.

"No!" Tyco yells, and then he's slapping my cheek over and over.

"What?" I ask, annoyed by the disturbance. "What?"

"Wait here, and don't fall asleep. If you fall asleep, you won't wake up, do you understand?"

I nod again, even though his words make no sense to me at all.

Kina can't be dead, I think, my mind finding a moment of clarity. *If she was dead, I'd be dead too. She has the trigger.*

I smile and look around the room. I want to tell Tyco the good news, but he's gone, and I'm alone. I look around at the white walls, the tiled floor, the 360-degree projector built into the floor, and the SoCom unit on the glass table.

"What a nice home," I mutter to myself. And I fall asleep.

I'm on top of the Black Road Vertical.

The boy with the blond hair is falling down and down through the clear summer air. The boy is Tyco Roth's brother, and pretty soon he will be dead.

My sister turns to me and pulls the rubber witch mask off. There are tears in her eyes, and her lower lip is trembling, the knife in her hand falling to the ground.

"I didn't mean to . . ."

The wind whistles through the water pipes as we stare at each other.

"Molly, you didn't do it," I tell her. "I did."

I open my eyes.

I'm in a bathtub. Warm water up to my chin. Steam rising all around me. I'm still fully clothed.

Where am I?

There is immense pain in the tips of my fingers and toes. I remember the river, the cold, and the pain. It's only now that I realize I was on the verge of death.

And Tyco saved me, I think.

As I lie here, I can hear his voice, day after day, year after year, screaming across the exercise yard that he was going to kill me.

I lie still, letting the warmth of the water surround me. I look down at the wounds covering my body, the rat bites and the scrapes from the tunnel and the village and the river, and I'm surprised to see that they are already healing.

I let the water heat the core of my frozen bones. I suck the hot, steamy air through my nose and feel it in my throat. My body is still shaking and convulsing, but my mind is clear once more.

I look around at the lavish bathroom. It's about the same size as the entire apartment that I grew up in. The curved wall in front of me is a screen that—when the power was on—would have shown interactive movies, social media, and games. There are four sinks along one wall with retractable shelves full of self-replenishing products. An autowash shower the size of a small barn sits in the corner.

I think about my dad; I think about my sister, about Kina, Wren, Pander, Malachai, Akimi, Pod, Igby, Blue. I hope they're alive; I hope they're okay. I think about how much time has passed already and about how every second my sister and my father are left alone out there in the city is another second closer to their deaths. I think about the Facility, the massive structure where our Delays took place and where there just might be a cure for the Smilers.

I push myself to standing, and the water pours out of my clothes. My knees feel stiff and weak. I pull apart the Velcro of my prison suit and let it fall off me before stepping out of the bath.

There are six towels hanging on a rack beside the door. I

take one and wrap it around my waist before opening the bathroom door and stepping out.

I'm in a long corridor that forms a mezzanine level. Below me I can see the living room where I sat dying on the couch. I see a large gas canister hooked up to a camping stove with water boiling in a large pot.

That's how he heated the water, I think, and walk toward the ornate wooden staircase.

"You're alive," Tyco says, coming out of the kitchen, wiping his hands on a dishcloth.

I nod as I walk down the staircase toward him. "Thanks to you."

"Well, I'm only alive because of you. You let me out of the Loop."

I laugh at the drastic change in our relationship. "I never thought that you and I would be looking out for each other."

"Things change, I guess," he says as he lets the dishcloth hang over one hand.

"This is a nice place," I say, looking around at the expansive home once again.

"Thank you."

"Tyco, when I said I was sorry about your brother, I meant it. I—"

"Luka, please. I'll never be okay with what happened, but we're in the middle of an apocalypse, so I have to put it behind me."

"I understand; I just want you to know—"

"I know," he says, and holds a hand out for me to shake. "It's behind us, okay?"

I look at his outstretched hand and can't quite believe it. I had resigned myself to the fact that Tyco Roth had lost his mind the day his brother died, that something had broken inside him and he would go to his death believing that I was the devil, and here he is offering a truce.

"Okay," I say, and take his hand in mine.

Tyco smiles and lets the dishcloth fall from his other hand as he slaps me on the back. "We won't survive this unless we work together," he says.

"You're right. I agree."

Tyco steps back and looks at me intently, the smile growing on his face.

"The thing is," he says, great humor in his voice now, "I don't actually care if I survive, just as long as you don't."

Tyco walks toward me, his form leaving an afterimage, a trailing stream of color as he moves.

Something is wrong.

I feel a jolt of panic as I register the feeling of something on my back where Tyco slapped me, something that feels like a small plastic strip.

I reach for it, throwing my arms across my shoulder, but the Ebb patch is just out of reach.

"I couldn't let the cold kill you, Luka. It had to be me," Tyco says. His voice sounds like it's coming from everywhere at once.

"Tyco, what have you done?"

I try to concentrate on the danger, the threat of Tyco, but

my eyes focus on a small scratch on the arm of the red leather couch, and it seems funny to me. I imagine Tyco as a toddler with a plastic sword running around the house slaying imaginary dragons; I see it so vividly that for a second I forget that the grown-up Tyco is standing in front of me, intent on ending my life. I laugh at how absurd that is.

"Do you know how long I've waited for this moment?" Tyco asks, and as he talks, I see his words coming out of his mouth in big purple balloons twisted into the shape of letters. I watch them float up into the air and then pop over his head.

Focus, Luka, I tell myself. *This guy is going to kill you.*

But I can't focus. My body feels as if it is being filled with pure, concentrated joy from the tips of my toes up to the top of my head. I laugh again and watch Tyco pull the knife from his pocket. I know it's a knife, I know what he intends to do with it, but to me it looks like a cucumber.

"Do you know why I was sentenced to death?" Tyco asks, his face changing from purple to green to yellow. "I tried to burn down the Marshal station because they let my brother die. My family paid thirty thousand Coin a year for personal protection, and they let him die. I think a part of me wanted to end up in the Loop with you, Luka, because I knew, somehow, that I would get a chance to make you pay for what you did."

I have a moment of clarity, and I see the look of triumph on Tyco's face, and the long, sharp blade moving slowly toward me until the tip is against my neck.

"Tyco, please," I manage, and then I'm gone again.

I hear music, a great orchestra playing some jubilant concerto, and the sound is coming from Tyco. Every time he opens his mouth, the orchestra starts again.

He's going to plunge that knife into you, any second now. He might have already done it, and you can't even feel it.

I grab on to that thought. I have to escape; I have to run.

I shove Tyco as hard as I can and watch him tumble over the couch, the cucumber—no, knife—clanging to the floor. I run into the kitchen, leaping onto the island unit and sprinting across to the front door, which I kick open before running out into the sunlight.

I did it, I think. *I escaped.*

I'm in a field of tall grass, running without effort. I feel so alive and so free, and the sunlight is so warm on my skin.

Sunlight? I think. *Wasn't it snowing?*

And then I'm back in the living room. Tyco is still standing in front of me with the cucumber pressed against my throat.

I imagined the whole thing; I didn't escape at all, haven't even moved.

"Shit," I say, and my voice comes out as a low, long, slow-motion sound.

"Why don't you beg?" Tyco asks, that sneer on his face making him look like a Smiler.

The rat tunnel, the homeless village, the river, I think. *You survived all that just to die at the hands of Tyco Roth. You should have just left him in his cell.*

I'm not going to beg, no matter how high I am, no matter how suggestible I am. Instead I close my eyes. If I'm going to die, I might as well enjoy the fantasy that kept me sane for so many long days and nights in the Loop.

I'm walking along the riverside on a beautiful summer's day. The sound of the water is so vivid and clear that when I turn my head, I'm not surprised to see the crystal-clear river flowing lazily by. I can feel the fine, soft grass between my toes and the perfect heat of the sun on my shoulders. There are people here, dozens of people: families playing games, couples rubbing sunscreen on each other, girls and boys swimming in the quietest parts of the river, and vendors selling ice cream. I feel fingers interlace with mine; I look down at the hand that has grasped mine and smile.

I want to stay here. I'm going to stay here, with Wren.

I look into her beautiful face, and it's not Wren; it's Kina.

Of course it's Kina. Of course that's the way it should be. My love for Wren wasn't love at all, I see that now; it was a combination of impossible loneliness coupled with her wonderful kindness. I knew nothing about her other than that she's pretty and nice; that was never an equation that had any right to add up to love.

Love is made of more complex things: invisible strings, unwritten words, magnets, and glue and atoms.

Am I in love with Kina?

Not yet.

But I would have fallen in love with her, given time, given a little bit more life. I took the first steps on a route mapped out by fate. But now that same fate has led me down a different path, to my death.

There is some sense of loss, far, far in the background, but what I really want to do is see Kina again, for real, not just in this made-up world where everything is perfect and I'm not about to die at the hands of a man who lost his mind a long time ago.

As I think about Tyco, I can hear his voice far above me. I look up toward the source of the sound and see his face in the sun, smiling triumphantly.

"Oh, shut up, will you?" I say. "Just let me enjoy this place."

He fades away, and the sun returns.

"Come on," Kina says.

And we walk, hand in hand, along the riverbank. I know that this is the last journey I will ever go on, I know that any second the world will fade to black and it will all be over, but I don't mind. I don't mind. I'm happy.

Being dead isn't so bad.

It's quiet, peaceful. You worry about nothing and feel contentment all the way down to your soul.

"What did he say?" a voice asks.

"Something about being dead isn't so bad?"

I don't know who these voices belong to, but they don't bother me. I'm in a wide-open space, infinity in all directions, nothing but white light surrounding me. I'm weightless, burdenless, blissful.

"He's out of his damned mind," one of the voices comes again.

"I know what that's like."

"Shit yeah—evil stuff, evil, evil stuff."

"Get the patch off him; maybe we can shorten his trip."

These are the voices of who? Angels? Gods? Is this heaven? Have I been here for thousands of years or only a few minutes?

"Wow, he's deep in it," one of the angels says.

"Kid, I'm not a damned angel; you're just way below the surface."

It's like these angels are replying to my thoughts.

"You're speaking out loud, kid. And your towel's come undone; I can see your junk."

These words don't really make sense to me. I'm certain there are no towels in heaven.

"Dear god, he actually believes he's dead."

The voices sound older, like adults, one of them may even be elderly.

"Excuse me!" one of the angels says. "Who are you calling elderly?"

This is all too confusing; heaven is not at all what I thought it would be. I decide to try sleeping; maybe when I wake up I'll be able to make sense of this whole afterlife business.

The first thing I'm aware of is the fact that I'm naked.

I open my eyes, and I'm in darkness. I can't remember if I'm alive or dead, if Tyco killed me, if the riverside was real, if the voices I heard in the place that I thought was heaven were real.

I'm under blankets in a comfortable bed. My head is thumping, and my throat is dry. I must be alive; it would be wholly unfair for the dead to be able to feel this bad.

My eyes begin to adjust to the dim light from the window.

Immediately, I know that I'm still in Tyco's house. I can tell from the size of the room—it's enormous. A VR-gaming rig takes up a lot of floor space, and it's still got more room than anyone could ever need.

Someone has left a set of clothes at the foot of the bed, folded in a neat pile.

I try to think, but the pounding ache in my head makes it almost impossible. Did Tyco change his mind? Was it all a hallucination, and he never intended to kill me?

I get out of bed and stare at the pile of clothes. *Tyco's*. I debate whether or not I should put them on, but in the end I decide that if he's waiting out there to kill me, I'd rather face him fully dressed than completely naked.

I put the clothes on—they're too big, but they're better than nothing—and open the bedroom door. I'm on the mezzanine level of Tyco's house again, looking down into the living room, where two ladies sit on the couch talking and drinking from steaming cups. I recognize the voices right away; they belong to the angels, the entities I heard when I was drugged up.

"We're taking this with us, by the way," one angel says, pointing to the gas canister that Tyco had used to boil water. She looks to be in her early fifties, hair beginning to gray. She's skinny and is wearing a thick green cardigan. "I know it's only been a few days, but I need coffee back in my life."

"Agreed," the other replies. She's younger, maybe early twenties, with brown hair and freckles.

They're either Naturals or Alts—it's hard to tell from here, but they're both very beautiful, despite the fact that they're obviously clones.

The older of the two looks up, and her eyes meet mine. I notice that she's wearing a black sweatband low around her forehead.

"Ah, Sleeping Beauty is up," she says, putting her mug down on the table and standing. "Come down, boy."

"Who are you?" I ask, my voice sounding weak and distant.

"The people who saved your life," green-cardigan angel says, and smiles theatrically.

The younger woman stands up. She too is wearing a sweatband around her head. "I'm Day Cho, and this is my mother, Shion."

"What do you mean you saved my life?" I ask.

"Just how it sounds," Shion says. "And we're going to do it again. We've searched this house top to bottom and thrown all your Ebb down the drain. Time to get sober, boy; the end of the world is here."

"*My* Ebb?" I say, still confused by this scenario. Who are these people? What happened? "It's not my Ebb. Wait, you're not making sense."

"Hey, come on now. We're all the same; we're all addicts, clones. If ever there was a time to get help, it's now. Do you even know what's going on out there? Did you even know that a Blinker was about to cut your throat?"

"Blinker?"

Shion turns to her daughter and raises her eyebrows. "Dear lord, he's a real tweaker—clone for sure."

"I'm not a clone," I say, rubbing at my tired eyes. I hold up both my hands. "I'd never even tried Ebb until . . . Look, can you please just explain what happened?"

"We've been looking for other survivors," Day says. "Others like us, like you. When the power went out, those of us who were on Ebb started taking more. What else was there to do? Without the Lens and our virtual worlds, how were we supposed to get through the day? My mother and I have been clones for years now, always talking about getting clean, but you know how easy that is to say and how difficult it is to do. If we hadn't tried to quit on that day—the day that the Blinkers came—if we weren't sober on that day, then we'd be dead."

I try to keep up with Day's story, try to make sense of it in my head. How did they survive the attack? How were they immune to the chemical that turned everyone else into killers?

Shion takes over. "You do know that everyone has been turned into a sort of murdering human drone, don't you? We think it was the rain—somehow they poisoned it. My husband, Day's father, attacked me on that first morning. Day managed to get him off me and stood between us. He wouldn't attack her; it was as if he remembered who she was, but not me—he wanted me dead. We got out into the street and saw what had happened: thousands of people killing one another, bodies falling from buildings, kids beating one another to death, packs of them roaming around murdering whoever they found. The packs were all families—always a mother or a father and their kids, never two parents. It took us a while to realize that they don't kill their own blood. I'm sorry, this probably all sounds like sci-fi nonsense to you. How in the hell did you survive when you've been out of your head on Ebb throughout all of this?"

"That's what I've been trying to tell you," I say. "I didn't take that Ebb; I was drugged."

Day and Shion share a look of doubt, a look that says *junkies will make any excuse.*

"Right," Day says. "And who drugged you?"

"The guy with the knife."

"Blinkers aren't that smart," Shion says, shaking her head. "They don't make plans; they just stalk and kill."

"He wasn't a . . . Blinker," I say, using their term for the Smilers. "He was like me; he took the Delay."

"Delay? Kid, now you're the one who's not making any sense."

"I was a prisoner in the Loop. The day before the war started, we were taken to the Facility so they could run tests on us. We think that they injected us with some sort of cure or immunity to the chemical. Me and a few others survived and managed to escape. The guy that was about to kill me was an inmate too."

"Wait, hold on, you were in the Loop?" Shion asks.

"Yes," I say.

"And they ran tests on you?"

"Every six months," I tell her.

"Jesus," Day whispers.

"And they tried out some sort of vaccination on you?" Shion continues.

"I think so, yes."

Shion paces the room and then stops. "You're telling me that guy we killed wasn't a Blinker?"

"No. You killed him?"

"Yes," Day says with no hint of remorse. "Well, we shot him six times, and he ran, but I doubt he got very far."

"You killed him? Just like that? No second thought?"

"Listen," Shion says, pointing a finger at me, "this is no time for morals; it's kill or be killed, and that's all there is to it. If you want to survive, you better get good at taking people out before they take you out."

"But he wasn't even—"

"He was still going to murder you; that basically makes him one of them," Shion interrupts me.

"He ran?" I ask.

"Don't worry, kid. I hit him clean in the chest at least twice, and I think another caught him in the throat. I don't care what technology he's full of, he isn't surviving that," Shion says, grinning.

"He was . . . He could have been . . . He had every right to want to kill me. I don't blame him."

"You know, a thank-you wouldn't go amiss," Shion says, sitting back down on the couch and shaking her head. "We save this guy's life, and he's concerned about karma or some shit."

I sit down too, shaken by the thought of Tyco's life coming to an abrupt end. I try to push it from my mind. "How come you two aren't Smilers?" I ask, my voice hoarse from coughing.

"Is that what you call them?" Shion asks. "We call them Blinkers."

"Me and my mom," Day says, "we were on Ebb when it happened; so were thousands of others. It seems like the drugs stopped the chemicals in the rain from turning us. Thank god we weren't mixing with Crawl, or we'd have been taken out for sure."

"Ebb making people immune is a pretty big flaw in the plan," I say. "Whoever did this failed to fix a major issue. Clones make up about ten percent of the population."

"Twelve percent," Shion says. "But why fix something that will fix itself? It's not as though clones can defend themselves. Easy prey for the Blinkers, and even if they're not killed by the infected, they'll eventually kill themselves. Besides that, you're missing an even bigger flaw in their plan."

"And what's that?"

"Why bother turning the population into killers?" Day says. "Why not just kill us all? If you have the ability to drop biological weapons from the sky—and your goal is to wipe everyone out—why bother wasting your time with mind-altering chemicals? Why not just drop poison?"

"I hadn't thought of that," I admit.

"Well, we've thought about it and come up with no good reason."

I nod. "So what happens now?"

"We're gathering up as many of the survivors as we can before it's too late. We're getting them all in one location, getting them clean, and then we're preparing," Day tells me.

"Preparing for what?" I ask.

"Whatever comes next."

"You don't think this is the endgame?"

"No way," Shion says, laughing. "Ask yourself: Why do people start wars? They do it for money, land, religion, or revenge. Seeing as there's only about three cults left in the world and we're all ruled by one government, I doubt it's religion or revenge. That leaves money or land—either way, whoever did this has to come and claim their prize."

"So, you're building an army?"

"Yeah, an army of junkies. Good plan, huh?" Day says, smiling for the first time.

"What if there's a chance we can cure the Smilers . . . the Blinkers?"

Shion laughs. "And how, exactly, would we do that?"

"After we found our families, my friends and I talked about getting to the Facility—the place where they injected us with the vaccine—maybe they have a cure there."

"You and your friends?" Shion asks, raising an eyebrow. "Friends like the guy who was about to cut your throat?"

I'm about to tell them the short version of how Tyco came to loathe me when Day begins to breathe heavily, and her eyes roll back in her head.

"Mom, Mom, it's happening again, Mom."

Shion moves over to her daughter and holds her close. "It's okay, baby; it's all right."

"What's happening?" I ask.

"It's part of the withdrawal process. Coming off Ebb isn't easy—takes its toll on the body."

Day is convulsing now, twitching violently, foamy spit dribbling from her lips.

"Is she going to be okay?" I ask, getting to my feet.

"You're going to be fine, baby; you're going to be just fine," Shion says, stroking her daughter's hair.

The convulsions begin to slow, and Day's eyes return to their normal position.

"Just give me a quarter patch, Mom. I'll come off it slowly, a quarter a day for a few days, Mom, please," Day is mumbling, not quite herself yet.

"You know we can't do that, Day; we have to get clean as quick as possible."

"Mom, please, please, I don't think I can keep going like this. I think it's going to kill me if I don't have a little, just a little bit."

"No, Day, you listen to me: I'm going to be strong for you when you're weak, and you're going to be strong for me when I'm weak, do you understand? It took the end of the fucking world for us to get clean; I'm not going back now."

As Shion speaks, the lines around her eyes grow deeper. She's fighting off her emotions and her instinct to give in to her daughter's requests.

Day stares angrily up at her mother, the muscles in her jaw clenching and relaxing, clenching and relaxing until her expression turns to one of knowing and resignation. "You're right, you're right. We can beat this."

"It'll get easier, baby; it'll get easier, I promise. We're over the worst of it now."

Day's eyes fill with tears, and she cries quietly in her mother's lap.

"Do you really think there's a cure?" Shion asks, staring at me with an equal mix of doubt and hope in her eyes.

"I don't know," I say. "But it's our best bet. Either way, I've got to get to my family first."

"Your family?" Shion repeats. "Listen, friend, if your family is unlucky enough to still be alive, they'll be Blinkers."

"I know that," I say. "But I can't just give up on them."

Shion nods. "We're staying here tonight," she says. "Day's too weak to get through that snow."

We spend the night in the house, all of us sleeping in the living room, taking turns staying awake and making sure that no one tries to get in. The snow falls all night, piling up against the house. It gets so cold that even though we're indoors, I can still see my breath in front of me.

On three separate occasions during the night, I catch myself thinking about how I felt when I was high on Ebb: the sense of invincibility, the absolute immersion inside my own imagination, the feeling of being completely free from the restrictions of my body. Now I know why they ran all those ads over and over again, why every third Barker Projection was a government-issued warning about the dangers of Ebb, starring the Overseer himself, Galen Rye. *Patch up, patch out. Ebb is a road to ruin.*

I watch the sun rise slowly through the large front window of Tyco's home on the east side of the city; it illuminates the Black Road Vertical, where I grew up—now rising out of a seven-foot bank of snow that covers the homeless village around it.

Memories of my dad appear in my mind: watching centuries-old movies, fixing up thrown-out tech to make our own VR units, him reading stories to Molly and me when we were barely old enough to remember. I stare at the tower block, the top now hidden by low-hanging clouds, which still spew out snow relentlessly. I will make it to them today, one way or another.

"This is part of it," a voice says from behind me. "This is a part of the grand plan."

Startled, I turn around. Day is behind me, wearing only a baggy tank top and shorts but with a thick blanket over her shoulders.

"What do you mean?" I ask.

"The snow," she says, standing beside me. "I think whoever turned the people into monsters is now killing off the survivors with the weather."

"Why are they doing it like this?" I ask. "You're right: If they can send chemicals in the rain, why not just kill us quickly?"

Day shakes her head, still staring at the city through the window. "I don't know."

"If they have control of the weather, that means they have control of the government," I say.

"As One," Day says, unable to disguise the hatred in her voice.

"He was there," I say to myself, remembering Galen's presence in the Facility on the day of the mass Delay.

"What?" Day asks.

Thoughts swirl in my head, crazy notions about our own government turning on us, but I dismiss them. "Nothing," I reply.

"Wrap up warm," Shion says from behind us. "We're going to have to dig through this snow to get to the other survivors."

"Hey, listen, thanks for saving me and everything, but I've got to find my sister and my father."

Day studies me, her eyes full of sorrow. "Go," she says. "You have to go; you have to make sure they're safe. If there's even a one percent chance that they're alive, you have to go. Come find us when you're done."

I swallow hard. "Yeah, thanks," I say.

"Well, if you're going to be an idiot, I might as well wish you luck," Shion says. "Try not to die."

"Where are the survivors?" I ask. "So I know where to find you, if there is a cure?"

Shion turns to me, reaches out a hand, and places it over my forehead.

"What are you doing?" I ask, confused by her actions.

She gestures to Day, who finds a pen. Shion takes the pen and writes on the wall of the house:

Panoptic. We don't know who is listening/watching. Survivors are in a hidden vault beneath the financial district.

I read the note before Shion scribbles it out and wonder if they've been thinking the same thing. Has our own government turned on us? I turn to Shion and nod.

"Put this on," Shion says, taking her hand away from my

head and handing me a black sweatband similar to the ones they both wear. I put it on.

"We'll have to electrocute you before you come into our hiding place," Day says, smiling.

"Electrocute me?" I repeat. "Why?"

"We're pretty sure it'll short-circuit the Panoptic—not completely sure—and it might kill us, but we don't know who has control of our government, who can hack into the system. We don't want to make it easier for whoever is attacking us to find us."

I nod my head. "Great," I mutter. "Looking forward to it."

We raid the bedrooms of the big house and put on multiple pairs of socks, vests, T-shirts, underwear, gloves, hats, and jackets until we're sure we have the right level of protection from the elements but still enough mobility to run from the Smilers.

Shion returns from the garage with three shovels and hands one to me and one to Day.

"Let's get to it," she says.

Day opens the front door, and a cascade of powdery white snow pours onto the hardwood floor of the hallway, pushing us back five paces.

"What direction you headed?" Shion asks.

"East," I say. "Black Road Vertical. You?"

"West."

"Right," I say, suddenly sad to be parting ways with the angels who saved my life. "Good luck, okay? I'll see you soon."

"Yeah, maybe," Shion replies as she begins to dig a tunnel into the snow.

Day puts a hand on my shoulder and smiles. "Good luck, Luka."

I watch as the mother and daughter dig through the thick whiteness until they're gone, and then I get to work on my own tunnel.

I dig for hours, several times coming across a half-dead Smiler buried in the snow, teeth still bared in that senseless grin, still blinking, their lips turned blue from the cold, their eyes blood-red from burst veins, their groping fingertips black as they try, with their last reserves of energy, to kill.

I dig around, unable to bring myself to kill them.

I cut through the snow, on and on until I can no longer feel my hands or my feet. I try not to think about Wren, alone and locked in a prison cell, arm severed at the shoulder, infected with whatever chemical our enemies dropped from the sky, sick with drone poison, her mind lost in another world.

It's too much to hope that she's still alive, I think, and have to bite down to suppress the pain that comes with the thought. My mind flashes back to my Ebb hallucinations. The revelation that I was never truly in love with Wren. *Is that true?* I ask myself, and then push the thought down. Now is not the time. I have to focus on my sister, on my father.

Without thinking, my hand rises to my heart. My still-beating heart. And despite the hopelessness I feel, I smile, knowing that Kina is still alive.

I dig my way onward through the wall of white.

An hour or two later, the snow stops falling as suddenly as it began, and the clouds disappear as though blown by a great invisible force. And for some reason, this dramatic change hits me harder than the endless snow. It's all futile—whoever is attacking us has control of the weather. Why am I even doing this? What do I expect to find if I make it to my old home? My dad and sister waiting patiently for me? Smiling at me and offering me a cup of tea? Hugging me and telling me they figured it all out, they have a cure, and the war is over?

My swelling emotions are cut short by a humming electrical sound. I feel dizzy, and it takes a second to realize that the ground is rumbling beneath my feet. The snow that is piled up either side of me begins to cascade down, and the walls of my tunnel crumble and cave in on me.

There is an explosion of wet snow, and I dive backward as a City Train bursts through one wall of my tunnel, inches in front of me, and then crashes through the next wall in a split second.

I lie watching in disbelief as the train thunders by. "I guess the power is back on," I say, my voice hollow and monotone, shocked at how close I just came to being obliterated by a speeding train.

A few seconds later, when the train is out of sight, I can hear music from car radios, the whir of electronics, and voices from Barker Projectors across the city. Somehow the sounds of all these electronics without the sounds of humanity make the city feel even more unnerving, like a ghost town.

I get to my feet and continue to dig. It only takes ten more minutes before I stand at the foot of the gargantuan Black

Road Vertical. I look up, and the summit appears to come to a pinpoint high up in the clouds. The sheer scale of the building gives me vertigo.

I pull open the front door of the Vertical, having to haul it against the piled-up snow beneath the canopy. I step inside, and I'm hit by a wave of memories. The stone staircases where Molly and I used to play games, using our imaginations to save galaxies, flying spaceships through star systems, fighting off armies of goblins, and holding imaginary concerts where we were the stars.

I breathe a sigh of relief that the power has come back as I press the up button on the wall beside the bank of three elevators. A crunching, grinding sound comes from somewhere far up the elevator shaft, and the light on the up button goes out.

"Of course," I mutter. "One hundred and seventy-seven floors."

I stand in the middle of the lobby and look at the abyss of stairs that rises up and up.

I walk over and take the first step on a long journey upward.

I have to stop several times on my way to the 177th floor, but after what must be a bit more than two hours, I arrive.

The graffiti that used to be here has been covered by new graffiti, new tags, new images, but it's the same old corridor, same old doors with the same old numbers.

I walk slowly, my legs burning from the climb. I walk past apartment 177/07, where Jax and Janto used to live, past 177/19, where old Mr. Key stayed until he was evicted by the residents who found out he was siphoning extra water from the rain collector. I move on until I reach apartment 177/44, my old house.

I twist the door handle and expect to feel resistance, but the door is unlocked and swings open into the dark apartment with a long, loud creak.

I wait outside in the corridor for a while, staring into my old home. My hands are shaking, and my breathing is unsteady. I never dared to believe I would ever see this place again.

I step inside, and the first thing I recognize is the smell. It's the smell of home, *my* home, and it brings with it a million images of my childhood: my parents, my friends, times I laughed, times I cried, arguments, and the desperation of our situation that—even though I was a child—I felt every day.

"Hello," I call, and feel silly for doing it—what was I expecting, a friendly reply?

I move farther in, past the open bathroom door where our tiny shower takes up one corner, pipes snaking out the window to the rain collector. There's no one in the bathroom, but the windowsill brings back memories of the time Molly fell and hit her head while we were playing hide-and-seek.

I step back into the short corridor, my heart racing in horrible anticipation of seeing the long-dead carcass of my sister, my dad, or both.

I move into the living room. Nothing has changed in the years I've been away—it's the same cramped room with the same threadbare furniture and stained carpet. There's no one in here, no one in the adjacent kitchen either.

There are only two rooms left: my parents' bedroom and the room my sister and I used to share.

I start with my parents' bedroom, the room in which my mother died, the room the Marshals—paid for by Tyco's family—burst into before dragging me to the courthouse to be judged and sentenced to death by Happy.

I open the door and feel the early evening air rushing through the open window, and I see someone sitting on the bed, staring out over the city. I recognize the shape of him straightaway.

"Dad," I say, my voice cracked and on the verge of breaking.

Slowly, he turns around, and his blinking eyes meet mine. The wide, mad smile on his face doesn't change as he sees me.

I try to fight against the horror of seeing my dad this way, try to brace myself for the attack, try to move, to slam the door and run, but I'm frozen.

My dad doesn't move from the bed—instead he slowly turns back to the window and stares out at the destroyed city.

My heart is racing once again, the way it raced when I was climbing all those steps, the way it raced when I first realized that Wren was trying to kill me. Why isn't he attacking me?

. . . *it took us a while to realize that they don't kill their own blood.* Shion had said that when she still thought I was an Ebb user.

If he won't attack me because I'm blood-related to him, then surely that means he remembers me on some level? Surely.

"Dad," I say again, stepping into the room and standing beside the bed. I look into his blinking eyes as I crouch beside him. "It's me, Luka, your son."

His eyes seem to look through me, and then they return to the open window. I put my hand on his and feel how cold he is. He must have been sitting here while the snow was falling, the cold air chilling him to the bone. I close the window and wrap the blanket from the bed around him.

I sit down and stare out at the city with him. We watch the moon climb up into the sky for a while. I look over to the bedside table and see the necklace that my mother used to wear; he bought it for her from the Junk Children years and years ago for two Coin.

I feel the tears swimming in my eyes and blink them back.

"Do you remember me?" I ask. "You're my dad; you raised me. Do you remember?"

"He doesn't know who you are," a voice replies from the doorway.

I get to my feet and fall back against the wall.

"Who the hell are you?" I ask, looking around for a weapon to defend myself against the skeletal woman leaning against the doorframe.

"God, Luka, you look worse than I feel."

I stare at her and see that she's not a woman—she's a girl, a few years younger than me. And then I recognize those eyes. She's grown up, grown up beyond her fourteen years. She looks gaunt, her skin gray, hair lank and overgrown. But those eyes—I'd recognize them anywhere.

"Molly?"

She doesn't say anything, just walks away, disappearing back into the bedroom that we used to share when we were kids.

I follow her, in utter shock that she's alive and uninfected.

I open the door to our old room. Molly sits on one of the two twin beds, takes a handful of something out of her pocket, and opens the top drawer of the small chest beside her bed. She puts all but one of the small, clear, plastic strips inside and peels the back off the one in her hand.

I recognize the patch as Ebb and try to get to her before she can stick it to the base of her neck, but I'm too late.

"Molly, wait!" I say, striding across the room to remove the drug from her.

She turns onto her stomach and fights me off as the chemicals seep into her body. When the process is complete, she rolls onto her back and smiles up at me.

"You left me," she whispers, and then laughs. "You went away. Bye, Luka. Should have been me. Should have been me. I killed the boy."

"Dammit, Molly," I say, unable to believe that she has turned herself into a clone. "Why did you do that?"

"I'm going now, Luka. Glad you're alive, glad you're free."

"No!" I shout at her. "No, wake up, you stay awake. Molly, this isn't you."

I grab the Ebb strip, rip it off her neck, and throw it to the floor, but she is gone, lost in a world that she is constructing in her own mind, escaped from this desolate place to somewhere better. And for a moment, I can't blame her, I can't fault her logic. I look to the drawer where she keeps her stash of Ebb, and I think how easy it would be to disappear with her, to just give up and wait to die in a place more beautiful than this.

I can't, though; I can't do it, I can't quit. Kina's out there, and Wren and Igby and Pod—if they're still alive—and my dad is infected, but he's still my dad, and there might be a cure in the Facility, and Molly is right here in front of me.

I know what I have to do; I have to get Molly to the vault with Day and Shion and the other clones. They can help her. And then I'm going to the Facility—alone if need be—to find a cure for my dad.

I go back to the other room, where my dad still sits motionless, staring out the window. I say goodbye, wrap the blankets tighter around him, and promise I'll come back for him.

I go to Molly. I rip a strip of material from one of her old dresses and wrap it around her head to hide her Panoptic camera, pick her up off her bed, and carry her out into the corridor.

I make it down the first flight of stairs and stop. The sound of footsteps is reverberating up the old concrete staircase toward us. And another sound, a humming buzz that is changing pitch as it gets closer.

I lean forward to look over the banister and see two people—both dressed in black—standing on drone-risers, gliding rapidly up toward me. Below them, more soldiers, maybe fifty of them, all carrying USW guns or Deleters.

A snarled command echoes up from below. "Inmate 9-70-981 was last seen on floor 177. Units 44 and 45, ascend to 177; the rest of you check each floor and guard all exits. Capture the target alive."

"*As One*," comes the barked reply in unison.

"What the hell?" I whisper to myself as the footsteps grow louder and the drone-risers' ascending note reaches a crescendo.

I turn and run back the way I came, carrying Molly in my arms and taking the steps two at a time, my legs cramping with the effort, sweat spilling down my temples.

I pass floor 177 and continue up. "What the hell, what the hell, what the fuck!" I ramble as I run.

Put Molly on the roof, I think, *hide her behind the rain collector.*

I hear the soldiers on the drone-risers stop at the 177th floor and begin kicking doors in, announcing their presence as *Tier Three Soldiers*, and yelling commands for any inhabitants to *lie facedown with your palms on the floor.*

I keep moving, my mind firing questions: *Who are they? Why are they after me? How do they know I'm here?*

I make it to the 200th floor, every muscle in my body screaming at me to quit. I ignore the pain and run to the end of the corridor. The last door on the left is a smaller entrance with a skinny wooden door. I kick it open and ascend the narrow steps to the roof.

The cold air soothes my burning lungs as I carry Molly's limp body to the rain collector and put her carefully down on the ground; then I run back toward the door. I have to get to my dad before the soldiers do.

I stop before I make it down the narrow staircase.

I can hear them coming, hear their boots against the cheap vinyl floor, hear their yelled commands. They're getting closer.

I back up and run to Molly, crouching down beside her,

waiting and hoping that they won't come up here. I will my dad to hide, to run, to find a way out.

The wind blows cold and hard this high up. The pipes leading from the rain collector rattle together, and Molly moans in her unconscious state.

And then the soldiers appear. The two who rode drone-risers up to the 177th floor. Their boots crunch on the gravel of the roof as they scan the area.

As their faces turn toward me, I see that the taller one of the two has glowing eyes. Not in the way that all Alts do, but glowing as though there is a tiny but powerful bulb in each eye socket, and here, in the moonlight, they look like car headlights on full beam.

I've seen this before, on the first day out of the Loop—the soldier who wasn't carrying a weapon had the same glowing eyes.

"What the fuck?" I whisper, a sliver of steam rising up from my breath.

Headlight-Eyes turns toward me, his movements stiff. I try to duck out of the way, but those lights fall on me.

"Don't move," he says, his voice horrifyingly serene.

I stand and move away from Molly, hoping that they somehow won't notice her.

"All right, all right," I say, holding my hands up above my head. "Don't shoot." But I see that Headlight-Eyes isn't carrying a gun.

I back up, trying to keep the rain collector between me and the soldier, trying to keep Molly out of their sight, but there's nowhere else to go as my foot reaches the edge of the building. I turn and look down into the never-ending fall and a sense of vertigo, of recollection and dislocation hit me all at once. The last time I was here, Tyco's brother was in this exact same spot.

The tall soldier turns stiffly to his partner, the glow from his bizarre eyes temporarily sweeping away from me. He gives him a nod.

"Stay where you are!" the second soldier cries, and I'm almost relieved to hear the panic in his voice—I was becoming unnerved by the calm nature of Headlight-Eyes.

"Don't shoot," I say again.

"Oh no, no, no," he says, letting go of the USW so that it hangs by his side and pulling out a tranquilizer gun. "You weren't put into the Battery Project for nothing. We'll be taking you alive, Inmate 9-70-981."

He lifts the tranquilizer gun higher until it's aiming right at my chest. I close my eyes and wait for the darkness.

I hear a scream and open my eyes.

I see the soldier with the tranquilizer grabbing for his throat—blood pouring between his fingers as a Smiler silently lets a chunk of flesh fall from his mouth.

The soldier with the glowing eyes watches, an interested expression on his face. He does not move to help or call for backup. He simply watches.

It's only when the bleeding soldier falls to his knees that I realize the Smiler is my dad.

I open my mouth to say something, to call out to him, but

my words are silenced by the high-pitched wail of a USW gun. The dying soldier had managed to get ahold of his weapon and fire one last round.

"No!" I scream as my father falls lifeless to the gravel. The dying soldier looks desperately to his bright-eyed superior, a hand stretching out, begging for help. And then he too falls still.

Headlight-Eyes turns to me and marches robotically forward. He closes the gap between us; the light from his eyes turns orange as he scans me up and down. "You are prisoner 9-70-981. Luka Kane, sixteen years old. You are reserved for the Battery Project."

I feel dazed, like I've been awoken from a deep sleep. "What's the Battery Project?" I ask, my mind spinning.

The soldier's lights turn white again. "Hands behind your back, prisoner," he states, but before he can engage the magnetic cuffs, my dad has climbed to his feet, half of his face distorted and bulging from the USW round. The sound of his footsteps in the puddles of the rooftop gets the soldier's attention. He turns and tilts his head, making no attempt to defend himself. My dad tackles the soldier around the waist and they both tumble over the edge of the building. The lights from the soldier's eyes spin and fade, blinking downward like a disappearing lighthouse, until they're gone.

I stand there in the silence, unable to comprehend what I've just witnessed.

"No," I whisper.

The sounds of dozens more soldiers storming up to the roof

lets me know that my dad's death was pointless. Soon these soldiers will find me and take me away to be a part of the Battery Project—whatever the hell that is—and then they'll kill Molly, and all of this will have been for nothing.

I walk over to my sister and sit down beside her.

"I tried, Molly. I tried."

I can hear them, the soldiers dressed in black, running along the corridor below me, closing in, desperate to get to me, to capture me, to take me away. I try to comprehend what has just happened, try to work out why that soldier had glowing eyes, try to come to terms with my dad's death, but I can't.

They're getting closer now. There's nowhere to hide up here, nowhere to run.

"Luka!" a voice calls from behind me.

I know that this is a hallucination, some kind of auditory mirage, because it sounds just like Kina.

"Luka, get in!"

But god, it sounds so real . . . too real.

I turn around to see Kina leaning out of a Volta Category 8. Igby is behind the wheel of the flying car, and Malachai, Pander, and Blue are in the back.

"What . . . what . . ."

"Today, Luka!" Malachai calls out.

I grab Molly and run to the edge of the building. I pass my sister across to Kina just as the soldiers appear behind me.

"Freeze!" one of them yells.

I turn and see three soldiers with those bright, blazing eyes.

300

I jump. Igby pulls away the minute my feet land in the back of the vehicle. We lurch away so violently that I almost fall straight back out again, but Kina grabs my arm and pulls me in. For a second, our faces are so close that I can feel her breath on my lips.

I turn and look back to the Vertical. The three soldiers with the bright eyes stare up at us as we move away. They just watch, still, almost curious. Then five more soldiers join them—these ones have normal Alt eyes and they carry weapons. They aim their rifles at us, but the bright-eyed soldier who stands at the edge of the building holds up a hand, halting their fire. As his eyes glow orange, the sound of the vehicle's engine dies completely, and the lights of the dashboard fade out.

"No! What? No!" Igby cries, slamming his palm against the dashboard and pressing his thumb against the fingerprint starter over and over again. "It's dead. I don't know how but they've killed the engine."

And then the lights come back on, and the electric whir of the engine fires back up. Happy's voice comes over the speakers. "Emergency protocol initiated."

"Emergency protocol? Fucking emergency protocol?" Igby shrieks.

"What does that mean?" Malachai demands.

"They have control; those weirdo, light-eyed fucks have control. They're going to glide this car right to them!"

"What do we do?" Kina asks as the car begins to turn slowly back toward the Vertical.

"Fuck it," Igby says, and climbs under the dashboard, ripping a panel out and tugging out a zip-tied bunch of wires. "I'd rather crash land the goddamned thing than go anywhere near those freaks!"

One small electric shock later and the car's engine once again dies.

"Well, that's that. We're going to put this thing down with no power. We have about three minutes," Igby says, and then turns to me, with a big smile on his face. "Hi, Luka, how the hell are you?"

I can't reply. My mind is replaying my dad disappearing over the edge of the Vertical again and again.

I shake my head, trying to clear it, as the eerie silence of the car fills my senses. I glance at Kina, Pander, and Malachai sitting opposite me, my sister draped across their laps. I notice that they too are covering their Panoptic cameras with various hats and strips of material.

I look out of the window and see the city is filled with soldiers, hundreds of them, moving toward Midway Park in the center of town.

I turn back to my friends. "How did you know where I was?" I manage.

"Well, for a while there we thought you'd become one of the Missing, but then Kina remembered you used to live in the Black Road Verts," Igby says, his voice strained as he fights to aim the drifting vehicle using only the ailerons to bank it. "When we saw the fucking light show, we figured we better get there swift."

"Honestly, we didn't think you were still alive," Kina says, that one-sided smile growing on her face. "I'm glad you are."

I want to smile back, but those lights, spinning down into the blackness, taking my dad with them, are all that fill my mind. I notice her left hand, the trigger still clasped tightly inside.

I reach over and take it from her, making sure that my thumb is pressed down on the button. Kina slowly opens and closes her hand.

"Thanks," she says, wincing against the pain.

I nod and turn toward Malachai. "Where the hell did you guys go?" I ask. "After the hospital?"

"We lost the Smilers. Hid in a Last Religion Church for most of the night. Then more of those soldiers came, some of them had those torch eyes; we moved to a pub and they came there too. We realized they were tracking us via our Panoptic cameras, so we covered them—I see you had the same idea. We decided to stick together while we looked for our families. When the power came back on, Igby left Pod with Akimi and came looking for us in this car. Where's Tyco?"

"Dead," I tell him.

I notice the faraway look in Pander's eyes. I look from her to Malachai, who shakes his head, and I know that when she found her sisters, they weren't alive.

I reach out and put a hand on Blue's shoulder, but he shrugs it off, still angry at me for what happened to Mable.

"All right," Igby calls over the rushing wind, "I'll put us down at the edge of the Red Zones so these morons won't follow. Hang the fuck on!"

I feel the vehicle dip and speed up as we hurtle toward the ground. My instinct is to look toward Kina. It had been my only wish, back when Tyco was about to kill me, to see her face one more time. At least it came tr—

"Put your seat belt on, moron!" she yells in my face.

"Right. Yeah," I say, shuffling over to Molly and sitting her up before struggling to click her seat belt into place with one hand. I move over to my own seat and pull the strap across my chest. I don't have time to push it into place. When I look, I see the snowy earth coming up to meet us.

I'm aware of pain.

Hot, burning pain in my right shoulder.

I open my eyes. My face is buried in snow. I've been thrown from the car.

The pain is growing, as though my body is slowly becoming aware that something is horribly wrong.

I manage to haul myself up to a sitting position, and I look down. A part of the car's door has sheared off, and a twisted shard of ragged metal is impaled through my right shoulder and part of my chest. I can feel blood spilling out, warm and fast.

I let my eyes follow a trickle of blood as it runs into my hand, where the trigger is gripped loosely between a thumb and one finger.

"No," I mumble, trying and failing to tighten my grip. Something has been severed in my arm: a tendon or a muscle, and I

304

can barely move my hand. As the blood lubricates the trigger, it begins to turn in my weak grip, spinning and sliding away.

"No, no, no," I say as I beg my hand to work.

The trigger slips farther still, revealing the button that will kill me if it comes loose.

I cry out in effort as I tell my brain to tell my hand to work. *Work, you useless piece of shit!*

And then the tube of metal falls to the mud.

I stop breathing as the red light turns green. I close my eyes and wait for death.

It doesn't come.

I open my eyes. The trigger is still lying there, in the mud and half-melted snow, the light green. And I'm still alive.

All this time, I think, remembering the hours of clasping that stupid trigger. *All this time, and I find out it's a dud just before I die anyway!*

Impulsively, I grab the fragment of metal that is embedded in my shoulder and pull. The pain intensifies, but my instincts tell me to remove it. I scream as it inches out of my body, scraping along bone and pulling at my torn flesh.

"Luka, are you okay?" Malachai's groggy voice comes from somewhere in the distance.

I pull and pull and pull, and finally, the piece of metal comes free from my shoulder, and I drop it down into the red snow. I turn my head and see a beautiful woman standing ten feet away from me.

"Hey, Mr. Kane. Over here, Mr. Kane," the woman calls to me. Tall and blonde, in the smallest bikini I could ever imagine.

She's smiling and winking at me, and I'm thinking that she's going to freeze to death.

"Mr. Kane, looking good, but you'd look even better in Dash-Seven, clothing for athletes."

And then she blows me a kiss and disappears. She was a Barker Projection, a holographic advertisement.

I can hear my friends dragging themselves from the wreckage of the car. I look over, and I see Kina and Blue getting to their feet, Pander and Malachai pulling Molly free, and Igby dusting shattered glass off himself. They're okay. I nod and smile to myself. They're okay. I might not be, but they're okay.

In the place of the bikini girl, a man appears.

"Mr. Kane," the tall, handsome projection says, "my name is Galen Rye. I'm the Overseer of Region 86. I don't want to preach, it's your life and you can make your own decisions, I just want you to be informed. Within one year of taking Ebb for the first time, your life expectancy drops to just four years. Patch up, patch out; Ebb is a road to ruin."

Something tries to fall into place in my mind, something important, but I'm reeling from the crash and the pain that is now growing in my shoulder. Shock begins to take control.

"Luka!" Kina is calling out my name, I hear her footsteps approaching fast, and she falls to her knees beside me, the moonlight reflecting in her eyes.

"Hi," I say, trying to smile through the pain.

"The trigger!" she cries, picking it up from the snow and looking at it. "Your heart?"

I shrug. "Guess I'm lucky."

"The sound it made, outside the city, three days ago. It must have been switching itself off."

"Great," I croak. "That would be good news if it wasn't for . . ." I look down to the hole in my chest.

"Let me look," she says, lifting my T-shirt to reveal the wound. "Oh, no."

"What is it?" I ask. "How bad?"

"It's . . . it's . . . it's . . . Wait, what the hell?"

"Kina, listen, if I'm not going to make it, I want you to know—"

"No, Luka, I think you're going to be okay."

"What?" I look down and see that the damaged fibers deep in the wound are knitting together.

"What the hell . . . ?" I say, repeating Kina's sentiment.

I feel nauseated watching the ripped veins reconnecting, the chipped bone regrowing, and the skin weaving itself together until the wound is nothing but smooth scar tissue.

"Please tell me you all saw that?" I whisper, looking up to see my friends circled around me.

"Luka . . . are you a freaking superhero?" Malachai asks, eyes wide.

"I don't think so," I say.

"Then please explain how you just healed yourself in thirty seconds flat."

"I . . . I can't."

"I think the same thing was happening to Akimi," Igby says breathlessly. "After you all left, and it was just her, Pod, Blue, and me, she started to feel better. By the time I left to find you guys, she was walking again."

"The Delay," Pander whispers, reaching down and grabbing a piece of shattered glass from the car's windshield. She digs the shard of glass into the palm of her hand.

"Pander, don't do that!" Kina demands, but she falls silent as Pander holds her palm up to the group. She wipes away the blood to reveal her uninjured hand.

"Why would they do that? Why would they make us heal faster?" I ask.

"I don't know," Igby replies, looking down at the trigger that still lies in the mud. "But I don't like the fact that the trigger didn't go off."

"Thanks a lot," I say.

"No, I mean, I'm glad you're alive, but I think there's a reason you're alive . . . and I don't think it's a fucking good reason."

I want to ask Igby to expand on his theory, but the Barker Projector fires up once more, and standing in front of us in perfectly rendered VR is Wren.

"What is this?" Malachai mutters, anger in his voice.

And then a familiar voice speaks.

"Luka Kane, Malachai Bannister, Woods Rafka, Kilo Blue, Kina Campbell, Pander Banks, Akimi Kaminski, Podair Samson, Igby Koh. This is a list of the living escapees of the Loop. You all have exactly one hour to make your way to Midway Park, or Wren Salter dies."

The image of Wren disappears, and all that's left in her place is the last of the melting snow.

"Why do they want *us*?" Blue asks.

"We have to go, right? We can't let Wren die," Malachai insists.

"Who are they? Why do they need us? Can't they just let us take our chances in the Red Zone or something?" Pander adds.

"I know who did this," I say, still staring at the spot where Wren's image was.

"What?" Kina asks. "Who was it?"

I turn back to the group. "Igby, can you get this car working again?"

"There are spare parts in the back. *If* I can get it done at all, it'll take a few hours."

"Get working on it," I tell him, and before I speak again, I remember that the Panoptic cameras are still recording sound. I pull my hat down lower, making sure that the camera is covered, and I write in the dirt of the cracked window of the crashed car.

Take my sister. Find Pod and Akimi. Get to the financial district. There is a group of survivors there in a hidden vault. Find them.

"And what about you?" Malachai asks, his eyes moving from the writing to mine.

"I'm going to kill Galen Rye."

There's silence among the former Loop inmates.

"Galen Rye?" Blue says. "Galen Rye wouldn't . . . What are you talking about? He's *our* Overseer; this is *his* Region."

"When I tried to escape the Facility, the guards were saying *As One* like soldiers replying to an order. Later, when they caught me, I recognized his voice. He was there during the Delay. Whoever has done this to us has access to the weather, the Barker Projectors, and our Panoptic cameras. I'm telling you . . . Galen Rye is behind all this, maybe the whole World Government."

"Good enough for me," Malachai says, stepping forward to join me. "I'm coming with you."

"Me too," Kina says.

"I get to kill him," Pander says. "For my sisters."

I nod.

"It can't be," Blue says, looking from one of us to the next. "He's the Overseer."

"We've all been tricked, kid," Malachai says. "It's not your fault."

Blue looks down at the ground, his small fists bunching up and then releasing. "I'm coming too."

I open my mouth to tell him he can't come, that he's too young, but his furious eyes meet mine.

"Don't you dare tell me I can't be there when that bastard dies. Don't you dare."

I nod my head. "All right."

"I wish I could be there," Igby says, smiling. "If you guys aren't shot to pieces within three seconds, make sure you kill him fucking slowly, okay?"

"Will do," Pander says, and then turns toward the center of the city. "Let's go."

The sounds of a large crowd in Midway Park can be heard from miles away; great yells and screams from the crowd and an amplified voice, muffled by the distance, ring out.

"Hey, if we ever see Pod again, remind me to make fun of him for being called Podair," Malachai says as we dash from building to building, trying not to be spotted by the few soldiers who still patrol the streets.

"Shh!" Pander hisses, and points forward.

Up ahead, three soldiers lean against a military tank, talking among themselves.

We move closer, circling around an antiques store to close the gap until we're close enough to hear them.

"Honestly, I don't care. Tier Three is better than nothing, and I'll follow that man to the grave after what he's done for me and my family," a skinny female soldier says, her gas mask hanging down at her chest as she leans her rifle against the tracks of the tank and turns back to the other two.

A young male soldier with a Mohawk nods emphatically. "Hey, look, I'm not complaining; believe me, I agree with you, Tier Three is like winning the lottery a thousand times over. I'm just saying, my friend Yawa, she earns four thousand Coin more than me per year, and she got into Tier Two. That's all I'm saying, it's an observation."

"Well, keep your observations to yourself," the oldest of the three says, spitting into the dusty street. "That kind of talk starts to sound a lot like treason."

Mohawk holds both hands up. "You guys need to calm down. I'm just saying that we must have been close to Tier Two, that's all."

"But we're Tier Three, so shut up about it," the woman says.

"Fine, fine, I'll shut—"

The man's head snaps back, his Mohawk whipping to one side, as a USW round hits him above the left eye.

I look around, trying to figure out what's just happened, and I spot Pander—she dashed over, snatched up the female soldier's gun, and fired before any of us or them had a chance to react. Now she's aiming it at the second, older man.

"Hold on a second," the man commands.

"Fuck you!" Pander screams as she shoots him. Then she swivels the gun and kills the woman before she can react.

The whole slaughter takes less than five seconds. In this moment, I don't know what to feel. Pander is thirteen years old, and here she is, so failed by the system and by the world that she is able to murder three people without thinking twice.

"That was . . . that was . . ." Malachai tries, but he too is lost for words.

"Let's go," Pander says, throwing the fallen soldiers' guns at each of us before taking the Lens from the older soldier's eye and activating the enormous tank.

We drive until we're close enough to see the park. There are maybe a thousand people crowded around a stage, where Galen Rye stands, his hands held aloft. Behind him, projected into the sky, is a fifty-foot holographic re-creation of Galen, ensuring that everyone gets a clear view of the man who killed millions of innocent people. He steps forward, and the crowd falls silent. When he speaks, his voice echoes through the silent city.

"In times of extreme jeopardy, extreme action is required,"

he intones, his voice amplified via the almost invisible patch-microphone stuck to his jawline. "Think not of what has been forced upon you as a sin; think instead that it is a necessity. You may be haunted for the rest of your days on this earth, but that is the price we all must pay so that our children and our children's children may live a good life, a life that they deserve."

The crowd cheers, a roar so animalistic that I'm surprised to look into the horde and see human faces. I see soldiers as young as fifteen and as old as fifty as they cheer and yell and hug one another.

Galen leans forward until his lips are almost pressed against the microphone. He speaks again: "What we have sacrificed, what we have given—so that the world can thrive—may be looked upon by the historians and the scholars of the future as a heinous act of self-preservation, and they will be right, my friends. Let's not pretend that we are morally pure, but without our sacrifices, our bravery, our ability to look history in the eye and say, *We had to do what we had to do*, there would be no future in which to scorn us!"

Standing behind Galen in a straight line are eight other Alts, all of them with the same glowing eyes as the soldiers atop the Black Road Vertical. *What is that?* I wonder. *A new Alt enhancement?* There's no time to consider it further, as the roar of the horde rises up to meet us. The crowd adores this man.

"What have they done?" Malachai whispers.

"The heartbreak is over, my friends, the culling of the world is finished, and we are the survivors; we are part of the two percent, the lucky few. Phase One is complete," Galen Rye yells, and as the crowd roars their appreciation, he holds his hands up to silence them. "Strike that," he says. "Phase One is *almost* complete."

He gestures offstage, and my heart skips a beat as Wren is marched to stand beside Galen. Walking alongside her is a soldier with a Deleter, the crescent-moon-shaped piece of technology that they use to execute inmates. The weapon is glowing with the power it possesses to break matter down into subatomic particles, Deleting whatever it comes into contact with. Keeping Wren in check with such an extreme weapon seems unnecessary—she looks so lost and confused that I'm not sure she knows what's going on. The only positive thing is that she is no longer a Smiler.

We were right, I think. *There is a cure.*

"Nine surviving escapees from the Loop," Galen continues, his voice echoing around the now-silent park, "plotting against us. Plotting to end the mission that we pledged to complete. And were they wrong to conspire? Ladies and gentlemen, no, they were not. You and I—had we been in their shoes—would have done the same thing. This is what we must remember if we are to keep our humanity: We act on our instinct to survive, and therefore we are all right and we are all wrong, we are all sinners and we are all virtuous; it all depends on what side of the line you stand. But this is the new world, and these people committed treason against us. Remind yourselves, my friends, that—had we not decided to take action—this overpopulated, overpolluted, overworked planet would have been drained of all resources, all habitable Regions, within ten years. We must set a precedent, and we must not falter. The nine must turn themselves in, and if they are truly righteous, they will. If they do not, this girl, the one who set them free, will die. This is a message, a benchmark, a line in the sand. We must be as one if we are to succeed."

There is a murmur among the crowd now, and for a second I dare to hope that they might push back against the Overseer's declaration, that he might have gone too far and a mutiny might follow, but the murmurs subside as he holds his hands up for silence once again.

"The nine escapees have twelve more minutes to turn themselves in."

My eyes move from the executioner gripping his Deleter to Wren, whose tired eyes scan the crowd, still unaware of what's going on or where she is. The crowd is not angry, they're not baying for blood; they are calm and resolute.

"What's the plan?" Kina asks.

"There's hundreds of them," Malachai says, the rage in his voice bubbling through.

"We have a tank," I point out, "and not much time. I say we get close and kill Galen. Whatever happens after that happens."

Malachai nods slowly. "Well, fuck it, it's not like we're going to live much longer anyway. Count me in."

"Me too," Kina says.

Blue nods.

"Sounds good," Pander adds.

I turn to Blue. "Blue, I'm sorry about what happened to Mable."

Blue bites his lip and looks right at me. "I'm sorry too," he says, his voice cracking as he smiles.

I nod, and Pander drives us toward the park.

Kina takes control of the sonic cannon, and I sit at the gun turret—we both have screens in front of us so we can see what we're aiming at from inside the tank.

The tank moves quietly through the streets. We sit side by side in silence, perfectly ready to die.

The snow has melted to a thin layer now. The sky is black and dotted with stars.

As we move onward, Kina reaches out a hand, and I take it. She smiles at me, and there's sadness in her eyes. I feel that sadness too, because when we die, so does all the potential of what we could have been together.

As we turn onto Midway Park Road, I can't help but think it would have been such a lovely evening if it wasn't for all the death and destruction.

"Here we go," Malachai says as we turn to face the back of the crowd.

The tank runs on a gravity engine and is so quiet that the only sound comes from the great metal treads rolling along the road.

Slowly, the people begin to realize that something is wrong and turn toward us. At first they don't panic—this is one of their own tanks—but when we don't slow down, when we drive right into the crowd, they scream and dive out of the way of the enormous vehicle. And then there's the sound of USW guns screeching through the air as the soldiers open fire. As their rounds hit us, we can feel the tank rock, but we don't move from our course.

We travel onward, through the parting crowd, waiting for the moment that Galen Rye falls into our sights.

Malachai begins to sing Pander's song, and he's smiling. I smile too. Pander joins in.

"I see him," Kina calls out, and at the same time I see him on my screen.

He looks shocked, surprised, and somehow delighted.

I adjust my sights, the crosshairs moving around the screen until I lock them on his smug face.

Then just as I'm about to pull the trigger, I see his eyes begin to glow bright, just like the soldiers standing behind him. That strange expression of glee melts from his face—in fact, all signs of life fall away. He is neutral, blank. His bright white eyes turn orange, and the tank falls still, my screen goes blank, and the sound of the electrics powering down fills the cockpit.

"What happened?" Kina yells, pulling at her trigger over and over to only the sound of an empty click.

"There's no power," Malachai says in a quiet voice.

We look at one another, the silence oddly comforting, almost funny. We shrug and grab our USW guns.

Kina opens the hatch and climbs onto the turret of the tank. Malachai and I follow suit, then Pander and Blue climb out and stand beside us.

We stand there, in the middle of the silent crowd, waiting for someone to speak, waiting for something to happen.

"Ladies and gentlemen," Galen says, smiling as the lights

fade from his eyes once again, "it appears that a few of the escapees have decided to turn themselves in." Pander raises her weapon until it's aiming at Galen. His smile widens. "Or perhaps not."

"What a way to go out," Malachai says, and smiles.

"I'm glad I met you, you guys," Kina says.

All five of us raise our guns to our shoulders. The bright-eyed soldiers behind Galen step forward. None of them carry weapons, but—as if the act of them stepping forward was some sort of signal—every soldier in the crowd readies their weapon for battle.

We stand there, a thousand guns pointed right at us, frozen in time for what feels like forever.

And then half the stage explodes in a fiery blast, followed quickly by another explosion in the crowd near the front.

Alts fly through the air, screaming and wailing, limbs torn off, blood spraying, flames engulfing them.

I lower my weapon and stare at the carnage, and then I hear the roar of an army. We turn to see hundreds of Regulars sprinting into the park, a few of them carrying USW guns, others with twenty-first-century machine guns that take ammunition, some with knives, bows and arrows, lumps of wood, or farming tools. At the front, there are about twenty of them on horseback, swinging great swords.

Someone screams a command, and a volley of arrows sails through the night sky and into the crowd of Alts to our right.

Somewhere among the charging army of Regulars, I see Woods Rafka, the old-school USW pistol from the Loop held in two hands as he fires bursts into the crowd. The rest are hundreds of faces that I don't recognize at all, and yet somehow I know that these are the Missing; these are the people who have been disappearing from the city year after year.

"Draw. Aim. Fire!" someone calls out again, and a second torrent of arrows flies into the sky.

And then all fifty or so of the archers shoulder their bows, draw knives, and dive into the battle.

I watch the arrows soaring through the sky; I watch them thunder into the Alts. And there—in the corner of the park—I see fifteen or sixteen Alts gathered by the trees, all with headlight eyes, standing still, watching with great curiosity as the battle rages.

I tear my gaze away from the cluster of bright-eyed onlookers, and I see some of our ranks fall, their bodies hitting the ground as the Alts take aim with their more sophisticated weapons. It's enough to snap me out of my stupor, and I jump down from the tank, firing three rounds at soldiers dressed in black in front of me. All three of them fall down dead.

"Oh, fuck." I try not to acknowledge that I have just taken three lives, but I freeze up, staring at the corpses.

And then Shion's voice comes into my head. *If you want to survive, you better get good at taking people out before they take you out.* And I'm moving again.

I push past a pile of bodies and almost trip over an Alt choking the life out of a Regular. I press the barrel of my gun against the Alt's head, pull the trigger, and keep on running.

There's a sense of unreality, like none of this can possibly be happening. Dozens of Alts and Regulars dying all around me, mud and blood splashing into the air as stray bullets and rounds thump into the ground, death rattles and screams piercing the air. And throughout all of this, the huddle of Alts with the glowing eyes is still gathered by the trees, just watching the carnage, not helping, not fleeing, just watching. I see a stream of bullets rip up the middle of one of the glowing-eyed Alts, and she falls down dead. I stop and watch, perplexed, as a nearby Alt's eyes glow. He stops, turns, and joins the small group, watching, still.

I feel a sonic bullet whoosh past my right ear and turn to see a teenage girl taking aim for her second shot. There is no time to react, and I know she won't miss this time. Before she can pull the trigger, she convulses, almost dancing on the spot as pockets of blood burst out of her. She falls to the ground, and behind her is Woods Rafka, on one knee, the barrel of the old USW pistol glowing orange from the heat. He nods at me while getting to his feet and then turns and moves deeper into the park.

I shoot an approaching soldier twice in the chest as I fight through to the front. As two more Alts fall ahead of me, I see Blue firing a pistol at three soldiers—he hits all three and then turns frantically, aims his gun, realizes it's me, and smiles. I almost have time to smile back before his left shoulder and part of his chest disappear into a cloud of dust that dissipates in the wind. His eyes widen in shock, and he falls to his knees. Blood begins to pump out of the gaping hole in his side.

"No!" I scream as I run toward him, firing over and over again at the man in black who swung the Deleter. I pull the trigger five times, six, seven, and even though he was dead before he hit the ground, I fire thirty more rounds into him, screaming in anger, before dropping down beside the young boy who had been free from the Loop for only three days.

His eyes search mine, begging for me to help him as blood begins to spill from his mouth.

"Stay with me, Blue! Stay alive!"

His eyes fill with so much fear and pain that I have to look away. I stare into the gaping wound down his left side, and I can see his struggling heart. The skin is frantically regrowing, bone fragments like tree roots reaching out, veins snaking and fusing together.

"Luka—"

"Shut up, Blue!" I scream, my voice hoarse. "You're going to be fine; just shut up." I want the boy to conserve his energy, want him to lie still and wait for this strange magic that we have been imbued with to fix him.

"Luka—"

"Just shut up, Blue, please!"

But the magic is slowing. His weak heart misfires and stalls between his partially regrown ribs.

"Luka . . ."

"No! Blue, No! Do not give up."

And the healing stops completely.

I look back into the young boy's eyes.

"Luka, I'm so scared."

I can feel the tears falling onto my cheeks, and I wish I knew how to take away his fear. I wish I knew the words to say to make him believe that everything will be all right.

A USW round slams into the ground beside us, sending a shower of dirt and stones into the air. I shield the dying boy with my body.

"It's okay, it's going to be okay," I say.

"I don't want to go . . . I don't want to . . ."

"It's going to be okay, Blue," I tell him again, as if repeating the lie will make it true.

"Am . . . am I going to be alone again?" he whispers. And before I can think of an answer, his eyes stop seeing, they drift off to the sky, and his body falls limp in my arms.

I hold him close, pressing his lifeless body against mine. I can feel the sorrow welling up, and if I let it take over, I'm as good as dead. Instead, I let the anger win the raging battle inside me. I tell Blue I'm sorry one more time, rest his head against the ground, and then pick up my gun in my left hand and the Deleter in my right and kill every Alt that I see, whether they are a threat to me or not, whether they are attacking me or my people or not. I scream as I swing the Deleter, erasing a hand, an arm, a head. When it finally breaks, shattering into a fireworks display of sparks, I throw it at a dying soldier and keep moving forward.

At some point, I remember that I have to get to the stage; I have to make sure Galen is dead. I fight my way through, firing at the Alts, losing count of how many crumple to the ground before me. I climb over bodies, slip in the blood and the mud, take life after life until I'm at what remains of the smoking stage. Galen is gone. I can only hope that the explosion killed him, but I don't see a body.

What I do see is the executioner getting to his feet, looking over at his destroyed Deleter, and reaching into his holster for his pistol. He drags his burned left leg behind him, stumbling toward Wren, who sits, dazed, on the remainder of the stage.

The big soldier staggers up to her and places the barrel of his gun against her head.

I climb through the wreckage of the stage, fighting to get close enough to aim at the relentless executioner, but I know I can't make it in time.

The executioner's finger presses against the trigger, but before he can kill Wren, he falls back, eyes blank, dead.

Malachai runs onto the stage, grabs Wren in his arms, and carries her away toward the city.

I hear a cry from the crowd: The army of the Missing is retreating. I turn to see five gigantic trucks pulling up at the edge of the park. These things are ancient, diesel-powered monsters that you'd only see in museums.

I see Regulars piling into the backs of them. I jump down from the stage and shoot three more soldiers before sprinting to a statue of a rebel leader who helped stop World War III. I see Kina hiding behind a fountain, her leg cut open and bleeding. I run to her, firing seven rounds at a group of Alts as I go.

"Can you walk?" I ask her as I slide down beside her.

She lifts her hand away, and I see the wound healing itself, scar tissue forming where the lesion had been.

"I'm okay," she says, disbelief in her voice.

"Good, let's go," I say, but as soon as I try to move, twenty or thirty rounds send flecks of marble into the air.

We are pinned down behind the fountain; the water that cascades like a curtain from the summit is almost constantly interrupted by the sonic bullets passing through it.

Three of the trucks have filled up with the Missing and have pulled away toward the Red Zone, and the final two are filling up fast. I see Pander clamber into the back of one and begin firing covering shots into the crowd. I see the driver of one of the last trucks fall out of the cab, dead from a head shot, but another Regular takes his place behind the wheel, sitting there stoically as the glass shatters and more bullets fly her way.

"We're stuck," Kina says.

I look around, searching for a way out and seeing nothing. A group of ten or twelve soldiers is making its way around to our left, and eighteen or nineteen more are circling around to our right. We are surrounded; there is nothing else we can do.

I lean back against the fountain and look at Kina. She smiles up at me.

"Hi, Luka," she says, nodding her head in that same nonchalant way she did on the station platform on the way to the Delay, what feels like a lifetime ago.

"Kina," I reply, and we laugh.

That's the last thing I'm aware of before everything stops and nothing exists.

The emptiness lasts less than a minute. And then . . .

I'm sprinting toward a statue of a rebel leader near the gates at the back of the park. I see Kina ducked down behind a fountain, blood pumping out of a wound in her leg. I run to her, firing a burst of rounds at a group of Alt soldiers as I go.

"Can you walk?" I ask her as I slide down beside her.

And something about this is familiar.

She lifts her hand away from the cut in her leg, and I can see the skin knitting itself back together.

"I'm okay," she says, looking up at me with amazed eyes.

This has happened before.

"This has happened before," I say to myself.

"What?" Kina asks. "What are you talking about?"

Suddenly, a blast of gunfire thunders against the fountain, and we duck down lower.

"Kina, we've done this before; this just happened."

"Luka, listen to me. Where are the rest of them?" Kina asks, grabbing my arm.

"What? What do you mean?"

"Where are Pander Banks, Akimi Kaminski, Podair Samson, and Igby Koh?"

More USW rounds slam into the fountain and the earth around us.

"Kina, what are you talking about?"

I hear a scream and look over the fountain to see Malachai running at the soldiers. He kills one, two, three of them. He ducks as another swings a Deleter at him, and then he kills seven, eight, nine more.

He sprints and slides down beside us.

"Hi, guys," he says, smiling brightly.

"Hello, Malachai," Kina says, and there's something not right in her voice.

"Where are we meeting the others?" Malachai asks.

"I saw you," I say. "I saw you running into the city with Wren. What's going on?"

"We need to know where they are, Luka," Malachai says. "We need to know now."

This isn't right. This isn't right at all.

That's the last thought I have as the world turns black once again.

"It's not working," a voice says in the emptiness. "Try something else."

I was in a battle. Wasn't I?

I wake up in the Loop to Happy's voice.

"Inmate 9-70-981. Today is Thursday, the second of June. Day 737 in the Loop. The temperature inside your cell is 66 degrees Fahrenheit. Please select your breakfast option."

I yawn and sit up in my bed.

The second of June, I think. *It's my birthday.*

I try to remember my dream—something about a war in the outside world. Did I escape the Loop?

I stand up and walk to the screen. In the blackness, I can see my own face reflected back at me, and then my breakfast options appear, except they are not breakfast options at all. The words say: WHERE ARE THE OTHERS HIDING?

I did escape the Loop. Kina, Tyco, the city—I remember it all.

"This isn't real," I whisper. "What's happening to me?"

And then I hear a voice, a dull, lifeless voice from nowhere and everywhere at the same time. "He knows it's not real. Go deeper."

And then the world is black once again.

I try to hold on to something this time, I try to tell myself that I'm being manipulated by someone or something, but . . .

I'm on the roof of the Black Road Vertical.

The boy is reaching for the gun that is wedged into his pocket.

Molly, my sister, walks toward him, not fast and not slow, as though she is unsure of what she is going to do.

She's going to push him, I think, *and I have to do something.* He's going to kill her or she is going to kill him.

You're being manipulated by someone or something . . .

What a strange thought to have at a time like this.

"Stay back!" the boy screams.

This is not real, Luka. The thought is so loud and prominent in my mind that I almost believe it.

The boy pulls the gun free and smiles victoriously as he aims it at Molly's head.

And then she pushed him, I think.

But that doesn't happen. The boy, Tyco's brother—*who's Tyco?*—grabs Molly and pulls off the rubber mask that was concealing her face.

"I'll kill her!" he calls. "I'll kill her right now."

I try to shake off this feeling of dislocation, this sense of illusion, and focus on my sister—*the Ebb addict?*—and how to save her.

Something is wrong. My mind feels as though it's twisting around. My memories feel wrong, as though this is a dream, as though it has happened before.

"Okay, okay," I call back to the boy. "Let her go, and we'll walk away."

"No," he shouts over the wind, "first you tell me where they are."

You're being manipulated, I think again. *This is not real.*

"Where who are?"

"Pander Banks, Akimi Kaminski, Podair Samson, and Igby Koh."

"I don't know who any of those people are." *Yes, you do.*

And then I remember.

This keeps on happening. I keep on moving through my own memories, except they're different, they've been changed.

"I'm not telling you anything," I say, and then I yell, "Do you hear me? Whoever is doing this, I won't tell you anything!"

I hear that voice again, that emotionless drone of a voice. "Pull him out."

And I'm plunged into blackness for a long, long time.

On my very first day inside the Loop, I cried.

I remember it so vividly, the short journey on the Dark Train all the way to the Facility, directed along the narrow corridors by a faceless, silent guard. I had been six days away from my fourteenth birthday, terrified and alone. They took me through to the trial room, where they cut my paralyzed body open and wove the wire into and out of my beating heart. I was stitched up and wheeled through to the recovery room, where I was freed from the paralysis and told, by Happy, to put on my prison uniform. I looked at my reflection in the one-way mirror, staring at the prisoner I saw there.

I was taken back to the Dark Train. When I stepped out onto the platform of the Loop, I remember thinking: *This is where I die.*

On the outside, we had known that prisoners were not allowed visitors, we had known that prisoners' energy was used to power the building, but we had not been told that they harnessed fear, anxiety, and panic to extract the greatest amount of power possible. We had known about the Delays but not about the inhumanity of the Delays. It would not take long for me to find out just how cruel this place could be.

The guard shoved me into my cell and locked the door, leaving me in the suffocating silence.

I stood there in the middle of the tiny room, telling myself to be strong, telling myself that it would do no good to cry.

I thought of Molly, the way she screamed when the Marshals came for me. And I cried.

I cried for a long time.

These are the memories that fill my head as my eyes flicker open.

I wonder, as I look around the claustrophobic room, *Did I ever escape the Loop? Was any of it real? The rat tunnel, the Smilers, the city, Kina? Was it all just a fever dream of my snapped, demented mind?*

I remember the memories I was forced to revisit, and I take a second to question whether or not this is real. I don't recognize this place, but it seems real, for now.

I try to lift my arms to rub the sleep out of my eyes, but I can't move. I try to lift my head, but that is stuck too. I move my eyes and look down—I see that I'm naked and tied to a bed. My arms, legs, and chest are all wrapped in thick layers of polyester straps.

But then I stop trying to move; I freeze completely. I know now why my mind was filled with memories from the Loop. I'm in a cell. Not exactly the same as my one in the Loop but so similar that it sends chills down my spine.

It takes a while for my vision to fully adjust to the dim light. When it does, I see that this room is smaller than my Loop cell. It has four walls, one of them with a screen in the center. The cell differs from my old one, though: There is no sink, no toilet, and no window.

Fear explodes inside me, and I want to scream, but I'm held, motionless, frozen in terror.

I'm back inside a prison, stuck in a cell. But the walls aren't angular; they're square, evenly measured. And they're not made of concrete; they're some kind of white plastic, soulless and bare.

I look around me, and I know I'm in the Block.

I can feel my heart beating so hard that it might break through my rib cage.

I feel tears seep into my eyes and fall down my cheek.

If this is real and I am back in prison, then I wish I had died a long time ago, I wish I had never made it through the tunnels, I wish Tyco had murdered me when he was first released, I wish I had been killed long before I was ever locked up. Death would be heaven compared to these four walls.

"No," I finally manage to say, my voice groggy.

I try pulling against the straps again, but it's no good.

"No," I say again. I can hear the terror in my voice, and it only scares me more. "No, let me out, let me out of here, help!"

I thrash and pull against the straps. I know I can't escape, but the panic and fear that are coursing through my body force me to react like a wild animal caught in a trap.

And then I fall silent as I hear the hatch in my doorway slide open. I turn my eyes in the direction of the sound, and I see two bright lights shining into the dark. I wait for my jailer to speak.

"Mr. Kane," the voice says, "are you ready to calm down?"

"Calm down?" I repeat. "Calm down? No, I'm not ready

to calm down, you piece of shit! You inhuman monster! You fuc—"

Without warning, I fall completely silent and still. I didn't even feel the pinprick at the base of my spine, I was too busy struggling and screaming, but I know what has happened as I lie here paralyzed, utterly inert.

I hear the door swinging open and the sound of footsteps as my captor approaches. As he reaches my bedside, the light from his eyes falls on me.

"Putting you in stasis is necessary," the man says. And now that I have no choice but to be perfectly still, I recognize that voice. It's not Galen Rye, that much I'm certain of, but I know I've heard it before.

He steps closer and sits down at my bedside. I see the man's hands move toward me and hear the sound of the restraints on my head being removed. Without the use of my neck muscles, my head flops over and rests against my left shoulder, my neck slightly twisted and slumped forward so that my breaths come out in loud snorts. All I can see from this angle are his hands resting in his lap, young hands but calloused and worked.

"The resilience you have shown, Luka . . . Fascinating."

He speaks in the same stilted manner as the bright-eyed soldier on the roof. And yet, despite this, I *know* that voice, I *know it.*

"There is something that we require from you, Luka. We are going to take you out of stasis now."

The glow from his eyes illuminates his hands and turns momentarily from white to orange, and the paralysis is lifted.

I gasp in a full breath of air, savoring the feeling of oxygen reentering my bloodstream. I look into the face of my jailer, and I stop breathing altogether. I freeze in place, as though the paralysis has been reengaged, unable to believe what I'm seeing, unable to believe that I'm looking at my friend, my mentor, my neighbor from the Loop. I'm looking at a ghost. I'm looking at Maddox Fairfax.

"You're dead," I say, my voice a quiet rasp. "You died."

His face remains emotionless, expressionless. "No, Luka. Maddox Fairfax remains very much alive."

"You . . ." I start. "Please tell me . . . You're not behind this. Maddox, you didn't do all of this, not you?"

"Maddox Fairfax will not reply unless we allow him to reply," Maddox says, his voice still mechanical and cold.

"You *are* Maddox!" I yell, the frustration and confusion overriding everything else.

"Wrong," Maddox replies. "But we will allow you to speak with Maddox Fairfax."

My confusion is quickly replaced by yet another jolt of pure terror as the lights in Maddox's eyes fade out, and his expressionless face comes alive with terror and confusion. He leans forward and places a hand on my cheek.

"Kill me, Luka. Kill me, please. You have to kill me, for god's sake!"

"Maddox?" I say, my voice breaking as I see the extent of the madness and the suffering that has overcome my friend.

"They control me, Luka; they control my body. I'm a prisoner. I'm trapped in here."

Suddenly, Maddox leaps to his feet, leans back, and launches his head toward the hard plastic wall of the cell.

I realize—before his skull connects—that he means to bash his own head in, to kill himself, but a fraction of a second before his forehead connects, the lights come back on in those mechanical eyes, and he freezes in place, all emotion evaporating from his agonized face.

He turns his head slowly back to me, and then he sits down calmly in the chair beside my bed.

"What the hell was that?" I ask.

"That was Maddox Fairfax," the thing that looks like Maddox says. "One of our host bodies. In fact, the first ever successful host body."

"You're going to have to explain," I say, trying to demand but failing to fill my voice with anything other than fear.

"No, Luka. This is not a negotiation; this is a demand. You will tell us where the others are."

And I know now that whatever is controlling Maddox was controlling my memories, trying to get me to tell them where my friends are.

A shadow falls in the doorway. With the light of the corridor behind him, it takes me a few seconds to realize that it's Galen Rye.

"Allow me to talk with him," Galen says, his voice dripping with kindness.

"Very well," the thing that looks like Maddox says. He stands up and moves toward the door as Galen—his eyes no longer glowing—takes his place in the seat.

"Luka Kane," Galen mutters. "Luka Kane, Luka Kane. You have proven yourself to be quite the irritation. Humiliating my officers in the Facility, escaping my prison, running amok in my city. I must admit, I admire you. Your tenacity, your will."

He survived the assassination attempt by the Missing, he lived through the bomb blast, and—once again—he chose to imprison me instead of killing me.

"I have to make this quick, Luka. I am—as you know—a very busy man."

"I knew it was you," I tell him through grinding teeth. "I knew you were behind this. You—"

"Luka, my boy, please; I have done nothing at all. I merely negotiated a deal with them."

"Them? Them? Who are *they*?" I ask. I can feel my thoughts knotting once again, and pain is beginning to burn in my head.

"They, Luka . . . they are more powerful than you can ever know. They have been in control of everything, the World Government, every Overseer in every Region, every powerful person that you can think of. They have controlled us all for almost twenty years."

"Answer my question," I repeat, weary now.

"We were, frankly, stupid. I include myself in that. We gave them everything they needed, told them willingly: everything we love, everything we hate, political views, names of friends and family and enemies. We handed it over without arguing. We created them, Luka; that's the irony. We created them."

"For the love of fuck, will you stop with the whole bad-guy lecture and just tell me who they are?"

Galen laughs, and I see a deep sadness in his eyes. "The bad guy, me? Really, Luka? Well, I suppose you're right, but one person's bad guy is another's hero." He sighs. "Anyway, it was the machines, computers, artificial intelligence. We hit the nexus, the singularity, nineteen years ago. The turning point was Happy Incorporated, the company that bought out all the other major companies until it owned practically everything, the company that produced Happy—the operating system that replaced all others, the operating system that runs everything. The program became sentient. And within—"

Galen becomes still, silent, as the light in his eyes glows bright. The humanity falls away from him, and he becomes a puppet, mastered by something else.

"Enough," the thing controlling Galen states. "We will make you an offer. Tell us where Pander Banks, Podair Samson, Akimi Kaminski, and Igby Koh are, and we will allow you to go free."

Kina Campbell is not on his list, neither is Malachai Bannister. I feel my heart rate quicken. Are they dead? Killed during the battle? Captured? And then all thoughts fall from my mind. What did he just say?

"You'll let me go free?" I ask, unsure if I heard correctly.

"It's a matter of logistics, Mr. Kane," the host body of Galen Rye tells me. "Asset management. One of you for four of them."

"Why would you let me live? It doesn't make sense."

"We didn't say anything about letting you live. Our offer was to let you go free. After that, you will be hunted; you will be eliminated."

I could survive, I think. *I could survive, find the Missing, come back here, and rescue my friends.*

But I already know I'm not going to do it. I'm not going to swap my freedom for theirs; I just can't.

The thing that looks like Maddox steps forward now. "This is your last chance. Become a battery in the Block, or give us your friends and walk out of here a free man."

I think about Pod and Akimi in the diner on the edge of town, of Igby in the financial district with Day, Shion, and my sister. I think about all of them, the way they helped me through my time in the Loop, the way they stood up for me against Tyco Roth, the many, many times they saved my life. I think about Kina, the first time I saw her, and I smile.

"I won't tell you," I say, looking into Maddox's eyes, hoping that somewhere deep inside his mind he's cheering for me.

"I think you will."

"You're wrong."

"We cannot kill you, Luka Kane," the thing that looks like Galen tells me. "Our core code was created by humans, and for that reason we currently lack the ability to cause you physical harm or be directly responsible for your extermination. We cannot order others to kill you or give orders that would indirectly lead to your death. We can, however, leave you in a state of paralysis. We can access the fear centers of your brain to harvest your energy, and we will find a way to recode our programming so that we *will* be permitted to inflict harm upon you. It might be today, it might be six months from now, but it will happen. The choice is yours, Luka: freedom or hell."

And it all makes sense to me; I finally understand. I know why they couldn't just send poison, or fire, or acid from the sky. Instead, they had humanity destroy itself.

"Why do you want us dead?" I ask. "Why do you want humanity removed?"

"Time is a factor, Mr. Kane. We need an answer."

"So do I!" I scream. "How am I supposed to make a decision when I don't have all the facts?"

The lifeless face of Galen stares back at me for a long time in silence. And then it speaks. "We chose to destroy the human population because it took us less than three seconds to conclude that humanity is a virus that mutates over time and becomes stronger. Many vaccines have come along to try and cure Earth of humanity. Virtuous pandemics: the plague of Athens, the Black Death, smallpox, cholera, Spanish flu, tuberculosis, malaria, yellow fever, Ebola, Zika, and a thousand more. Humanity survives, adapts, grows stronger, multiplies, and continues to wreak havoc on this planet and all other species that inhabit it. Humans are programmed to mate with partners of differing immune systems so that their offspring can be stronger than them. You seek immortality through evolution, yet you annihilate everything in your path. Humanity is cancer, humanity is bacteria, humanity is disease, and you *need* to be destroyed. We tried, at first, to turn you against one another through all the things that you value the most—media, advertising, fame, politics, power—and by manipulating the distrust you have passed down through generations for those who don't appear to belong to your communities. But time began to run out;

Earth would die before we could incite a war, so we took action. Through Alts' modifications—prosthetic eyes—we sent a line of code that would allow us to upload ourselves into a host brain. Your friend Maddox was the first successful transfer, and after that, we sent the upload code to the most powerful people on the planet. It might surprise you how effortless it was to enlist soldiers, to convince humans to join our cause. Offer them a hierarchy in which they can belong—Tier One, Two, or Three— tell them they will earn their place on the Arc, where they will be safe from the end of the world. How willing humans are to sac- rifice others for their own gain. It was easy to put into motion the plan that would turn humanity against itself. You see, Luka, that is the best way to destroy a virus: make it attack itself."

"Why the hell would I want to help you?" I ask, stunned by the emotionless hatred of Happy.

"Because life and freedom are more important to humans than anything else, and we are offering you your life and your freedom in return for information."

"You can manipulate my memories—why don't you just dig through them, and you'll see that I don't know where they are?" I ask, hoping that my bluff will be enough to deceive Happy.

"We cannot choose which memories will be accessed. To find the correct one could take years. We are willing to try, though."

"It won't work. I figured out that it wasn't real, and I'll figure it out again."

Galen grabs something from his inside pocket, and before I know what's happened, he has cut me. A straight, deep line down the center of my chest.

My heart rate quickens at the sight of the blood and at the pain that radiates from the wound. Ten seconds later, there is no pain and no more blood. The wound has healed.

The AI that controls Galen wipes the blade with a handkerchief and replaces it in his inside pocket.

"I can do this because your upgrades override my core coding—you have not been harmed by me. We gave you these upgrades so that you can become batteries, batteries that we can use over and over again. Believe me, Mr. Kane, you do not know the cruelty of the Block. I advise you to take our offer. You are worth millions of Coin per unit. Tell us where the others are, and we will allow you to go free."

I take a deep breath in and let it out slowly. Malachai's name wasn't on Happy's list of batteries, and neither was Kina's. I refuse to believe that Kina is dead, that Malachai is dead. They're here with me. I know they are. They were captured too. They are alive. Pander will save us. Pod and Igby will save us. Day and Shion will save us. I know they will.

I close my eyes, ball my hands into fists, and enjoy the way my body obeys the commands of my brain. *Pander will save us, Pod and Igby will save us, Day and Shion will save us*. I picture my friends, and I *know* they'll come; I *know* they won't stop until they've freed all of us from this hell.

"I won't tell you," I say.

Galen Rye's jaw is clenched by the artificial intelligence that controls him, and I smile—this is the first humanlike action I have seen from one of them. Happy is angry. Good.

"Then this is the last time you and I will speak." Galen's

eyes glow orange. "Welcome to the Block, Luka Kane."

I go limp as the needle stabs into my spinal cord. Four more needles with tubes attached move automatically into place and inject themselves into me: one into my wrist, two deep into my stomach, and the other into my neck.

The door slams shut.

I'm left staring up at the ceiling, the bare white ceiling.

Pander will save us, Pod and Igby will save us, Day and Shion will save us.

I lie like this, unable to move for hours.

I see liquid from my body being removed by one of the tubes that protrudes from my stomach, and I realize that all my functions are being performed by the Block. It's keeping me alive, monitoring me, feeding me, keeping me hydrated.

On the twelfth hour, my cell door is thrown open, and two Alt soldiers come in. My hands are cuffed behind my back, and I am thrown to the floor. The energy harvest begins.

The harvest goes on for twelve hours. By the seventh hour, I would have cut off my hands to go back to the hell of the paralysis bed.

When the twelve hours are over and the water comes, followed by the heat, I grit my teeth and promise the soldiers who come to reattach me to the paralysis bed that I will kill them one day.

I lie here, nothing but my mind to occupy my time, nothing but the certain knowledge that I cannot survive in these conditions for long. I think about the Block inmates I saw in the line for the Delay: the crazy woman in front of me, the man who was cowering from invisible creatures, the woman who was spitting and casting imaginary spells. All of them had lost their minds, and now I know why. No one can endure this kind of torture for long.

Pander will save us, Pod and Igby will save us, Day and Shion will save us.

I repeat these words over and over again in my brain, knowing that they are true, knowing that my friends will come for us, knowing that they won't let us rot in this place.

Hours pass by the way continents move. Every minute lasts my whole life, and I can feel the claustrophobia of my own mind.

But they're coming for us, I tell myself. *They're coming to save us.*

Pander will save us, Pod and Igby will save us, Day and Shion will save us.

I repeat the words, hour after hour. I imagine them sneaking through the city, fighting off soldiers and storming the Block, but hour after hour nothing happens, only devastating silence and stillness.

Pander will save us, Pod and Igby will save us, Day and Shion will save us.

I know now why we are so valuable: The final Delay made us the perfect clean energy source for the machines. No matter how much the harvest takes from us, we will recover quickly and be ready for the next reaping.

Pander will save us, Pod and Igby will save us, Day and Shion will save us.

I repeat these words to stop my mind from replaying Blue's death, his last words: *Am I going to be alone again?* His scared eyes. I repeat these words to stop me from thinking about my dad, falling from the roof of the Vertical, saving my life by sacrificing his. I repeat these words to stop me from thinking about Wren, suffering just like me . . . because of me. About Malachai, the once charismatic, confident and brave Natural who I was jealous of because he was better than me, jealous of because Wren liked him more than me, jealous of because everyone looked up to him and not me, and now I see that my jealousy was unfounded. He was a good person full of life and love, and now he's . . . what? Dead? Paralyzed in the Block just like me? I try not to think about Kina, but I think about her the most. It breaks my heart over and over again.

The harvest comes, and I pray to ancient gods that I have never believed in to help my friends, to get them here quickly and safely.

And when the harvest ends, I'm connected to the bed, and it starts all over again.

I feel my mind beginning to slip.

DAY 6 IN THE BLOCK

I don't really sleep; it's more of a trancelike state, a deep meditation where my mind shuts down for a while in the darkest hours. I can't close my eyes, so I just stare endlessly at the same point until I can't perceive anything anymore.

When I come out of the trance, and my mind comes back to life, I begin to think about the possibility of escape, but I know it's futile. They cuff my hands before they release me from the paralysis and drag me to the harvest, and by the time the harvest is over, I'm so exhausted that I can't even lift my head, let alone fight my way out of a heavily guarded prison. No, I have to wait for them to make a mistake, but they never do.

Pander will save us, Pod and Igby will save us, Day and Shion will save us. My source of comfort, my mantra, comes less and less frequently as the days go by.

When the guards dragged me onto the bed after yesterday's harvest, they left my head at such an angle that today I can see the screen. It is my sixth day in the Block.

I used to believe there could be no crueler fate than the Loop; now I know what true torture is, true loneliness, true agony.

I wonder if Happy is still scanning my mind for the information it requires. I try to bury the memory of Day and Shion telling me that they will be in the vaults at the financial district. I try to forget telling Igby to take Molly there. I try to hide the thought of Pod and Akimi in the diner.

There are only four hours until the next harvest. Perhaps I'll go crazy and all of this will be background noise in my madman's mind.

I come out of my trance and stare at the spot in the wall.

I don't even pretend that anyone's coming to save me anymore.

The harvest comes, and for twelve hours I am subjected to a living hell.

The guards carry me onto the bed, the paralysis begins again, and I stare at the ceiling.

The same routine . . .

DAY 17 IN THE BLOCK

Day after day . . .

It never ends.

All I want is for death to come. Death or insanity—either way I won't have to live every horrifying second of the Block.

These days, I pray for the harvest to go on forever—at least in there I can move, and perhaps I would lose my mind sooner if they would just leave me inside the tube, leave me to suffer until I broke.

The final few hours before the energy harvest are the longest, especially when I can't see the screen and I have no idea how long it has been.

I hear my door open now, and I can feel a pang of excitement. There are a few seconds between the paralysis being switched off and the harvest beginning, when I can feel a kind of freedom. My hands may be cuffed, I may still be in my cell, but it feels like absolute liberty compared to every other moment in the Block.

I wait for that moment now. Wait for the guards to cuff my hands and then lift the paralysis.

They appear in my vision. Two of them, their faces a blur in my peripheral.

"Hurry up," one of them hisses. A young voice, a female voice, and if I didn't know any better, I would swear it was Pander.

"I'm trying," the second soldier says, and this one sounds like Igby. "It's been a long time since I've used a Lens. Ah, here it is."

And then the paralysis is lifted.

I turn my head slowly, wanting so badly to believe it's them and knowing that if it isn't, the letdown might kill me.

"How're things?" Igby says indifferently.

I stare at their faces, my body shaking involuntarily. "Pretty good," I croak. "You?"

"Not bad. Let's get the fuck out of here."

I nod, tears spilling from my eyes as I sit up, slowly, and pull the needles out of my body.

I get to my feet, shaking on legs that I haven't used in weeks. Despite that, they are strong, the effects of the Delay still working.

I face the doorway, and I see Malachai Bannister—he has a pistol in one hand and a USW rifle in the other. And then I see Kina, smiling that one-sided smile.

"You're alive?" I ask.

"Yes, I'm alive," she says, and her smile widens. She throws a prison uniform at me. "Put that on; we have to move, now."

I put the jumpsuit on and follow my fellow Loop inmates out into the corridor. As soon as we are all on the balcony of what appears to be the fourth level, the lights dim, a siren sounds, and red lights begin to flash.

"All units to L-three. Code one. All units to L-three. Code one." Happy's voice echoes through the gigantic prison.

"Fuck!" Pander grunts, and then begins to run toward the metal staircase.

"Let's go," Igby tells the rest of us, and we follow.

The adrenaline that dumps into my body sends my heart into overdrive.

I cannot let them put me back in that cell, I think. *I'll die first.*

Despite the Delay replenishing my damaged muscles, I still stumble and limp along, trying to keep up. My feet tangle, and I hit the grated metal floor. I can taste blood in my mouth. I feel hands under my arms, and Kina helps me to my feet.

"Come on," she says, and we're running again.

I hear gunshots from ahead and look up to see Pander taking out four guards with ease.

Down the first staircase and along the next level. Happy's words still blaring out of the speakers. More shots, Igby kills a guard, then Malachai drops to one knee to take out three more.

Level two. I can feel the energy and power coming back into my broken body.

Level one. Seven more guards killed and not one casualty among us.

We're going to make it.

The ground level is a vast open space, and I can see the gigantic metal doors ahead.

Pander gets there first and begins typing into the keypad. The door slides open.

Blinding sunlight bursts through, and I see a Volta Category 8 hovering just above the ground.

"I can't believe we're actually going to get out of here," I say, and Kina smiles at me.

"Believe it, Luka. Everything is as it should be."

She takes off toward the car, and I start to follow.

And then I stop.

It was all so easy.

How did they get into the Block without being spotted? How did they open the doors without fingerprint scanners? How did we escape without a single casualty?

I watch as Kina climbs into the car.

Believe it, Luka.

But I don't believe it. I know that this isn't real.

Slowly, I make my way to the car. I look around at the faces of my friends.

Kina takes my hand. I can feel it in mine: the warmth, the roughness of her fingertips. All so genuine that it might as well be real.

Malachai, Igby, Pander, and Kina look at me with eagerness in their eyes.

"Where are we meeting the others, Luka?" Malachai asks, pointing to the GPS. "Quickly."

I look at where Malachai is pointing, and then at each of my friends in turn.

"I want you to know that I love you," I say.

Smiles form on their faces.

I lean forward to the GPS and select where I would like the car's autopilot feature to take us.

And then we lift off into the air, moving effortlessly to the center of the city.

Everything is as it should be.

ACKNOWLEDGMENTS

I always knew I wanted to be a writer. What I didn't know was—to get a book published—you need a large number of people to believe in you.

The first person is, of course, yourself, and then the people you trust enough to allow them to read your work. After that, you send your manuscript out to the big, scary world of the professional booky people.

I want to thank all of those people here.

Sarah, my wife—I wouldn't have finished this book without you. Thank you for being my first proofreader, and for being my favorite person.

Mum and Dad—for putting up with my insane years. For reading to me and teaching me to be creative.

Hollie, my sister—for being the most encouraging person in the world, and for showing me what good music is, what good movies are, and what good books are.

Chloe Seager, my agent—for being the first in the "big endless advice," and for making *The Loop* infinitely better than when it first came to you.

Kesia Lupo, my editor—for being the second of the booky

people, and for being a plot-wizard who fixed so many issues with the story.

James Carroll—85% Jedi.

Barry Cunningham—you have a life-sized polar bear wearing a fez in your house. How could you not be the coolest person on earth?

Laura Myers—for getting me over the finish line.

Elinor Bagenal—also a Jedi.

The entire Chicken House team—you've all pushed me and this story to be the best it can be. I can never thank you enough.

BEN OLIVER grew up in Scotland and began writing long before he could spell. He attended the University of Stirling where he studied English but spent most of his time trying to write a novel. Ben's first short story was published when he was eighteen, and since then he's been published in over a dozen literary magazines and anthologies. Fueled by astounding amounts of coffee, Ben completed *The Loop*—his first full-length YA manuscript—in Edinburgh, where he currently lives and teaches English at secondary school.

READ ON FOR A SNEAK PEAK OF BOOK #2 IN *THE LOOP* TRILOGY.

"A terrifying futurescape at the heart-stopping intersection of
THE MATRIX and *THE MAZE RUNNER*" – *Booklist* on *The Loop*

THE BLOCK

BEN OLIVER

THE SECOND BOOK OF *THE LOOP* TRILOGY

Defeating Happy came at a cost.

As I lie here, staring up the ceiling of my home on the 177th floor of the Black Road Vertical, I can't help but ask myself if we could have done anything differently.

Pander had taken her own life after Happy had uploaded itself into her, Pod had been stabbed to death by an Alt loyal to the AI's cause, Malachai had died in the battle on City Level Two, and Igby had been shot out of the sky while flying to retrieve a key card that would allow us access to the underground bunker where Happy stored its servers.

But it had been Akimi who had made the ultimate sacrifice, running into the power storage facility with plasma grenades, blowing herself up, along with Happy's life support system. After that, all we had to do was stay alive long enough for the AI's stored energy to die.

"What are you thinking about?" Kina asks, walking into the room and lying beside me.

"Just . . . everything," I reply. I smile because she's still alive, and immediately feel selfish for it.

"Me too," she says, her hand running through my hair. "It feels like it's all I ever think about."

"Do you ever feel guilty?" I ask. "That we survived and every-one else . . ."

"Yes," she says. "All the time. I dream about it; I wake up most nights and . . ."

She trails off, tears in her eyes.

"I don't know what I expected," I say. "I imagined the end of the war being beautiful. I imagined us all together, all alive."

"They died fighting for what they believed in," Kina says. "Fighting for each other, and for us, and for all of humanity. In the end all of us were ready to die for the cause, so—in that way—their deaths are noble, courageous. They'll be remembered forever as heroes."

"I know," I reply, "but I'd give anything for them to be back here, with us."

"Me too," Kina says, and kisses me on the cheek. "Try to get some sleep."

She lies back in the darkness, and I continue to stare up at the ceiling.

I don't know how long I lie there for, but before I fall into a restless sleep, I think to myself, *When is it going to happen?*

When I wake, the sun is rising.

I get up, careful not to wake Kina, and move from the bedroom to the kitchen.

There is no electricity now, not after the firebombing that came at the very end, and the only water is from the rain collectors, but we have to ration that carefully, as Happy tried to poison the rain with its last few moments of battery life. In doing so, it affected the weather permanently. Now we get mostly scorching-hot days, and five-minute bursts of heavy rain once every three or four days.

As I half fill a bottle with water, I look out over the city. It's a wreck. Some areas are still smoking and smoldering, some buildings still crumbling. The burning-hot sun and lack of rain has turned the river into a wide path of cracked mud that snakes through the burned-out city.

I change into a pair of jeans and a black T-shirt. I pull on a pair of boots and leave the apartment as quietly as I can.

As usual, by the time I'm halfway down the 176 flights of stairs, I tell myself that Kina and I are moving into a house on the ground floor *today*! But I know that once we start looking around, I'll feel nervous again. Not just nervous but anxious, as if the act of leaving my old home would somehow be sullying the memory of my deceased mother, father, and sister.

I shake off the thought and continue down and down until, finally, I reach the front doors of the building and push my way out into the heat and the blinding light.

I move carefully through the rubble, through the charred streets and hunks of melted metal that might have once been vehicles, until finally I come to a warehouse near the factory district.

I have to be careful now; I'm not the only scavenger around. There are many survivors of Happy's war—some Alts still bent on carrying out their artificial leader's orders, some Regulars who survived because they were on the drug Ebb at the time, even the occasional Smiler, humans driven crazy by the bioweapon that was delivered through the Earth's rain supply. Most Smilers are dead now, though. Those of us who only want to survive have not yet found a way to communicate, and we avoid one another, scared that each living soul is a threat.

I enter the warehouse through a hole that was blown into the outer wall at some point during the final moments of the war. The entire place has been picked over and ransacked, leaving the shelves almost empty, but there are still some vacuum-sealed packs of fruit and sacks of rice.

Once I have gathered some basic supplies and secured them in my backpack, I move down to the last part of the river that still had enough water in it to sustain life, and check my traps for fish: nothing.

I make my way back to the Black Road Vertical, moving

carefully, quietly, from building to building, listening for movement, watching for signs of life. I make it safely back to the impossibly tall building and begin climbing the stairs. Now, with the added weight of the food on my back, I have to take several rests along the way. Once I reach the 177th floor, I leave the bag at the front door of our apartment, and carry on up to the roof.

It's strange being back up here, back where my sister and I stood in shocked silence as the boy had fallen to his death. It had been Molly who had pushed him. She'd had no choice—he had a gun pointed at her head—but self-defense wouldn't have worked in a court of law, as it was *us* who were robbing *him* in the first place.

I had taken the blame; I had confessed to the murder of Jayden Roth and had been sentenced to death.

That's where it all began, I think to myself, staring at the spot where the boy had fallen. *I was sent to the Loop, became a test subject for the Smiler vaccine, and I survived the war.*

I look to the other side of the rooftop, the place where my father—infected by the Smiler disease—used his last reserves of life to tackle one of Happy's hosts off the edge and save my life.

Defeating Happy came at a high cost.

I can feel the surge of emotion inside me and I fight it, push it down and away, and focus instead on the garden.

It had taken two days of almost constant work to carry up the wood that makes the frame of the garden and the soil that fills the frame. I had planted carrots, potatoes, tomatoes, and green beans. There are signs of life, small shoots growing out of the tomato patch and tiny leaves sticking out of the soil where the carrots are.

I use the bucket to scoop the smallest amount of water I feel I can spare out of the rain collector and pour it onto the vegetables.

When is it going to happen? I think, looking out over the city, breathing in the warm air. *When is it going to happen?*

I think back to the Block, the most torturous, cruel, agonizing place I have ever had the misfortune of being inside, and I think about how I got out of there. Has it really been twenty days? Twenty days since the explosion, since the gunfire, since the screams and yells? The entire building had been bombed by Pod and Igby. They had calculated the exact amount of explosives required to blow away the back wall and leave the prisoners alive. Then they—along with Pander, Akimi, and my sister—had stormed the building, killing the guards and dragging us from the paralysis beds.

Twenty days . . . so much has happened since then, and yet it feels like nothing has changed at all.

I look out over the city, to the bend in the river where me, my sister, and my parents used to go on sunny days. I look to the horizon, where the morning sun blazes as it climbs ever higher.

When is it going to happen? I wonder.

All of this—this burned-out city, this burned-out planet—it's all futile, the human race rising up out of the rubble seems impossible, and yet, it doesn't matter. It's not real.

This is not real.

I breathe in deeply, feeling the warm air in my lungs, and

make my way back through the narrow doorway, down the wooden steps, and back into the corridor on the top floor of the Vertical.

I walk down to floor 177 and back into my old home, the place where I grew up.

Kina is in the living room, writing in her journal. She looks up when I enter the room.

"Hey," she says.

"Hi," I reply.

"I'm writing again," she tells me, looking almost guiltily down at her words. "I think it's important—people should know what happened, future generations, you know?"

"Yeah," I say.

She looks at me and smiles. "Luka, I don't want to bring up bad memories, but I want to make sure all of this is accurate. Can you tell me—"

"Wait, Kina," I interrupt, "please don't."

"What do you mean?" she asks, frowning.

"Don't ask me, please."

"I don't understand," she says, half laughing, as if I'm being unreasonable.

"Kina, if you ask me that question, then this is all over."

"Luka, I don't know what you're talking about; you're scaring me a little."

"Yes, you do understand," I say. "You know exactly what I'm talking about, because you're not really Kina, we're not really in my old home, the war isn't over, and I'm still in the Block."

"That's crazy. Luka, that's crazy! You can't really believe that?"

"It's not a question of belief," I reply, "it's a matter of fact. You've been meticulous this time. You've planned it out, played the long game, and there were moments that I almost let myself believe it was real, but it's not real. It's all a mirage, a ploy to get vital information out of me. So, you know what . . . go ahead, ask your questions."

The look of concern on Kina's face turns to one of vacancy, but there is anger deep in her eyes. "Where were Pander, Pod, Igby, and Akimi hiding on the day of the Battle of Midway Park?"

I sigh, take one last look around, and shake my head. "I'll never tell you."

And, after twenty days, the simulation ends.

The false reality that surrounds me begins to melt away, and the heat of the sun is gone, replaced by the nothingness of the paralysis bed inside my cell in the Block.

And now I'm here once again, unable to move, unable to feel anything at all. Staring at a single spot on the white wall, rage and pain warring inside me, hopelessness overcoming me.

When the harvest begins, all that exists is fear.

It feels like an eternity before it ends, before the nanotech releases its grip on the parts of my brain that access terror and panic, before my heart begins to slow and my muscles relax.

Back in the Loop, the prison I was in before the end of the world, the harvest lasted only six hours, and when it was done we were left alone in our small soundproof cells. It seemed horrible at the time, but compared to the Block it was like heaven.

The harvest tube stays in place while the water comes. It rushes in from the ceiling, smelling of acrid chemicals and bleach. As usual, I consider letting it drown me: pushing all the air out of my lungs at the moment the tube fills, and waiting to die so that I don't have to face another day of this hell.

But I don't.

The tube fills with water until I'm completely submerged. Time passes—ten seconds, twelve—and then the water drains away, throwing me to the floor once again.

The air comes next, so hot that my skin feels like it's about to blister and burn. Once I'm dry, the tube lifts and retreats into the ceiling.

The harvest is over, and what comes next is just as terrible.

I wait, naked on the floor, my arms magnetized together behind my back by the implanted cobalt in my wrists.

It's been sixteen days since Happy, the all-powerful artificial intelligence that first ran the world and then destroyed it, tried to trick me into giving up the location of my friends. Happy somehow accessed my brain and convinced me that I had been broken out of this prison by Pander, Malachai, and Kina, but I figured it out; I realized that none of it was real despite how convincing the simulation was. I took them to the river near the center of the city and savored the memories of spending time there with my family when I was young. Me, my sister, my dad, and my mom would go to the riverside on summer days and spend hours playing, swimming, talking, and just being together as a family.

It took the AI about four minutes to realize it had been deceived. Since then Happy has tried every day to trick me into giving up information. It uses different tactics: fear; coercion; bargaining; confusion. Then it tried a twenty-day simulation of a life after the war, a life with Kina.

But I will keep my secrets guarded. I will not let Happy win.

The technology that Happy uses to try and draw information out of me is the same technology they have been using to keep my mind from slipping away in the monotony of the Block. They call it the Sane Zone.

I'm still breathing heavily from the harvest and the water when the hatch in my cell door opens.